I0634168

FANG

VOLUME I

Edited by Alex Vance

Bad Dog Books

2006

FANG Volume 1
First publication 2005
First revision 2006
Second revision 2007
Third revision 2010

ISBN: 978-90-79082-13-1

Edited by Alex Vance
baddogbooks@gmail.com

Published by Bad Dog Books
www.baddogbooks.com

All stories copyright their respective authors.

All works here are printed with expressed permission from their authors.

No portion of this work may be reproduced in any form, in any medium, without expressed permission from the copyright holder.

BAD DOG BOOKS

TABLE OF CONTENTS

PREFACE

What you now hold in your paws is the first revision of the inaugural volume of FANG. Months of preparation on the part of the editor and countless sleepless hours on the part of the authors have culminated in the first volume of the 'little black book of furry fiction'—which now, in its pocket-sized format, honestly deserves that name.

Slip it in your back pocket, toss it in your backpack (dog-ears are cool) or make a neat row on your bookshelf. Where you put it really doesn't matter, because you will probably keep picking it up again to have a flick through. Books are for reading, after all.

FANG is dedicated to providing furs around the world with high-quality fiction of various themes. The editor stands behind this whole-heartedly and has very few qualms about informing a hopeful author that his work needs improvement—as many of the authors included in these pages can attest.

But so far, these authors, mostly 'amateurs', seem to have

taken those harsh words in the spirit in which they were intended and have sharpened their work until it reached a level of excellence worthy of inclusion between FANG's sleek black covers. And as a consequence, even a hard-nosed editor such as—well, modesty prevents me—might be forgiven a few tears at being forced to reject some rather good fiction simply because there weren't enough pages.

The future of FANG would appear to be safe, considering the volume of material already submitted, but the editor remains adamant that erotica should not be the be-all and end-all of this publication. Clean fantasy, science fiction, romance, horror, children's fiction—all of these themes may yet have a volume of FANG devoted to them.

And so FANG, after a strong start and is sure to continue in the same vein, providing furry authors with proper pages on which to display their work and eager readers the comfort of paper from which to read it.

"We don't have much time…"

The staple of all sex stories has always been the chance encounter, two people who know nothing about each other meeting and copulating. The raw sexual honesty of such stories is what makes them so arousing to read and the fact that a long lead-in is hardly essential makes such stories little work to write.

Consequently, there are a great many very poorly written 'chance encounter' stories. A little setting—and it's off to the races, sexual equipment is whipped out and tabs are inserted into slots.

Fortunately there are also more than a few exceptionally well-written such stories. The format allows for an unprecedented intensity of description—since the reader hasn't had to get to know the characters involved, the only way they can be truly engaged is if they're swept away by the vividness of the scene, if they can visualize the action and taste the mood it evokes.

"Hit the showers" by Red Swampwulf is an example of how such scenes should be presented. Dripping with detail, the richness of its descriptions borders on sensory overload.

HIT THE SHOWERS

Red Swampwulf

"Leo, my boy," muttered the brawny, narrow-hipped lion to himself, once again unconsciously shaking his head at the less than imaginative name his parents had stuck him with at his birth. "You have got to get laid, dude, and soon."

With a broad, strong paw he reached up and redirected the showerhead so that he could more easily wash the soapsuds off his belly and the hefty, throbbing maleness that had arced up toward his belly as he had languidly washed it clean. He shuddered gently as he brushed the soft pads of his palm across the pink pointed tip that peeked from the loose pucker of the foreskin like sheath that encased it, lightly stimulating the hypersensitive nerves bundled there.

With iron-willed determination he did not reach down and stroke the turgid meat despite the urge to do so, not wanting to rush his long, leisurely respite as he washed the chlorine from his fur after the late workout session in the school's natatorium in preparation for the upcoming state semi-finals. With a broad paw he directed the hot stream of water down over his velveteen-encased balls.

Unhurriedly he sluiced the lather from the oversized orbs that had earned him many jealous, teasing comments from his teammates about the almost obscene bulge that the twin spheres and the thick, meaty shaft made in this wrestling singlet. The formidable mound that the combined flesh created had earned the fairly beefy lion the nickname 'Schooner' due to his prodigious 'keel' and his daily routine in the pool to refine his already remarkable muscle tone. The college junior chuckled huskily and ran a finger over the thin, sparsely furred skin that encased his rampant maleness, savoring the tingle that it brought to the hard flesh.

Idle thoughts of the wrestling team coach's promise to take them on an illicit 'field trip' to a local house of ill repute several counties distant if they managed to bring home the trophy this year, and what he and the other fellows on the team would do there with the 'ladies', made him hard as a rock. The lust-filled thoughts of his first sexual encounter—well, his first with a girl anyway—had him hornier than a vixen in heat.

Knowing that it wouldn't take very much more to make him blow off his wad he stopped the teasing play and reached over to squeeze out another dollop of soap from the small bottle of shampoo that had brought with him from his locker to the empty showers. He took his time wringing the soap into a thick sudsy lather in his hands so that he could wash the long, gently curling, golden-red locks that he refused to cut short despite the unhappy looks they constantly garnered him from Coach. He also began to scrub the small dense patch of coppery fur that lay between the firm mounds of his well developed pectorals that he knew would spread to cover his wide chest as he reached his full growth. That is, of course, if the thick luxurious thatch that covered his father's chest and trailed down over his still firm belly was any clue. He grinned crookedly at the thought of the line pointing to the thick bush that always sprouted like an unruly patch of turf when the middle-aged lion wore shorts when relaxing around the house.

The thought of fur covering the well-developed torso that he had worked so many long and hard years at to bring to its current state of development made him frown momentarily. The unhappy look was soon replaced by a toothy smile as his hand finally slipped down to grip his cock firmly. He began to stroke slowly as he thought of how much he admired a nice thick pelt on a hot guy. The knowledge that his own mane, slowly filling in over the past few years, was blatantly advertising the fact that he was a man now, and not a boy anymore, appealed to his sense of vanity. "Just another week and I'll be balls deep in some nice juicy *poontang*, then we'll see what all the hollering is abou…"

His squeezing, slowly milking hand stopped in mid-stroke, the fleshy skin of his scabbard worked halfway down the fat, red shaft, as his reverie was shattered by the sound of clopping footsteps in the locker room. They were coming from just around the corner from the entrance to the showers that the rowdy collegiate athletes called the 'cattle chute'. The distinctive sound of heavy hooves against the concrete floor instantaneously told him that the head football coach, a massively built ex-pro tackle that everyone at the school referred to as 'The Rock', was still here… *and was coming back toward the showers!*

"Shit!" he cursed quietly as he looked pretty much blindly around for his towel. It was a few moments of desperate panic before he remembered that he had left it carelessly on the low wooden bench in front of his locker after he had stripped off the skimpy low cut swim trunks he had worn during his workout.

Shitshitshit! Soapsuds from his thickly lathered hair slipped down even further into his eyes his vision blurring even more despite the 'No Tears' label prominently displayed on the travel sized, yellow bottle as he looked down with horror at the more than obvious erection still held loosely in his fist. He desperately tried to figure out what to do. With no other options available to him he simply turned his back to the entrance, and tried to buy himself some time for his erection to subside, before sticking his head under the hard spray to try and rinse out the lather so he could get to his locker and get his towel wrapped around his waist to hide his implacable erection before…

"Hey, Schooner." The deep bass voice of the bull resonated in the large, completely tiled room after he stuck his horned head around the corner to see if the shower was in actual fact occupied or whether one of the kids had carelessly left the water running again. "You're here awful late, even for you, ain't ya?" queried the bull in his usual slow manner as Leo tensely worked his fingers across his scalp, hastily trying to get the soap completely out of his mane as quickly as he could.

Fuck! the younger feline thought to himself in frustration, *Busted!* before answering aloud, "Uhhh, hey, Coach Anderson," a somewhat lame response, even to his own ears, to the friendly inquiry. *Aw, man! Why'd it have to be him,* he silently lamented as his flagging erection began to rise anew as half forgotten masturbatory fantasies involving himself and the handsome, ebon coated bovine flashed through his already testosterone-drenched brain. "Yeah, uh… gotta be ready for the tournament next week. Gotta have that edge, y'know?" Now that the suds were sensed from his eyes he was able to see more clearly and he turned his head to look over his shoulder, carefully keeping his torso turned so that the Coach couldn't see his stiff woody, just his backside, only to see the heavily thewed bull step into the room in only an overstuffed jock.

"Mind if I join you?" he was asked rhetorically as the bull took a second casual step into the steam-filled space. The already small room felt instantly tiny with the massive form filling the open doorway leading out into the darkened room beyond. "Heard the water running after getting through with some red tape in the office and figured it wouldn't be a bad idea to hose some of the stink off me before getting into my street clothes."

The half panicked feline snapped his head back around to face forward as the winningest coach in the school's long history slipped his thumbs under the elastic band that rode low on his wide, solid hips. In what felt like slow motion he bull slid the sweat stained, woefully inadequate XXL supporter down and off so that he could step out of it and be as bare-furred as the drenched cat.

"N-No... Not at all, Coach. B-be my guest." The sound of the big male's hooves clopping closer made the normally confident, almost cocky feline want to curl up and hide somewhere, *anywhere*, and just die despite his brave words just moments before. The simple fact of the matter was that there was simply nowhere else to go at this point. The only entrance and exit to the narrow room lay past the authority figure he had lusted after for so long and there was no way he was going to dash past the bull like some scared kid with his dong bouncing side to side before him.

Truth be told, the reason that he hadn't joined the football team immediately after transferring in from his former alma mater in the middle of his sophomore year the season previously, despite the fact that he had been first string, and in line for the quarterback position after this year's seniors graduated, was the fact that he wasn't sure if he could cope with stripping down to his bare fur day after day in front of the astoundingly built staffer without totally embarrassing himself. The mere thought of doing so made his stomach churn sourly and his brain twist itself into knots, so he had opted for the wrestling team instead. He most definitely had the build, the drive, and the determination to be successful at the rough and tumble sport. The chance to test his agility and strength while rubbing up against some of the best-built athletes in the school and to cop the occasional feel on the sly didn't hurt his feelings in the least.

The sound of an additional shower being turned on made him look hesitantly back again only to see the Coach lifting one of his massive arms up over his head to wash the sweat from the deep pit under his arm with a thick-nailed hoof like hand. The young lion's eyes dropped momentarily down as the ex-linebacker turned his face into the water with a low satisfied rumbling. There was no way that the lion could pass up the chance to view, with no hindrance for the first time, the enormous bovine genitalia that he had so often fantasized about. It arced out slightly, pushed forward by the bull's massive balls. Now unconstrained by the jock or the tight coaching shorts that the staff always wore it swung in a lazy arc, slapping back and forth between the massive, trunk like thighs that supported the broad torso. What seemed to mesmerize Schooner though were the amazingly low-hanging balls that reached nearly halfway down to the bovine's knees like a pair of baseballs in a dark chocolate colored suede sling.

Oh, fuck! he thought to himself miserably, his breath catching in his throat audibly, as he brought his head back forward again to look back down at his own now drooling shaft as it slapped against his belly demandingly. *I'm not gonna be able to get you to go down for at least a week at this rate,* he reflected miserably as he considered his demanding erection.

The deep, rumbling sound of the bull's drawl made him jump guiltily at the thoughts flashing through his mind as the Coach asked him, "You got enough soap there to share with a buddy in need, Schooner? I figured there'd be some out here but it seems like the janitor did a decent job of cleaning out this swamp for a change."

Keeping his eyes turned away he answered "No, uh, no soap, Coach, but I got a some shampoo here if that'll do." The lion's voice was somewhat shaky, his control of it seeming to slip from him with every syllable that rolled off his thick, fuzzy-feeling tongue. He reached for the bottle, resting precariously on the narrow ledge designed to hold only a small bar of soap, not noticing the slight quaver in his hand that matched the one in his voice.

The bull nodded, the gesture unseen by the nervous youth, "Hey, any port in a storm, bud." Coach Angus Anderson's self-control was marginally better as he'd had years of practice at repressing his reactions to situations where his 'interests' were better left unknown to those around him.

Leo's hand, shaking with both a touch of nervousness and repressed excitement, knocked container over and off the ill designed shelf making it tumble in a lazily spinning arc toward the floor. He made a futile, lunging grab for it as it fell, missing it by inches. The plastic bottle bounced a few times and came to rest just out of reach from where he stood looking dumbly down at it. After a moment, exasperated with his bumbling move, he took a half pace forward and knelt to retrieve it, his tail instinctively lifting high to help him keep his balance as he did so.

An almost inaudible snort from behind him made him sneak a curious look back between his legs for an instant, to see what had prompted the sound, only to catch a fleeting glimpse of the virile male bull staring with narrowed eyes at his upturned ass. His heart leapt in his chest as he stood slowly back up. *No way!* was the first gut wrenching thought that burned into his brain. He thought about what he had seen. It was more than obvious that Coach Anderson had been licking his lips as he stared as his ass. *Does he maybe... maybe think that I'm kinda hot too? Could he wanna fool around with me as much as I wanna fool around with him?* The thought roiled in his brain as he stood numbly rinsing off till something in him seemed to snap.

With the impetuousness of the young he made the decision to find out. With all the bravado he could muster, he turned as nonchalantly as possible, ignoring his hard-on utterly, and handed the bottle to the bull. The Coach grinned as the only slightly smaller lion pivoted gracefully, giving him a perfect view of the up until that time hidden arousal.

An arched eyebrow and an unperturbed "Looks like I'm not the only one in need, eh, Schooner?" was the bull's only comment on the more than obvious lance that arced up from the thick, curly bush of the lion's crotch. With a broad thumb Coach Angus flipped the cap of the bottle open and squeezed a hefty quantity of the thick liquid into a huge, ham-like hand and began to massage the pale yellow detergent into the fine fur that covered his hyper-defined abdominals.

Letting some of the resultant suds drip down over the flaccid maleness that dangled below Angus continued to slowly rub himself watching with a probing, though casual, gaze as the youth stood before him mutely. He noted with bemused pleasure that the feline's light jade green had eyes locked onto the motion of the hand as it slipped slowly lower and lower toward the flat plane of his pubic region.

The Coach's smile widened ever so slightly as the lion took more than obvious, wide-eyed note of his pubic fur, or rather lack of it. The older athlete kept his pubic hair trimmed so short as to render it almost invisible against the sleek layer of fine black fur that covered him almost entirely from horns to hooves. "You like the look?" he asked nonchalantly as he slipped his hand down much lower to encircle his hairless, low hanging ball-sac in a bunched fist. He trapped the heavy nuts at the bottom of the sac where they had rested, swaying in counterpoint to his thick, flaccid cock before pulling them up. His fist tugged them up toward his belly, stretching the silky smooth skin tight till the flesh shone with the pressure being applied to it before soaping up the hairless flesh, making it glisten even more in the hazy light of the shower area.

"I'm surprised that the Chief… " he continued, pretending to be oblivious to the small gasp that escaped Leo's mouth as he stood before seemingly nonchalant male, while referring to the retired Navy otter who was in charge of the schools wrestling team, "that the Chief hasn't already taken a razor to you himself. He's threatened to in the teachers' lounge often enough." The bull rubbed the palm of his hand leisurely across the twin, fist sized lumps indolently, almost as if polishing the stones to an even higher luster as he continued to watch the youth's face assessing his reaction to the suggestive show. He was ready to instantly make light of the circumstances at the first sign of uneasiness on the broad, fine boned youngster's handsome face, but all he saw was arousal.

The feline, far from seeming repulsed, his jaw dropping to almost rest against his chest in lustful awe at the lewd sight of the bovine playing with himself so boldly. In a husky, guttural voice he choked out, "Yeah, he's on my case about my mane and... s-stuff all the time. Says it gives an opponent one more handhold, b-but..."

As the feline's voice faded off uncertainly and catch in his throat, the bull came to a decision himself. "C'mere." chuffed the grizzled sports veteran commandingly. He added a small beckoning toss of his head as added encouragement to Leo as the lion stood there, arms hanging limply at his sides. The bull's gentle milk chocolate eyes were watching the lion's wide, hungry ones as they remained locked, almost as if mesmerized, on the equipment that the Coach gave such intimate attention to.

The big cat took a plodding step forward, readily obeying the order. The pace brought the feline to within a foot or so of the subject of many a late-night jerk off session. He looked up at the bull as he stood with his broad back to the spray of the showerhead, waiting for him.

Casually the hoofed male released the hand from his balls so that they again dropped back down, coming to a jerking halt at the end of their tether to sway and bat down around his knees. He took one of the adolescent's hands and brought it to his rippled belly and used it to rub in the slick suds into the chiseled musculature. He watched the youth's lower lip quiver slightly as he guided it lower down, slowly following the path his own hand had taken a few moments before till it rested on the flat plane of his pubis.

The side of the athlete's hand rested against the root of the Coach's slowly thickening shaft which dropped bit by bit from it's scabbard to gleam, in stark contrast with the background of his slick ebon fur, with a surprisingly delicate pale pink. "Feels good don't it?" Angus asked huskily as he took a half step closer to the almost breathless cat that slowly brought his head up to look the handsome bull in the face.

Schooner's voice was strained and clipped as he answered honestly, his mind so fogged with lust that he didn't think before replying, "Yeah, it does. Feels hot, Dude... umm, I mean, Coach." The rush of blood to the inside of his ears that made then burn with an almost coral red belied his embarrassment at saying what he had said to the staffer so bluntly. He was sure he had managed in those few words to make an utter and complete fool of himself.

The bovine muscle-god chuckled deeply in his chest, the sound more felt than heard even at the close range that the two were standing "Hell, just us guys here, Schooner. Call me Rock, all my friends do." He looked down to where the hunky cat's fingertips grazed over the almost bare surface of his groin just above the join where his calf-maker extended like a piece of rubber hose from his snug sheath, "You know feels especially hot, Schooner?" he asked in a voice at least an octave lower then the already deep masculine rumble he normally spoke in. "It feels *really* hot when I'm pounding a nice piece of ass and can grind it against some bare butt, y'know?"

The lion's knees almost buckled at the Coach's words. The thought of the massively framed male thrusting so deeply that he could grind his hips against someone's rump as he bred them, made already wavering vision briefly go grey as the blood rushed from his face. Leo's hand was freed from its gentle guidance, obvious permission to continue its explorations of the only previously imagined region granted by the relaxed, easy-going look on the short muzzled face of the male that towered over him.

When the bull reached over with a beefy hand to take hold of the feline's steel-cored member near the tip Schooner did, in fact, wobble a bit before reaching out with his free hand to support himself against the adjacent water-slicked tile wall. When the older male ran a coarse, broad thumb tip over the oozing tip of the student's cock, coating it with a layer of slick, glistening discharge before bringing the digit up to his muzzle and slipping it past his thick lips to suck it clean he was positively flabbergasted.

"So..." chuffed the bovine, pressing close enough for the two strapping fur's chests to touch, "You wanna feel what it's like?" The question was asked casually, as if he were asking what the time it was or what the weather report was for the next day, but the bull's eyes were locked onto the decidedly meek-seeming younger cat's face with a near blazing intensity.

The lion looked bewildered for a moment, his head filled with a jumble of thoughts and unexpected sensations, "Feel what? What's it's like to shave off my pubes?" The cat's brows furrowed in open confusion as his mind refused to grasp the meaning behind the question.

"No" replied the bull, a lewd, crooked grin crossing his rugged face, already more than sure that the youth would agree with his proposition, "What it's like to have my short hairs rubbing up against your ass while I fuck you."

Leo looked down quickly between the tightly pressed bodies, his head already beginning to unconsciously nod in the affirmative, gaping at the still only semi-erect shaft that already dwarfed his own, momentarily making him feel inadequate despite his rather generous endowment. "Really?" he asked, a touch of fear mixed with obvious eagerness in his youthful voice.

This is a dream come true! thought the lion as he only pretended to momentarily consider the offer. Of course he wanted to lose his 'cherry' to this obviously potent, amazingly virile hunk of prime beef! "I-I'd like to try, Sir, uh... Rock, but... but what if..." he looked up toward the entrance of the shower room almost as if expecting to see someone else walk in at any second and catch the two at their illicit play, "What if someone comes... "

The brawny bull shook his head cutting him off, "The doors are locked. I chained 'em shut myself. Only way in is through the Office entrance and everyone else who has a key had already left for the weekend when I sat down to do that paperwork a while ago. We won't be bothered." The utter and complete confidence with which he spoke reassured the nervous jock.

"Then, heck yeah, I wanna." the buff lion replied, still nervous but eager now, as his hand slipped from where it had been rubbing the bristly plane to tentatively grip and stroke the massive shaft that was quickly rising up now to poke and prod against his leg. "If I could've picked anyone could be my first..."

"Your first?" interrupted the Coach again, one thick brow ridge arching at the unexpected declaration "Good lookin' stud like you ain't never fooled around before?" Angus' already half hard maleness surged and became nearly instantly to full throbbing attention at the knowledge that, if what Leo told him was true, he'd bee entering virgin territory by becoming intimate with the college Junior.

Leo blushed at his clumsy, unintentional admission and lowered his eyes to the tiled floor. "No... Well, Yeah... I mean I've fooled around some... jerked off with a couple of the guys but I haven't ever... ever... you know... "

"Gotten laid?" finished the bull-man for him with gentle amusement, "That's cool." He nodded approvingly, "Gotta watch it you know. You don't wanna knock up one of those cute cheerleaders. It'd be a shame to have to quit school so that you could get a job to support a family at your age, and it can be kind of a challenge to work up the nerve to ask a buddy to do 'other stuff' with you."

Leo looked up smiling widely now. He had expected to be poked fun at due to his inadvertent confession. It was obvious from his words that the bull understood perfectly how he felt. Leo didn't feel like explaining right then to the massive bull that the simpering, too delicate females on the cheerleading squad did absolutely nothing for him. They could all be lesbians for all he cared. He liked *guys*, big men, and brawny studs just like the one he was stroking to full erection right now! Not that he had anything against women of course. He was as eager as any young male to get his first piece of pussy, and had his eye on that nicely built female hyena goalie on the soccer team, but for right now, his thoughts were solely on the massive, towering porn fantasy come to life standing before him in the locker room's shower licking his precum from his thumb.

The young lion hefted the cock in his hands, his confidence returning in spades at the unexpected results of his bold action, up from where it still pointed down despite it's obvious fullness, gravity keeping the almost alarmingly formidable pole from pointing in any other direction. He lifted it toward the bull's belly so he could get a better look at the thickly veined meat. "Damn, dude. Yer fuckin' *hung*!" growled the feline lustfully. Wrapping both hands around the now fully hardened length, amazement showing in his smiling eyes at the sight of the several inches that still jutted, gleaming wetly as the water cascaded over it. Slowly, gingerly, as if he were afraid of snapping it off he began to jerk the bull's meat as he asked somewhat shyly, almost hesitantly "You ever... I mean do you think you can... W-will it..."

Coach smiled toothily again both at the compliment and at the rising reluctance as his shower buddy began to think through the daunting task he had agreed to so readily only moments before. His gleaming, broad flat grass-eater teeth showing starkly against the darkness of his face as he finished the awkward question. "Will it fit up yer tight little butt?" He nodded sagely. "Yeah. I've managed to get it wedged into some pretty tight places before. I'm pretty sure that we can figure something out."

"Not," he added quickly, "that I've done this sort of thing too many times before mind you. I don't jump just every student's bones you know... I've gotta be pretty damn certain that they wanna play too." He reached down and tickled the feline lightly on the underside of his cocktip, making it jump up and down with the added stimulation, "But when I saw this bad boy slapping up against your belly, all hard, and dripping like a leaky faucet, I knew that you wanted to screw around as badly as I did."

The young lion, put at ease by the obviously much more experienced bull's confident manner, simply nodded in acquiescence. "All right then," chortled the youth, obviously eager again to get on with the deed, "so where..."

Coach Anderson pondered the answer to the second unfinished question and briefly considered the Hydrotherapy Room. It had a nice padded bench that the PT guys used to give rubdowns. He almost immediately dismissed the idea, as he and Leo would have to exit the sanctuary of the Locker Room to use it.

Besides, the bull thought half frowning as he considered. *I did almost get caught pounding my pud in there just last week.* He snorted quietly at the memory of trying to explain to his star linebacker that the bellow of release his long ears had heard was due to his stepping on a pebble and not because of the especially protracted orgasm he had. The cross-armed, brow-arched, look of disbelief that he'd earned from the rabbit as he tried to cover up his still dripping erection with a hand full of unwashed jockstraps that he had just *happened* to have in his hands was enough to make him reluctantly decide to keep it somewhere closer.

"Well, let's get dried off before we do anything else, 'kay?" the bull spoke slowly as he dismissed one or two more possible spots. "You might have a set of gills hidden under that long mane of yours but I ain't real partial to getting a face full of water when I'm tryin' to have some fun… an' besides, this tile'd play hell on my busted up ol' knees pretty quick, an' I plan on takin' my time with you, boy."

The bull reached around and gripped the lion's firm rump with his work callused hands and growled, "Why don't you go on ahead? I'm gonna go double check the office door and grab some supplies. I'll be right there." The bull smiled widely at the youngster's obvious reluctance to move from the hold on him, just as he was reluctant release the new toy that he still gripped possessively in his hands. He gave one hard cheek a playful swat and continued soothingly, "I promise I'll give you as much of *that* as you want in a minute."

Schooner nodded and grinned, reassured slightly, and decided that he'd let the massive bull direct the festivities thus far and he might as well continue to do so. The older male watched with open hunger now as the lion pulled away and headed toward the exit to the muggy room. Angus once again licked his lips, but openly as he leered at the feline's ass as it swayed seductively as he walked, tail twitching from side to side with excitement. The bull gave the youth a playful wink as he paused and turned to look back at the massive bovine again before heading out into the dimly lit room beyond. "Go on…" the bull prompted, shooing the wrestler out with a wave of his hands, "I'll be there in just a bit."

Angus couldn't help but smile widely at his new friend, who returned the smile with a broad one of his own. Leo then did as he was asked and hurried off to retrieve the towel that he was now thankful he had left. He neither saw the bull look down at the potent rod that tried mightily to rise up more than a foot from his crotch as blood pounded into it nor did the feline hear the low rumbling murmur of the bovine as he addressed his prodigious member. "Betcha he's gonna be so tight that he's gonna pinch you off at the root, buddy-boy." The shaft seemed to nod in mute agreement as the trainer hurriedly finished rinsing the day's accumulated grime off before hustling off to fetch the bottle of KY from the office. The surprisingly well-used one that was kept hidden behind the rest of the supplies in the well-stocked First Aid Kit that hung on the wall by the door inside the office.

Leo left a dripping trail of water behind him as he practically raced to his locker and snatched up the small, dingy white towel and began to ruffle it through his hair hurriedly, wanting to be ready when Coach, no, not Coach but rather *Rock*, came back from checking the door and making sure they wouldn't be interrupted. With broad sweeping strokes he wiped the better part of the moistness from the fine fur that covered his shoulders and arms before swinging the short cloth over and behind his back to saw it back and forth to dry it before rubbing quickly down his legs, saving the still sodden balls and erection that continued to hammer in time with his heavy heartbeats for last as he knew that it wasn't just water that dripped from them.

The tawny pelted feline flopped down onto the bench that stretched from almost one end of the room to the other before the rows of cages, thinking as he always did of all the buttocks that had, over the years, polished the wood to a high glossy sheen. He couldn't help but chuckle with the thought of adding a little more luster to the surface, as he reached down and methodically dried his feet, careful to make sure he got between his toes.

The big cat jumped at the sound of a door slamming shut. The sound of it echoed in the empty, now almost silent room. The hollow sound of a solitary set of unhurried clopping footsteps that immediately followed the jarring noise made him relax as it told him this was the bull approaching. Schooner unconsciously reached down to grip his steel-cored tool again, knowing that there would be no turning back now. That which he had only dreamed about was finally going to come to pass. He was going to get fucked, *royally* fucked, and by one of the hottest guys he'd ever laid eyes on. His gaze was aimed toward the corner that he figured that the Coach would be coming around any second, and he was rewarded with the sight of the bull's still hard, jutting cock appearing just a moment before his broad torso followed it out of the deep shadows.

The massive bull stopped almost immediately, his features obscured by the low lights of the cool, suddenly still room, "So cub," his gravelly, husky voice echoing back and forth among the hard edges of the utilitarian room, sounding almost harsh, "You ready to be made a *man?*"

The young lion swallowed hard and replied almost meekly, his bravado vanishing like a snowflake on a hot grill at the tone and nature of the question. "Y-yeah, Rock… I think so." The lion's tongue swiped across his suddenly dry lips as he openly stared at his long-time secret idol as he stood in the darker shadows.

The bull casually clopped forward into a puddle of glowing illumination cast by one of the emergency lights that had automatically come on when the main overheads were turned off to show the broad, friendly smile that he wore on his thick muzzle. "Good." he chuckled, the sound resonating in his broad sculpted chest, "Cause I'm more than ready to make ya one."

After plodding ponderously closer, looking like some ancient Minoan statue come to life, he stopping only when he stood towering over the young jock. He reached down with thickly thewed arms and pulled the lion's head against his belly in a surprisingly gentle hug that brought the youngster's muzzle up against the flat ramp of his groin, giving him an unobstructed view of the straining shaft that would soon be deep within him, "Just relax and let me show you what to do." He ruffled the damp fur that coursed down over the feline's shoulders. "I promise I'll go easy on you this time and we won't do nothing you don't want to. You good with that?"

The lion could only nod in wordless agreement, the coarse, short-trimmed fur of the burly bull's pubic area combing across his face. He relaxed after a couple of beats of his thundering heart against the bull and stroked his face against the wall of flesh that held him close, grooming himself while at the same time marking his 'catch' unconsciously.

The staffer pulled back just a bit from the lion so that he could gaze down at him with hot, almost burning eyes and chuffed, "Then why don't you just lay back and let me get a good look at you, boy. Lemme see what I'm about to get myself into."

Schooner looked up with nervous, excited eyes and again nodded agreeably, "Sure thing, Coach. Whatever you want." Letting the towel that he had been clutching tightly in his hands drop unheeded to the floor he slipped a leg over the bench to sit astride it before lying back. It was uncomfortable being stretched out on display like he was. This made him feel somehow more exposed than he did in the shower. Schooner craned his neck a bit to hold his head up at an awkward angle up from the hard wooden surface of the wood as he tried to see what the bull would do next.

Not sure what to do with his hands as he lay there his legs splayed wide, and his cock arching up like a not so miniature flagpole Schooner simply folded them across his tense belly and tried to smile. In his mind the lion felt a bit foolish lying like he was, like some porn star posing for a camera or some lame male model selling some new cologne.

The staffer however had a completely different opinion of what he saw and stood there a moment, arms akimbo as he took in what he thought was the simply magnificent sight of the feline feast of flesh laid out before him and rumbled, "Niiiice, Schooner… very, *very* nice. I can see why the Chief lets you get away with throwing the occasional practice match."

Leo jerked his head up startled, "W-What do you mean? I never… " The feline's eyes were wide and his face drained pale under his fur as his most secret of secrets was spoken of quite casually by the nude male towering over him while he lay utterly vulnerable.

"Oh, please," snorted the bull, "I've seen you do it myself. Pit you against a guy with a nicely packed singlet and you'll roll over every time and let him pin you just so that you can feel his big'ol basket rub up against yer butt."

Leo blushed crimson all along the inside of his laid-back ears, aghast at the thought that his actions on the mat were so transparent to the casual observer despite his best efforts to keep them hidden.

"S'what gave me the idea that you might like to try swingin' on this rope of mine in the first place." The Rock stepped closer to the youth's head, letting the long slender shaft brush against the gawping youth's mouth, the tapered, slightly twisted tip brushing against the athlete's lips lewdly. "Relax, no one around here could give a huge rodent's rectum if you're partial to guys. Even if they did," he chuckled, "it's not like you couldn't mop the floor with them if they gave you any shit for it, y'know?"

Leo started to feebly argue his innocence, but as his mouth opened the bull standing beside him pushed his hips forward just a bit. The first few inches of his cock slipped past the lion's lips to press against his tongue, quite effectively silencing the mumbling, half-hearted protests. Leo's eyes grew wide as he got his first potent taste of the aroused male bull and he did indeed relax, knowing that he couldn't deny the simple truth of the older male's words.

A low purring moan rose from the feline's throat as he clamped his thin, black lips around the thickly veined shaft and began to hesitantly suck noisily at the moist tip. At first he wasn't sure if he liked the taste, but after a moment he strained his neck even more so that he could lift his head even further, taking another inch or so of the turgid tool into his mouth, letting it slip deeper in. The flavor of the musk that coated the bull pendulous penis was strange and completely unlike his own. The taste of the goo was stronger, and slightly sweeter than the bitter essences he'd licked experimentally from his own fingers occasionally. But the rich arousing nature of the musk that filled his nose overrode any initial distaste and quickly made him hunger for more.

"Oh, yeah… that's it, boy… suck on that dong… just like a calf nursin' at his Momma's teats." The bull reached down and ruffled the youth's long hair again, encouraging him gently to take even more of the hard cock into his muzzle, "Don't try to take more than you can handle… just suck on the tip." Angus snorted, his legs stiffened, and almost immediately had to resist the urge to disregard his own advice. The urge to force more of his cock into the moist, swirling heat of the nearly full grown feline's mouth became a silent battle as Leo instinctively worked his coarse tongue across the web that connected the underside of the slight flare of the bovines cocktip to the rock hard shaft.

"Oh, fuck yeah, Schooner, that's *real* nice." the horny bull groaned gutturally, "Got some natural talent showin' there… If I wasn't so hot for that ass of yours I'd give you a nice muzzle full of bull-milk to start things off right." With slow deliberateness the Coach pulled his hips back just a bit before rocking them back forward again, giving the youth time to adjust to his movements, slowly starting to muzzle-fuck him. "Betcha you'd make one hell of a cocksucker if you practiced at it just a little bit."

Leo's face flushed hotly and his ears burned red at the softly rumbled words. If someone had said that to him just yesterday he'd have not thought twice about pounding him or her till he couldn't walk, but with a rock-hard, drooling cock in his mouth decided he couldn't deny the attraction of the thought of practicing on the bull till he perfected his technique. The inexperienced lion, having at least read about what it was like to get and give a blowjob decided to take a little of the initiative and began to bob his head back and forth in counter-stroke to the bull's shallow thrusts so that their efforts combined created a slow steady rhythm as old as life itself.

Seeing that Leo was beginning to get into the mood of the illicit act, the bull gradually slowed his thrusts, then stopped them completely, letting his companion take control of the action for just a moment. He used the free moments to carefully down and pick up the towel from the floor so that he could bunch it up and place it behind the feline's neck to alleviate some of the strain of the position. The bull then stepped forward a pace moving over the now more relaxed cat so that he could step over both the bench and feline, straddling both. He moved his hips slowly again once he was in position so that his balls dragged back and forth across the tawny chest that heaved in time with the loud snorts of breath that were sucked in through his widely dilated nostrils.

He was careful not to dislodge his cock from the eager, hungry maw that tried to devour just one more inch of the tool that was so willingly fed into it during the maneuver. He was pleased to see that the lion was able, and

19

quite willing, to take another bit of his cock into his longer muzzle so that almost half of the stiff length was pressed past the long framing fangs that guided him toward the back of the youth's throat.

The feel of the bull's balls dragging across his chest made Leo moan lustfully and reach up with both hands to frig the stiff tool, stroking what he couldn't suck, milking it for more of the strong-tasting precum that oozed constantly from it now due to his inexperienced but eager efforts.

After a couple of long intense minutes of oral play the bull pulled his hips back and took a shaky step back, pulling the shaft from the youth's mouth with a wet *pop*. "Damned if you ain't already got me close to bustin' a nut, kid." He reached down to cup the balls that had begun to rise up toward his groin and almost growled roughly "Nuff of that for now though. I wanna see if you like my cock up yer ass as much as you like it in yer muzzle... you think yer ready for that?"

Leo, licking his chops, looked up at his hero with lust-glazed eyes and replied huskily, "Yeah. I wanna feel your cock up my ass, Coach. I wanna feel you fuckin' me." Leo felt dizzy as he confessed his desires to his playmate openly. Saying what he'd secretly desired for so long felt liberating, almost as if a weight he'd never known was there had been lifted from his shoulders as the words left his muzzle.

The bull snorted and chuckled as he caught sight of the jock's cock bouncing up and down with unrestrained excitement, reinforcing his words. "Well, alright then," he said and took another couple of careful, shuffling steps back till his legs brushed alongside the laid-out lion's. "Why don't ya move your legs so I can get comfortable, Schooner." Leo did as he was told, opening his legs wide to make room for the bull to sit between his thickly muscled thighs.

The bull lowered himself so that he was sitting astride the bench and his cock was laid alongside the youth's throbbing maleness. "Now go ahead and lift your legs up so that you can wrap them around my hips," murmured the bovine. As he instructed the lion into the new position he bent over to grab the tube of slick ointment that he had placed on the floor when he picked up the towel earlier. "Gonna have to get you slicked up but good if I wanna have any kind of chance of getting my pecker up yer ass, bud... So just lay back and relax," he instructed. "You'll like this part. I promise." He uncapped the gel and squeezed a more than generous amount onto two of his fingers. With a sure hand he reached down and spread the tense buttocks open a bit wider so that he could smear the ointment across the pink, unbroached pucker gently.

Leo shuddered at the sensation of the cold, slippery substance being applied to his nether passage. The feel of the bull's hard cock brushing along the side of his nuts, his steadily jerking shaft, the fingers pressing firmly in wide circles around his pucker, and the feel of the bull's callused, work-roughened hands parting his ass distracted him enough so that he didn't notice when the first finger slipped past the tight ring into him. He did however most definitely feel it when the bull began to massage the hard lump of his prostate with the thick digit, writhing like he was being branded at the new, unexpected sensation. "Wha... ?" He lifted his head to try and see what the older male was doing but the stern look that his action earned him made him lower it back to the pad of the towel and simply enjoy the sensation. "Damn, Coach... what're you doin' down there?"

The bull continued to stroke the hard little nut and chuffed. "Just got my finger up in you. Feel good?" He knew the answer before asking the question as he'd been in the exact same position that the lion was in on several occasions himself, but he was curious to hear how the younger fellow would express himself.

Leo smiled widely, his earlier anxiety allayed by the wonderful feelings coursing through his groin. "Yeah," he replied quickly, "just wasn't what I expected." He'd assumed that it would just be painful at this point, but was pleasantly surprised that it felt wonderful.

"You ready for another one?" asked the bull. The lion just nodded this time and pressed his hips down to try and force the pleasure-giving digit further in, but the bovine withdrew it teasingly so that he could coat it, and a second thick finger, with the thick, water soluble goop. "Alright, just a little more and it won't be my finger up in that tight ass of yours, Schooner... It'll be my cock. Just lay back and enjoy the ride." The feline couldn't help but tense a bit, clamping his ass tight as he felt the pressure of the almost cock thick girth of the two fingers press insistently at his entrance. "Just relax," rumbled the bull soothingly, "Just pretend you're trying to take a dump... it'll make it easier."

Leo did as he was instructed. The words may have been inelegant, but they were effective. He relaxed his belly and pressed down with his guts. The fingers slid in relatively easily now, stretching the pucker open wider that it ever had been before.

The bovine held them there, just past the second knuckle, taking as long as it took for the feline to relax a bit. He let the youth become accustomed to the feeling for several timeless moments before pulling his digits out to help spread the slickness more evenly only to press them back in more deeply. Only when he felt the tight sphincter relax did he begin to saw them back and forth slowly, giving the youngster a hint of what was to shortly come. "You alright?" he asked the lion who lay there, eyes screwed shut with the intense, almost but not quite painful, feeling of having something so thick plugging his hole.

"Yeah," he replied the feline shakily, opening his eyes to look down at the staffer as he played with his throbbing ass. "Kinda burns a little, but it's not that bad."

The Coach nodded. "That'll go away pretty quick. Just give it a minute." Feeling the urgent need to fuck the lad rising in his loins the bovine decided to speed things up a bit and wrapped his free hand around the lion's up till now neglected cock and began to stroke it slowly in time with the probing of his fingers. From the reaction he got the action was both completely unexpected and most definitely welcome. The muscles of the youngster's ass clamped down almost painfully tight on the now deeply buried digits as the jock arched his back up off the bench in an unquenchable urge to speed up the stroking of his over-stimulated cock.

The soft, but steadily rising grunts coming from the lion's chest told the older more experienced male that it was time to move on to the next step of his seduction and he stopped the stimulation of the youth's shaft and withdrew his fingers from the now hungry hole, earning him an almost whimpering protest form the now eager athlete.

"W-why'd you stop?" mewled the big cat, "Did I do something wrong?" His ears were laid back and much to his chagrin his voice was almost pleading as he asked the question to his companion.

"No," chuffed the big bull as he slid back a bit further down the bench, "You done everything just right, Schooner. It's just that I think we're ready for the next step." He took the tube and squeezed the contents down along the foot of his steel-cored shaft, coating it liberally with the slick contents before wrapping a fist around it to stroke the goop evenly all along it's length. "I just gotta get my pecker up in you soon or I'm gonna pop my wad all over your belly an' I wanna be as close to balls deep in you as I can get when I do that."

Leo, despite the pleasure he had experienced at the hands of the gentle giant, felt his breath catch at the thought. He still wasn't quite sure if he was ready for this, but as he felt the bull reach down and take hold of the end of his cock and rub it in a slow leisurely arc across the ring of his ass he laid his back on the towel and moaned in utter abandon. The feeling was just too wonderful for him to ask the bull to stop. "Go ahead," he urged the more than willing bull, "Fuck me. Pop my cherry, Coach. I want it. God, I *need* it so bad right now."

The brawny male needed no further encouragement and carefully aimed the tapered tip of his shaft at the tight, well-lubed sphincter and rumbled holding it just at the winking entrance, "Remember, just relax and press down. It'll go in a lot easier that way."

Leo again did as he was told, not caring at this point what he had to do to get the bull to breed him, just so long as he could have that majestic piece of meat up in him, scratching roughly at the intense itch that the ass-play had roused deep within his gut.

Carefully, slowly, the bull pressed his hips forward toward the upturned, waiting ass, letting the slim, narrow tip of his tool part the tight ring till just an inch or so of his formidable length was pressed into the snug passage. He stopped as he felt the tightness snap down on the shaft just behind the tapered head of his cock, gripping it like a clenched fist. "There… it's in."

The young lion grunted and raised his head a little to smile at the male topping him, "That wasn't so bad." He groaned as he felt the bull's calf-maker surge and jump so that it tugged at the quivering ring of muscle that encompassed its tip.

The bull returned the smile breathlessly and chuckled, "Well, it's not all the way in mind you, just the head, but you took it that easily then from here on out it's bound be a piece of cake."

Leo dropped his head back down onto the towel limply, his ass clenching over and over around the shaft just barely inside of him, trying of its own accord to try and force the invader back out.

The coach snorted as the tight passage seemed to chew toothlessly at his pecker and managed to choke out a gasping, "I'm gonna try and go real slow… you let me know if it starts to hurt. Okay?"

Schooner nodded and tightened his legs around the bull's hips, silently spurring him on. The feline's mind raced with a half dozen conflicting thoughts and emotions. *I'm having sex. I'm getting fucked. I have a cock up my ass. It feels good though. How is this going to change me? Will anyone be able to tell I'm different because of it? Does it really fucking matter? How much more of there dick is there to go before he's all the way in?*

Rock reached down and took the youth's narrow hips in his massive hoof-like hands and pulled the lion toward him, inexorably downward onto the shaft, slowly letting inch after inch of the meat slip into the pulsing heat that slowly encased it. His milk chocolate brown eyes looked down, slowly moving from the erotic sight of his shaft pressing into, stretching open the virgin passage that it pierced. They then moved up a few inches, past the cat's large balls to the throbbing shaft that rose stiffly upward, straight as a post from the lion's crotch. He watched with narrowed eyes as the angry red shaft pulsed even thicker, surging wildly when his cock slid across the swollen prostate hidden just inside the quivering entrance. He rocked his hips more firmly, grinding his tool against the pulsing gland and forced it to spit out a thick wad of precum that oozed from the slit at its straining tip so that it drooled down the quivering shaft down onto the youth's hard belly in a long silvery strand. Finally his eyes finished his visual journey, letting them finish sliding up past the broad, heaving chest to the handsome face that was pinched tight with concentration. He smiled then as the lion looked oblivious to anything but the feel of his ass being filled slowly with the slender but formidable cock.

The Coach stopped when he had just a little more than half of his turgid cock firmly entrenched in the spasming passage, giving the youth a moment to adjust to the length that had been so gently pushed into him. "You still doin' all right, kid?" the bull asked conscientiously as he let the inner heat of the feline's rectum soak into his flesh.

"Yeah, It feels like... like... " the big cat shook his head, unsure how to explain the feeling of being taken like he was. "I dunno what it feels like, but I'm doing real good so far." Leo couldn't help but return the smile that was plastered across Angus' face, the knowledge that he was making the bull feel good somehow made the discomfort of taking the length of hard meat up his ass more bearable, desirable even.

The massive ex-tackle nodded and pulled out a bit. "We're 'bout halfway there," he grunted, "You're doin' fine... " He reassured the youngster. "Just keep concentrating on how good it's gonna feel when I get it all the way in."

Receiving no reply but a set of heels pressing into his hips pulling him back in, Angus shook his head and muttered to himself, "Hotter'n a fuckin' firecracker, and probably gonna pop real quick." and pressed in again, this time not stopping his ingress till he was a good eight inches in, almost three-quarters of the way to the ebon ring of skin that was bunched in a tight pucker around the root of his tool. He shuddered, then paused, rallying his self-control once more before beginning to short-cock the youth, pistoning his shaft back and forth in shallow, steady strokes that long experience had taught him felt especially good to his partners.

Leo raised his head a bit and looked down with now wide eyes, "You all the way in now?" His voice was tremulous, quavering as he struggled to keep from squirming too much on the narrow, sweat slicked bench, but he felt his discipline slipping away from him with every thrust of that rod against his prostate.

The Coach shook his head, "Nope, almost, but not quite... wanna try and make sure that you're loose enough for me to get myself hilted in you." He smiled as the youngster writhed almost bonelessly beneath him at the sensual feel of the shaft rubbing against the nerves lining his inner recesses.

"Your cock feels so good up my ass, Coach, *so* good," the feline hrowled gutturally at the added stimulation caused by the steady gliding movement of the fleshy spear piercing him, stretching him, probing deep into his gut.

The bull silently agreed, nodding a bit as sweat began to form on his brow, and began to lengthen his strokes as he tried, and failed, to remember a time when he'd felt so tight an ass around his dong or one that accommodated him as if made for him.

Now putting a good three or four inches of length into the strokes of his raging hard cock, he kept up the slowly increasing pace till he began to feel his balls rising in excitement, coming perilously close to spewing his seed. "C'mon… let's try something just a little different." the older bull rumbled as he stopped. He rubbed his hands along the firm muscles of the feline's thighs encouragingly. "Lift yer feet and put 'em up on my shoulders… that'll open you up a little more and might let me get all the way in you before I cum."

Leo moaned and shuddered, not sure just how much more of the shaft he could accommodate. The pressure of the bull's dick already seemed to push up against the bottom of his lungs. His trust was complete, however, and he limberly lifted one leg jerkily upwards, then the other to the broad shoulders offered to him. He bent easily due to the long hours he'd thrown into his routine so that he didn't become muscle-bound like some of the larger guys he'd known.

"Yeah," rumbled the older jock as he felt the almost painful grip on his cock lighten considerably. "That's much better," as he eased back in. The shaft continued to sink further and further in, to the point it was before, then past it, inch after inch swallowed whole till he felt his hips brush up against the upturned ass offered up to him.

Leo groaned as he felt the coarse fur of the Coach's groin press against his buttocks. *I did it! I managed to take the whole thing!* a small corner of his mind shouted jubilantly before being washed away in the rising tide of lust.

The old male grunted and held himself in position, enjoying the feel of being balls deep in the handsome young lion before announcing in a somber, teasing tone, "Congratulations, Schooner. It's not every guy that can take me all the way to the sheath. Seems you got lots of hidden talents, eh?"

The young athlete made no reply, as he didn't hear the guttural words. His mind was ablur with the feel of what felt to be a core of seemingly molten lead burning within him, stoking his own inner fires higher and higher. The youth began to struggle wildly, not away from but against the pole pressed so deeply in him, the thing that made his nuts swell and then burn with a liquid fire that began to creep from them up into his cock, making it buck and throb wildly of its own accord.

Coach Anderson lowed deep in his chest as the channel that held his cock so tightly began to ripple in a series of pulses from root to tip along its length. He felt himself teetering on the edge of orgasm from simply that and snorted in frustration that this wouldn't last long. Seeing the look of complete abandonment of the young male pinned under him on the bench he knew it really didn't matter if he blew of immediately though. They were both about to cum. Nothing was going to stop that. He knew this deep in his bones and so let himself go and began to fuck the youngster like he'd imagined he would ever since he'd seen him stripped down at the physicals some months before.

The bull began pounding roughly into the spasming rectum, pulling almost eight inches of the rigid, unbending shaft out before hilting it in. He kept his eyes desperately open despite the sweat dripping steadily down into them from his fevered brow, not wanting to miss a moment of seeing the reaction his cock had on the straining, bucking feline beneath him as his balls began to draw up again. This time he did not slow his pace. He knew from the delicious ache in his balls that it was just moments before he flooded the willing lion's ass with his potent, jell-like spunk. Knowing this the bull reached down to grasp the big cat's cock to bring him off along with him only to have his fist batted away by wide hands with claws extended.

"No!" screamed the feline hoarsely, "Just fuck me. G-gonna cum... gonna *real* quick... " Schooner heard the voice coming from his muzzle, but wasn't totally sure where they came from. He felt almost trapped in his body as it took on a life of its own, feeding the hunger that had haunted it for so long and that he had denied it for no reason that made any sense to him at the moment.

The bull snorted at the words ringing in his ears. His nostrils dilated wide and he simply took the lion by his waist to hold him in position so that his solid thrusts didn't push the impaled feline away from him. "Gonna cum too... " he almost hissed, "You know, *Ughn!,* the best part about that, boy?" he asked honestly not expecting a reply, "The best part of that is it's not just milk that comes in quarts... so... *DO... I!*" With his last, shouted word he rammed in as deeply as he could, hilting himself utterly bottoming out in the widely stretched ass and began to pump wad after wad of thick, sticky cum into the guts of the lion who continued to thrash wildly under his assault.

Leo's world became a roaring in his ears, his vision turning grey and dimming as the rising pressure in his loins built to a crescendo. The throbbing of the bull's cock as it began to unload in him was enough to stimulate him more than enough for his cock to start bucking and spewing its own load, the thick meat completely untouched by either of them. The pearly white gobs of kittenbatter flew fast and far, the first several wads flying completely over his shoulder to land in broad wet spatters on the bench over his head. The next half dozen or so landed on is face, chest, and his shoulders. Only as his balls became more completely drained did the flow slow enough to land on his belly and groin.

As the lion came back to his senses the first thing he became aware of was the fact the bull was *still* thrusting into him with shallow strokes and the torrent of potent spunk was still pumping from the shaft just as hard as it had been when he'd lost his battle of restraint. Each gout of jizm flushed deeper and deeper into him till he felt something give way somewhere within his gut and a slowly spreading heat began to fill his belly. *My God!* the feline thought as he strained to continue to take the rampaging shaft, *He's an animal... I've never even heard about anyone being able to cum like that!* The lust-driven bull continued to ride that ass for several long moments, causing it to make lewd slurping sounds as the back pressure of the enormous load finally forced the thick fluid to start leaking from the now not so tight ring that slid up and down it.

The bull's hips continued their almost mechanical thrusting, each accompanied by a meaty smack and a husky grunt of satisfied pleasure that only began to slow after his balls too were utterly drained and the red curtain that had seemed to drop over his face lifted. The spent bovine then shook his head, sending droplets of sweat flying in an arc across the room, as if shaking himself out the trance he had been in. He looked down at the young lion, with a dazed, slack jawed expression on his face that quickly turned to one of concern. "Are you okay, Schooner? Did I hurt you? I-I must have lost it... gone out of my mind. I didn't mean to."

Leo laughed at the concern on the older males face, making his ass clamp down tightly again around the now sensitive shaft still buried in him as he reached up and wiped away a splatter of cum that threatened to drip into his eyes. "Does it *look* like I'm hurting, Coach?" He continued to chuckle making the bull winced at the added pressure around his cock forcing him gingerly to withdraw it. The chuckle quickly turned into a gasp as the bovine uncorked himself and the pent up seed literally blasted out past his exhausted, limp sphincter and washed the front of the massive male from navel to balls in a thick coat of bullspunk. The feline looked down wide-eyed at the spectacle and breathlessly asked, "Do you always come so much?"

"Yeah," replied the bull shakily as he lowered his head to try and keep it from falling off and bouncing across the floor. "Runs in the family. My brother does too... I can remember one time when we... " he stopped breathless as he watched his load continue to flow from the ass, onto the bench and then the floor underneath, leaving a quickly spreading puddle, "Well, maybe next time I'll tell you about some of the things we used to do till my Pa caught us one time and tanned our asses but good." He reached down and gripped the still half hard lion's cock, shaking it. "But for right now, why don't we hit the showers."

One Night Stand

A favorite variation of the chance encounter, and a far more realistic one, is the one night stand. People go to bars and clubs often for no other reason than the hope of hooking up with someone who's as eager for some physical entertainment as they are. Sometimes it's honestly about meaningless sex, sometimes the people involved hope for some sort of relationship to grow out of the experience.

The following story, "White Night" by Kyell Gold, is an example of how story elements such as random one-night-stand pick-ups, nervousness and confidence, hot sex and the potential for some manner of relationship can be presented with maturity and restraint, staying well shy of sentimentality without having to rely on grimness and depression to convince the reader that the author has a grasp of drama.

WHITE NIGHT

Kyell Gold

Jason yawned and stretched his lithe frame. He'd been in the library for five hours and didn't think he could open another book. He pulled his jacket on over his bare, white-furred chest, slung his backpack over one shoulder, and walked toward the front door, white tail bouncing behind him.

The evening air was cool and crisp, but that wasn't why he wore the jacket. Arctic fox fur was plenty warm even for the coolest nights in Chicago. The jacket looked cool—black leather—and had lots of handy pockets for putting things in. Jason favored tight jeans, and when he tried to cram things in his pants pockets, they produced all kinds of unsightly bulges. There was only one bulge Jason wanted showing in his pants.

That bulge was warm as he reached the street, making him hesitate at the crosswalk. His dorm was to the east, in the quiet residential area, but there was a little bar, only half a mile in the other direction. He'd been meaning to check it out ever since he'd heard about it a couple weeks ago, but hadn't worked up the courage. Now was the time, his hormones were telling him. His brain finally conceded, not that it had much chance; the test wasn't 'til ten o'clock tomorrow, and would provide a convenient excuse for him to leave early if he needed one.

The bar was moderately busy, but there were several tables free. He picked one back in the corner, ordered a beer, and scanned the other patrons, who were mostly just turning around from looking at him. An interesting mix met his eyes: some hares, a few other foxes, a couple polar bears. A few of them were attractive, and a couple of them were trying to make eye contact with him. He glanced at them and then looked away, nervous, while he finished his search.

There was one table he couldn't quite see, in the opposite corner. He could see enough shadows to pick out the silhouette of the single occupant: large and well-muscled, from the look of him. Looking closer while trying not to stare, he noticed a long, bushy tail under the table.

As he sipped his first beer, his eyes kept searching the shadows in that table. Most everyone else in the bar was ignoring him now, except for a desperate-looking hare who actually wandered up to his table. "You've got a great chest," he said without preamble. Jason turned to him to say "Thanks," but as he did, the corner of his eye caught motion: the bushy tail under the shadowed table had started twitching.

"You can see mine if you want," the hare went on. He was wearing a t-shirt that didn't promise anything spectacular underneath.

"I just came here for a beer," Jason lied. "Sorry."

"Oh." The hare wandered off, ears drooping, and as he did Jason saw the tail stop twitching. He finished his beer and signaled the waiter for another one, keeping an eye on the table. A green gleam flashed at him from the shadow, making him sure he was being watched in return. He scrounged in his pockets and found two singles—enough for his second beer—and a five. He held the five thoughtfully.

The waiter, a skinny hare wearing nothing but tight shorts, plunked his beer down on the table. Jason decided, what the hell, and handed him the five, heart pounding. "I'd like to buy the leopard at that table a glass of Blue Ice. Make sure he knows it's from me, and you can keep the change." The hare nodded and took the five, unimpressed. Jason watched him go to the bar, pour a glass, and take it over to the table. He perked his ears, but the noise level was too high for him to hear what was said. He smiled, sat back, and sipped his beer, deliberately not looking at the leopard, but aware of the feline eyes on him.

He was surprised. He'd given up on the leopard and almost finished his beer when a shadow fell across his table and an empty glass slid next to his beer. The smell of Blue Ice wafted up to his nose, followed by the subtler but more alluring smell of the snow leopard. Jason's amber eyes followed the table over to the jeans, sporting their own promising bulge, and then up a taut, white-furred stomach and muscular chest. The leopard was wearing a black vest, showing off his well-developed arms, and a silver chain around his neck. Looking up from the chain, Jason met a pair of blue-green eyes, mostly curious, but with an unmistakable underlying power that made his tail bristle for a moment.

It took him only a moment to regain his composure. He gestured to the seat beside him, and the leopard slid into it with fluid ease. They watched each other for a few moments, and then the leopard gestured at the empty glass.

"What's in that?"

His voice was a low bass rumble. Jason's ears flicked. "Blue Ice. Traditional Northern drink. Made from iceberry roots." He tilted his muzzle to one side. "You like?"

The tip of the leopard's tongue curled out ever so slightly, tracing a line around his lips. He glanced deliberately over Jason and then smiled. "So far."

Jason let his tail beat lazily against the chair, trying to hide his nervousness, and smiled back. He shifted his legs to accommodate the sudden swelling in his sheath. "It's an interesting taste."

The leopard purred softly. "You look like you would be full of interesting tastes."

Jason felt his smile widen. "I like to think so."

"My name's Trey," the leopard said abruptly, extending a paw. The other remained on the table near his empty glass.

"I'm Jason." Jason extended his own paw and leaned over to exchange scents. Trey's paw was firm and cool, with pink leathery pads like Jason's black ones, and similar long white fur surrounding them. He held Jason's paw while the fox drank in his scent. He could smell it clearly now, without the alcohol in the way, and it was rich and musky, holding hints of arousal, as he was sure his own did. It told him that Trey was only a little older than he was, and there was no tension that would have signaled nasty intentions on the leopard's part—only the tension of anticipation, which made Jason's ears and tail twitch sympathetically.

Trey smiled as he leaned back, and tapped his empty glass with a claw. "So, Jason. Do you have a place near here?"

"Just the dorm." He inclined his head. "Down that way. Usually a hassle to bring visitors in."

"Mmm. Then I guess it's my place. If that's okay?"

Jason nodded. "Oh yes." He grinned; it was no use trying to seem nonchalant. His tail was nearly wagging. Trey's tail was lashing, too, betraying his excitement.

They walked out together under the eyes of the other patrons, who redoubled their efforts to find someone, both encouraged and made more desperate by the view of a successful match.

Trey lived about five blocks away. They exchanged some small talk on the way there, where Jason told Trey he was a new English graduate student at the college, and Trey told Jason he was a firefighter.

"You're putting me on! Good heavens, why haven't I seen you around before?"

"I just got transferred to this station last week. I don't have any family, so I moved to be closer to work." Trey flashed a toothy smile. "Took me a few days to figure out where the best places were."

Jason grinned back. "Oh, you haven't seen the best places yet. But you will." He was amazed at his own daring, but he felt like someone else entirely. He'd actually picked up this gorgeous creature at a bar.

Trey chuckled, stopping at a grimy door. The smells were thick and not all pleasant, but Jason tried not to wrinkle his nose.

"Sorry about the smell. I guess I got used to it." The leopard looked at the fox's longer muzzle. "Probably bothers you more, too. I promise it smells better inside."

Jason smiled and made a show of brushing his nose against the leopard's fur, inhaling. "I'm sure it does."

Trey wrapped an arm around him and laughed, and half-pushed him up the stairs inside.

The apartment was a small studio, decorated mostly with cardboard boxes. A sofa-bed in one corner was open, sheets rumpled across it. Trey looked uncertain for the first time that night. "I haven't really had a lot of time to set up."

Jason grinned, his tail brushing the floor. "You've got a bed, right? Then no problem." He glanced around the apartment and was just going to comment on the antique-style radiator under the window when the leopard's powerful blue-grey arms circled him from behind, pulling him back against the muscular chest and stomach. He shivered, then pressed back into the embrace, sliding his bushy white tail between the other's legs. Trey's arms held him tightly, and just above his tailbase, he could feel the snow leopard's warm arousal through his jeans. He grinned and rubbed his rump up and down against it, and was rewarded with a low purr that reverberated through his shoulders.

"You are an adorable fox," Trey said softly into his ear. One soft paw slid down his stomach, ruffling the soft white fur, and then continued over his jeans to cup his sheath through them. Jason closed his eyes and swished his tail back and forth at the light pressure of the pads through his jeans. He felt his sheath expand still further, becoming almost physically uncomfortable in the tight pants. Trey's warm paw curled around it, and then before Jason knew it, both snow leopard paws were tugging at the catch of his jeans, opening it. He gasped and slid his arms back to hold the snow leopard's thighs.

"Tsk, no underwear?" Trey chuckled softly as his paws pulled the top of Jason's jeans open. They slid down his hips, claws out now and just brushing the fox's skin through the fur on either side of his swollen sheath. "Naughty and adorable."

Jason whimpered softly. He could feel the chill of the air on his fox-hood's tip as it hardened, sliding out of his sheath. "Too restraining," he murmured, trying not to squirm at the exquisite touch of those velvety paws.

"I can see why you wouldn't want to restrain this." Claws teased the base of his sac, making him gasp again, and then they moved up the length of his sheath, slowly and sensually. The touch on his sheath was delightful enough, but when the claws moved to his bare skin, it was almost more than Jason could bear. He pressed back against the snow leopard's groin, feeling the warmth of his sheath even through the jeans.

Trey responded with a stronger purr, slipping his paw slowly around Jason's exposed foxhood and grasping it. With his other paw, he worked around the fox's jeans and moved them slowly down his legs, caressing the soft white fur as he did so. Jason's tail swished back and forth against the leopard's chest, brushing his muzzle when he knelt to push the jeans past Jason's knees. He kept his warm paw on the fox's stiffness, taking his time with the process, until Jason's feet were almost stamping impatiently to get the jeans off. Finally, his second foot wriggled through the fabric. Trey tossed the jeans to one side and abandoned the erect foxhood to draw his paws slowly up both legs as he stood. The fox gasped in pleasure as the gentle claws left tracks in his white fur, ending at his groin, where one returned to his length while the other cupped and rolled his sac. He pressed back again, feeling the snow leopard's sheath larger than before, and they stayed like that for what seemed to Jason like hours. He rubbed his paws up and down Trey's legs and closed his eyes, savoring each touch of the snow leopard's warm paws on his soft white fur, until he was gently propelled toward the bed.

He smiled as his legs touched the bed frame. Trey nuzzled his ear and said, "Now, can I have a look at what my paws have been doing?" Jason turned, slowly, curling his tail across his groin and then slowly dropping it to expose his full, stiff erection. He watched Trey's smile broaden, and his purr deepen.

His own eyes wandered downward, and his paws followed. "My turn," he said. "That looks painful." The snap on Trey's jeans popped open easily with only a little help from Jason's paws, and Jason slid the snow leopard's underwear carefully down over his erection, murring softly as the thick cat-hood came into view. He dropped to his knees and took his time working the pants down the snow leopard's muscular legs, staying at eye level with the pink erection. He traced it with his eyes down to where it disappeared into a snowy white sheath, and followed the sheath down to the soft white sac, which hung temptingly below it. As he pulled the pants off of each white-furred foot, he let his nose just brush the sheath, drinking in the snow leopard's rich musk.

Jason smiled up at the naked feline and put one paw on each side of his hips. He meant to stand up, but couldn't look away from the long, pink length bobbing in front of him. He sighed, then slowly drew his tongue up the warm sheath and kept going until he reached the musky tip of the warm shaft. Trey's hips shivered in his paws as he closed his lips over it, letting the taste and scent fill his nostrils and muzzle. His tongue curled around the tip, and then he slowly lifted his muzzle free and smiled up at the feline.

Trey smiled back and rested a paw between his ears, ruffling the fur gently. Jason's tail swished slowly back and forth as he brushed the snow leopard's shaft with his nose and then drew his tongue slowly up it again, exploring every delicious inch of the pink hardness as it pressed back against his soft tongue. On the third lick, he tasted more pre, and lapped at the tip greedily.

Trey's tail twitched, and the snow leopard giggled and moaned at the fox's tongue. Determined not to let any more get away, Jason slid his muzzle over the engorged shaft. It fit nicely, warm and full, and he took it all down to the sheath, holding it for a moment. Trey's purrs grew louder, and his paw more insistent between Jason's ears. Jason brought one paw up to cradle the sac that hung just below his muzzle, feeling the weight and roundness of it, then gripped the base of the thick shaft and slid his muzzle back, slowly, teasing with his tongue as he went.

"Very naughty," Trey murmured. "But quite good, at the same time." His tail lashed happily.

Jason took the long shaft into his muzzle again, letting his tongue play over it, taking in the shape and taste of it. He pulled back and then let it fill his muzzle, holding it steady with a white paw. His ears swiveled, taking in Trey's purrs as he worked the stiff cathood. While his body lost itself in the sensations, his mind wandered, comparing the beautiful snow leopard to others he'd known. There weren't many with his muscle tone and soft fur, and Jason found the blue-grey spots particularly beautiful. He had a nice, gentle manner, and a good sense of humor, it seemed. And then, of course, he couldn't forget the nice, stiff part that his foxy muzzle was currently sliding happily up and down on. That was very nicely sized—not the biggest he'd ever seen, but it fit very well into his paw and muzzle and it tasted quite good. He found himself thinking that it would also fit very well under his tail.

He'd lost track of time when Trey took his head gently and stopped him. He realized the snow leopard was panting and smiling. "Let me... sit down." He chuckled and moved carefully with the snow leopard, who helped turn him around on the ground, keeping his muzzle in place the whole time.

Trey sat down on the bed and pulled the fox between his knees. Jason grinned, leaning comfortably on one muscular thigh as he resumed his suckling, this time moving his paw up and down as well. The thick shaft trembled in his paw, and Trey's purrs seemed much louder than before. They were getting rougher, too, and interspersed with soft moans. The snow leopard's large padded paw had moved to the back of his head, helping him move up and down, claws flexing in and out as he did.

Jason could smell the musk and taste it in his muzzle, noticeably stronger now than when he'd started. Patiently, enjoying every bit of the experience, he stroked the long cathood with his paw and caressed it with his muzzle, tongue curling around and pressing against it with every warm stroke. Trey shivered, panting harder above him, and Jason wondered as he felt the warm breath on his ear if the snow leopard would finish in his muzzle or wait for some other location. Or, maybe, both. Certainly the paw on his head made no move to stop him, so he bent eagerly to the warm stiffness in his muzzle, stroking it with his paw and tongue in a quick, firm, up and down rhythm. The snow leopard's sheath and Jason's paw grew wetter with saliva as he worked, listening to Trey's purrs become halting and urgent. He could taste the other's arousal and need, and his own length trembled stiffly in sympathy.

A shudder ran through the snow leopard. His paw tensed, claws pricking at Jason's skin, and Jason was ready when the feline length spasmed against his tongue, and his muzzle filled with warm, musky fluid. He held the cathood as Trey leaned over him, the snow leopard's other paw holding his shoulder, and swallowed as fast as he could.

"Ohhhhh!" Trey moaned, body tense against Jason. The fox felt the rush of warmth into his muzzle slow, and finally halt. Slowly, the tension drained out of the arms and legs he was pressed against. Keeping his muzzle warm around Trey's erection, he glanced upward to see the snow leopard looking down and smiling.

"Well... that was wonderful, fox," he said, still panting slightly. He leaned down further and kissed Jason gently between the ears. His panting slowed. "I'll have to see what I can do to return the favor."

Jason smiled. He circled the base of the snow leopard's still-hard cock with his paw and slowly slid his muzzle off it, flicking his tongue at the tip and grinning as Trey shivered. He kept his paw there and stood up, bringing his erection up to the same level. He touched his nose to Trey's. "You don't have to offer twice."

"Mmm." Trey's soft paws had slid down his sides, and now returned to his sac and foxhood, which was as hard as if they'd never left it. Jason closed his eyes and sighed happily as the soft-furred paw moved up to his tip. It rubbed around there for a moment and Jason could feel the coolness as Trey spread his pre around. "Looks like you need to be cleaned."

Before he could respond, the snow leopard's muzzle was replacing the paw, a soft tongue washing warmly up his cock and eliciting a happy moan from him. Trey slid his muzzle down over the foxhood and washed it thoroughly with his tongue, so that Jason couldn't help but squirm.

The muzzle slid off, leaving his damp foxhood chilly in the cool air, and when Jason opened his eyes, Trey was looking up at him. "Seems that no matter how hard I clean, it just gets messier," he said softly, grinning. Jason grinned weakly back. "I think I have an idea. Hang on."

He gave Jason's cock a quick squeeze and then flipped over, lying flat on the bed and rummaging in a box on the floor on the other side. His tail was lifted, and Jason couldn't help but stare at the firm white rump underneath it. He reached out, half-wanting to stroke the tail, but stopped himself in time. They weren't that close that he could do it without permission. He let his paw trail down between the snow leopard's thighs, which brought a chuckle from the other side of the bed.

"Be patient now—ah, here it is." Trey rolled back over and sat up holding a small bottle of Slick. He smiled at the fox's surprised expression, deliberately misconstruing it. "I know you don't need it," he said softly, "but I do."

"You sure?" Jason watched as the snow leopard drew his knees up, exposing his rear.

Trey shook some Slick out onto one paw and held it between his legs, then met the fox's gaze. "Sure. Are you?"

"Oh, yes! I mean, it's just that I can't... if I've just come, I can't take someone inside. It just doesn't work. Are you gonna be okay?"

"Cats have good stamina. So do foxes, I've heard." He winked and slowly lowered his paw to his tailhole, rubbing in a slow circle, slickening it. Jason watched, licking his lips, his cock trembling and already dripping again. "So is it true?"

He tore his gaze from the waiting rump and looking back at the feline muzzle. "Huh?"

"About foxes. And their stamina."

Jason laughed a shuddering laugh. "I'm so turned on right now that I don't think I'll be breaking any records this time."

"That's okay. We have all night." Trey reached forward with the slick paw and grabbed Jason by the foxhood, rubbing Slick all over it and pulling the fox forward. "C'mere, fox."

Jason found his tip pressing against the tailhole, almost sliding inside already, and he whimpered. He could already feel the swelling of his knot. Mentally, he tried to steel himself to keep control, but as he pressed forward and felt the tight warmth press in on his cock, he gasped and his control fled. He slid in up to his knot, glanced down at Trey to make sure he was okay, saw the half-closed eyes and heard the purr, and slid back out and in again. "Ohh.. oooooh."

Trey's ears flicked at his moans, and his smile widened. He curled his feet behind Jason's back, holding the fox to him, and reached up as Jason leaned over. His clean paw brushed the fox's muzzle, and his purrs grew louder with each thrust. "You feel very good, fox," he said softly. "Let me feel all of it."

"All?" Jason's hips kept thrusting—he could hardly have stopped them now—as he nuzzled Trey's paw and looked down at the snow leopard's smiling muzzle. Most non-canids didn't like to be tied, especially by one-night stands.

"Mm-hmm. All of it. Get that foxy knot in there." Trey's feet pushed Jason insistently.

"Ohhhhh… kay…" Jason moaned again, too close anyway to care about anything else through the haze of pleasure. He thrust in up to his knot, then gently pressed harder. Trey's slick paw was helping, and the snow leopard was pushing and then all of a sudden Jason felt a lightning pulse of pleasure radiate outward from his groin, and he was locked inside Trey and his body was shuddering as he emptied himself into the snow leopard. His legs weakened and buckled, but he locked them in place to stay upright, moaning and yipping at the flood of sensation from his climax.

He dimly heard Trey's giggles, and then as his body slowly relaxed, heard them more clearly. He looked down; Trey laughed up at him and pulled him close.

"What?" He was panting, grinning himself, feeling like he was being laughed at but too warm and happy to be upset.

"I'm sorry. You just—your tongue was hanging out and those little high-pitched yips are so cute…"

Jason tried to feel offended, but found he still couldn't, so he settled for nipping the snow leopard's chest. "No fair! I wasn't looking at you when you came!"

"Yipe! I know, I know. I don't mean it meanly. It felt nice, and you still feel nice in there, and I'm just giggly after sex."

"Mmm. Well. I can't complain. That was delicious." Jason tentatively slid his arms around the snow leopard and rested his head against the soft chest fur.

"C'mon, that can't be too comfortable for you." Trey tried to pull him up onto the bed.

"Nah, 'sfine," Jason murmured.

"Silly. Come on, get up on the bed."

They managed it gingerly, and soon had Jason leaning back against the wall and Trey straddling him, nuzzling his ears, still tied together. Trey traced Jason's sheath gently with a claw. "How long does this last?"

"You've never had a canid before?"

"Never been outside my species before."

"You're kidding. I didn't know there were that many gay snow leopards in the city."

"Only two that I know of."

"Wow. So you don't do this a lot."

Trey shook his head. "You're my first bar pickup. I've heard stories from my friends, though." He grinned, showing teeth. "You're not going to run off now that you've had your way with me, are you?"

"I don't think I could." He shifted his hips and tugged gently, but his knot wasn't ready to come out just yet.

The snow leopard winced dramatically. "Oooh! Not without me, that's for sure." He smiled back at Jason's chuckle and tilted his muzzle, softening his voice. "Do you do this a lot? Pick up guys, I mean."

Jason slid his ears down. "Not as much as I'd like. Probably more than I should," He brushed Trey's chest with a paw.

The snow leopard nuzzled his ears. "I don't mind, you know."

Jason chuckled. "I don't know why I'm embarrassed. Only ten since I turned eighteen. None since I've been at school here."

"None? I'm the first?"

"Well, I always used to go with my friends. It's different on your own."

"I guess it would be. You don't have a steady, then?"

Jason shook his head. "You?"

"No." Trey sighed. "I sort of moved here to get away from my last ex."

"Oh. What—"

Trey's muzzle brushed his ear. "Sh. Some other time."

"Okay." Jason smiled, letting his paws play with the warm sheath in front of him. The cathood had disappeared back into it, but it began to swell again and Trey purred softly. "So anyway, it's usually only about fifteen minutes."

Trey shifted his hips. "Feels a little looser." He grinned as the fox squirmed. "Still sensitive?"

"A bit." Jason smiled and drew his claws along the soft sac resting on his abdomen. He could feel his knot loosening, but it wasn't completely ready to slide out yet. He wasn't ready to slide it out, either. The warm snow leopard around him was nice and tight and felt too good. His fingers slid around the curve of the warm sac and up the sheath, playing with the pink tip he could now see. "Hm, looks like someone's ready for more action."

Trey glanced down, purring more. "Must be the inspiration of a certain cute fox."

Jason's white fingers circled the pink tip, pulling the sheath down and holding the cathood warmly. "Seems like a lot of inspiration for just a fox." He could feel the snow leopard's muscles tighten around his cock as he squeezed the cathood.

Trey kissed him between the ears. "He's a very inspirational fox."

Jason nuzzled up and smiled. As he arched his back, he felt his knot loosen and his foxhood slid out of Trey. "Mm, look at that," he said.

A warm paw reached down to hold his foxhood. "Trust me, I am."

Jason's tail beat lazily against the sheets, and he sighed happily, returning the gentle caress with his own paw. Trey moved slowly over to lie on his side next to the fox, keeping both paws firmly in place as he did. Jason turned to lean against him, and closed his eyes as they both played and teased and explored with their paws. Jason found himself playing his version of the mirror game, where he would note what Trey's paws were doing and mimic the action with his own. As the snow leopard's fingers slid delicately along Jason's sac and up his once-again hard length, the fox's paws almost of their own volition wandered down to the soft roundness between the cat's legs and then blazed a similar trail upwards.

After a little while, or perhaps a long while—it was a warm, wonderful, blissful haze—Trey's paw brushed for perhaps the third time against Jason's tailhole. It lingered there, pressing lightly and then rubbing, and Jason let out a soft sigh to let the snow leopard know the attention was appreciated. Trey nuzzled him gently and let his paw wander in that area a little more, drawing his claws through the soft white fur and along the rim of Jason's tailhole.

Jason let out a soft moan and didn't mirror the action this time, choosing to brush his paw along the tip of Trey's erection, now dripping slightly again. He reached down with his claws and brought them up the warm skin, feeling the snow leopard's body shiver slightly as he did. He smiled, then gasped at a clawless fingertip pressing into his tailhole. He opened his eyes and found Trey's blue-green eyes looking back playfully—and hungrily.

"You feel ready," the snow leopard purred.

Jason panted, for effect, a wide grin splitting his muzzle. He rolled onto his stomach and lifted his bushy white tail in a high arch, exposing his rear. He glanced sideways at Trey and wiggled his rump back and forth teasingly.

Trey watched him, his own long tail lashing against the bed, then smiled and reached over for the bottle of Slick. He grabbed it with one paw and then straddled Jason, his warm weight pressing the fox into the bed. Jason pressed his hips up against Trey's groin, and the snow leopard laughed. "Patience, you."

Jason chuckled, and then murred as he felt something cool applied to his tailhole, and then into it with a well-lubricated finger. His tail twitched, and he spread his legs a bit more.

The snow leopard took his time, making sure that first one, then two fingers could move in and out easily. He nuzzled Jason's tail as his fingers played and rubbed underneath it, and then took the bushy fur gently into his muzzle, biting just hard enough to hold it in place.

Panting harder now and rubbing his firm erection into the sheets, Jason whimpered in anticipation. He heard Trey's satisfied "Mmm" and then felt the fingers leave his tailhole. He tried to relax, but couldn't help swiveling his ears back to catch the sound of a paw applying some Slick to an eager cock.

"Give me your paw," Trey rumbled.

Jason obediently stretched one arm back, paw up. The Slick felt cool on his pads as Trey coated them with it. The snow leopard's paw guided his to his cock and closed his slick pads around it. "Just leave that there," he said, removing his paw, and Jason, who had started to stroke himself automatically, stopped with a small "Mm-hmm," though it was all he could do to keep his paw still.

Behind and above his ears, he heard Trey's slow inhalation. A finger brushed his tailhole again, and then… and then a different sort of pressure, larger, warmer, and more welcome. He felt the shifting of the snow leopard's weight on his hips as Trey leaned forward, lying on top of him and circling his chest with two strong arms. Jason had only a moment to reflect on the warmth and comfort those arms provided before Trey entered him, the long cathood sliding slowly and easily into his tailhole and driving all other thoughts momentarily from his mind.

"Ohh," he moaned, and right next to his ear he heard Trey echo his moan. The arms around him, the weight atop him, and especially the warm hardness filling him and his slick paw around his own hardness made his body shiver. The snow leopard squeezed him in response.

"You okay?"

Jason nodded. "Uh-huh. Oh, way more than okay."

Trey laughed and licked his ear. "Is that all? I think we can do better." He shifted his hips, pulling his length slowly out almost to the tip and then pressing it back in. Jason exhaled with a half-moan, half-whimper. The snow leopard moved again, in and out, and moved the fox's body slightly with his own, so that Jason's cock slid up and down in his paw with every thrust.

It usually took Jason much longer to come his second time in a night. This time, the slick tightness of his paw (which he couldn't help moving just a bit, to help out) and the smooth motion of the snow leopard's large cathood pressing in and out, gaining speed and urgency, were quickly overwhelming him. He tried to distance himself, to let the pleasure build in his body without letting his mind get caught up in it, but was only partially successful. Shivering again, he let out a soft moan to let Trey know how he was doing.

"I know," the snow leopard purred throatily into his ear. "Me too. You feel so good under me, Jason." His arms tightened, holding the fox to his chest, and his purring began to break up into a series of moans as his erection pressed even more quickly in and out.

Jason panted harder, his paw tight around his trembling foxhood. He liked to be tied, liked the warm full feeling that someone's knot gave him, but there was something sexy about the way non-canids could keep thrusting in and out all the way up to their climax. He moaned louder as the back and forth built up more quickly on both sides of his hips, and then felt that warm tingling build and grow, expanding from his cock up through his chest and bursting from his muzzle in a loud collage of moans and yelps a moment before his seed spurted out into his waiting paw, his whole body shuddering in delight. Dimly, he heard the snow leopard's deep moans of pleasure as his cock thrust hard into Jason, over and over, and his body tightened above the fox's.

As Jason finally relaxed, letting the warm afterglow take him again, he felt Trey slump atop him as well. "Oooh," the fox managed to say. He brought his free paw down to hold one of the snow leopard's on his chest.

"Yeah," Trey purred sleepily. "Mm. That was very good."

"For me too."

Trey nuzzled his ear gently. "And I can pull out whenever you want." He chuckled.

"You can stay a bit longer." Jason grinned. "I'm used to having big knots under my tail."

"Sorry I can't provide that."

"I'm not missing anything right now." In fact, he thought hazily, he felt he would like to curl up and sleep here with Trey, something he didn't often do with pickups. Usually, even if the sex was okay, or better than okay, they would've already done something to make him dread waking up next to them. With the snow leopard, he felt very at ease. He sighed, relieved that he wouldn't have to use the excuse to leave. What was it again?

"Oh. Crap."

Trey nuzzled him. "What?"

"I have a Shakespeare test tomorrow at ten."

There was no immediate response, but he felt some tension return to the snow leopard's body. A moment later, the cathood slid out from under his tail and Trey released his chest, sitting up astride him. "Okay." He patted Jason's back just above the tail and then got up and off the bed.

Jason rolled over onto his side. "Trey…"

Trey tossed Jason's jeans and jacket onto the bed. "It's okay, I understand." His ears were back, though.

"Trey." He said it more insistently, and the snow leopard stopped to look at him. Jason thought he saw a trace of hurt in the blue-green eyes.

"I was just going to ask if… maybe you could set your alarm for nine?"

He watched the eyes lighten, watched the muzzle break into a smile, and then threw his arms open as the snow leopard gathered himself gracefully and pounced onto the bed, grabbing Jason and rolling onto his back with the fox gathered to his chest.

Jason laughed. "Wow. Two times and you still have the energy for that? I can barely keep my eyes open." He did, anyway, happy to see the laughter in the snow leopard's lovely eyes.

"I'm a firefighter. We have to have reserves of energy for when necessary."

Jason wriggled against the still slightly-firm cathood. "You sure know how to handle that high-pressure hose of yours."

Trey grinned. "You get to use that one exactly once. From now on, Mr. English Student Fox, you have to find better metaphors."

"Now on?"

The snow leopard got the guarded look on his muzzle again, but only for a moment. He relaxed and scritched his claws down Jason's back. "Yeah. Now on. I think I'd like to see you again."

"Mm. Good. Me too. You can meet me for lunch after my test tomorrow if you like."

"I do. Unless there's a fire."

Sleep was fast overtaking Jason. He smiled and rested his muzzle on the broad chest. "Then we'll just have to come back here and put it out." He yawned.

"I'd rather put it in." Trey giggled.

"That too."

"Okay, okay. Get your rest." He held Jason in his arms, and the fox held him back, and within moments, both were sound asleep.

Far-Fetched Chance Encounters

Some stories are just too far-fetched to be believable, so far out there and so unlikely that they defy our ability to suspend our disbelief. These are often the greatest disappointments, especially in the case of erotica, where a lack of realism can make an otherwise enjoyable piece utterly unconvincing.

However, it is very possible for a piece to be so vivid, so thoroughly visual that the mere sensory pleasure of reading it, immersing oneself in that world, lets one suspend disbelief to far greater heights than usually possible.

For instance, "Full-Service Fox," which follows hereafter. An honest to goodness 'yiff' story that makes no apologies for its raw sexuality—yet it's set up with a care and a patience that makes the setting, as the cliché goes, leap off the page and into the imagination.

By the time the sex occurs we find ourselves so immersed in the richly detailed, dry and dreary world of the protagonist that the sexual connection the characters make doesn't seem so far-fetched at all and even if it does that fact alone isn't nearly enough to dampen our enjoyment.

Full-Service Fox

Whyte Yoté

An ebony ribbon of oil carelessly spilled onto a warped, rusted piece of scrap metal, Nevada County Highway RR wound its way haphazardly around crags of ancient stone carvings and in between stands of Joshua trees. RR stood for Red Rock, a county that found itself lonely in central Nevada, far from any interstates and, consequently, civilization as well. A tall bluff stretched its arched back to the unforgiving sky, lazing away another desert day.

The road itself was subject both to the hellish heat of the day and the barren chills of nighttime. When the sun set reluctantly over the western horizon, the temperature dropped fiercely, sometimes by forty degrees or more when there were no clouds in which to trap residual heat. Despite these harsh circumstances, the Double-R (as the locals chose to call it) was lightly-trafficked and needed rare maintenance. Its smooth asphalt surface was surprisingly free of cracks, its double yellow line shining as brightly as the day it had been painted.

The ghost-shadows of passing clouds made their way along the sprawling scorched valley, painting the land in two shades of iron-rust red. They moved swiftly but there was no breeze. The air was still, dry, but stifling nonetheless. From a distance came the soft staccato caw of a lone crow, most likely in search of dinner. Or maybe complaining about the heat.

At the intersection of the Double-R and County Road W-M was a stoplight. W-M was short for Warren-Main, because the road turned into the Main Street of Warren, Nevada, a bustling metropolis of seventy-seven. The light stood dead, its triple-eyed stare unblinking in the bright day. It had not worked since 1996, but no one had ever seen fit to take it down. It was a sign of the lifestyle out here; things happened slowly if they were important, and not at all if they weren't. The power lines attached to it sagged like useless umbilical cords waiting to be cut. They yearned to be free, just like the person who was staring at them from inside his cramped little office.

Beside the stoplight, a few cliffs of red rock and the occasional coyote or wandering vulture, was a gas station. Built first during the silver boom to refresh and provide miners with equipment, the site had seen many incarnations in the ensuing years: Pony Express stop, law office, speakeasy, squat house for hippies, and porn shop. Since 1981 it had stayed a gas station, but the sign out front often changed: Chevron, Amoco, Sinclair, and now Shell.

Its single pump stood under a gigantic awning painted white with the typical yellow-and-red coloration of its parent corporation. The colors were obnoxious and out of sync with their naturally beautiful surroundings. The entire station consisted of the one pump, an office about the size of a Port-a-Potty (at least in the attendant's humble opinion), a junk pile out back and a large white cylindrical tank that had once been used to pump well-water for weary miners.

The sun shone straight down and cast almost no shadow from the building, which was good because Toby had been avoiding the shifting light all morning. He was easy to perspire, and the longer he could put off having to go outside for anything, the better. Eight vehicles had passed the gas station since he opened up at eight o'clock that morning—a busy day so far—and two of them had stopped for gas, both serving themselves and not entering the office at all. This had left the fox plenty of time to catch up on his sketching.

Toby had his bare feet propped up on the counter and was busily pondering them as he drew his pencil furiously over the pad. Since they were covered in black fur from the knee down, he had to imagine light and shadow out of the diffuse indoor shade. His pencil flew in circles and long, quick lines. After a few moments, he uttered a curse under his breath, drew a big X over the page, and tossed pad and pencil onto the counter. There was no denying it: he was absolutely certain sure that he had never been this bored in his entire life. The endless tick-tocking of the dated Pepsi clock on the wall behind him, half-obscured by stacks of cigarettes, seemed to prove his point.

Of the citizens of Warren, Toby was one of the few who had ever been more than a county away from his hometown. Having spent one summer in Los Angeles, and now forced to be a gas-jockey this summer, the fox pined for life outside the box of Red Rock County. Day by day he could feel his creativity waning, sucked from his soul by the unforgiving sun. The sketchbook, which lay half-open on the counter, its contents splayed out like a Chinese fan, was filled with half-finished pencil works, a multitude of five-minute doodles and page after page of dark X's. He had seen not one piece to completion, and it drove him crazy.

Soon, he thought. *As soon as I find a decent school I'm gone. I don't care what Mom and Dad say... I need a life!* Mom and Dad, who had left town only once for Toby's birth twenty years ago, wanted him to stay and work on the family farm. They never stopped to consider their son might not want the same thing. So in a way, being fifteen miles from home every day had its advantages. It got him out of the house and away from farm work, plus he could make enough money to skip out and go to school where there were people who would appreciate him.

None of that mattered right now, as Toby sat and watched the dead highway. He would leave when he was ready, but getting through the day without going mad was more important. Sighing, he picked up the sketchbook again, but not before reaching over to turn on the ancient transistor radio to his right. It crackled to life with a hiss of static, and a quick twist of his claw proved that, like every other day, there were no radio waves to be picked up this far out in... well, nowhere.

Toby turned the radio off and settled for counting himself lucky that at least the small fan in the office worked. He flipped to a blank page and closed his eyes, feeling the gentle breeze in his spiky blond headfur, the only rebellious thing his parents hadn't grounded him over because it would eventually grow out.

Out of the shadows of his mind came flashes of disjointed light, images and color. He sifted through a mental clipart collection, looking for a freepaw subject. In a matter of seconds he considered and discarded hundreds of potential objects, tossing them to and fro with abandon. He stopped for a moment, and settled on a nude torso. It floated and rotated, and he took in the curves of muscle, saw the dark cleaves made on its surface by the direction of the light, the detailed pinpoints that were the nipples, and each and every fur that covered the form.

His paw flew, outlining the image and then sketching it raw, the details growing more intricate as he filled them in on the paper. Encouraged by his sudden wave of creative energy, Toby watched as the torso emerged where blank white had been. After a while he didn't even need to think about it; two dimensions became three with deft strokes of his pencil.

All was quiet, save for the scratching of lead on paper and the fox's shallow, anticipatory breaths. His brown eyes were wide, clear; finally he felt like his artist's block had been broken!

His entire concentration was centered on the sketch in front of him, but his black-tipped ears perked at the sound of an approaching low rumble from the west. Toby's hearing had improved since taking the job at the gas station, and when the wind was right he could hear a car coming from a mile or more away. He looked up and through the open door, which gave an unobstructed view of where the highway curved and disappeared between two tall cliffs of rock. Far off in the distance, where the sky met the horizon, the blue melted into a ruddy brown dust. The vehicle had to be booking it across the desert to make dust fly on the asphalt like that.

Still reclined in his chair, feet up on the counter, the fox now watched intently to see what was traveling so fast in his direction. The sound was almost lost to his sensitive ears, but then came back full-force as a glint of chrome topped the curve. The flash reflected off the car's windshield and covered the office's interior in stars and sparks of light. Then it was gone in an instant as the convertible (Toby could tell that much now) roared around the gentle curve, dust flying behind it in a futile effort to keep pace.

At once the vulpine knew this was no ordinary car, and certainly not one you would want to take for a *Cannonball Run*-type drive around the desert. His feet left the counter and he stood, swaying a bit as blood rushed to his head. He padded out from behind the counter and to the door, leaning on its frame with his right arm raised for support. He squinted, and the car started to take shape as it rushed toward him, seeming to carry the sun on its shiny surface.

It disappeared below a rise, only to leap into full view again, bullying its way along and straddling the double yellow lines. A splash of color in an otherwise dull landscape, its sea foam-green body rocked and settled on its springs, taking the undulating road with deft authority. Polished hubcaps shone within giant white walls of rubber, the smooth treads eating up the last half-mile of road before the intersection.

Toby licked his whiskers. His throat made a dry clicking sound. Even if the car didn't stop, his day had already gotten much more interesting than usual.

The 1955 Ford Thunderbird's throaty American V-8 lost volume, signaling that the car would at least slow down. When it reached the intersection, the fox was standing just outside the front door, thinking that it would pass up such a sorry-looking place for better facilities downroad. But, like an afterthought, the sculpted front end swerved toward the fox, the whine of shifting gears accentuating the spray of gravel that fanned out behind its skirted rear fenders and showered the old pump.

The driver slammed on the brake, sending the car into a low-speed angled skid, and the T-Bird stopped in a cloud of dust, its fuel-filler door less than two feet from the nozzle. Toby sighed, partly in relief, and partly because he hadn't breathed in a while.

Wind whirled the cloud from in front of the car, revealing it in all its chromed and painted glory. Toby approached, almost reverently, taking in the surfaces, which looked to be free of imperfections and concourse-quality. It was almost too much to look at; a car that was almost fifty years old shouldn't look that good, and definitely shouldn't be anywhere near a sun-drenched desert. As he rounded the pump he noted the rare continental kit mounted on the back bumper and—his heart jumped a little when he saw it—the fake foxtail tied to the antenna. It was a relic from the era of rock 'n' roll, no doubt about it.

Smiling now, because he actually had something to do, Toby walked around to the passenger side to see the driver. The ground was hot on his footpads, but he maintained a smile nonetheless. "Hi!" he said in a cheery voice, although he had already begun to perspire. "What can I do for you, sir?"

The fox's smile evaporated when he saw the driver, who stood as he exited the convertible. The tiger was enormous, noticeably older than him and at least a head taller. He raised his bulky frame from the T-Bird and shut the door with purpose. Even in the shade his dark orange fur screamed against black stripes, the white of his neck and chest contrasting with the black leather vest and pants he was wearing. A plain gold chain adorned his thick neck, and there were three studs in a line up the side of his right ear. His face was shaded by a black leather driving cap, but when the tiger removed his sunglasses his green eyes fairly glowed the same color as his car.

"What can I do for you?" repeated Toby in a much smaller voice. Although the car separated them, he still felt intimidated by the big feline.

"Top it off, I suppose," the tiger said in a throaty baritone as he removed his driving gloves and turned to walk toward the station. Toby nodded at the broad back and swaying tail, then opened the fuel door and proceeded to try and fill the vintage automobile without touching its perfect surfaces.

When he was finished (the tank had already been half-full, but fuel was scarce in this part of the country), the fox made his way back into the gas station, wiping beads of sweat from his brow and off his snout. He made sure to close the door to keep the heat out, and when he glanced up he was surprised to see the big tiger sitting in his chair, feet upon the counter, looking at *his* sketchbook.

He blushed, something he did whenever anyone else looked at his work, and wondered how to handle this situation. He didn't like anything in that book; they were all junk, but he also didn't want to do anything to piss his customer off. A few items sat on the counter, waiting to be paid for. There was no harm to just let the big male satisfy his curiosity, so Toby decided to wait.

The leather-clad feline hummed an unrecognizable tune as he studied the sketchbook, his head cocking this way and that. He tapped his foot-pads absently on the countertop, and the fox found himself oddly thinking that the chair would be warm when he next sat down on it. Smiling at such a silly thought, he walked back to the storeroom to get a mop and bucket for the daily floor-cleaning. He rolled the clunky contraption back to the front, where the tiger still sat regarding the pages of drawings. The fox couldn't help but be glad for the company.

Toby was just turning around to retrieve some detergent when a deep bass rumble vibrated the hairs in his ears. It tickled, and they flicked in re-action to such a low frequency. The fox looked up toward the tiger, but his face was hidden. Slowly, carefully, he crept up to peek around the pad.

The big cat's face was drawn into a savant grin, his upper lip trembling slightly as he growled... no, purred... at what he saw on the page. Curious as to what sketch of his could elicit such a reaction, Toby looked in the direction of the tiger's gaze, and fought to suppress a low moan of embar-rassment when he saw what was there.

It was only a pencil-sketch, but it was something Toby had drawn months ago, in school. He had been in Life Drawing, and the model that day had been an exercise in physical perfection. Toby had taken the time and opportunity to focus all his efforts on recreating the model in his en-tirety, all the way down to the pubic fur curled slightly around his sheath. At the time, he had only been concentrating on the details, but the more he looked at it the more it excited him. Not only the fact that the model was good-looking, but the fact that he had actually *drawn* that well. The fox had been trying to repeat that all summer, with little to no success.

The fox turned away, clutching his face in his paws. His heart beat wildly inside him; he had never meant for anyone to see that, but he had forgotten it was even there! At least the tiger hadn't reprimanded him for his 'lack of discretion,' as his art teacher had put it.

A claw scritched behind Toby's right ear, and he shuddered all the way down to his tailtip.

"Hey, kid. What's your name?" The voice had an added trace of lustful vibrato now.

Toby turned around and faced the tiger, who despite his reclined position still seemed intimidating. He realized the tiger had tapped him with a toeclaw. The sketchpad lay on the counter, its dark, unabashed lines open to all the world. Toby couldn't help but glance at it, then up at the tiger, his eyes falling for just a split-second on the bulge in his pants that seemed to flex of its own accord. His head felt light and airy.

He cleared his throat and managed to speak, "Toby." It felt more like an act of supplication than a polite address to a customer. Had he actually wanted to add the word "sir" to the end of that sentence? "If I may ask," he said, feeling uncomfortable for being so forward with a stranger, "how much did the restoration cost?"

The tiger chuckled, his body shaking under his weight. "Restoration? That, Toby, is one hundred percent original."

The fox's eyes went wide. "How do you come up with something like that?" he practically shouted, leaning over the counter. He didn't know much about cars, but he did know that anything fifty years old and looking that good had to have been at least a frame-off.

The tiger's paws were crossed over his broad chest. "An old couple. Some wedding present they never liked and didn't want to sell for forty-some-odd years. All I cared about was its original condition."

"Dang," Toby muttered. The tiger's eyes were on the sketchpad again, and the fox knew what was coming. He blushed again, cursing himself for doing so.

On his feet now, the big tiger came around the counter to stand behind the fox. Toby could practically feel his body encircling him, and he knew that if he looked up a white-furred chin would be staring into his face. It wasn't enough to make him uncomfortable, though. The stomach behind him growled loudly, almost enough so that Toby could feel it on his back.

"These are good," the tiger admonished, exuding an intelligence belied by his body and clothes. "By the way, the name's Thor. Not my real name, but good enough." He offered his paw, extending it across the vulpine's chest, and Toby offered his in return. Thor's grip threatened to crush the fox's fingers, but he held on just the same.

"There's only the one that I like, the one you looked at. The rest are junk I couldn't finish." Toby was finding it a little hard to speak with the big cat standing right behind him.

Thor chuckled and flipped a couple of pages back from the nude. "Maybe it would be easier if all these X's weren't in the way." A heavy paw came to rest on the fox's left shoulder. "See here?" he said, indicating a model sitting, facing away from the viewer. "On his back, the way you drew the spine? Either that's spot-on, or the model had a perfect back."

Warmth surrounded Toby's face, and he could feel red creeping into his ears. "Actually," he said, trying not to sound too boastful, "I drew that freepaw."

"Bullshit." It came out more as a statement than an exclamation. "How do you do something like that from memory?" He cleared his throat, challenging the little fox to answer.

Toby thought hard. How could he find an explanation for it? He just picked something out of his mind and concentrated on it. He would memorize everything about it, and just start drawing. The rest just kind of came as the picture took shape. As he pondered all this, what came out of his mind was a stammered "I-I don't know." Toby was surprised that Thor was interested at all in his work; he also hadn't expected the tiger to be so forthcoming. He hated that he couldn't explain himself in a more thorough manner, but it was all he knew. He'd never thought about it before.

Thor flipped forward in the sketchbook again, and stopped when he saw the torso Toby had been sketching when he pulled up. Considering it for a few moments, he scratched his chin, his dark green eyes glinting and reflecting the bright outdoor light.

"This is very, very detailed, Toby. It isn't crossed out, so I take it you like this one?"

"Actually, no." The fox stared at the floor, feeling the bulk behind him. "I was doing that one when I heard your car coming. I haven't had a chance to finish it yet."

The tiger traced a claw over the lines of the torso's muscles. "Hmm... Oh, I know!"

"What?" Toby asked, perplexed.

Thor pointed repeatedly at the drawing, as if he were trying to jog his memory. "I thought I saw something weird, and it's clear to me now. Do you see here, where the abdominal muscles come together?"

The fox nodded, happy to be receiving feedback of any kind, even criticism.

"You have the angle just slightly off. See, you have the abs straight across the chest." Thor turned away and spread his vest, exposing his bare chest. Toby backed away a bit, finding all he could do was stare at the sculpted mass of snowy white fur in front of him. The tiger shrugged the leather vest down. "In real life," he pointed to himself, outlining his abs for the fox to see, "the muscles angle slightly downward as you reach the side. Here, feel."

Before Toby could react, the tiger grasped his wrist and drew the vulpine's paw to his hard chest. The muscles were hard to the touch, and gently undulated with his rumbly breath. They did, indeed, fall off a bit as he traced their outlines to the sides and down. Except now Toby wasn't thinking at all about drawing correctly. His claw ran over the bumps of muscle, and before he knew it he was just above the beltline of Thor's leather pants. Coming back to the world, he jerked his paw back as if from a flame, heat rushing over his face. He knew his ears were beet-red. Also, he couldn't deny the tightness behind the zipper of his jean shorts.

Thor closed his vest back up and scowled a little, looking down at the vulpine. "Is something the matter?"

Forcing himself to look the tiger straight in the eyes, Toby said, "No, no... I guess I was wrong about the abs. I'll have to fix it later." He smiled weakly, and Thor seemed satisfied.

"Lift up your arms," said the big cat suddenly. Toby had no idea why he should do this, but there was something hidden in Thor's voice that told him to obey nonetheless. He complied, and his shirt was lifted off of him in one solid motion. He yipped in surprise, quickly covering his mouth at the adolescent sound.

The tiger looked him over appraisingly. Then he was on his knees, his head level with Toby's navel. The fox stood still, not knowing the intent of his very unusual but very attractive customer, and when he clasped his paws just above his tail, he realized they were trembling. If he couldn't remain decent now, there was no way Thor wouldn't notice. Big, pink-padded paws smoothed down where the shirt had pulled his white chestfur against the grain, running up to his neck and down to his belt, his claws even curling under a little bit. Still, Thor's touch was platonic and nothing more.

The wide muzzle smiled, then turned down in concentration, and finally relaxed. "Dang, I was going to say you could practice on yourself if you wanted to draw muscular anatomy, but you're not as defined as I thought you were. Just wanted to check."

"Sorry."

"Don't apologize; no big deal. That doesn't mean you can't *find* somebody to pose for you, just for practice. I would, but I'm kind of on a tight schedule."

"That's all right. Just you stopping here made my day. Usually I'm lucky if I get to talk to two people a day working here. I'm sure I can get back to sketching in no time." Toby couldn't stop the thought of Thor posing for him from entering his mind, and his sheath pulsed against the cotton of his briefs, right in front of the tiger's eyes. He swallowed again; his throat was as dry as the air outside.

There was an awkward silence from both furs: Toby looking down at the kneeling feline, Thor gazing pensively at the floor. Only the faraway call of a crow penetrated the office's open door. No cars had come since the T-Bird.

Toby's breath was consciously slow, and he was unable to think of anything to say to carry the conversation. He didn't have to, because in the next moment Thor thrust his head forward, turning it slightly, and bit around the fox's covered hardness. The tiger inhaled sharply, snarling, and let go with a sigh of pleasure. His eyes were closed but fluttering as if he were dreaming... or fantasizing. The fox felt the tip of his penis rubbing his briefs; his knot was becoming painfully obvious through his shorts.

At once Thor stood up, blushing and embarrassed. Toby was surprised to see such an expression on a rough-and-tumble exterior. The tiger turned to the counter, sighing again for a different reason, and braced himself. "I apologize, Toby. I was out of line. You should not have been subjected to that. I'd best just pay and be on my way." His tone was submissive and distracted.

The fox, still a bit stunned but as hard as ever, could do nothing but watch the big cat as he opened his wallet, fumbled with weak fingers, and pulled out a fifty-dollar bill. Toby saw the bill and became alarmed.

"This should cover it," said Thor, refusing to meet the vulpine's gaze but handing him the bill. Toby took it but knew it was of no use.

"I can't accept anything bigger than a twenty," he said, and Thor's face flashed past anger, and grew into slight worry.

"Do you take credit cards, then?" he said, sounding annoyed to make up for his embarrassment.

Toby cringed a bit, but his eyes were someplace not on the conversation. Thor was wrapping and unwrapping the fifty in front of his zipper, which still stood out quite easily from the crotch of his pants. "We only take cash," he muttered apologetically.

"Oh, great... " Thor rolled his eyes and scratched behind his head with one busy paw. He sighed a third time, obviously uncomfortable. "I don't know how I'm supposed to pay for this, so unless you have any big ideas we're both screwed." He was looking at the ceiling now, and when the fox didn't answer he brought his head down. Toby was thinking hard, all right... but in a much more obvious way.

A rustling caught his ear, and he realized Thor was twirling the money in front of his crotch. Self-consciously, he put the bill on the counter and his paw into his pocket, but Toby's eyes remained glued. All of a sudden he didn't feel as bad about giving in to the temptation to smell the little vulpine. The money forgotten, he watched, flattered, as Toby licked his lips, looking for all purposes like a hungry predator. It contradicted his personality, or at least what the tiger had gathered so far.

Entranced, the fox saw Thor put the bill up but couldn't move. He kept remembering the day with the perfect model, and how he had memorized every small detail about him. He almost whimpered from the uncomfortable pressure between his legs, but he dared not move or make a sound. The money problem was all but forgotten for the moment. He licked his lips; his whole body felt dried out and needy. Finally, he looked up at Thor's face, unable to hide anything.

The tiger's right paw came out of its pocket and up over the leather-clad waist, under one sleeve of the vest and pulled the material off, so now both furs were shirtless in the stuffy office. He leaned against the counter, the pressure on his tail enough to make his hips jut out just farther than the rest of him. Carefully, and without leaving Toby's stare, Thor hooked a claw on the zipper of his fly and brought it down slowly. The noise seemed deafening in the heavy silence. Following it was a barely audible groan of relief from the tiger.

Toby still looked into Thor's green eyes, but when he caught a flash of white from a place lower he averted his gaze. As the zipper came down, soft white fur filled the space where black leather had sealed it off. The feline finished by undoing the button on his pants, and it snapped open to reveal its pink-tipped prize, full but not yet exposed. The vulpine's heart felt about to burst.

As much as he was aroused, he couldn't help but notice the way light and shadow peaked and bottomed out over his defined torso. At last he found the strength to speak. Smiling and giggling, he managed, "Man, I would love to draw you…"

Taking advantage of the comment, Thor moved closer to the fox, his sheath bobbing a little further from his body. Leaning in past the russet muzzle, he simultaneously pinched the vulpine's trapped bulge and whispered in one ear: "You would, now?"

Thor's purposeful vagueness was teasingly infuriating. Whatever the tiger was going to do, he'd better do it now. Even walking away would bring an answer, and relief of its own kind.

But then Thor was on his knees again; as Toby watched he buried his broad, pink nose between his legs and sniffed hard, then clamped down around his concealed member, gnawing up and down its sheathed length and making him *meep!* and *yip!* and *erf!* in falsetto. One paw made its way easily under the loose fabric and went all the way to his balls, tickling them with a claw as the other undid his fly. The shorts came open, and then both them and his pre-stained briefs were around his ankles.

The tiger took a moment to admire the vulpine's tapered tip of flesh before licking its seeping entrance and pulling the white fur around it down and over Toby's growing knot. The fox stared into space now, thankful to be freed from his clothing. No attention was paid to the fact that a car could pull up for gas at any moment. There were more important matters to be addressed.

Thor stroked the seven-inch foxcock, narrow but shapely, noticing its pink surface was splashed with a black birthmark on one side. It was an amoebic shape, resembling nothing, but it was cute. The big tiger kissed it and stroked some more, keeping Toby's leaking tip free of fluid.

He stood up, placed a paw on each of the red-furred buttocks, lifted, and carried him to the counter. His sheath was just inside the cleft of Toby's rump, and he murred at the feeling. After setting the fox down, Thor spread Toby's legs so that the foxcock was unobstructed and his crotch fully exposed. The member bobbed slightly and twitched with a quickened, excited pulse.

"Hold on," the tiger warned, and Toby clutched his burly shoulders as he bent down to the fox's most vulnerable area.

Toby saw the striped muzzle go for his length, watched the tiger take every inch down to the knot, but he was beyond belief that what he was feeling could be possible from the simple touch of lips to skin. He was aware of his toes curling under, and the sound of claws being dug into the countertop.

Thor sealed his muzzle tightly around the shaft, slowing his movements to an agonizing pace. He started with his lips only, first in a straight up-and-down motion, then twisting his head to increase friction and Toby's resulting pleasure. Each of his paws was rubbing a corresponding thigh, scritching as they went, feeling the contours of the fox's sinewy muscles and soft buttocks. The vulpine's cock contrasted with the bright white of his sheath… at least what cock he could see in front of his nose.

Grasping the counter for balance and dear life, Toby closed his eyes to the pleasure. It was still only early afternoon, and the strong light penetrated his eyelids. The fur inside his ears and his whiskers swayed in the gentle breeze from the lone fan, and his wagging tongue felt cooled for the first time that day. Beyond the soft *whirr* were gentle wet slurps and Thor's breathing through his nose as he serviced the fox.

Satisfied that his partner was sufficiently warmed up, Thor struck out his tongue on an up-thrust, and caught the underside of the fox's head with its rough surface. He heard a yelp from above him, and suddenly his wrists were bathed in sharp pain, but he couldn't tell if the sound was from discomfort or pleasure. The big cat kept up his ministrations, and the fox settled into a series of strained moans, which meant he was doing something right.

Toby let go of the tiger's injured wrists, making a mental note to apologize later for hurting him. At the moment, however, the cat's raspy tongue was making quick work of him. He placed his palms flat against the counter and thrust upward to meet that wonderful warm muzzle. Since he couldn't touch himself, he raised his head back, out of the harsh light a little, and fell victim to the orgasm that quickly built up in his loins.

Humming in a low register around the fox's cock, Thor slowed up again, opening his jaw wide enough to just take in Toby's knot. He felt the balls below his chin draw up tight against the vulpine's body, and he darted his tongue out one last time. The poor fox jerked and held onto his forearms with determination, and the back of his throat was sprayed with hot fluid.

Toby gritted his teeth and held his breath, only to let it out again forcefully. Little streams of saliva fell from in between his teeth; he felt like he had no control over his own body. The fact was, Thor had all the control right now, and that only made his climax twice as strong. He felt it leaving his body in great spurts, felt the tiger's throat working to swallow all of his seed, that rough tongue caressing his knot and the stretched sheath close to his body.

The rest of the fox's load trickled out of him as Thor eased off the swollen knot before it could trap his muzzle open. He retreated, drawing a lower fang over his urethra to milk the last out. He stood to his full height again, licking his lips and smiling. That was one of the better tasting loads, to his knowledge, that he had taken.

"I've never tasted fox before," the big cat said, wiping himself on a forearm to make sure he didn't miss anything. He could see deep furrows in both the counter's top and sides, from four sets of claw marks. Toby's head was lowered, his tongue flaccid and moving with every ragged breath he took. After catching his breath, he slid off the counter, but his legs buckled beneath his weight. He stumbled into Thor, who caught him before he fell all the way to the floor.

He did fall far enough, however, to bump his nose into a couple inches of tigercock peeking out of leather. Before Thor could pull him up, he gave a few bobbing passes to the barbed member. A loud growl signaled the tiger's assent.

Toby finally got to his feet… and to his senses, pulling on his shorts just as soon as he was resheathed. One last drop of cum glistened at the tip, and the fox swiped it up and onto his tongue, smiling cheekily at Thor across from him. "I've never tasted tiger before, either."

"I've got a better idea," Thor said, zipping his half-hard member back into his pants and leading the fox by the paw out of the station.

"Where are we going? I can't leave the office unattended," said Toby as they passed around the corner of the building and into the clearing of dead brush between the station and the old white well-cylinder. He was practically dragged behind the structure; tumbleweeds scraped his bare footpads. When Thor had gone far enough so that the cylinder blocked any view from the road, he turned to face the fox.

The tiger had a smile on his face. Whatever he was planning, it couldn't be done inside. His curiosity was piqued when the tiger asked him, in a hushed whisper even though they were alone, "Have you gone to the bathroom yet today?"

Toby paused. "Actually, no." But just the thought of answering such a question stirred his bladder into announcing its fullness. He did have to piss, now that he thought about it.

"Good."

"Why do you want... oh, no. No, no, no." The fox started to back away slowly, but halfheartedly. Thor followed him, imploring.

"Come on, Toby. Do me a favor and mark me. Who's it gonna hurt? Oh, God, I sound like a Saturday morning special." The big, built tiger ran his paws through his headfur and laughed in a high, barking tone. He saw that Toby was thinking, so he walked up and embraced the smaller fox, holding him in his tight, huge arms. "Please?" he asked, although he knew the answer already. He let go of the fox.

Toby didn't have to think very hard. Yeah, it was weird, but who cared after what Thor had done for him? He turned around to answer, but held his tongue when he saw the feline was already naked, kneeling before him, muzzle wide open. It was funny, and a little unnerving to see a tiger, who had pulled up leather-clad in *the* classic American sports car, the very picture of masculinity, submitting before him in the dusty backyard of a desert gas station.

"You're crazy," the fox stated incredulously, and stepped forward while unzipping his shorts again. Thor ran his paws through his chestfur, tweaking his nipples so hard he made himself yowl in pain. Nonetheless, his half-hard cock sprang to its full nine inches, the length emerging straight out from his groin. As the fox released his sheath, a drop of precum oozed from Thor's tip, stayed there for a moment glinting in the sunlight, and drooled to the ground, never breaking. The tiger milked his member, and more added to the small puddle.

60

One eye scanning around, the other watching the begging cat, and his ears waiting for the sound of approaching engines, Toby drew the first few inches of his penis out and down, aiming directly for Thor's muzzle. The big cat stroked himself vigorously, his paw slick and matted with pre, and his mouth opened wide. The green eyes focused on the vulpine cock aimed at him, awaiting a rare treat he seldom had the pleasure to experience. He was actually whimpering a little.

"Um, Thor…" Toby was finding it difficult to let himself go. He tried, but his bladder refused to cooperate. "I don't think it's working."

"Fine then," said the tiger authoritatively, reaching out with his free paw and using a light touch to massage just behind Toby's scrotum. As the fox moaned from the massage, Thor extended a claw and dug it into the skin, hard. Toby jumped; his bladder let go in a sudden rush of acidic warmth, and he had just enough time to aim before a stream of yellow fluid arced out of him and directly onto Thor's broad nose.

The big tiger drew back and let the warm spray shower him from the head down, his broad tongue lapping up whatever happened to land upon it. Toby aimed lower, soaking the white chest, watching the fur mat, the nipples harden. It pooled in the sheath that was bunched up around the base of his cock, his paw catching it and flinging urine and precum over the ground in front of his legs.

"Mmmm, oh yeah," he mumbled in between breaths and swallows.

Toby saw the look of pure simplistic enjoyment on the tiger's face, and began to see a little bit of what the feline was getting out of this. He smiled and renewed his efforts, aiming to cover the rest of Thor, whose solid chest now heaved with effort.

Eyes closed, the tiger felt the warmth penetrate him down to the skin, tasted salt on his tongue. The craving grew along with his arousal, and he covered the short distance to Toby on his knees. Toby's stream was dying but still strong, and Thor had to finish before the flow reduced to nothing. He rooted around the fox's groin, snuffling and taking in the very essence of vulpine… young, sweet and unspoiled. Then Toby's member disappeared, his paw shoved out of the way as Thor sucked what little he had left to give.

A grunt emanated from his crotch, but Toby paid it no mind. The fox's head was lifted to the sky to release a constant breathy sound that would have been a moan, were there more power behind it. His right leg felt as if it were in a vice, and then Thor slid off his cock, which had released all it had to give and started to harden again. At last the big tiger exhaled, his body collapsing from the effort of strained muscles. Leaning back on his knees, he looked up gratefully at the fox, who shook his head in disbelief.

"I really need to do that more often," Thor muttered, looking at his cum- and urine-stained chestfur. There was quite a load mixed in with the white, and spots also covered the orange and black stripes on his thighs.

"That was... different." Toby meant it to sound slightly sarcastic, but in his mind he had actually enjoyed it... and wondered what it would feel like to trade places with the tiger. At the moment he was too spent to care. Then, he snapped to reality with a sickening thought. "How are you going to wash all that off? I don't think you wanna get dressed like that." He offered a paw to Thor, who took it.

The tiger pulled himself up and said, "No need to worry." He pointed to an old garden hose, attached to a rusty and peeling spigot in the side of the cylinder. "I never do this sort of thing unless I have a way to clean up. I may be a little kinky, but I'm not stupid." He reached down and, with an effort that made his body tense up and give the young fox quite a show, turned the knob. There was a rush of brackish, rust-colored water for a time, then it ran clear and cold.

Toby was nonplussed. "Huh! I never thought that thing actually worked."

"Could you help me?" Thor handed him the hose, and the fox rinsed his friend down with the freezing water, watching him dance and shiver, making sure to put his thumb to the spray and jet several crucial areas of his body. After Thor was satisfied, he held onto a ladder on the cylinder and shook himself vigorously. The air was full of rainbows, and then they were gone. He picked up his pants and slid them on, then both furs walked in silence back to the station's office.

"I still don't know how I'm going to pay for this stuff," Thor muttered as he held the door for the fox.

Toby went behind the counter where the bill still sat, looked at it in the light and opened the register. He made change and handed it back to the tiger. "I'll just go to my house in town at the end of my shift, get change from my parents, and come back to the till. The bill's good, and besides..." the fox jingled something in his pocket... "I have the keys." The tiger chuckled. "People are too trusting in this fucking town. I've been here way too long."

"I could tell that the minute you walked out that door and offered to fill up my car. Seeing your sketches there, I feel sorry for you being stuck in this hellhole. Tell me... why are you pumping gas instead of selling your art?"

Toby almost laughed, but knew it would be inappropriate. He swiped his arm in a wide, encompassing arc, then turned to the tiger with a look of practiced dejectedness. "All these people want are cowboys, God and mountains, on sale at Wal-Mart. I'm sick of all three, and I don't even want to draw the first two. Tell me how I'm supposed to sell anything, or even hope for a job." He couldn't help the note of cynicism in his voice, and suddenly he felt very alone.

"You have a degree?" Thor inquired. Even though it wasn't his place to ask, Toby felt genuinely flattered by the question. Still in the last remaining stages of his afterglow, his mind was forced to go back to thinking normally when, in fact, the fox was still trying to come to terms with the fact that he'd just scentmarked a tiger just about twice his size. This same tiger was now making small-talk. As odd as it was, Toby suddenly felt very comfortable in Thor's presence. Actually, he had never felt *un*comfortable at all. He was glad for the attention.

The fox smirked facetiously. "Yeah, a bachelor's in unleaded." He saw the hurt in Thor's eyes and immediately recanted, sighing. "I'm sorry. No, I came here directly out of high school. Nobody has money to pay for something like that. I'm trying; that's why I'm here."

"You know there're scholarships all over the place, don't you?"

"Not enough for art school."

The non-sequitur smile that crossed Thor's large muzzle made Toby wary. "I'll tell you a little secret," he said, mimicking the do-you-wanna-know-a-secret excited whisper of a sideshow barker. Pulling the fox's ear closer, he whispered, sending little puffs and vibrations into his head. It was almost too distracting to listen to the words. "I deal in historic cars, Toby. I hold auctions all over this country, meet the most interesting people you could ever hope to meet, and pull in a salary closer to seven figures than it is to six."

Why is he telling me all this? If this is his idea of a pep talk…

Thor paused for emphasis, then, in the quietest rumble he could manage: "I don't have a degree. You don't need one."

"Bullshit." It was a blatant and vulgar statement, and Toby regretted it, but it was the God's-honest truth. He didn't believe it.

"Believe it," the tiger quipped, stepping back and gesturing with his arms reassuringly. His eyes glowed with feline intelligence and an almost giddiness at being able to give Toby such good news. "Listen, kid. You're good. I don't pretend to know a hell of a lot about art, but I like what I see when I see it. It's rare when I find something I like, too. Really."

"But I don't even have a résumé!" the fox found himself whining, already more fully into the conversation than he had wanted to be. But they were talking about passion, something both obviously had in common. Thor motioned for him to listen, and he relented.

"One thing I learned growing up was that you don't need a piece of paper with letters on it to say you're good at something. All it says is that you got a bunch of A's and made your teachers happy. But if you don't do good work worth a shit, you're no use to anybody *in real life*." The ease with which Thor's words came together and was accentuated by the robust arm gestures which gave him credit with the still-doubtful fox standing behind the counter.

The tiger watched his statements have no visible effect on Toby, and his whole body seemed to fall limp. "Look," he said, "I'm not going to pull any Lifetime television speech crap on you about following your dream and never giving up. I'm just saying that, when you ever get to interview for jobs, your potential bosses aren't going to ask you for a degree. They're going to ask for your portfolio. You would have one, too, if you'd quit drawing X's over everything you do."

There it was. The sentence that practically broke Toby's humble heart. Sure, he'd been told he was good before, but for someone… anyone… to sit there and spout out advice, when they had a hundred better things to do? The unsolicited generosity emanated by the tiger was overwhelming, and he had to regulate his breathing to hold back a blubbering sob of gratefulness. Instead, thankfully, he smiled broadly.

"You really like my stuff? Good enough for a job?"

"I can't say anything other than my opinion, and I definitely can't make promises, but you impressed me. And I've been around. With money like mine, you can't help but have taste." A vision of Thor, leather-bound and seated at a glass-topped table sipping tea with his pinky out, came to the fox's mind.

Oh, the juxtaposition! he thought, and giggled aloud.

"What?"

"N-nothing."

"Okay," said the tiger, rolling his eyes, pseudo-satisfied. "I'd better get going. Wanna make it to Cali before the sun goes down." There was tangible regret in his voice. He looked at his wrist, which was watchless, for emphasis.

"Yeah, okay." Slowly, Toby came back to feeling like a kid again, now that Thor had changed the subject. He was again the simple gas-jockey, but he still held on to that residual feeling of specialness left by the tiger's words. He followed Thor out to the pump, carrying his few purchases through the claustrophobic heat of the Nevada day, and set them in the passenger seat. He came around back to Thor to bid him farewell, now finding himself actually attracted to him on a more-than-superficial level.

"You're all topped off."

"Thanks, Toby." The tiger started to bend down into the T-bird, stopped, and stood again. In one quick, furtive motion, he bent over at the waist, lifted the fox's chin in his meaty paw and planted a gentle, affectionate kiss on Toby's forehead. Such grace from such a big buff person totally blew him away. There were no words, in his mouth or his head. "Good luck, kid. Don't know when I'll be out in this part of nowhere next. But I'll be thinking of you."

Without waiting or watching for a response, Thor slid easily into the convertible, its relatively fresh springs squeaking under the added weight. The door shut heavily, the big engine roared to life and settled into a throaty idle.

The tiger glanced at Toby through the rearview mirror, and saw the expression of abandonment on his muzzle. There was a sting of regret in his gut, but he gunned the engine a little. Toby, now a bit recovered from the kiss, smiled at hearing the exhaust note, and they were both okay.

He wanted to yell "Thank you!" as Thor sped away down the road, dust flying behind the T-Bird as it headed west, to the city. But even if he could have been heard above the pistons and gravel, what would he have said to reciprocate Thor's actions? Maybe it was best to leave it alone after all; maybe that was the way the tiger would have wanted it left. And just like that, silence took the day back for itself.

The fox walked back to the safe, cooler shade of the office, humming a Beach Boys tune as he did so. Closing the door and sitting back down, he quickly replayed what had happened in his mind. There were lots of questions, there were bound to be a lot of questions, but instead of pondering them the vulpine accepted this abnormal day in Warren at face value.

He hummed the tune absently. His feet went back onto the counter, crossed, his pawpads leaving traces of dust on the surface. The young fox leaned back and closed his eyes for a moment. They jerked to and fro, as if searching for something. Suddenly they reopened, and his muzzle spread into a wide, knowing grin.

His paw flew, tracing circles and lines over the paper into a familiar shape, only minutes old in his mind. This time he had a perfect reference.

On Hooking

Pornography, a word with which we are rather familiar these days, literally refers to 'the depiction and description of prostitutes and their activities'. It is only fitting then, that two such works should be included in this volume.

The first, "Nocturnal Emissions," is the story of a typical night in the life of a young feline 'working boy', making a living in the harsh city. This piece indulges more even than it explores the themes of co-operative exploitation, of the curious dynamic of control and submission that exists in a situation where sex is paid for and provided as a service.

Nocturnal Emissions

Mikori

The streets were cold at night. But you get used to it. In the city, working the alleys was one of the best ways to get fast money, if you had the body for it, and the desire.

Most people didn't go into prostitution willingly. There were always circumstances, like your mother was sick and needed money fast, or you had lost your job and needed to pay rent, or perhaps you had gambling debts. The list was endless, and unique stories weren't hard to find. There were people, though, who whored themselves out because it was an easy way to make money. Because they enjoyed the thrill and didn't care about the social repercussions. Jason was one of them.

Feet nearly silent on the sidewalk, the young serval and his canine friend walked down the sidewalk. Overhead, various insects, mostly harmless, were visible circling the stark white glow of the streetlights. The occasional car rumbled past on the road, bathing both males in yellowish light. It wasn't a common occurrence, considering it was just past ten at night. Far beyond rush hour.

"How're ya feeling tonight?" the wolf asked Jason. The young feline smiled quietly up at the canid in return, and nudged him on the side with an elbow.

"Feelin' great. If I'm lucky, I'll make a couple hundred tonight. You know, Bret, you really oughtta try this, instead of that stockroom crap you have to do at the store. Pays a lot better." A dainty, long-fingered hand was passed through the feline's blond hair. "And it's more fun, too."

A wry grin passed over the black lab's face. He nudged Jason's hip in return with his own, and replied, "No thanks. Unlike some of us, I have plans for the future. I don't think law school would approve if they found out I was earning money in… less than legal ways, hm?" A casual smile was cast Bret's way in return.

"Suit yourself. More for me, then."

Both feline and canine came to a stop next to Bret's apartment building. For a moment, Jason felt a twinge of regret. The two had grown up together, and a few years back, Bret had asked if the serval would move in with him. Jason had just turned eighteen, and had just gotten his first fifty from sucking off some tiger after the bars had closed. It had been so easy to fall into that world, to allow himself to become entranced by any guy willing to fork over a few bills, and that's how things had been going for the past two years. Occasionally, Jason wondered how things would be now, if he'd moved in with Bret rather than getting his own loft downtown, amidst the nightclubs.

"Well. Seeya," the wolf called over to Jason, who lifted a paw and smiled in return. It was only a moment of reflection. He was happy doing what he did, he decided, and it was nice to be able to walk Bret home after the canid's shift at the warehouse. It gave them some time to catch up on things.

It was only another block until the serval's usual prowl. It was a good spot, a street corner that was easily visible from a pair of bars. One of them was a strip joint. Most of the guys who came to him from there were aroused from watching the women, and were either involved and frustrated, or between girlfriends. They weren't looking for much, just a willing mouth and a little eagerness. If they had a problem with guys in general, most of the time, Jason was just girly enough to convince them that it'd be okay 'this one time'. The serval figured that probably nine out of ten of his clients came from here.

The other establishment was a little higher end. Most of the people who frequented the "Lunar Eclipse" were there to relax after a hard day managing their company. Champagne flowed like water and most emerged late at night to be driven home in their BMWs by a (hopefully) designated driver. On the rare occasion that one of them didn't have a few harlots waiting at home and noticed Jason, they paid well. Really well. Once, he'd been able to take a whole week off once after putting up with just a few hours of rough sex.

Jason eventually came to a stop, on his corner. He reclined up against the streetlight, and carefully slid a few fingers through his light hair, making sure everything was in place. "Damn this awful lighting," he thought to himself. The artificial brightness cast over him never presented him at his most flattering.

Now came the hardest part. Waiting, and trying to entice interest in the slender, young body that he'd worked so hard on making attractive. As a serval, he had tall ears, about eight inches' worth, that poked through the golden-blond hair that topped his head. Just a little under six feet tall and about a hundred and forty pounds, his body was covered in black spots of varying shape and size, over a coat of tawny fur. Most of the guys who he'd serviced commented that they liked the way those spots led right down between his legs, both in front and on back, so what he wore was designed to emphasize that. A black leather vest, too small for his body, was worn open over his torso. It occasionally revealed flashes of silver from where barbells pierced both nipples. Further down, a black stretch-velvet thong was all that covered the feline's crotch and ass. Jason's opinion was that the cops hadn't bothered him yet because they liked looking just as much as everyone else.

Every now and then, a single male or a group would emerge from one of the two clubs, usually moving with inebriated awkwardness. It wasn't that Jason really minded the alcohol. After all, their money was as good as anyone else's. But it was tricky, trying to tell the mean drunks from the guys who had just had one too many.

A pair of guys wandered nearby. Two gazelles, laughing quietly among themselves. They glanced briefly his way, and the serval cocked his hips their way, and offered the two a tantalizing smile and a lick of his lips over to the two herbivores as his tail snaked around over that nearly naked rump of his. The only response he got was a nervous look, and hurried steps.

"Ah well," Jason murmured to himself. "Not every fish will bite." There was plenty of time left in the night, after all.

Hours passed slowly. Business was usually slow until around midnight or one, when people began to file out of the clubs more frequently. Now, things were beginning to pick up. Some of the cheaper boys had already left with their clients, leaving just Jason now with a few of his chief competitors'. Jason's eyes shifted over toward one of them, a leopard girl, a few years his senior. She was in the process of seducing a stallion who looked more than a little intrigued. It was so much easier for the women.

"Hey, kid. You looking for something?"

The voice was deep, masculine, intriguing. Jason glanced back over his shoulder at its owner.

There were two men standing behind him. The one who had spoken was grinning down at him from a height of probably around six and a half feet, blunt teeth white and shiny. Two long, curved horns extended from the top of his head, and a thick silver ring hooped through both nostrils. Stereotypical for a bull, but somehow it looked right. Amused brown eyes met the serval's, and he actually felt himself blush a little. That hadn't happened in ages.

The other male standing there was a lion. Only slightly shorter than his partner, the feline had an arm looped casually around the bovine's waist. A black mane, tied back in a braid that hung over his back, framed a broad tawny-muzzled face with amber eyes. Both of the males were powerful. It was every hooker's dream… two guys you'd probably sleep with even if you weren't getting paid.

The bull, who seemed mostly to be in charge, didn't seem like he wanted to waste much time. "I'm Jack," he declared, jabbing one thick thumb against those broad pecs of his. "This's Vic. And your name ain't important. Yer gonna take care of us tonight. Got it, boy?"

Vic, quiet up until this point, shifted. Both males were decked out in leather, both wearing pairs of those tight leather pants that showed off your ass and package like you weren't wearing anything at all. The only difference was that Vic was wearing a vest similar to Jason's, while Jack's powerful torso was bared. Leather creaked as the silent lion pulled something from a pocket, and extended it toward the serval. Between index and middle fingers was held a pair of hundred dollar bills. Jason's eyes widened a little. This was perfect. He reached up, took the money from the lion, and slipped it into the inner pocket of his own vest. This was all the acceptance that Jack needed. He reached down, grasped Jason by the collar of the vest, and pulled the stumbling feline along behind him. Vic assisted, with one paw around the serval's wrist.

Jason tried not to get too excited. This was business, after all. But, there was something about the way that the two guys were treating him that was really pushing his buttons. It was something about Jack's overwhelmingly cocky demeanor, and the way that Vic just watched him, like it wasn't even worth his time to speak his desires. Eventually, the serval settled into a quiet pace between the two larger males, following wherever they led. Somehow, it just felt right.

Once again, they only went a block, down to a rundown Motel 8 that Jason was familiar with. It was one of the most convenient places to bring a client, and these two men seemed to know the place as well as the serval. After all, the dog tending the counter only grinned, and tossed Vic a key when Jack pushed through the door and nodded to him.

The staircase creaked as the three males made their way upstairs, Jason sandwiched between the bull and the lion. While Jack fumbled with the lock, a quiet growl was breathed into the smaller feline's ear as Vic pressed up behind him, and the serval was treated to the sensation of that warm, leather-clad package pressing up under his tail. Subtly, he pressed right back.

"Awright, loverboy, inside," Jack sneered over his shoulder at Jason. The young serval's tall ears folded back, and he bowed his head in reply. Jack looked pleased. He had no idea how Vic felt about it. The lion's steely gaze was expressionless. The only way he could tell how the larger feline was feeling was the increasingly prominent bulge between his legs. Jack thumped into the room, followed by Jason, who was not-so-gently pushed inside by the lion, who closed the door behind him.

For just a moment, the three stood there. Jason looked between the two tall, powerful males, simply admiring the view for now. Surprisingly enough, Vic was the first to make a move. Casually, the big feline shrugged out of his vest, and tossed it onto the floor. The serval's green eyes snapped over to the lion's body as Vic lifted both brawny arms, and flexed. A quiet sigh escaped Vic, as he indulged in sensuous stretches that relaxed his body and prepared him for the 'ordeal' that was coming. It was about the most noise Jason had heard him make all night. Almost at the same time, a heavy hand came to rest on the serval's shoulder.

"Strip," Jack growled into one of his ears. "Show off that pretty little body of yers, cat. Show us both what we're payin' for."

Aah, something familiar. Having something to concentrate on was a brief respite for Jason, who'd been fighting to control an erection. "Whatever you say," he purred in reply. Jack's lips were tugged upwards into another shit-eating grin, even as he released the hustler, reached down, and casually unbuttoned the front of his dark leather jeans.

Jason closed his slanted eyes. Usually, he'd have a beat or something playing on the radio that he could used to establish a rhythm. He didn't have either with Jack and Vic. The only sound that permeated the room was the heavy breathing that he could hear from both of them, broad chests that looked as if they'd been worked on for years rising and falling. So, he went with what he had.

The young feline nudged his hips forward, reached down, and slowly slide those slender fingers of his up along his inner thighs. As his hips rotated silently to that mostly imaginary beat, his paws drifted over his own slender body, caressing that concave belly, his chest, the fur down right over his knees. He was going to make sure that the two guys got their money's worth.

"Oh, good boy. What a hot little piece he is, ain't he, Victor?" Jack growled under his breath, brown eyes flicking briefly over toward the lion. The large bull was standing there just a few feet away, casually massaging a thick bulge in his trousers. It snaked down one pant-leg a little bit, thick and impressive. Jason was jolted out of his reverie momentarily as he glanced between Jack and Victor. The lion simply nodded in reply to the bull's question. What had the young serval distracted was what he saw as the lion, quite without pretense, simply pushed those leathers down over his legs and stepped out of them.

Victor was big down there. Those leonine legs were powerful, toned beneath the short tawny fur that covered them. The pelt between his thighs was a little thicker. Already erect and holding his maleness in one fist, the lion's jutting cock was around seven inches of pink flesh, nicely proportioned all over, sheath pulled back around its base. But what really made Jason falter were the heavy balls that hung beneath. They were huge. Probably about the size of peaches. The serval tried to keep his mouth from watering as he thought about what a load the silent male would probably shoot.

Jason had barely managed to keep moving as he watched Vic disrobe. It made the lion grin, sharp canines visible over each corner of his lips. He angled his swollen erection up toward the serval's mouth, even as a glob of clear, crystalline precum trickled from that slick glans. Quietly, the young feline shrugged out of his vest. His thong was already bulging with a prominent erection, and his scent, along with that of the bull and lion, was easily distinguishable in the air. There was no hiding his arousal now.

"Good boy," the bull murmured again, one big hand squeezing himself down where the leather barely concealed his own erection. "Now. Off with the panties." Large fingers wrestled his button and fly open, and the bull began to slowly push his own trousers down. Jason was looking forward to the view.

Carefully, the serval eased his fingers down into the edge of his thong. Each movement was deliberate, planned, and the two big men watching him obviously appreciated it. Though, those erections were probably more likely a result of anticipation for what lay ahead than just watching him dance. Pulling the elastic of the waistband outwards, he nudged it carefully around his own cock, then down over his legs. The serval was proud of his body. A modest six inches of circumcised dick dribbled between his legs. He wasn't huge, but then, most of the people he slept with weren't after his cock. It was the other side that saw most of the use.

Jason's ass was tight and almost femininely rounded. Gold, black, and white fur all sloped down between his buttocks toward the tight little pink ring right under his tail. Though well used quite often, the serval's rear always healed quickly.

With a grunt, Jack pushed his own trousers downwards, and slipped legs that were even more impressive than Vic's out of the leather. This time,

Jason really stared. What was probably a full nine inches of human-style meat, glistening black at the glans and lighter in the drooping foreskin that mostly concealed his glans, hung heavily from between the bull's thighs. The big male's cocky grin only widened. Even as he curled one fist around the base of his shaft and began to pump slowly, the bull reached over, lay a heavy hand atop the serval's shoulder, and pushed him down to his knees.

Jason was almost amazed at the large male's strength, even though he wasn't exactly putting up a fight. Resting down there on the motel's old rug as Vic and Jack both closed in on him, the serval couldn't believe how turned on his was.

"Ya know what's comin' kid, don't ya?" The bull's voice had taken on a husky edge, an almost dangerous growl that made Jason shudder with arousal. Vic's amber eyes continued to stare down at him, half a grin pulling at his lips as the lion's hips nudged forward, brushing his heavily dripping cockhead over one of the serval's cheek. A few strands of fur were matted down, and Jason inhaled the heavy scents of arousal abruptly presented to his face. It was exquisite, like this whole night was ending up, powerful musk that made him forget all about the money, all about the job. He just wanted to make these two men feel as good as he possibly could.

"Yer gonna suck him off," Jack continued. "And I'm gonna plow that pretty ass of yours." Vic nodded, silently. "So ya better get me nice and slick, before I decide just ta stick it in as is," the bull finally concluded. Green eyes flicked up to meet Jack's for a moment, and he nodded, ears folded back. Jason understood his position here. Reaching up to carefully grip the thick base of the bull's uncut meat, Jason spent a few second simply staring at it. It was beautiful, the way the black flesh throbbed, the way it felt in his fingers. Once again, the serval's reverie was interrupted when Vic's furry paw curled fingers through his hair, and shoved his face up against Jack's erection.

The bull groaned, heatedly. That broad chest expanded, then retracted as he took deep breaths. Vic knew exactly what he liked, and apparently, the boy they'd hired liked it too. The eager little prostitute moaned heatedly down there as his face was smeared across foreskin damp with precum and sweat.

Jason's eyes fluttered. He panted directly up against the bull's fragrant cock as Vic 'forced' him over it. A few seconds later, the bull took over, tugging firmly on the serval's blond hair with one hand, and prying his jaws open with the other. "Suck, boy," he muttered under his breath. Almost too quickly, that musk-heavy erection was fed between the serval's lips. He closed his mouth around it, sealing Jack's still thickening meat inside his muzzle.

Just a few inches away now, Vic continued to gaze down at his and Jack's prize. He squeezed one of his own hips sensuously in one paw, even as he continued to pump his slippery cock in the other. As Jason was quickly finding out, the sheer size that Jack possessed was easily made up for by how much liquid the feline seemed to produce. Little droplets of clear fluid trickled over Jason's face, dripping off his chin and down onto his chest. The slim feline shivered subtly as he felt the soft fur on his face grow even damper.

This was one of the things that Jason enjoyed the most, and despite the excitement he experienced just because it was sex, he didn't often get to *really* enjoy his work. Something really turned him on about having a hot guy get him slick and sticky with precum, and then their load afterwards. He knew it was perverse, but who really cared in this job? Everyone had their interesting kinks.

The serval nearly choked as Jack grunted, pulled his head further up, and just about hilted those thick nine inches inside Jason's throat. His cock tasted like… male. Almost bitter. Musky. He loved it. With the slick sound of Victor's paw sliding back and forth over his own shaft close in his ears, the smaller feline reached up to brace his paws on Jack's powerful thighs. He took a deep breath, pushed his muzzle up further, and swallowed the big bull's erection to the fur around its base.

Jack snorted loudly, and his fingers unconsciously pulled tighter on Jason's hair. The boy was better than he'd expected. Two hundred wasn't much to Vic and him, but it was nothing he'd ever casually thrown away. The night was definitely looking up. He could tell from Vic's expression that the lion was feeling the same way. Brown eyes flicked down to watch the serval who was so skillfully nursing on his twitching erection, and with an almost reluctant sigh, he pulled the boy's dark lips back off of his now glistening shaft.

"Awright, boy. On your knees." Jack almost sounded impatient, now. After he'd pulled Jason's lips back, the bull had reached down, grasped his erection, and begun stroking it firmly to keep it as hard as the young male had gotten it. Vic was starting to get a little tense as well, toes curling, a faint growl building in his throat.

Jason, still trying to regain his breath after swallowing that huge, uncut erection, simply nodded up at Jack, and shifted his slim body away from the bull. He arched his back, glanced over his shoulder momentarily, and flicked his tail upwards.

Jack licked his lips with that broad tongue of his. The serval's ass looked perfect, spread so willingly like that. This was going to be fun. The bull crouched down over Jason's boyish body, and pushed that meaty cock of his up between those taut buttocks. A thin trickle of precum, aided by the young feline's saliva, dampened the little furless spot underneath Jason's tail. The little cat moaned heatedly, as if on cue. At the same time, Vic was moving in from the front.

Jason's slim body trembled with anticipation as he felt Jack's hot flesh sliding up against him. It had been a while since he'd taken anyone as big as the bull was. It was going to be intense. Vic's own scent continued to grow more intense. Without a sound other than that constant, deep growl, the lion pushed that copiously dripping erection up against his lips. The young serval lifted his head to meet the slick glans of the large feline's cock, opened his mouth, and slid the first few inches of the lion's dick across his tongue.

It was even more delicious like this, fed directly to him rather than dripping off of his nose or cheeks. This, combined with the nearly bitter, musky taste of the lion's flesh, made Jason moan softly with arousal around his mouthful, and Vic grunted and nudged his hips forward again. Jack's grin widened again as well. It looked so right, having the slim little spotted cat pinned between them. The large bull's big hands both rested on Jason's slender hips now, while Vic had tangled his fingers through the serval's silky blond hair.

Jason felt both of the bigger, powerfully muscled males begin to work him between them, slowly and leisurely at first. Jack's erection throbbed with need as he pulled his broad hips back, and positioned his engorged cockhead right at the young feline's tight little anus. The warm spot that he felt gradually yielding to his shaft glistened with his precum, which was making things a lot easier. The bull's eyes fluttered closed, and he snorted, a tremor coursing through him.

"Fuckin' tight little bitch," Jack growled, more to his leonine partner than to the young feline between himself and Victor. The big lion's broad grin only widened, and he nodded once in reply. Perhaps a little more roughly than he intended, thick fingers kneaded at the serval's taut buttocks while his brown eyes remained fixed on the sight under Jason's tail. He loved watching himself slip into an eager young male. Hearing the smaller of the felines whimper and pant really stroked the ego.

Jason was in heaven. He'd only been fucked by two guys at once a few times before, and this was definitely the best of them. Even better because he was getting paid so well for it! Supporting himself on the ground with one paw, the other had found its way to Vic's sizeable balls, which he was gently kneading and tugging on. The serval's shapely little muzzle slid back and forth slowly along the lion's erection, which was dripping more than probably anyone else he'd ever been with. It was virtually a steady flow of precum, and he had to swallow every ten or fifteen seconds just to keep up with it. Just as often though, he'd let that warm fluid simply spill out from between his lips, running slickly down over his chin and neck.

He was unbelievably aroused. The serval had to fight not to shoot off without touching himself. He found himself trying to think about mundane things, math problems, old teachers. Women. It worked a little bit, and he gradually fought back that approaching climax. It was only a matter of time, though.

Above him, Vic had begun to growl more loudly. That tawny-furred body was shaking, and Jason was picking up the telltale signs of an approaching orgasm. He was only a little surprised at the big feline's hair trigger. The serval had begun to pull back a little, an attempt to prolong the feline's orgasm, when abruptly, he felt those fingers tighten in his hair, and those hips shoved forward, hilting all twitching seven inches in the serval's throat. His eyes snapped open and teared up a little bit as he fought not to gag on the intruder that was unexpectedly throbbing in his throat. The powerful bovine abruptly slapped the serval's slender ass, which made him shudder all over.

"You ain't goin' nowhere," Jack growled, not even looking away from the slim ass he was continuing to push into. It was obvious how well he knew his partner. "Vic here's gonna hose ya down. Get ya all nice an' gooey, since that's what slutty little boys like you enjoy." Once again, Vic seemed perfectly happy to let the bull do the talking. His amber eyes were squeezed shut, lips drawn back into an aroused snarl, fingers pulling harshly on Jason's hair.

Jason shuddered as Jack's words elicited a few delicious mental images. With the amount of liquid that was flowing across his tongue, the serval almost could have been fooled into thinking that the lion was coming already. He'd tasted so many loads in the last few years though that it was usually pretty difficult to fool him. Vic abruptly shuddered above him, and the tug on the young serval's hair became painful. The lion's cock surged in his mouth, and a sudden splatter of syrupy cum filled the young male's muzzle.

Jason gurgled as he felt that first massive spray of semen flood across his teeth, coat his tongue in salty warmth, ooze down his throat. He swallowed reflexively, even as the older feline's shaft swelled again, and fountained another thick gush of semen between the serval's lips. It was intense, almost bitter, and claws bit into Jason's scalp almost hard enough to break the skin. Abruptly, Vic shoved the teenager's head back, closed a fist around the base of his thick feline maleness, and began to beat himself off. That deep growl remained a constant, even as the serval felt rope after rope of hot cum jetting over his face.

Jack's eyes rose from the slender little ass he was penetrating with those thick inches of uncut meat as his lion cohort began blasting the little serval's muzzle with his load. As always, Vic's orgasm was intense. The whimpering, obviously aroused young feline held his head high to receive what the older cat was giving him.

By the time Vic's climax had faded, probably almost half a minute later, Jason had slumped down just a little bit on shaking arms. Thick globs of semen hung from his chin, drooling thick and long down to the floor. Streams of it ran down his cheeks to soak his neck and chest. A big drop oozed slowly down over the ridge of his nose, and some had even soaked into his hair. The young feline was completely overwhelmed. In all his time turning tricks, he'd never encountered two guys as intense as this. Jack had taken firm, almost vicious hold of the serval's hips, and was hammering roughly into Jason's ass. Seeing Vic shoot off like that had sent him over the edge.

"G-Gunna… Fill yer ass up… with a hot load, you little slut," Jack growled above him. Jason was having to grip the floor with his claws now to keep from being shoved forward each time that huge, uncut bullcock shoved up inside him. It didn't help that Jack was so massive, he was slamming the little feline's prostate with each thrust, and Jason was at the edge of tears. Still. There was something incredibly hot about it. About being used like an object, just a hole to shoot a load into, a body to coat with fluids.

Vic had settled back onto the edge of the bed, was hunched forward slightly, and was sliding his fist slowly over his own cock. Incredibly, he had regained any strength his erection might have lost through his recent orgasm in only a few seconds. Jason was so far gone at this point that he barely even noticed, though.

Jack grunted, eyes squeezing shut as he felt himself quickly passing the point of no return. He exhaled roughly through his nose and mouth, and his powerful, gym-built muscles tightened beneath his short pelt. Jason knew what was coming. Another hard slap made his ass tense up, a sensation that Jack certainly seemed to enjoy. In front of the young serval, the lion who'd climaxed just a minute or so ago had already risen to his feet again, visibly swelling as he jerked himself off. It was all too much for

Jason.

The feline prostitute shuddered violently under Jack's assault. The huge load that had been splattered across his muzzle, the massive cock that was pounding under his tail, the domineering attitudes, all of it combined to make an intense, earth-quaking climax course through the spotted cat. Parting his lips, Jason let out a loud, almost desperate yowl of intense pleasure. His cock flexed, and a powerful jet of semen leapt out to jet across his stomach before falling to the floor beneath him. Waves of mind numbing pleasure very nearly made the serval pass out. As globs of cum continued to rain over the rug, the young feline's rear spasmed sensuously around Jack's own nine inches, and it was this that completed the experience for the bull.

Both of Jack's powerful hands gripped Jason's slender ass, and spread it, almost painfully. Large balls tightened up, and the bull was almost caught off guard as his first blast of cum exploded into Jason's rear. It was intensely pleasurable, better than anything he'd felt in ages. Probably something about how the boy seemed to eat up the sensations he and Vic were piling on him.

Jason was one of those people who had a hard time feeling it when someone came in his ass. It wasn't that he wasn't sensitive in there, quite the opposite, it just didn't usually stand out as a separate sensation from the erection it was pouring from. This time was different, though. Jack was shooting so intensely that he could feel the impact and splash of that hot cream in his rear, and it only made Jason's orgasm more intense. On the other side, the big lion growled heatedly. He obviously knew what was going on inside the smaller cat's bowels. Tightening his grip around his own cock, drooling clear fluid once again, he leaned closer.

"F-fucking whore..." Jack's speech was slurred and broken. His mind was centered on Jason's ass, and the words escaped more as an afterthought than anything else. The young feline swayed unsteadily underneath Jack as his own orgasm tapered off into a gooey flow, supporting himself on shaky arms and knees. He hadn't come without touching himself since he was fourteen. Gradually, he felt the pulses of the large bull's erection begin to taper off. Jack slide one hand off of the young feline's rear to grip the base of his cock, and pulled himself free with a suddenness that jarred Jason's already exhausted body.

Following that twitching, uncut maleness came a hot flood of seed. It ran thickly down over Jason's buttocks, trickling down to drip off of his balls, streamers matting the fur on his legs down. Still trying to catch his breath, the serval lifted his head as he felt Vic's own cockhead brush over his face, still soaked from the lion's first load. He licked one of those thick globs of semen up before it could fall from his nose to the floor.

He was spent. The serval's arms shook, his ass was sore, and his balls ached. Jason was a professional, though, and he'd keep going until they were finished. Even if he hadn't been having as much fun as he was. He shifted his soaked ass back and forth, wriggling it back against the heavy meat Jack had thumped between his buttocks, savoring the sensation of the bull's final squirts of semen dampening the base of his tail, then trickling down to drip off of his ballsac.

He'd just finally caught up with his breath when he felt a large hand grab him by the chin, and lift his slippery muzzle up to gaze directly at Victor's throbbing erection. A glistening cockhead, glazed with both cum and pre-cum, slid over his lips.

"You're gonna… cum on me again," he whimpered. It was less of a question than a comment. Vic just grinned, showing off sharp fangs. Once again, it was Jack who replied.

"He must like ya," the bull growled from behind. One hand had settled on Jason's rump, where he'd begun to slowly smear those ropes of semen through the serval's fur. Jason shuddered again with arousal. Eyes fluttered closed, his slim little mouth parted, and he awaited the shower that Vic was about to treat him to. The lion's growl deepened, muscles quivered, and that deeply swollen cock swelled for the second time that night.

Jason was already soaked. His face had been splattered before, there was some that had dripped down to his chest and stomach, and his ass was possibly even more caked than the other side. His next shower would feel great. But for the moment, the young serval felt like he wouldn't trade this moment for anything.

Again, Vic's erection exploded in a fountain of juice. He was squirting much more forcefully this time, though it was thinner, more watery. Jason gasped as a few powerful jets sprayed right across his tongue, and reflexively swallowed as some of the lion's cum tickled the back of his throat. Another glob drew a white line up across the bridge of the young feline's nose, another splashed off his cheek, and more still hit Jason directly on the chin and neck. Vic tightened his grip reflexively around the smaller cat's chin, and yanked him right up against his crotch as his second orgasm of the night began to taper off.

Jason whimpered quietly once again. At this point, he just couldn't help it. He felt thin rivers of the lion's hot fluids streaming down his face, running down across his neck. He felt his face being smeared over the lion's erection, really completing the image. He'd been thoroughly dominated.

Soaked in cum. Fucked deep and hard. It'd been an awesome night.

Vic slumped back onto the bed, and exhaled heavily. Jack pulled back as well, gradually softening cock drawing a trail of cum with it. He settled down next to the lion, and murmured something into one of the big feline's ears. Vic reached down, fished around in his discarded trousers, and pulled a twenty out. He tossed it over onto Jason's lap, even as the serval settled back onto his haunches and glanced down over his own cumsoaked body. He looked up again a moment later, over at the two on the bed.

"Ya did good, boy. Keep the room, and get some rest fer the night. Bill's taken care of." Jack's impish grin was back. Both of them gradually found their footing, and re-dressed, Vic quiet as always, the bull occasionally muttering comments about how nice the serval looked caked in their semen. Jason smiled up at the bull through the glaze of cum that slicked his facefur.

"Thank you very much, sir," he demured, licking his lips. It was all still a game, and he wasn't about to disappoint now. "I look forward to seeing you both again."

"Oh, you will, ya slut." Jack's grin widened again, even as he pulled the door to the hallway open. Victor tossed the serval a casual two fingered salute. They both left, and closed the door behind them.

Jason finally found his feet. He made his way over to the bed, and collapsed bonelessly atop it, emitting a heavy, content sigh of pleasure, heedless of the goo that was soaking into the sheets. He'd sleep well tonight.

Mikori

And Whoring

The following is another adventure of a young feline prostitute. This time our hero is hired by a stallion—not for his own sexual gratification, but that of four 'friends' of his. Which only goes to show that there is still such a thing as altruism in this world.

This story is about the thrill of submission, the excitement and pride that come with having your limits pushed and liking it. It's also about really hot sex with dogs.

STUD SERVICE

Kohai

Mikori washed his hands at the only sink in the bathroom that looked clean enough to use. The walls were covered with scratches and graffiti, most of it obscene. He'd ducked in here for two reasons: the first was to answer nature's call. The second was that he felt like he was being followed. He'd been shopping in the mall, and in store after store he'd kept feeling like someone was watching him, keeping track of his every move.

The young cheetah heard the door swing open as he shook the water off his hands. He recognized the stallion who walked in. He'd seen him whenever he'd looked around, trying to see who was following him. The stallion was dressed in a pair of dark grey slacks with a red shirt on and a multi-colored tie around his neck. His sleeves were rolled up, showing off an impressive pair of arms that looked like they had put a weight-room to a lot of use. He looked like a businessman on his lunch hour, though it was well into the evening by that point. Mikori felt the hairs on the back of his neck rise, feeling like he was cornered.

The tall horse leaned against the blue-tiled wall, brown-furred arms crossed over his broad chest, and simply regarded the young cheetah. He stared him up and down, like he was sizing him up. Mikori and the horse watched each other for several seconds, the cheetah feeling his muscles tense, readying himself to run in case the man was dangerous. Finally, the horse spoke. "You're Mikori, right?"

Mikori paused, blinking as the stallion said his name. "Uh… yeah, that's me. How'd you know that? Who are you?"

The stallion reached into his trouser pocket and fished out a black leather wallet. He pulled out a pair of fifty dollar bills and offered them to the cheetah. "My name's Max. I want to hire you. You came highly recommended."

Mikori felt his throat catch as the horse held out the money. He felt butterflies in his stomach, having a pretty good idea of what the horse was offering. "Hire me for what?" he asked quietly.

Max broke into a grin. "Well, fucking, of course. One hundred dollars to put that little body of yours to use any way I want. I hear you're into that, aren't you?"

The cheetah blushed, a pretty pink color under his golden fur. "Um… sometimes. You want me to, um… take care of you."

Max shook his head, his dark mane swaying as he did so. "No, I'm not gonna fuck you. But I've got a bunch of guys who'd love to. From what I hear, you'll love it." The horse took out another fifty dollar bill. "Here. One hundred fifty, if you're good."

The cheetah felt the early risings of arousal squirming inside of him. Here was an attractive stranger offering him money to service some guys he'd never met. He knew it was wrong. He should say no and walk away. But underneath that, the cheetah wanted to go and do it. He had a feeling it would be… intense. He hesitated, torn.

The horse drew out another bill, offering the wad of green paper to Mikori. "Here. Final offer. Two hundred fifty. You come with me, do what I say, and have the ride of your life. Guarantee you'll love it."

Swallowing once, the cheetah nodded. "Um… okay. Deal." The horse handed Mikori two fifties. "The rest when you're done. Whore," he added, reaching out to squeeze Mikori's shoulder.

Max took Mikori to his car, a black BMW convertible, and the two drove off. They didn't speak during the ride, the big stallion keeping his eyes on the road, the little cheetah staring out as the scenery sped by. They arrived at a white house at the edge of a circular driveway. Max lived in a well-off neighborhood with attractive houses and sizeable yards. The horse escorted Mikori inside, hanging up his tie on a coat-rack as they passed into the hallway.

Mikori had half expected a group of business execs waiting to grab him and put him to work, but the house seemed to be empty. Mikori peered about apprehensively, wondering if he'd made a bad decision in going off alone with a stranger. Max pointed to a relatively barren side room. There was a pink, plush carpet lining the floor, and a pair of metal rings dangling from one of the walls. One of the walls was lined with mirrors, clean and well polished. "In here, slutty cat," he directed, giving the cheetah a shove on the rump.

Mikori stumbled in, gave a graceful recovery, then turned to look at

Max. He crossed his arms over his chest and cleared his throat, trying to sound unconcerned. "Ahem. So... where are all these guys you wanted me to... take care of."

Max kicked off his shoes in the corner of the room, settling his large feet into the soft carpet. "Downstairs in the basement. In the kennel." He stared at the cheetah, waiting to see his response.

Mikori took a moment to grasp what the horse was suggesting. His eyes widened and he gasped as he figured out what the horse wanted to pay him for. Bestiality. The horse wanted him to service his dogs.

Max grinned as he watched Mikori's moment of realization. He nodded. "Yup. I've got four prize purebreds downstairs, and they're going to make use of you. That's what I'm paying you for." Propping himself against the arch to the hallway he explained: "I'm a professional dog breeder. I've got four studs here. My boys. Business has been slow, and so they've had to go without for months. They need it real bad. I don't like having my boys all pent up like that." Max stepped toward the cheetah. "And that's where you come in. Or... more like where they come in you. I bring 'em up here. Four dogs fuck you, however they like, hard as they like. You get two-hundred fifty dollars for your service. Deal?"

The poor cheetah felt dizzy as he comprehended what the horse was offering. Mikori wrung his hands, caught between the humiliation of what the horse suggested he submit to, and his own undeniable arousal. He felt lust building in his belly and his groin, strong and almost palpable.

The well-dressed equine saw Mikori's hesitation. "Well? You interested or not? If not, then I'll just call you a cab and you can go home. I was told you'd be totally in to this though."

Mikori peered up at the horse, muzzle down, voice soft. "Wh-who told you that?"

Max bobbed his head. "Your pimp, the little tiger guy. He said you loved dog cock. I didn't believe it to look at you." He lifted a few fingers under Mikori's chin and turned it from side to side, examining the cheetah's face. "I mean, it looks like you're bred from good stock. Pretty, soft features. Nice physique. I'd never have guessed it to look at you, but your pimp seemed really adamant." The horse released Mikori's chin. "So what's it gonna be? Service some dog cock for money? Or head home and I'll find someone else to do it."

Mikori was blushing a bright cherry red under his fur, giving him the impression of innocence. He swallowed once and murmured, "Yeah. Yeah, I'll do it." The cheetah draped his hands over the front of his pants, where a rather firm bulge pressed out at the fabric. He always felt embarrassed at being spoken of like that. Even more so at how it managed to unfailingly arouse him.

Max grinned, showing two rows of strong, pearly teeth. "Great. I'll go get the boys. Be naked by the time I'm back." With no more instruction than that, the big horse turned and walked down the hallway. Mikori heard him open a door and descend a flight of stairs. He stood there for a moment, then began unbuttoning his shirt. He slid it down over his slender shoulders and folded it up in a corner by the door. He took of his shoes and set them by his shirt, then unfastened his pants and discarded them, leaving him naked. He looked at himself in the wall of mirrors. He was fit and trim, with barely an ounce of fat on him, making him look almost dangerously slender. He was also quite erect. His cock, rather large on his slim-looking body, was stiff and uncut, standing up before his tummy. A trickle of shiny precum had dribbled halfway down the belly of his shaft.

Down the hallway Mikori heard the sound of claws scrambling up a flight of steps, the sound of dogs' paws clambering up toward him. He turned to the entryway into the room, and a few moments later Max emerged with a pair of leashes in each hand. Each leash was attached to a dog, each one a beautiful specimen. There was a German Shepherd, a Dalmatian, a husky, and a Great Dane. All of them very male. The dogs all strained toward Mikori, tightening the leather of their leashes, but Max held them in check. "Whoa, hold on there boys! One at a time for ya. I promise, every one of you will get your turn." He led the canines to the two rings set into the wall, strapping their leashes there. He reached down and stroked the fur on the Shepherd's head. "Sorry, boys. I just don't trust you to share nice. We can't have you hurting our little kitten here, not when he's gonna be so nice to you."

Max grinned over at Mikori, gesturing to the four dogs assembled for him. "Do you have a preference on which to start with?" He pointed the dogs out, starting with the German Shepherd. "This is King." He pointed to the Dalmatian, "And this is Prince." Ruffling the husky's ears he said, "Here's Rex. And this is Caesar," patting the Dane's back.

Mikori felt his mouth drying up, finding it hard to speak. "Um, whichever you want," he murmured.

The horse unfastened the husky's leash, trotting him toward the cheetah. "We'll start you out with Rex then. He's been without it the longest. Poor boy, it's been nearly four months for him."

Mikori blinked. If these dogs had been without for that long... then they'd all be quite productive. He'd be a mess by the time they were all through with him. Max led Rex in front of Mikori and told the dog, "Sit,

Rex." The dog lowered his hindquarters, settling onto the carpet. "You get down there too, Mikori," he ordered. "Take a look at what he's got."

Rex cocked his head, giving Mikori that curious dog look as the cheetah slowly crouched down on the carpet. He imagined he could see the dog's testicles swelling with arousal, nestled below the grey and white sheath that poked out from the dog's belly. Mikori felt his face hot with embarrassment and arousal. He knew what he wanted to do, in front of a stranger, and he knew he was about to do it anyway. He reached out a paw and stroked it through Rex's chest-fur. It was soft and clean, a pale white leading down to his thighs. Slowly he stroked lower, 'til he reached down and gently cupped his palm around the dog's balls.

Rex shifted about on his haunches, but Max ordered him, "Stay, Rex. Just sit still and let the cheetah get you all wet. Gotta get you all slick before you can fit inside him. Stay, boy." The dog let his tongue loll out, panting, but he held still.

Mikori looked up to Max. "He's very obedient."

Max nodded, "I've trained them all real well. Since he's being such a good boy, why don't you give his sheath a kiss? He needs it real bad. G'wan, show him how much you want what he's got." Max's voice was deeper than before. Mikori could see a thick length pressing down one leg of the horse's pants. Max was enjoying this a great deal.

Mikori slowly stroked the dog's sheath, tugging gently on the furry holder, stroking it against the length it hid inside. A few moments later, the beginning of a pink cock began to slide out of the tip. "Kiss it," Max told him. Mikori took a deep breath and dipped his head between the dog's thighs.

He picked up the dog's scent, his soft fur and the growing musk coming from between Rex's legs. Mikori licked his lips once, wetting them, and gave the tip of the dog's cock a kiss. Rex held still for him. Taking a deep breath, Mikori dropped his neck a little lower and sealed his mouth around the crown of the husky's dick. It was warm between his lips, and he felt it swell, giving up another inch of cock as the cheetah pressed his tongue to it. Gently he nursed, gradually coaxing out more and more of the canine dick, letting it ease into his mouth. Max watched over Rex's shoulder, catching the sight of a dog's cock pushing past the cheetah's dark lips.

Mikori began to taste something. It was familiar. A thin watery trickle, but very clear. The dog began to leak precum into the cheetah's mouth, wetting his tongue with it. Mikori pulled off, regarding the dog. The husky sat before him, fit and healthy, and with a thick erection sprouting between his thighs. It was just a bit longer than the average guy's, though with a tapered end. Wrapping his fingers around the base, Mikori rubbed the sensitive flesh. It twitched once, spraying a wet shot of preseed against the cheetah's whiskers.

Max murmured, "Get your mouth around it again, cat," putting a hand behind Mikori's head and guiding it back between Rex's legs. "You'll want it as wet as you can get it, 'cause he's gonna be fucking you in just a minute."

The cheetah examined the doggy erection his fingers were encircling. It was rather thick and long, but he thought he could take something of that size. Dipping his head low, Mikori recaptured the canine prick between his lips. It felt much more swollen than the last time, and he felt it twitching against his tongue, slathering it with gooey precum. Slowly the cheetah pumped with his mouth, the horse watching the throbbing shaft pass between those dark lips, the stud dog panting and starting to whine as the young feline serviced his cock.

The sticky fluid dribbling into Mikori's mouth began to thicken, the taste growing stronger and the texture more slimy. The dog was being prolific with his preseed, injecting hot gobbets of it onto the cheetah's tongue. Most of it trailed down Mikori's throat. The rest, that which he couldn't manage, flowing over his cheeks and down the dog's dick. Rex's nutsack was painted with rivulets of slippery liquid drooling over his balls.

Mikori felt a hand tangle in his hair and pull him back from the dog's cock, leaving it twitching in the air. "That's enough," said Max. "Hands and knees, slut." The spotted feline swallowed, gulping the last of the juice in his mouth. His chin and lips were stained with it. Mikori panted softly through his nose as he knelt in position, hands braced in front of him. He knew what was expected and he raised his tail up, hiking it off to the side, leaving his taut rump bare and exposed, ready to be covered by the stud he was there to service.

He felt snuffling behind him, and a wet tongue and warm breath under his tail. Mikori shivered, shifting his weight as the dog examined him. The horse put a hand on Mikori's back, pushing down firmly. "Keep still, whore. He's ready for ya. This is for his pleasure, not yours." Max lifted at the dog's collar, urging Rex to mount. "Hup, boy. Take 'im, he's waiting for you." The dog clambered forward, up onto Mikori's back, wrapping his forelegs around the cheetah's slender waist. Kneeling beside the two, Max reached out and took hold of Rex's sheath, the other hand holding Mikori's hips steady. With a practiced hand he angled the dog's cock between the young cheetah's buttocks, nestling the tapered end against the tight tailhole.

The dog humped forward, dragging his cock up the cleft of the cheetah's rump, to eager to gain penetration. Rex's dangling cock left a glistening trail of precum between those furry cheeks. The dog shifted a half step and drove his hips forward more slowly, the head of his reddish prick touching Mikori's anus. Slick with saliva and that clear juice, it began to slide in. Mikori gasped as the dog began to fuck him, blushing a pretty cherry red under his fur. Rex began to swing his hips back and forth, picking up the pace as he pumped his cock deeper and deeper into the young cheetah. "Yeah, that's good," Max encouraged. "How's it feel to be pleasing my boy?"

Mikori stared ahead, ears burning with embarrassment of what he was doing. It was not the first time he had played with animals, but he had never before done so with a whole pack of dogs in exchange for money, particularly with an older, stronger male watching and urging him on. "'s good," the cheetah murmured. The little feline's dick was quite hard, bobbing between his slender thighs, the swollen glans dripping with shiny juice. It jerked and emitted a thin shot of precum as Rex's cock nudged his prostate.

The large dog was pounding harder now, his animal lust forced to endure long abstinence. Mikori could feel the dog's swollen nutsack slapping against his rump, full and heavy with its messy burden. The spotted feline whined as he began to feel a bulge at the base of the canine shaft pressing at his tail hole. He knew that the dog was growing a knot, and that soon Rex would drive it in him, locking them together. Dogs are driven to bury their cocks in to the hilt, bracing their partners open to receive their load, forcing it to be held inside. Mikori would allow these dogs to ejaculate in him, dumping their gooey loads into his body, and he was doing it for money.

The cheetah's breath caught in his throat as he felt that bulge slip past his puckered anal ring, holding the throbbing cock in his bowels. Rex gave two more vicious thrusts, driving his prick as deep as could be into the squirming feline. A moment later, Mikori felt hot, syrupy liquid running down over his ass as the bulge at the base of the dog's cock swelled to the size of a lemon, a thick knob locking the cheetah tight. It was more than a little uncomfortable, pressing out at the walls of his tight rectum, rubbing with shallow humps of the dog's hips. The lake of gooey dog semen made things very slippery, though. The messy fluid matted down the golden fur on Mikori's ass and thighs, soaking them in cockslime.

Max clapped a large palm on the top of Mikori's head and ruffled his hair, grinning. "That's a *good* boy! Rex's been needing it bad, just like my other boys." The strong horse strode over to the wall and unfastened the leash of King, the German Shepherd. He was handsome, with short-trimmed fur over his taut body. His reddish cock was already halfway out of its sheath, dangling between his thighs. Max guided the shepherd over toward the prostrate feline. "Your turn boy." He coaxed the dog up onto his hind legs, the forelegs resting on the cheetah's back. King and Rex stared at each other, panting from atop their bitch.

Mikori knelt there on shaky limbs, a leaky dog cock implanted in his rear, and another soon to be sliding into his muzzle. He'd earned a quarter of his money so far. Gently, the stallion curled his fingers under Mikori's jaw, tugging the feline's mouth open. Mikori saw Max's other hand come into view, clasping the dog's dick between strong fingers and angling it between toward the cheetah's lips, the horse murmured, "Suck that dog's cock, you whore." He pulled his hands toward one another, pushing Mikori's mouth right onto the canine prick. Immediately the cheetah's mouth was alive with the flavor of drooling precum. His eyes widened as the horse continued to urge him on, forcing his mouth deeper on that cock so that it was getting hard to breathe.

Max held him there, keeping the cheetah's lips collared around the base of the dog's shaft, his nose nuzzling the fuzzy end of King's sheath. Just as he was getting lightheaded, the stallion allowed the cheetah to ease back off the stud dog's cock, 'til only the tapered glans was buried in that feline mouth, pumping in regular jets of thin, watery juice. Mikori judged the entire cock was about eight inches long, thick and red and pointed right down his mouth.

The cheetah winced and whimpered as Rex's knot slowly deflated to the point where the dog could be free of Mikori's clinging ass. The canine did not remove himself gently. He scrabbled with his feet, pulling back until the shrinking knot slurped free of the cumlogged anus. A river of messy cockslime splattered out onto the floor, soaking the cheetah's legs and tail.

The hot, slimy juice continued to trickle down the cheetah's thighs, matting down his fur and staining it with the scent of a dog's semen. It would be with him for days afterwards. His mouth was similarly adorned, though the German Shepherd hadn't begun to truly orgasm yet. The strong canine was still drooling thick, rich precum into Mikori's mouth. The cheetah's tongue was floating in it, the excess flooding out the corners of his lips even as he sucked and swallowed. It was already as abundant as several guys' full cumloads.

There was a clink of chain over by the wall as Max retrieved the third dog, Prince. He was a handsome Dalmatian, very sleek and youthful. His long dick was dangling low from his sheath, and there were stains on the carpet from where he'd been emptying his precum. Prince was excited, straining hard at the leash, his reddish cock hardening before the cheetah's eyes. Perhaps this wasn't the first time Max had used someone to service his dogs. The Dalmatian left a trail of shiny liquid on the carpet as he approached.

Max led the canine up behind Mikori's sloppy, well-used rear. "Here he is, boy, Rex got 'im all slick for you to use." The equine knelt by the cheetah and pressed a hand to the underside of Mikori's throat. He could feel the feline's Adam's apple bobbing rhythmically as he swallowed in a vain attempt to keep up with the flow of hot liquid King was producing. "Get ready, kitten," the horse murmured. "Prince is real young, but he's got a real big dick on 'im. Be glad I had Rex get you all lubed up first."

There was another rattle of chain as Max coaxed the Dalmatian onto Mikori's back. The dog's paws scrabbled on the feline's back, searching for purchase, and he woofed once, standing face to face with King. Mikori felt something prodding at his anus, something very thick, as Max aimed Prince's dick between his sodden cheeks. With an obscene wet noise, Prince humped forward, driving his cock into the cheetah's rear, dog semen squelching around it as it wormed deeper into Mikori's rectum. The poor feline gurgled on dogcock.

Prince was far bigger than Rex or King had been. As thick as several fingers, the dog's bloated prick was at least ten inches long, including the swelling bulge at the base, which was getting larger by the moment. The Dalmatian dragged his hips back, hauling half of his meat out of the squirming cheetah, and then pumped it back in. Rex's semen leaked out in thick pools with each thrust of canine shaft.

The load of cum Rex had dumped there made penetration possible. If not so thoroughly soaked, Mikori might not have been able to accept the dog's sizeable cock. It was already uncomfortable trying to accommodate the pulsing meat as it throbbed and probed at his deepest parts. From each end, a four-legged dog pounded into him, rubbing its slickened meat against tongue and ass. He could feel two canine scrotums, weighted down with heavy, dangling balls that bespoke much need, slapping against his chin and cheeks.

Suddenly Mikori heard a deep grunting and growling from the German Shepherd's chest. Max's hand slid into view, reaching behind the turgid knot on the canine dick and squeezing in an imitation of a slick body clasped to it. King snarled, baring his white teeth and drooling on Mikori's back as he gave three final strong pumps of his powerful hips into the cheetah's mouth and then held still. The dog's prick shuddered once, then throbbed powerfully between Mikori's lips as a thick foamy load of semen splashed into the kitten's mouth. Mikori's throat worked frantically to swallow, gamely attempting to keep up with the dog's climax. Long, thick ropes of cockslime spilled from his lips, running in syrupy strands down over his neck and splattering on the floor.

Behind him, Prince whined and yelped, his long cock straining to bury itself deeper into the young feline. The cheetah moaned around King's dick as the Dalmatian slid the apple-sized knot into his used-up ass. The Dalmatian's fuckjuice filled him, mingling with Rex's seed as the two dogs marked the feline with their pent-up loads. Above him, the canines snarled and growled as they emptied their balls' contents into their whore, soaking the cheetah from both ends. It went on and on, Mikori nursing on King's meat with his fingers, coaxing him and milking him to the dregs, while the young Dalmatian worked the cheetah's ass with shallow thrusts. The milky cum was smeared thickly over Mikori's mouth and ass, the remnants of it painting his legs, neck and chest. Some of it even ran down his arms and trickled onto his hands.

Gradually the two dogs calmed down and allowed their cocks to be withdrawn from the clasping body of the cheetah. The German Shepherd's cock gave a final twitch as it slid from between those cloying feline lips, spattering Mikori's nose with watery cum, heavy with the smell of dog and sex. Mikori felt his face burning his embarrassment, unable to turn and look at the equine beside him. He was nearly done. Only one canine remained to be serviced. Caesar, the Great Dane.

Mikori looked at where the canine stood over by the wall. Rex, King and Prince had all finished making use of their feline whore, and were busy lazing about on the rug and lapping at their cocks as the slid back into their furry sheaths. Caesar stood proudly, head erect and regal as he regarded the cheetah kneeling before him. Mikori thought the dog to be looking at him in disdain. He could almost hear the dog thinking, "You filty little cum-covered whore, groveling there in front of me. Why should I even allow you to touch my cock?"

Max stood, adjusting his dick as he did. There was a soaked wet spot in his trousers from the amount he'd been leaking. The equine must have been dripping since the cheetah began his work. Mikori's eyes lingered on it. Striding over to the final dog, Max unchained the Great Dane's metal-studded collar. The dog sniffed once and nibbled at one of his claws, as though he were in no hurry to acknowledge Mikori's presence. The cheetah knelt before him, sopping with cum from each end, blushing as he was made to wait to earn his money.

Caesar slowly trotted over Mikori, sniffing at him a few times. The cheetah's scent was saturated with lust and semen from the three other stud dogs who lay a few feet off, tongue lolling out as they watched. Max laughed and the cheetah's eyes flicked over to him. "Caesar doesn't put out for just any little whore. You'd better ask him nice for it."

Mikori looked at the horse, unsure if the taller male was being serious. "Umm… can I have it, please?" the cheetah attempted.

Max frowned. "C'mon, slut, you can do better than that. And it's his dick, you better ask him. Remember, if you don't service all the dogs you don't get paid," he warned.

The feline stared over at the dog, whose dark eyes watched him coldly. Though it was silly, he could imagine Caesar saying, "Well? Beg for it if you want it, you little fuck."

Mikori swallowed, gathering his words and forcing down his pride. "C-caesar, please let me have your dick. I'll treat it real good. I promise."

Caesar snorted and turned his head away, as though to say, "That's it? All I get is a promise from a dirty whore that you'll try to make me feel good?" Max grinned, watching, stroking his own immense shaft through his trousers.

The cheetah tried again. "Please, sir, let me service your cock. I have a skilled mouth and a nice tight ass. I'd love to feel your cock sliding into me." The feline swallowed, ashamed at begging a dog to be allowed to touch his cock, but unwilling to give up.

The Great Dane sniffed at Mikori again. The spotted feline saw a hint of reddish cock beginning to protrude from the thick canine sheath. The tapered head was as thick as the Dalmatian's had been, and it was not even fully erect. Caesar was the true stud of the four. Mikori would have to earn the right to pleasure him. The cheetah begged again, words becoming more heated, "I want your dick so bad. Please, Caesar, let me touch it. You've been saving that pent up load for so long. Let me help you spill it out."

Mikori heard the shivery sound of a zipper from over by the wall. Max unfastened his trousers and shucked them down over his legs. They were strong and toned, the calves and thighs those of a man who keeps his body in pristine condition. The true prize lay between those thighs, though. The horse's cock stretched up to the bottom of Max's ribcage, a size to match any of the dogs. His thick, blunt meat was black with a streak of pink on the underside, with milky fluid drizzling down the belly. Max gripped his shaft and moved to take position by the feline. "C'mere, Caesar. He's worth it," the horse said simply.

The dog trotted up shoulder to shoulder with his master. Max put an arm around the canine, helping him up onto his hind legs, the dog's cock hanging before Mikori's cumsoaked face. Caesar's cock had slid out all the way from his sheath, and it was quite a tool to have pointed at a young cheetah. Longer and thicker than Prince's, it was a match for the horse himself. The two pricks wagged in front of the cumlogged feline, both in need of attention.

Caesar eased forward, nudging his cocktip against Mikori's lips. At the first touch, there was a heavy squirt of gooey liquid, hot and sticky. Immediately another followed, and another and another. For a moment Mikori was afraid the dog had simply shot off his load. Then his tongue flicked out and he tasted it. It was a strong, lewd flavor, but not semen. The juice was clear, as thick and sticky as it was, but it was only precum. He'd had males who were very abundant with their semen who gave off less with each shot. The cheetah drew in a deep shuddering breath in anticipation. How much would the dog give after being denied orgasm for so long?

Beside him, Max gave off a low groan that began deep within his barrel chest, and the horse's cock throbbed, sending a fountain of pearl-sized droplets of prejizz over the cheetah's face. The two large males were washing away the jism King had deposited on Mikori's face, though the feline know they would soon be replacing it with a mess of their own.

The canine slid his cock past Mikori's lips with surprising gentleness. The cheetah had been afraid the dog would shove that thick cock into his throat, but Caesar seemed willing to work it in slowly. Inch after inch of angry red bloated meat pushed its way into Mikori's mouth. The feline had to swallow with each squirt of Caesar's prick. The gooey precum was so heavy that he could feel the liquid weighing down his belly. It was rich and thick, smooth and tasting of musk and slightly bitter.

The cheetah was forced to close his left eye, so potent were the splatters of prejizz on his face from the stallion's cock, chest heaving as he breathed, Max pumped his meat like the consummate stud, working himself off as he coated his shaft with slimy fluid as though oiling it to make it shine. The stallion looked down, seeing half of his stud dog's cock buried in the cheetah's mouth. Experienced as he was, Mikori could only manage so much of the massive prick. It stretched his jaw to the limit, and if the cheetah pumped with his mouth or Caesar humped with his hips it could catch on a tooth.

Max reached down, his strong hand caressing the base of Caesar's dick. Those fingers slid around the drooling meat, slickening it with the stallion's own copious precum. Mikori could feel the cock throb powerfully in his mouth as the stallion's fist encircled the Great Dane's meat, and he had to swallow twice to catch the entire load of prejizz that the stallion milked from the dog's cumslit. Max spoke to the feline, voice much deeper now with arousal. "You jus' keep swallowing and licking. Lemme take care of his dick. You treat my boy real good."

The stallion inched forward on his knees, shifting into a better position to jerk and caress the dog's swollen member. This left the equine dick mere inches from Mikori's face, those strong hips occasionally nudging forward to rub the flared glans against Mikori's cheek and smear in that pre-juice, gooey slime from King's orgasm rubbing off onto Max's dicktip and increasing the lewd wet sounds of a slippery stallioncock being masturbated. The cheetah could hear Caesar panting hard above his head. The stud dog kept his hips still, content to simply let the cheetah caress the turgid meat with his lips and tongue as the young feline nursed on his erection, while his equine master pumped his meat with slick fingers. "You're gettin' a real treat, kitty," Max informed the cheetah. "Caesar's a purebred all the way, a perfect specimen. A load of the size he's gonna give is worth over a thousand dollars." Mikori's eyes widened at the sum, as Max's fist brushed his lips while working over the dog's meat. "Be sure to drink as much as you can. Don't waste it."

Mikori could sense the two males nearing their peaks. Each began breathing harder, panting as they approached the finish. Their precum became more thick and voluminous. They were grunting, the almost-painful sound that males make to signal the pleasure is becoming too much. The air was hot and thick with musk and wet sounds of two males being serviced, each a stud in his own right. The Great Dane hunched over, his cock shifting slightly in Mikori's mouth, and growled hotly into the cheetah's ear. The sticky slime pumping into Mikori's mouth began to thicken and issue forth more frequently, gradually turning from clear slimy juice to proper semen, hot and messy.

"Cup your hands," Max snarled, "Catch it all, you little fuck." The horse grabbed the cheetah's wrist and brought it up under his chin, just beneath the stud dog's meat. The feline brought his other hand up to meet it, forming a small basin under his mouth. He did it just in time. Only a second later, semen began to foam from the corners of his lips. He felt it drooling down his face, tasting perversely strong. The stallion milked and squeezed the dog's knot as Caesar's shaft shook between the cheetah's lips. Were it not buried so deep in Mikori's mouth, the spasms that accompanied each ejaculation might well heave torn the dog's cock from his mouth.

Mikori gulped it down as well as he could, though there was no way he could match what the dog was producing. The stud injected him with semen that had been building up for weeks, the jizz running over tongue and lips even as Mikori nursed and lapped at the spurting meat. He could feel a thick pool of hot dog semen puddling in his hands.

The stallion's hand faltered on his own dick, groaning inarticulately as he watched the dog empty his balls into the cheetah's belly. The black horsecock throbbed dangerously beside Mikori's cheek, and immediately it covered half of the feline's face with slimy egg-white jizz. The horsedick shot again, splattering Mikori with opaque white fluid hard enough that it hurt a little. Finger-thick shots of white honey pounded the cheetah's face and side, messing up his features, throat and chest. The two stud males grunted and shook against their whore, pumping meat and squirting semen, leaving him a cumsoaked, sloppy mess.

With a snort, Caesar pulled his hips back, sliding his cock from the cheetah's saturated maw in one smooth motion. With no more recognition than that, he chose to lie down with his canine brothers, tongue sliding out to lap at his cock as it slowly returned to its furry holder.

The horse reached down and ruffled Mikori's hair, smearing in a fair amount of the matted-down cum. "Good boy. Now clean your plate." Mikori peered down with one eye at the large, slimy pool of dog jism in his cupped hands. It was almost running over the sides of his fingers. "Slurp it up quick before you lose it. You're holding hundreds of dollars worth of semen, kitten." Mikori inhaled once, too exhausted to protest. He craned his neck down and raised his hands, bringing that pool of dog jism to his lips and slowly began to nurse it down. A few trails of slimy white liquid ran over his lips, vanishing in the mess already there. Tipping his head back, the cheetah's throat bobbed as he drank the last of the Great Dane's semen, lapping the gooey fluid from his fingers and palms.

Max grinned. "What a *good* boy you are." He grabbed his pants and fished around in the pocket, withdrawing three $100 bills. "Here ya go. A little extra for you, since you worked so hard for me and my boys." The stallion laughed, giving the cheetah's cumslimed ear a tug. It was so slick that he couldn't hold on. "I'll keep you in mind in case my boys need serving again." The stallion stood and gathered his clothes, tossing the cheetah a pink towel from the corner of the room. "Clean yourself up, I'll call you a cab." The stallion walked out into the hallway, leaving Mikori kneeling there with the dogs, mind reeling and body soaked.

He knew he would go without hesitation if the stallion called him again.

Coming of Age

The coming of age tale is notoriously the most attractive story for an author who wants to evoke not only arousal but give his characters a genuine emotional journey—and one of the most difficult to pull off.

The greatest problem lies in the fact that the protagonist teeters on the cusp of two states of being—youth and adulthood. The author is faced with the challenge of writing both convincingly, and very few can manage that. Young authors often lack the life experience and perspective to convincingly describe grown-up life, while more experienced authors can't resist imbuing their youthful characters with a cleverness and maturity they really ought not to possess.

At the risk of displaying favoritism, the editor humbly admits that this story has long been one of his favorites. The splendid balance between youthful ignorance and mature perspective makes the protagonist's innocence charming rather than grueling.

And sex never looks as exciting as through the eyes of a budding young male…

BITCH-BOY

André "Badger" Blaireau

Memory is *so* weird. And it's not just those funny little stupid things that stick in your mind like they were the biggest thing that ever happened to you. The really strange thing is what sets off the memory of the funny little stupid things you can't forget.

Every morning, just about, unless I'm sick—too sick to make a fist, I mean—I think of the same thing. Something that happened a long time ago—years—and really didn't mean much. At least I think it didn't.

Sometimes I wake up first. I look at the rangy little critter next to me in a rust-colored pelt, and right away this old memory comes back to me. But more often, I guess, I come to when I feel a tongue on my muzzle and get an eye open to see my darling's sweet red-and-white face, with its perky black accents, smiling a little, and a soft "Hi, guy." Tick's voice still sounds young, to me, despite the grey hairs here and there. And a fox's features are small, I guess, like their bodies. All of which makes them seem permanently young. Younger than their age, anyway.

But that's not the weird part. The weird part is that just about every morning, I remember something about the day I met *Dennis*. Oh, I remember the day I met Tick, too. Don't get me wrong. The week doesn't pass without me thinking about it. The day, hardly.

The memory that won't leave me alone, the Dennis thing, is just an instant, really. A snapshot. It was a perfect morning in the late spring, full of wonderful scents. I felt horrible, though. Frustrated, uncertain, my guts twisted tight with a craving for—something, but I didn't know what. In a word, your typical adolescent. I was making my way along the creek that flows about a mile from our place, where it runs through an old woodlot, not really hurrying, certainly not actually going anywhere.

If I was thinking about anything in particular, it was my folks. Dad and

99

Mom had been "doing it" a lot in the last couple of weeks. Okay, for some months, now. But now it was like they couldn't get enough of it. I could tell something really intense was going on between them, like the whole rest of the world just disappeared for a few minutes. There was something beautiful about it, too. I mean, I'm not talking about the fact that Mom and Dad are good-looking. Dad especially, I mean, he's a handsome guy and when he's with Mom, especially like he was then, he seems so strong. So totally male. Mom isn't the same, either, when he's like that. Eager or something. Excited. Not at all like her way around us kids. Or around Dad, either. I mean, there was never any doubt that my folks loved each other. That showed in a jillion ways, not just obvious ones like nuzzling and licking. But, wow—*this* stuff was something else.

It was sort of scary. They turned into some other kind of animal. The girls, Thistle and Firefly, pretended nothing was happening. They had to be pretending. You'd have to be a moron not to see what was going on.

Well, maybe I'm the moron. I commented to Thistle that Mom and Dad were behaving real differently, and I couldn't figure out why there was this sudden change from nuzzling and hand-holding and ruffling each other's fur and the occasional friendly lick, to grunting, groaning, up-to-the-nuts *sex*. Morning, noon, and night, too.

"Oh, that's *easy*, silly!" Thistle said, primly. "Us kids are going to make our own families. Soon. And move out. So-o-o, Mom and Dad are going to have some more babies, that's all. Except that Mom—"

She broke off in a little fit of giggles.

"Mom what?"

"Well, *Mom* says she's in no hurry. She says this stuff is the best part of having a husband."

"What is?"

"Doing what they're doing."

"Oh."

Really. It looked to me almost like he was hurting her. But considering how often Mom started it, I had to think I was wrong about that.

Thistle gave me this knowing look. "He'll get him a litter, all right. When Mom feels like it."

"Feels like what?"

More giggles, and she said something dumb about minding my own business; it was women's stuff.

So suave. Well, it was true, though. Both Thistle and Firefly were, well, starting to do the same thing as Mom and Dad. With dates. Trying them on for size, Thistle said.

How many times do you have to try the same guy on? I wanted to know.

She looked arch, said you learned something more about a boy every time.

Maybe so, but how they kept score, I'll never know. They were getting it so often. Just about every day, sometimes. Even oftener. I wasn't snooping or anything. I mean, it's not snooping when you come home in the middle of the afternoon and find your sister and her date 'relaxing' right there on the couch. Relaxing, my foot. Not a stitch on, arms around each other, and anyone could see they were just waiting for the knot in Buckthorn's, um, root to let him free. You might have thought they'd be embarrassed, at least a little, but they hardly even noticed me come in the room. And then ten seconds later, Oak and Firefly came out of the bedroom, all casual, holding hands and still nuzzling and licking each other's necks. They were dressed, at least, but Oak's hand was under Firefly's top and his fly was open. Firefly spotted it and buttoned it up for him. With her own hands, I mean! I just about died, Oak just stood there, stupidly looking down his front at it, while she fiddled with his *crotch!*

Don't get me wrong. Us furs are not really shameless. Or exhibitionistic. For sex, or even just lovers' conversation, we prefer privacy. *Some* privacy. At least go off somewhere. Not necessarily very far. Behind a tree will do. Or another room. But especially when a bitch is stirring up a boy, I guess it's easy for everyone to just forget where they are. They may just move off a few yards, as they get ready, say. Maybe not even that. You can be with friends and just notice that a couple of them are into it a lot deeper than hugging and kissing. Mom and Dad, it's their house of course, and especially when Mom gets Dad all excited, on purpose, I guess it's not surprising that they don't always go to their own room before they start. But I have to think it's pretty easy to get Dad to lose control. I mean, while I was growing up I don't remember the folks doing much of that sort of thing at all. And now! Wow. It's a wonder they haven't broken something.

I got a thrill out of watching couples screwing. Of course; who wouldn't? But what I liked most about it was the wrong thing. I didn't realize it was the wrong thing. I did know it was different. My brother and the other young males I knew, they were almost as fascinated by the *idea* of having sex with a bitch as actually doing it. At least they talked about it all the time. *All* the time. Bragged. Not about what a rush it was, no, it was all about how good it was for the bitch. And announcing their plans of who they'd lay next. Dopey as I was about that stuff, I figured out for myself that *that* part of it didn't fit with "how good it was for the bitch".

Me, before I had a bitch myself, I was happy just watching.

The boys.

I knew that. I mean, I knew I was fascinated by the boys. But I didn't think anything of it. I supposed everyone was like me. Most of the action was the boys, after all. The girls didn't just lie there, exactly, but there was something beautiful about the boys. Glorious. So totally physical—all that striving and struggling, panting and whining. The muscles all over their bodies under the fur, you could see the muscles moving and sliding around under the skin. So limber and strong at the same time. The first time I watched a wolf ejaculate it was Dad. I'll never forget it. I was amazed. I could feel the fur stand up on the back of my neck. It was so powerful. Frightening, in fact. Of course, I didn't *know* it was "ejaculation". I knew that whatever it was, it was awesome. (And Mom seemed to think so, too.) Anyway, it never failed to amaze me, whether it was Dad or one of the fit young guys my sisters were 'trying on'.

When bitches are trying out their boys, they mostly do it somewhere close to where the girls live. In the yard, on the porch, even inside. Wherever, but not far away. Parents like to know who their daughters are having sex with. If a bitch goes off alone somewhere to 'meet a guy', you automatically guess there's something fishy about it. A married guy, say. Wrong side of the tracks. Or worse. Maybe even as bad as doing it with a *fox*.

Anyway, that meant I hardly ever saw Briar in action. He's my brother. The few times I did, it was impressive enough. He was a hunk, no matter what; but when he was putting it to a bitch he was marvelously *male*. A few times I saw him together with Willow, the bitch who lives closest to us. Nice girl; they got married, too. I liked that. I figured she'd be a good match for Briar. Anyway, I saw them twice, when she was trying him on. The first time they were doing it a little different, her on hands and knees. She was reaching back between her legs and playing with his nuts. And Briar, he was something else. His head was back and his mouth was open and I thought he was having convulsions. Sex-*xy!* But not as sexy as the other time, when he was lying on her, regular. Boys always look so strong when they're hugging a girl like that, seems like every muscle in their bodies is moving, hackles up, grunts and growls, throaty, deep, urgent. Desperate-sounding. But they'd swear they were having a good time. At least the bitch was (like the guy was just going to a lot of trouble to do her some favor!).

Most of the boys my sisters were dating were a little older than Briar Jr. and me, which is probably why I didn't know them real well. But I was seeing plenty of them now that they were dropping by to court my sisters, and we'd get to chatting. One time Oak and Bristlecone showed up at the exact same time. They had dates with the girls, who were late getting ready. While the boys were waiting they got into this quarrel about who would date who. Pretend quarrel. I think they were showing off. For my benefit, I decided. Going on about what kind of sex they aimed to have, while trying to tease me about my own inexperience. Which I suppose comes to the same thing. It was pretty exciting, and being included in this raunchy man-talk conversation, or even just kind of included, didn't exactly work, if it was supposed to be teasing. It made me feel grown up.

Also, you learn stuff from teasing. For example, Oak said something about Thistle being the better date, on the whole, unless you happened to mind having your moves compared to Bolt all the time.

This was news to me. I knew Thistle was *dating* Bolt, of course, but she hadn't mentioned any special feelings for him. For my part, I thought Bolt was the handsomest of her beaux. Well, 'handsome' isn't quite it. He certainly was that, but so was Buckthorn. Handsomer. And I guess I found all of them wonderful for some reason. Neither Oak nor Bristlecone was what you'd call really good-looking, after all, but they fascinated me even more than some of the handsomer boys. They seemed especially—something. I actually kind of put myself in the girls' shoes, thinking weird stuff like if it was up to *me* I'd rather try on Bristlecone 'for size' than, say, Alder, who was so handsome, everyone agreed, but, I don't know, Oak was more—well, more something. He certainly wasn't more handsome.

I was old enough to date, myself, and I knew Briar Jr. had left his juices in a bitch or two, already; but for some reason I was backward. Part of the story was that next to the older guys who were dating Thistle and Firefly, I felt like a dopey little half-licked fur-faced cub. I dreaded asking a bitch for a date. I just knew that if I did, she'd say no. Or something worse.

Bolt would make almost any guy feel inadequate, I think. He was special. Actually thrilling. I guessed it was because he was like Dad. Intense. Strong. *Always* randy. Well, the other boys were, too, but Bolt was sex in the form of a wolf. Even in his sleep. Once I watched Thistle and Bolt, for the longest time, napping after, well, really wild coupling. They were perfectly still, but it *looked* like sex. Or anyhow, *I* thought it was almost as fascinating to watch them sleep as it was to watch Bolt just about coming out of his skin in trying to bring off his third or fourth juicing of the day.

I assumed that Bolt could have any girl he wanted. It isn't quite that simple, I now realize—there were actually one or two bitches who didn't like him, and others who definitely preferred some other young man for some reason—well, take me and Oak—but I was terrifically impressed to find that he seemed to be paying special attention to Thistle. And I was thinking she ought to be totally thrilled whenever she had that hunk.

But to be honest I thought the same thing about most of the boys that were courting my sisters. Oak and Bristlecone, to name two. Not handsome, especially Oak, but young and strong and *so*—something—I didn't even know what it was that impressed me. But what I did know was that I loved being around them, even when they teased me.

Well, when the girls showed up, it was almost embarrassing. The boys started talking even more crudely about who would date who; and the girls, they took up where the boys left off—talking right out loud, in front of them (to tease them, I guess), about their physiques, the texture of their fur, whose 'love-lessons' were most arousing, teasing them about awkward events on their first dates, and debating such questions as whether it was true, as the saying had it, that 'the better the fathering, the worse the father'. *Right there!* With the guys listening and bragging and teasing and poking fun at one another. I mean, this was stuff Firefly had never even *whispered* to me. And even Thistle had never said anything about Oak being 'hung', before! (It confused me, too, because I only knew the word in connection with lying quietly together after sex, like that time I came in on Buckthorn and Thistle. But eventually I figured out that they were talking about something a little, um, unusual in Oak's pants.)

Thistle's question set the boys off on another pretend quarrel. Stuff like, 'it's not what you got, it's what you do with it', and Oak coming back with 'there ain't nothin' wrong with *having* it, too', and Bristlecone said, 'You know what they say about guys with big dicks'.

I didn't, but somehow the whole idea of these guys—and my own sisters—talking dirty right in front of one another was exciting me to bits. Finally, Bristlecone gave a yank up on his belt and kind of twisted his trunk sideways. From where I stood it made his shoulders look huge compared to his waist. He said something like, "Well, bitches, what'll it be? Quality or quantity?"

This set the girls to giggling and squealing and saying things like, 'Oh, you *bow-weez*! There's more to life than sex!'

Oak sort of ambled over and put an arm around Thistle's shoulders and said, "*What* did you say, honey-bee? More to life than *sex*? Like what? Who says? —Look, you sweet little ball o' fur, what say we go somewhere where we can talk over this crazy idea of yours." She was rubbing his chest with her hands. Then she left off licking his cheek and licked his tit, the one with the ring in it.

"He-e-y-y!" he said, with a little laugh. Grinning, he briefly licked her muzzle. "Where did you learn stuff like *that*?" He licked her muzzle again, as his free hand slid up her side and *right under her top*. He cupped her breast. I could see the nipple under the light cloth, and his thumb sliding around on it. Thistle inhaled.

"Oak! *Please!*" she said, grabbing his wrist. "You *boys!* Can't you wait until we're behind the house, at least?"

"Okay," he said, in a funny voice, but he was still holding on to her, still had a hand on her breast, and after a lick or two more I could see he was playing with her again, even before they started to stroll off.

Meantime Bristlecone and Firefly were lost to the world, hugging each other and licking each other's ears and muzzles. They were so pretty, I thought. The young man glanced up at the other pair as they moved off, and whispered something to Firefly. They set out, to follow Oak and Thistle, obviously, but Bristlecone stopped for a second and turned to look back at me. Like he was thinking about something. Almost like he was looking me over.

"Hey, kid, y'know my cousin, Clover? Yeah, well—she thinks you're cute." A tiny grin while he licked his muzzle. Elaborately. "She'd kill me if she knew I was telling you that. Well, pup, see you around—c'mon, babe," and the two of them ambled off after Thistle and Oak.

I thought it was incredibly exciting, all that teasing and talking about sex, and the guys were so male and self-confident. As well they might be! Later, I asked Thistle what was going on. Mainly I was a little puzzled by the fact that she'd gone with Oak, because I had the idea somehow that she was sweet on Bristlecone. And by now, trying on Oak could hardly hold any surprises. She'd had him a lot.

"Oh," she said, with this foxy twinkle, "Yeah, I do like Bristlecone. But, listen, fur-face, give me a little credit. I know what I'm doing. Those boys have more than one arrow in their quivers. *A-a-a-and*, since it takes them longer to fire off the second or third shot—well, now, that's a plus—a *definite* plus—if it's Bristlecone drawing the longbow." Her face took on a dreamy look for a moment, then she chuckled and looked at me sideways. "After the first round we changed boys. And Firefly's insides got a *real* good shaking-up, I bet."

"Oak?"

"Yes, indeed. Oak. Don't get me wrong. I like Oak. Getting it from Oak is—well, special. Sometimes he's a little much, that's all."

"Is this that quality-quantity thing they were talking about?"

"Well, yes, I suppose, but mainly they're just different. By now, after all, they're both pretty good." She grinned. "I mean, Bolt is still—well—but both of those boys are nothing to sneeze at, these days." Her smile turned dreamy again.

"You mean, guys get better with practice?"

"Sure do," she said. "Don't you get better at *everything* with practice? Look, angel-face, I've done it with one virgin. Before I knew it he was in the wrong hole. *And* dropped his load."

"Who was that? A boy actually did *that?*"

"Listen, pooch, instead of asking questions, why on earth don't you just get started?" She was kind of yanking my cheek-tufts. "Find out for your-self—? Look, Bristlecone says Clover has her eye on you. So just go over there and ask her for a date. It couldn't be simpler. Besides, you could do a whole lot worse. Clover is a dish. *And*—" she was still holding my tufts and licked my muzzle a couple of times "—she's got good taste. She's had a few boys. You can bet on it. And now she's telling Bristlecone she has her eye on *you*. So hop to it. Before Oak gets to her and stretches her all out of shape."

Oak again. Oak's reputation of course made its impression on Briar and me. To different effect. Briar was inclined to scoff and sneer. More or less along the lines of Bristlecone's assessment. Not me! I was fascinated. Whenever I was around him, I couldn't hardly take my eyes off his crotch, not that I could see anything different from Briar's or Ash's or any other boy's. But from what girls said, what lurked in his sheath was different enough to talk about.

But the one thing Briar and I did completely agree on was Oak's nipple-ring. I mean, this, like, *jewel* only it wasn't in his ear, it was on his *chest*. Stuck right through his tit. It sort of made me wince just to think about it, but in our eyes it was the sexiest thing imaginable. We decided we want-ed one too. Briar and I nagged and whined and wheedled and pissed and moaned. You know how kids are when they want something.

Mom thought we'd lost our minds, I think. Dad was more direct: 'What? Over my dead body! No son of mine is going to go around with jewels stuck through his tits like some degenerate', and so on.

I thought that was real odd. I mean, it didn't make any sense: Oak, de-generate? *Oak?* How? He certainly seemed upright enough to me. But to-tally. A hunk, in fact. So male it made you squint to look right at him. I think Oak was the among the first guys I actually thought of as 'sexy'.

Well, whatever Dad's opinions about nipple-rings, we were total pests about it. Whining and pleading. Finally Mom and Dad relented as far as saying we could have an earring if we wanted. *One* earring. Anything else was right out. Dad actually said that if either Briar or I showed up with a 'candy-ass' nipple-ring he'd rip it out of our tits with his own hands. And he meant it, too.

I guess we were both pretty disappointed. We didn't want an *earring*, we wanted nipple-rings like the one Oak had. I think we both had this lame-brained thought that there was some sort of connection between Oak's success with girls and the nipple-ring, and we doubted that an earring would 'work'. It was funny: Briar had dreams of somehow acquiring Oak's stamina, but I was convinced there was some sort of connection between the pierced tit and Oak's sexiness. He was so virile. Maybe it did add something, but Oak would have *dripped* sex even if he was hanging by his tail and covered with shit.

Well, you know how kids are. Neither of us really wanted an earring, but we decided to get them anyway. Out of spite, as much as anything, since we knew Dad didn't really approve of an earring, either. So we trooped off and got our ears pierced. Briar got a sort of big silver loop in his left ear, with a string of little light blue stones set in it. It looked pretty good, actually, against his silvery fur. I opted for something gaudy, figuring that if I was going to wear an earring—out of spite, moreover—I might as well do it up brown. So I picked out a big, dangling thing. Heavy, too. I felt like I was walking sort of sideways until I got used to it. In my right ear. I didn't know any better. I just didn't want it on the same side as Briar's, and he'd gone first.

So far as I could tell, it didn't work. First, until I forgot about it, I didn't feel sexy. I felt self-conscious. Briar looked great in his, but there was something humpy about him anyway. I mean, he wasn't any Oak or Bolt, but he definitely had no trouble getting bitches to try him on for size, and he had no trouble getting them back to the table for second and third helpings.

I was the backward one in the family. (I've said that already.) The girls were going on dates and must have had sex almost every day not counting stuff like that double date with Bristlecone and Oak, where the four of them spent just about the whole afternoon screwing themselves cross-eyed. Briar Jr. was dating, too. And of course, there were Mom and Dad—

Especially when Dad and Mom were being, well, *that way*, but sometimes in between as well, Briar would be panting in my ear about his own bitches and talking over the plusses and minuses of this and that that he wanted in a bitch, debating with himself whether it was more fun laying the bitch from the front or the back, and wondering if there was 'something wrong' with him because he could only get it up 'two or three times' on a date, and how easy or hard it was be to get a bitch to do extra—you know, *different*—stuff. He told me he and Willow had figured out how you could lick each other between the legs at the same time, and that was *really* neat.

Oh, yes, and he was always trying to get me to agree that small ears were *totally* sexy.

My problems were a little different from Briar's. I didn't know *what* was sexy. I was fascinated by sex but couldn't figure out what anything meant. I mean, sure, I got all excited watching the girls necking, and talking over stuff with Thistle. I got real excited watching sex. I've already said that watching a guy come was about the most thrilling thing I knew. But there was just something special about the young men in general. All by themselves. Like that time Firefly buttoned up Oak. I just stared. Wondering. I suppose if I were less dense I'd have figured out better why I worshiped Oak, why I felt so tickled just to be in his company even if he ignored me. And the same was true of five or six of my sisters' guys.

Well, so, that's the picture. Yours truly, Thorn, one totally clueless adolescent. This is where my memory comes in, the one that won't leave me alone, after all these years. I was ambling along by the creek a couple of miles from our place, my brain buzzing with all sorts of confusing thoughts. I was frantically yearning for something but I didn't know what (or who) it was. I was dying. I was practically in tears I was so frustrated. Why I didn't just put my head down and run against a tree, I'll never know. *And* every time I thought about the fiasco with Clover I got so embarrassed all over again I moaned aloud. I'll tell you about that, later.

Everything made me feel sorry for myself, including the fact that it was a perfect day, and the little creek was pretty, everything all cool and dim in the shade of the bushes and trees. I spotted a big blue butterfly sitting on a leaf and sort of opening and closing his wings, and I crept up on him, trying to see how close I could get, amazed at the color of it.

I just about jumped out of my pelt when I heard this 'wurf' not two feet away.

There was a little wolf, he'd been drinking from the creek I guess. He was right in front of me, too, but given the cross wind I startled him as much as he startled me. I'd never seen him before. In fact, I'd never seen a wolf *like* him, before. He had this white face, the snowy fur continuing down over his neck and chest. And he was looking at me with the strangest eyes I'd ever seen. Blue. Fiery blue. Ice blue. I blinked. For a second I thought I could tell those eyes were staring right through me, looking at my bones or something.

He stood still, then (to my relief) switched from looking through me to making friendly gestures. His tail went up—a curved plume of a tail—and when he started bowing and leaping, and I couldn't help it, I was friendly back.

Then it hit me. This wasn't a wolf at all. He was a dog. A *dog*. I know we're not supposed to be friendly with dogs. To say the least! But—but—I took a deep breath and told my racing heart that killing dogs wasn't my job. Not all by myself anyhow. Not that I'd ever been put in the position of—

And besides, not *this* dog. Something was just plain wrong. There was something wonderfully likable about him. No, that's lame. Not just likable. I could feel the fur standing up on my neck with a funny kind of thrill. Whatever, I felt so strange. Giddy. Like I say, I haven't forgotten it, and I suppose I never will: just standing there looking at this guy made me feel happy. No; that's lame, too. What happened was that I had this *rush* of happiness. Total happiness.

I'd never felt anything like it.

So that's my memory. Stream, mild day, tension and anxiety on my part, and suddenly coming across this *dog* whose blue eyes looked out of a handsome face and right through me.

Of course, there's more. There's a whole story more. Happy-sad.

Well, I've come this far, you might as well hear the rest. It does have a sort of bearing on my fox, Tick. I mean on Tick and me. And the pooch I met that day is after all a member of the family, sort of.

It was unreal. The dog was bouncing around, splashing in and out of the creek, affable as all get-out. He was hardly more than a puppy. He was wearing shorts, and his body was compact and athletic under his fur, which was thick and fine. Well, like I say, at first I had a hard time deciding whether he was an actual dog or a wolf, though his markings definitely weren't like any wolf I'd ever seen. Or his eyes.

"What's your name?" I asked.

"Dennis," he said, skipping over and licking my cheek before springing away. "But that's not my *real* name."

"What's your real name?"

"Longchamps Sir Denali-de-Vere of Walworth. I mean, they *call* me Dennis. What's yours?"

"Um, unh, Thorn."

"Thorn? Thorn-what?"

"Just 'Thorn'. My, um, folks' names are Briar and Violet. That's all. Hey! I bet you can't catch me, Sir Dennis-de-Vere of Pinkle-Dick!" and I sprang over his back, splashed through the brook, and squeezed through the brush to the grassy openings beyond.

With a woof and a yelp Dennis was right after me, plumy tail in the air. He caught me, of course. Well, that's the whole point, isn't it? He tackled me and we rolled around in the tall grass, growling like crazy and chewing on each other's throats and kicking. Then a breakaway, and it was me chasing him, and when I jumped him he rolled over and we were chest to chest, gnarring and yipping and giggling like crazy.

I'd rassled with playmates before, naturally, Briar and others, but this time it was *the* most fun I'd ever had in my life. No question. But I didn't know why it was such fun. I mean, I was feeling different from anything I'd ever felt, but I didn't know why and I didn't know what. Except that I was happy. No; I was *flying*. That's all I knew. The smell of his fur, and the feeling of his body on mine, the feeling of my arms around him, it was all so much fun, or anyhow made me feel really great. Just being in the same field with him made me feel great. Watching him streak along in the tall grass. It was like night and day—going from being miserable and anxious to having so much fun that I thought my heart was going to burst.

"Hey," he said, once, "You're a mouthy one! If I chewed on things the way you chew on me, I'd get spanked!"

Right away I had this dreadful feeling. I didn't know exactly why. I started apologizing like crazy, but he smacked me on the bugle and yarfed, "Can't catch *me*, Thornbush!" and ran off.

I was bigger than Dennis, and stronger, but that guy could *run*. Even when I tackled him, as often as not he'd just keep going unless I could get him off his feet somehow. Finally, after a whole lot of roughhousing and galloping around and calling each other dirty names, we just fell in a happy, panting heap. Well, I was panting. He hardly seemed winded. I asked Dennis what kind of dog he was.

"Husky," he said. "*Siberian* Husky." He sounded little conceited I thought. "What about you, guy?"

"I don't know," I lied. "I, um, don't think I *am* a breed. I mean, we just live out here. I have a brother, Briar, like my dad, I mean that's his name too. And Mom, and two sisters, Firefly and Thistle. And of course I have all sorts of other brothers and sisters, somewhere. I only know a few of them. I'm, actually, well, *pretty* sure my dad is actually a brother. Half-brother, I mean. He's much younger than Mom, anyhow."

Dennis sort of sniffed at that. I could tell he was feeling pretty superior to a kid who doesn't even know what breed he belongs to, and who only has one dinky name.

And after it was too late. I wished I hadn't said anything about my mom being Dad's mom too.

I could have saved myself grief over *that*. Dennis kind of allowed, casual-like, that he never even met *his* dad. In fact, the only relatives he'd ever even seen were his mother and his litter-mates, both of who had names as fancy-ass as his. His dam had sometimes talked about her other kids, who had won all these prizes (whatever they were), and bragged about how many times 'they' had let a guy named Denali Shah-Jehan Kumara of Broken Ridge 'service' her—whatever, exactly, 'servicing' was. But it sounded important. Dennis had doped out that it had *something* to do with this Denali dude being his father, though how exactly was hazy. Anyway, his mom attached a lot of importance to the prizes. *Everybody* who'd serviced her was just dripping with prizes, and besides they were all these gorgeous studs. But she'd said time and again when he was a little pup that the most gorgeous was his father, this guy Denali Shah-Jehan Kumara of Broken Ridge.

It was all pretty confusing, since neither one of us really knew what he was talking about. He was just telling me what his mom had told him. He'd never set eyes on even one of these 'service' gents or their 'prizes,' and was pretty much at a loss about what the connection was between 'service' and 'prizes,' though there definitely seemed to be one. As for his two brothers, he'd never given any thought to whether either one of them was 'gorgeous' or what, though his mom had often told all three of them how handsome they were and how much they took after Denali Whoop-De-Do of Broken Prick.

I admit I was kind of shocked. I mean, it was okay for teenagers like my sisters to get hung on just about every date, but they were shopping around for a husband after all. I mean, a sex-addict like Wasp was different, but every other guy I knew understood that screwing a bitch was a kind of proposal of marriage. She 'accepted' you when somehow she let you make babies inside her. And while I couldn't even guess what Wasp would be like if he ever became a father, I was totally sure that every one of these guys who were laying my sisters, randy and sex-hungry as they were, once they had kids, they would be different. I knew Dad wasn't Mom's first mate (obviously), but I was sure that once they were mated she never did it with anyone but him. Well, guys didn't even *try* to make her. It wasn't done. Someone like Wasp, who went around trying to have sex with guys' wives, was just weird.

Dennis said his people (I pretended to know what he meant by that) had just moved to this farm over the opposite rise. He said, in this kind of superior way, that they were talking about arranging for bitches for him to mate.

"Do you know *how?*" I asked him.

"Of course," he said.

"You've done it?" I had the oddest feeling. A little excited, but there was something else, too. Not a happy feeling.

"Er, well, no. Not exactly."

(I didn't think 'not exactly' was a possible answer.)

"Then, you've watched other guys?"

"Um, well, no, er—"

"Well look, bonehead, how're you going to know what to do when these bitches put in an appearance?"

He mumbled something about it can't be too hard to figure out. So of course I immediately thought about Thistle's eager young date trying to plant a litter under her tail. Anyway, thanks to Mom and Dad being so open about their love-making, these days, not to mention watching the girls and Briar at it from time to time—and also Thistle had been telling me *all* about her dates—I was hardly in doubt about what to do and how to do it, long before I first found out for myself what it felt like. Even if I had no personal experience at that point, I was an expert compared to this pup. And I was about to start in, when—zing!—Dennis's ears flew up.

There was this funny squealing sound, I hardly noticed it, but he jumped up and said he had to go, he had to go, had to go right away, had to go, he was being called. He was making whimpering noises about the burrs in his fur, but kept saying he had to go *right away*, so he couldn't let me help him get cleaned up. He seemed almost frantic about taking off. We quick-licked each other's cheeks one last time, and off he ran.

Leaving me feeling as empty as a milkweed pod. I'd never felt like that.

The whole thing was too confusing: high as a kite one minute and, well, still high but feeling lost and hollowed-out the next.

I lay there, thinking my scrambled thoughts. About Dennis. About his screwy upbringing and my own. Funny, about parents and fathers and whatnot. My dad was very important to me. I was afraid of him, I suppose, but I really looked up to him, too. Ever since I was little I had funny thoughts about Dad. He was so strong and handsome. And of course kind of scary. At the same time he was real comforting. I mean, he wouldn't put up with any nonsense from us cubs at home, but if there was any trouble he was there. I remember once some older boys—Buckthorn and Oak, no less—were kind of knocking me and Little Briar around and all of a sudden, Dad was right there. The bullies were very impressed. I mean, he didn't tell the other guys to leave us alone. He just told them to behave. (They did, too.)

Once, on a picnic we'll all remember, a bear showed up. Dad was awesome. All hackles and teeth. I'd never seen him like that. I was scared shitless, as much by Dad as by the bear. But I think it was just at that moment—I mean, as soon as I calmed down—that I had this boyish thought about how I wanted to be just like Dad.

Of course, it doesn't work like that. By now I knew I'd never be 'like Dad'. Briar junior was a dumb sight closer, and even he didn't really measure up, either. I guess I'm resigned to it. I'll never be big and rangy like that, and my fur isn't going to get any more strongly marked than it is, and my mane is a real wimp-out. Still, for some nutso reason all the females in the family keep telling me I'm good-looking. That sometimes makes me feel more okay about myself. But I know I'm not good-looking the way Dad is. And speaking of 'wimp', I'm afraid of my own shadow, and most of the time I think I can't do anything right.

Mom is the best mom in the world. She really loves us. She really loves Dad, too, though I wasn't ready for the fur-flying, off-the-wall sex that had been going on for several months. Amazing. I mean, Dad is so masculine all the time, there weren't any surprises there. But what Mom turns into when they just *talk* about coupling, these days… well, it's awesome.

You're getting the picture. It's totally different from Dennis's family. No dad; a mom who *boasts* about the number of different guys who've made her a mother. Boy, did that sound weird. Girls, now, it's normal for them to have dates with all the different guys they feel like. But a *mom?*

Of course, it's not like nothing at all like that ever happens. There's some funny business in my own family, I know. I've never gotten the whole story. The folks don't seem to want to talk about it. But—well, like I say, Dad's a lot younger than Mom, obviously, and she's said a couple of things that sound like he's her own son. What happened to *his* dad, then? If he died or something, why not just say so? Anyway, I don't have any trouble seeing why a bitch might be attracted to a guy like Dad. My own sisters think he's perfect. I don't suppose they talk about it to their dates, but *I* sure get the rundown, about how their young men don't measure up.

I sometimes try to fit it all together. If I'm right about Mom and Dad, I *think* that means that Mom is also my granma. On my dad's side. I mean, if she's my dad's ma, isn't she my granma? And Thistle is my niece as well as my sister. Also my aunt. Confusing. I sometimes wondered who my grampa was, I mean Mom's first mate, and what happened to him. He must have been quite something, to have a kid like Dad.

Well, Dennis didn't have to think about stuff like that. He never even saw his dad. I bet for all *he* knew, he had only two great-grandparents, total.

On my way home I decided this Dennis thing wasn't anything I could talk about to anyone, except maybe Thistle. I was real close to Thistle. But even so I wasn't sure I could talk to her about something like *this*. I mean, making friends with a *dog*. Never mind asking her if she had any idea about what was going wrong with me, how I could be feeling so goofily happy and buzzard-miserable at the exact same time. But it seemed to me that the girls were smarter about things that mattered. So if I got a chance, I told myself, I'd see if she had any ideas.

But, well, it just never seemed like the right time to bring it up. Meantime, just about every day, I was out by the stream. And every day Dennis showed up. Every minute I was awake, just about, I was thinking about Dennis, and when he was actually there, I was just tickled to pieces.

Every time.

I would nearly burst with happiness when I saw him loping toward me over the grass, or walked up the creek to the pool and saw him lying there waiting for me. I felt totally wonderful when he was around. Mostly we raced each other and rassled and roughhoused. I kept getting my pants dirty and getting yapped at by Mom. But I was in another world. Since meeting Dennis I was just crazy. I didn't want to eat. I couldn't hardly sleep. All I wanted to do was play with Dennis. Play rough. And sleep with him. I mean, sometimes we'd just work ourselves into a tuckered-out frazzle and fall asleep. I really liked that. Or on the hotter afternoons we'd pant in the shade and talk. Not talk *about* anything. Just talk.

Meantime, I was feeling sort of horny and unloved but I was feeling, well, self-confident in ways I hadn't, ever, before, and I actually felt up to picking the scab off of my encounter with Clover, that cousin of Bristlecone's.

What a flop. Thistle had been asking me almost daily if I'd talked to Clover. Then, just before I met Dennis, out of a blue sky Mom started in on me about this darling Clover bitch. Saying she was such a nice young lady and I really should get out more and how Clover was so petite and refined, and it would be just like a *nice* girl like that to be swept off her feet by a boy with nothing but his virility to offer (that wasn't exactly the way Mom put it), and then she'd be miserable for the rest of her life with some thug when she *could* have had a sweet-natured and considerate husband. Meaning me, I guess, which told me something about *my* virility. (Actually, when she talked that way my mind tended to wander. I couldn't for the life of me see anything at all wrong with the boys I knew who had virility to spare. And 'sweeping a bitch off her feet' just set me to thinking of all the times I'd seen a guy do just that. In fact, I think the type of guys Mom was talking about would be happy doing it standing up, but none of Thistle's and Firefly's dates were so crude.)

And then one day Mom said she'd been talking to Lacewing, Clover's mom, some sort of cousin of Mom's I think, and how *she* was just *full* of compliments about what a *nice* young *man* I was, and made it clear that Clover thought so too. So Mom just up and asked me if I'd ever had a bitch. I said no, and she looked at me in this sweet way, drying her hands, and said, "Thorn, dear, Clover is just *waiting* for you to ask her for a date. So, ask. Do yourself a favor. You've got to start somewhere, and you could do a whole lot worse than starting with a darling little girl like Clover. Besides—" she had this funny twinkle in her eye—"before you can say 'jackrabbit', that busy brother of yours is going to have her. Well, he'll have her sooner or later anyway, I expect, but wouldn't you rather have her comparing *him* to *you* than the other way around?"

Nothing like a little sibling rivalry to top off Mom's wheedling.

So I got all my courage together in one place and paid a call on this Clover.

Sure enough, I hadn't hardly flustered out a couple of idiotic non-sequiturs when Clover said, why yes, she'd go out with me, and told me to come back in half an hour to get her. Which I did.

She was indeed a pretty little bitch, I thought. A little quiet, maybe. I mean, I'm happier with someone like Thistle, who has some sparkle to her, but Clover was very nice. Sweet face, soft voice, nice and gentle.

Not much of a talker, but by and large I thought our first date went fine.

Of course, it popped my balloon when I got home and Briar asked me what kind of sex I'd had. He was so elaborately incredulous when I said it hadn't come up I thought he was play-acting. I was kind of cross at his nosiness. And just as cross at myself for answering his stupid questions. So imagine my surprise when I go inside and there's Dad, and right away he grabs me—puts an arm around my neck and hugs me, kind of hard, and knuckles up my fur with a Dutch rub. He was obviously in a great mood.

"Well, big balls," he said, just about cracking himself up. "Pussy is popular for a reason, ain't it? Ain't it?" Then he gave my ear a lick, and another hug that almost broke my neck, and sort of smacked me across the cheek.

Dad didn't do that sort of thing often. Hug us and such. Usually it was kind of special, but I was just embarrassed, this time. Really embarrassed.

The very next day I met Dennis. And that did a lot for my self-esteem. So maybe two weeks later, like I say, I decided to try going out with Clover again. Lecturing myself about being a little more manly this time. And maybe Dad's raunchiness was infectious. Pussy certainly was popular, I knew that, and I thought I was ready to find out why, for myself. This time.

It almost didn't work. I mean, I was so *awfully* backward, and Clover was her usual clam-like self. What little conversation she was making was divided between talking about who was dating who, and stuff about how good-looking I was and how gentlemanly and how lucky the bitch would be who carried my litter, and so on. And she was looking at me with these big, serious eyes. I figured it was kind of a hint, but I couldn't for the life of me figure out how to go about making the first move. I mean, just grabbing her or something wouldn't do. Or asking her to open my fly. I'd seen my sisters and their dates start out with the bitch opening his fly, but I had the definite idea the girls just did it. On their own.

I thought of bringing up the subject of sex by asking her something like who was the last boy to screw her, but I'd already started the sentence when I decided that that wasn't a good approach, either.

I suppose it would have ended the same way as the first date except that after another of many long silences, Clover just put a hand between my legs. And squeezed.

I gasped. The hair stood on end all over my body. I was startled, but mainly I'd never felt anything like that in my life.

Clover said something in her soft, feminine voice about 'doing something' about the 'trouble down here'. She was slowly unbuttoning my shorts, calling me her 'poor boy' and so on.

I was horribly embarrassed. A girl, practically a stranger, too, seeing what was in my pants. In general. Never mind that I was fully out of my sheath with excitement. I was about to die, but whether it was excitement or shame I couldn't tell.

She'd only undone my fly when she put her muzzle to the opening and did something with her tongue that made me just about jump out of my pelt. Then, when she got my shorts pulled down a ways, she started licking me between the legs. I mean, I wasn't prepared for anything like that. I thought my heart was going to come out of my ribs. I literally couldn't talk. Not that I really wanted to talk.

Well, I may have been a virgin, but I knew perfectly well which hole to put it in, and at some point when Clover and I were both more or less naked, I decided a proposition wouldn't seem so stupid. Under the circumstances, 'no' wasn't a possible answer, but even so it seemed crude to me just to crawl on top of her and put it to her. But it also seemed sort of crude to say right out loud that I wanted to screw her.

While I was dithering over these things, Clover took matters into her own hands. Once again. When we'd been necking for a while, she looked up at me and murmured something about me being a big boy, and asked me if I wanted to get wet.

Get wet? That was boy-talk. Pure boy-talk. I'd never heard my sisters say such a thing. Since Clover didn't have any brothers I decided Thistle had to be right, she was no virgin. (I'm so smart.)

I figured I didn't have to say anything, now. I just gathered her up, like I'd seen the guys do so often, with my arms around her shoulders, and said, "Like this?"

I hope she couldn't tell I was shaking, but she probably could. In any case, something stiff and black found something warm and wet, all right. Both of us groaned. I was totally surprised.

The very first sensation was incredible.

But it was nothing compared to the last one.

It was over almost before it started.

As I lay on Clover, seeing spots, Dad's words were echoing in my head. My goodness. Whoa. *Whoa.* Pussy is indeed popular for a reason. Oh, my. I had no idea it was anything at all like *that.*

Well, I dated Clover some more, and got a whole lot better about making my way, all by myself—I mean, without Clover coaching and prodding and groping—from cuddling to licking to coupling to screaming orgasm. I even got the idea of licking her between the legs all on my own. She liked it, I think. Anyway, she *would* keep trying to pull my ears off while I was doing it.

I kept thinking I was doing something wrong, though, because once I was in her, it was over as soon as it started. And then I felt bad. Well, not *bad* bad, just stupid and embarrassed.

It was a little better with the two bitches who were the only cubs of Star and Larkspur—a young couple, also some kind of relatives of Mom's. Quiet, kind of shy. I think the girls were their first litter, so of course it was small. Just the two bitches, Cricket and Blackfoot. My brother had spoken highly of the girls, and kept telling me to 'get my ass over there' and lay them. But I was completely at sea about how to 'try out' two sisters. Cold, so to say: in Clover's case, it was a given that she was interested in me.

To my surprise (and relief), when I went over to their place, the two bitches as much as said right out loud that they knew why I'd introduced myself. Also, they obviously took it for granted that I'd be into both of them. After a little conversation, Blackfoot just said, "Look, Thorn, I'm expecting Hornbeam in a little while, so why don't you go and show Cricket a good time? There's a stand of sweet grass behind that little shed that's just perfect for that kind of, well, thing. No one will disturb you, you can take as long as you like."

I mumbled something gallant, I suppose, anyway Cricket had her ears up and cocked her head and smiled sweetly. I took her by the hand and she led me off to the grassy spot, which was in fact a great place for sex. Cricket got right to the point, too. Without a word she just slipped out of her clothes and lay down on her back, looking at me standing there fully-dressed.

"Come on, Thorn," she said. "Peel down to fur. Let me see what you got."

Taking off my own clothes while a girl watched me would have been embarrassing even if she hadn't been making remarks about my body and looks the whole time. But coming from such a cute bitch, and being pretty complimentary—me, the family spaz—I guess it was thrilling at the same time.

Cricket was a good lay. More experienced than Clover, or something, anyway she seemed to know a lot of little ways to make me feel more and more excited.

I'd dated her a couple times more when I showed up, this one time, hoping she might be up for a little fun, but she wasn't there. Her sister Blackfoot told me that Cricket was 'out'. Off somewhere, that is, with a young wolf. Then she said it was Wasp. Well, no 'young' wolf. Wasp was as old as Dad or older. He was famous. He seemingly was hard twelve hours a day, and had gotten into more than one fight over screwing guys' *wives*. That was just weird. Also, everybody had to know that he didn't have a particle of interest in settling down. I never actually heard a bitch say this, but the guys all claimed that Wasp was really great sex. They'd say stuff like how you don't want to be the first guy into a bitch just after she's had the Wasp treatment, because you'll bomb.

"You ever dated Wasp?"

She said something evasive like "Who hasn't?"

"Is he really hot? How many times did he come?"

"None of your business, wolf-boy. Anyway—" she looked at me out of the corner of her eye, "as soon as she recovers, I'm sure Cricket will be more than glad to get back to something—substantial. If you know what I mean. Of course—" she paused and cocked her head a little, "I'm not a gossip. I mean, when *I* talk about what a guy is like on a date, you know I'm speaking from *personal* experience. Though from what I *understand*—" she shrugged her shoulders and peered at her nails; "from what I understand, if Wasp was built like a certain wolf-boy in, uh, certain ways, he'd be a *real* danger."

Blackfoot just kind of stood there, like she was waiting for me to do something.

"I suppose there's no point in waiting for Cricket," she said. "I do hope you aren't too disappointed. I mean, I know how *excited* you boys can sometimes be when you're looking for a date."

Nothing like hinting a little more broadly if the first two or three hints don't work.

Well, so it wasn't more than a half-hour before I was blissfully holding Blackfoot in my embrace in the sweet grass and nibbling on her ears while waiting for my knot to set us free. She played with my cheek-tufts and ruffled my fur and arched her back and said the gossip was true.

"You mean, that I'm a gentleman?"

"That too, actually." She looked at me dreamily. "But after all, Thorn, with what you've got, you don't really *need* to come on like some macho sex-athlete. Just let your, um, nature do the talking and you'll come out all right."

Everybody always talked about what a looker Blackfoot was, and I guess they're right. And she was pretty responsive. Maybe even voluptuous. I mean, right after I came, she did something new to me: put her hands on my butt and held us together. Tight. Holding me in her. It really made me feel like she was enjoying me. Not that I could have pulled out of her right away anyhow. But Cricket was a tad more perky than her sister, and I sort of liked her company. I guess she reminded me of Thistle more than most bitches did. Giggle and tease, even after a good screw.

While we were still hung, apart from a word or two praising my 'nature' and a little moan when I made a move to see if I was free yet, there wasn't much conversation. There was only so much that could be said about my cock, and I couldn't really contribute anything since I had nothing to compare it to, so I was casting around for something to say when I made the mistake of saying that her dark socks and gloves were almost like a fox's.

I thought it was a compliment, but she didn't seem to be at all pleased. In fact, she was so pissed she just about pulled my hung-up prick out by the roots.

I guess I learned something. Two things, actually. First, really pretty babes are often less fun; and second, not to say unrehearsed things while you're hung.

Despite my gaffe, Blackfoot didn't cut me off totally. In particular, there was the once that Briar and I double-dated. It was Briar's idea to call on Cricket and Blackfoot. I just sort of tagged along, figuring I'd play it by ear—if just one of the girls was free, maybe we could take turns, that sort of thing. But they were both there, and *they* steered the talk to sex, and I couldn't believe it when Blackfoot put an arm around my waist—actually she was sort of feeling me under my tail!—and said something like, "You get Thorn all the time, Cricket; it's *my* turn".

In the course of the afternoon, Briar and I took turns with both girls. We humped ourselves to a complete frazzle. It was the only double-date I ever went on, and it was far and away the most exhausting sex of my life. I thought I'd have to crawl home. (Easily done. All it required was staying in the same posture, more or less, that I'd been in all afternoon.) I guess that Briar and I were sort of inspiring one another. Well, I know he was inspiring *me*. And either he's a sex-machine, or else he was inspired too.

However, that was right around the time when I began to worry seriously about something being wrong. Dating was fun but only *sort* of fun. Dad was right: pussy's popular for a reason. And sometimes, like that double date with Briar, I had the illusion that me and my iron cock could go for twenty-four hours a day. But—even so—and even though Cricket was cute and a funny tease and I liked her company, and she seemed to like mine—well, I don't know what happened. I just sort of stopped calling on her.

I'd sort of given up on Clover, too. She was pretty, even glamorous, and dainty and shy in a way that turns on a lot of guys. Once she'd gotten over the thrill of conquest, I knew she'd pass me up anytime for a whole bunch of guys, starting with my manly brother. She was taken with his virility, and I could hardly object. Briar Jr. was a pretty busy boy, by then, and it didn't help a bit that from that time on, *every single* bitch I humped mentioned somewhere along the line what a hot screw my brother was. This was a kind of code for saying that I may be 'a gentleman', and may have 'nice looks' and, unless talking about the size of the guy's cock is standard sweet-talk among the bitches, it seems I must be a little special 'down there'—*but*—one or two lays from me and we'd both sort of lose interest.

Mind you, that's not to say I wasn't having fun, and a couple of times when a bitch was licking me between the legs I thought it was something I'd like to do for ever, if I could. But mostly it wasn't even screwing for screwing's sake. It was orgasm for orgasm's sake. I wondered if that was unusual. The other guys sure enjoyed coming. At least they talked a lot about how often they came, on a date, and talked about what made it more intense for them, and so on. But as far as I could tell, for the other guys the *idea* of having sex was almost as fascinating as actually doing it, while for me, sex and orgasm were the same thing. Warm and wet was only a preliminary—a pleasant enough preliminary—to the intense thrill at the end.

And there was a crisis. A horrible experience with Waterleaf. She was one of the sisters of one of my sister Firefly's regular lays, a quiet boy named Teal. Nice looking. It was like our third date, Waterleaf and me, and we were on the floor in her living room and I was up to the nuts in her and humping away for dear *life* and looking forward to an *excellent* orgasm, and Waterleaf was chewing on my neck and tearing my fur out by the handfuls and talking about how she'd never felt a knot like mine, and then—then—I lost it. Just *lost* it. Poof. Couldn't finish.

I can tell you, I was pretty confused and embarrassed.

Waterleaf was nice about it, but I was awake half the night, replaying our conversations. It didn't help a bit when Thistle said to me, the next *morning* (can you believe it?) "I hear you lost your stiffie while you were inside Waterleaf, yesterday".

I was mortified enough when I thought only two wolves in the world knew I'd started something I couldn't finish. And now it turned out that, well, almost everybody—

But I had Dennis. The very happiest moments of my life were when I was with Dennis. He was so much fun, and I felt so relaxed and so happy around him. Totally relaxed, totally happy. Being with Dennis was different from being around wolf guys, and different from dating. It was so easy and so pleasant. We played and ran and roughhoused and rassled and napped. And talked and talked. He told me fantastic stories about his 'people'. I told him about my 'sexploits', all except for the fiasco with Waterleaf, that is. (Since he was a dog, I figured he wouldn't hear any gossip, and I was grateful there was at least one person I knew who didn't know the story of Thorn Lame-Dick.)

Dennis was interested, I could tell, but a little at sea. I tried to explain screwing. He wasn't exactly getting it, I could tell. He wasn't even quite getting the connection between my 'dates' and his mom's reminiscences about being 'serviced' by males. (I'd boned up on the terminology with Briar.)

I got the bright idea of showing him. I mean, he was so clueless. He somehow had the idea that the guy sort of *backs up* to the bitch. (Where do people get such ideas?) I said no, there were basically two different ways. One was like horses. Well, he didn't know what I meant by that, either, so I told him to get down on his hands and knees and I went behind him and felt between his legs, and told him how if he was a bitch he'd have another hole, right here, just about where his balls were, and the guy would be kind of on the bitch's back, and so on and so forth. Kind of demonstrating. But I mean we both had our shorts on and everything.

But, I said, most of the guys I knew, and my own folks too, preferred doing it from the front. I didn't know what to call it. I told Dennis a joke on myself, about how when I was a little younger I honestly thought I'd figured out for myself that doing it from the front was called 'screwing' and doing from behind was called 'humping'. I could have lived the rest of my life with that mistake making no trouble for anybody, but one day I managed to embarrass myself horribly, in front of one of the older boys, by asking him whether he preferred screwing a bitch or humping her.

So there we were, Dennis on his back and me lying on his chest. We'd done that while rassling all the time, but this time I was explaining sex to him and describing what the boy does and what the bitch does.

I don't even know how it happened. Without any warning, Dennis started trying to push me off him. Real rough. I mean I had no idea he was even that strong.

"*Hey!*" he said. There was a real strange edge to his voice, and he was looking at me funny. "Cut that out!"

"What?"

"Cut it *out!*"

"Cut it?—Dennis! Please—!"

"No! Quit it!"

Dennis looked like he was crazy.

"Look," he said, scrambling to his feet, brushing off his clothes, "I gotta go, okay? Okay?" And he shot out of the tall grass into the field, back toward home.

There was an edge to his voice. It sure didn't *sound* 'okay'. And if he'd hit me with a stone I couldn't have been more startled by the look he gave me. Dennis's eyes were a little weird at the best of times. That pale blue. Ice blue. Fire blue. Normally they just made him look exotic and handsome. But *now*, oh help me, now every time I thought of the look in his eyes before he turned and ran off, I wanted to die.

I was sick. Confused, mainly. Excited—shaking with excitement, in fact, but sick, too. With dread. I had this feeling I'd made sweet Dennis really mad. Or something. But since I didn't know what he was thinking, and I didn't know why, I was left with this helpless feeling. It was physical, like getting punched in the stomach. I wanted to please Dennis so badly, I wanted to be around him, and I now guessed I'd done something really bad. I—well, I don't know, I'd been holding his head in my hands and licking all over his muzzle. And I guess—I *guess*—I'd been moving my body— this is so embarrassing—moving my body between his thighs, like I do when I'm working a bitch—I mean, it felt so good, I didn't even know *what* I was doing.

I lay in the tall grass, muzzle in my hands, and whimpered and cried and moaned.

It was almost dark when I finally pulled myself together enough to drag my poor body home.

I couldn't even go inside. I was sitting in the yard when Thistle came over to me.

"Thorn, my goodness, what's wrong with you? You look like a hare two cubs have been fighting over."

I just shook my head. I tried to say something but it came out as a sort of whimpering whine, and I started to cry again.

"Is it Dennis?" she asked, lying down next to me.

"Wha—"

"Your friend Dennis. Has he been mean to you? I know he's your best friend. A *dog!* You're just lucky I didn't tell Mom."

"How come you know so much, little Miss Smarty?" I asked, hotly. I had something new to be upset about. At least it made me stop feeling dead inside.

Well, she explained it all easily enough. She'd noticed I was acting funny—fidgety, restless, half-there. First she figured it was because of some bitch, which naturally fascinated her. But that didn't check out.

Then she decided I was having an 'affair'. Screwing some guy's *wife.* That was *so* exciting! Her own brother, another Wasp! So she followed me sometimes, but I never visited anybody's wife. It was just this dog. And a boy-dog, too. But she'd watched Dennis and me playing, and figured out that he was special.

"And, he's *cute!*" she said. "I admire your taste in dogs."

"What on earth are you talking about?" I was pretty steamed.

"—a *dish.* And he's—more—more something—than any regular wolf. I mean, just look at him. A *real* gentleman."

I wondered what that meant. My dates kept calling *me* a gentleman, which only seemed to have something to do with not being very good sex.

"He's got to be a fancy breed, too," she continued, her eyes shining, "he has such wonderful fur, the gorgeous markings; he—"

"I don't know anything about that stuff," I said, crossly. "And what about Bolt? I thought your pussy belonged to Bolt."

"Bolt? Nah-h-h. I mean, well, of *course* I'm *sweet* on him, you dope, who wouldn't be? And, well, of course, he *is* special—"

"That's what I thought. In fact, it beats me how come you aren't pregnant. Seems like every time I turn around he's emptying his nuts—"

"None of your business, you needle-nosed twerp!"

It was Thistle's turn to be huffy. She looked at me with this superior face. "I'm not pregnant because I don't want to be. I haven't made up my mind about Bolt, anyway. He's—well—not without his, er, charms. But he's like little Briar. He thinks the only part of him that matters is between his legs."

"I thought you *liked* what was between his legs."

"Well, yes, of course—"

"Better than Bristlecone and Buckthorn and Oak?" (Even the famous Oak.)

"Of *course*," she said, her eyes flashing. She was so cute when she was cross. And there was something funny about her sudden primness. "I've *said* I like him. You've told me often enough that *you* liked Bolt best, too."

Well, true. Bolt was like Dad. I mean, great markings; rangy; strong. And oo-oo-oozing sex. He was just a kid, maybe a year older than Thistle and me, but there was something about him. Some kind of presence. A questioning glance from that 'kid' and you started shaking. Thistle told me that the first time she *saw* Bolt she went all to pieces, because she just *knew* what he was thinking and she both dreaded it and wanted it. Of course, a boy at that age—hmffh! A really cute girl, like Thistle, hardly has to be a swami to know what he's thinking. There wasn't anything actually wrong with the other boys, especially (in my eyes) Buckthorn. Oh, and Oak. But if Bolt just standing there was impressive, Bolt in action was *awesome*. Every muscle in his body, man, it was *work*, and he made the most amazing noises in his throat. I couldn't imagine what it felt like. I mean, what it felt like either to *be* Bolt, or to *have* Bolt.

"Anyway," Thistle said, putting an arm around my shoulder and licking my cheek, "this pooch you have a crush on is so *cute*. I want to meet him. Introduce us. You've got to. C'mon—you've *got* to. Besides—if you won't introduce us, I'll just do it myself."

Wha—" I was astounded. "A dog? Thistle, really! Well—OK, okay, you win," I said. Reluctantly, "I'll take you tomorrow. I bet he doesn't like you though. So *there*. And, say—what's this rubbish about me having a crush—?"

"Well," she said, kind of smart-ass superior, "it's mainly that you've been behaving the way *I'd* behave if I had a thing for this Dennis-dog. Exactly the way. And besides—" a little girlish toss of her head, "I got eyes. I can see why you might be that way. He's very—well—elegant. Smart. Just look at that tail."

"You never 'behaved' in any particular way around Bolt," I said, crossly, "or any other of your *countless* boyfriends. Unless—speaking of tails—you count holding your tail to one side as 'behavior.'"

"Who says I'm in love with Bolt?" she snapped.

"You just did. Sort of."

"Oh—well—I didn't mean it *that* way. He's, uh, he's all boy. He flatters me. He makes me feel special. And he's so—affectionate."

"You mean 'tireless'?"

"Don't you wish!" she said, sharply, and was about to taunt me about Waterleaf, I think, but then drew herself up and gave me this arch look. "Of course, that's *really* just because the big silly wants to make me pregnant so I'll marry him. But that's *my* choice, not his."

I personally suspected that Bolt's single-minded devotion to the nooks and crannies of Thistle's body had as much to do with his worship at the Altar of Orgasm as with marriage, but Thistle's remark derailed me.

"Wha-a-at?" I yipped. "I mean, how can you be so sure? I mean—day after day, you two *do* it until Bolt drops from exhaustion. And he doesn't exhaust easily. And not just Bolt." It was my turn to be arch. "If you were to get pregnant, my dear Thistle-Down, how ever would you know which of that gang you give tube-rides to, just about daily, actually put the pups in there?" But that wasn't the point. I couldn't see how could she be so busy with her boy friends and still confident she wouldn't have babies. But like I say, the bitches seem to know more about just about everything than guys do.

In any case, the next day when I was about to go off to the place where Dennis and I usually met, Bolt was on the scene. As usual. I mean, he'd had Thistle once already, in the morning. I guess it was sort of mean, but I watched them until Bolt was just wheezing out his last creamy sigh and they were good and hung, and then kind of ambled over and said I was off, couldn't wait for her, but she could meet Dennis some other day.

That set Bolt off, and as I trotted away I heard the two of them spatting. I guess he thought she had enough cock in her life already. He wanted to know who this new guy Dennis was, and she was telling him it was none of his business. All while his knot was locking him inside her. Tee-hee.

For some reason the panic and dread of the day before had lifted and I was feeling okay as I went to the place where Dennis and I generally met, near the fringe of underbrush along the creek. It was a specially pretty spot, where the water ran over some rocks and made noise and fell over this ledge into a kind of pool.

No Dennis.

I just about collapsed. Well, in fact I *did* collapse. I was whining and cringing and my tail was between my legs so tight I don't know why it didn't snap off at the root.

Of course, I wasn't thinking. Thistle knew, generally anyhow, where Dennis and I got together, and particularly with my whimpering and whining she had no trouble finding me. And she doped out what was wrong right away.

It was no great achievement, since I was hysterical. Which only confirmed her cockamamie idea that I had a crush or something on that moth-eaten bag of bones, him and his fancy-ass name, like he had four balls or something. Dog. A *dog*. Whore for a mother. Nothing but a slave. That's right, a slave. Him and his collar and his shots and his spankings and his dog-whistle. Being put in a room with some bitch he's never even seen before and *told* to screw her. And looking *forward* to it!

Anyway, Thistle was trying to comfort me and I guess I was glad she was there. I was lying half in her lap and boo-hooing and whining and groaning when I heard a familiar voice say, "Well, now! Well, well, *well!* And who have we *here?* Thorn, you old rascal—you all right? Hey, guy, why didn't you *tell* me you had a girl-friend?"

Dennis came over and gave Thistle a sniff. "Oh, *well*, hey, I can't blame you, guy—such a gorgeous bitch, no wonder you keep her hidden away. —So, what's your name, honey-blossom?"

"Oh, do you really think so?" simpered Thistle.

I was all red-eyed and hiccuppy but I managed to sort of prop myself up and say, "She's not my girl-friend, you mangy buzzard, she's my sister."

"Izzat so?" said Dennis. His ears were so erect I thought they'd pop right off his head. "Better and *better*. You told me you had a sister, jocko, but you never said she was gorgeous. *Gor-gee-ous*. So, eh-heh-heh, baby, what's your name?"

"Thistle."

"Oh! Yeah! Wow! A beautiful name for a beautiful bitch."

"It's a prickly weed," I said, still sniffling, but I was as cross as a bear with a sore nose. "Good for nothing."

"Oh, I'd bet *this* 'thistle' is good for something," said Dennis, kind of puppying around, but not too boisterously. Just showing off his muscles and all. Him and his big chest and tiny waist. Making his pickled little unused slave's sheath look bigger than life.

"Do you really?" said Thistle. She was really laying it on with a trowel, batting her eyes and giving his muzzle a lick and putting her hand on his cheek. "You know, I was thinking that a boy as pretty, um, I mean, handsome as you are must have a regular string of bitches yipping and whining all day for the favor of your—ah—attention—"

"Naw, gosh," he said, bashfully. "Er, well, I dunno … my people have talked about 'breeding' me, if that's what you mean—I think it has something to do with girls, but—"

Thistle had pulled the cork out of the bottle, and now I had to face it. I worshiped everything about that animal. Everything. I was his. And while the two of them were talking I could almost feel my heart shriveling up. And all my other internal organs as well.

I still didn't know what on earth was going on, only that Dennis made me feel fantastic sometimes and miserable sometimes. And the miserable part seemed to be uppermost, recently. Right now, for example. If I could have *willed* myself to die, I swear I'd have given it a try.

"Hey, want to come down and take a look around the farm? It's kind of neat."

"Oh, I'd love to," said my dear, dear little sister. (*Snake in the grass.*) She'd been licking his cheeks and playing with his ears. I couldn't believe it. She was actually coming on to him. Overflowing with Bolt's second load of the day, and *coming on* to this mutt!

"Are you just trying to make Bolt jealous?" I asked. (I figured, why should I leave all the trouble-making up to Thistle?)

"Bolt? Who's Bolt?"

"Her boyfriend" I said. "Well, they're practically married. I mean, since he skr—"

"*Thorn!* Pipe down! Sheesh!" She turned to Dennis and gave him this super-sweet look followed by another lick.

"You have a boyfriend?" Dennis was plainly concerned.

"You can say that again," I said. "Not just one, either. Bolt's in her morning, noon, and night, but she still manages to find time for a whole pack—"

I didn't think Thistle was even *capable* of the look she shot me.

"Pack—?"

Dennis was only half paying attention, he was so busy exchanging licks with pretty little Thistle. I don't know where she got the business with a guy's tits. I never saw her do it with Bolt. I could see it pleased Oak; and it was getting through to Dennis.

"Yeah, pack. You know. Us wolves."

"*Wolves!*"

I've never seen anything like it. In a blink of an eye, Dennis's ears were flat against his head, and he dropped into this ghastly stiff-legged crouch. The hair was standing up around his neck and down his back, and if the look in his eyes wasn't bad enough, his face was all teeth. Nothing but teeth. He was slowly backing away, with an awful, low growl I'd never heard him make before, like he was breathing in instead of breathing out.

"Oh, for heaven *sake*," said Thistle, briskly. "*Dennis*, sweetie, don't be *archaic*. You're practically a wolf, yourself. In fact, from a distance I thought you were. Besides, you've been playing with Thorn for weeks now and nothing's happened. And I wouldn't *dream* of hurting you. Or letting anyone else, and, listen, honeysuckle, you've never seen a wolf in action until you've seen a bitch protecting her man. Oh, Dennis, *darling*, you're so *adorable* when you're scared. Come on. Stop it. Listen to me. Put your ears up. Stop that. Just *stop* it. Come over here and lick my face, silly cub."

Well, Dennis gradually got the power of movement back again, and did as he was told.

And then some. After about ten minutes of hugging and slobbering over each other's faces and ears, they started rolling around. All arms and legs. And somehow or other—and I was watching the whole time, but I didn't really see how—Dennis opened his shorts. Or probably it was Thistle who did. Anyway, her hand was right in there.

They were glued together, almost, and then, in the middle of all the kissing and growling and muttering, Dennis let out this groan and slowly went all stiff and humped up his back.

Humped is right.

I died. I just died. I was sick to my stomach.

Thistle is the most special person in my life and the main thing I want out of life is for her to be happy. And as awesome as I found Bolt, and as much as I—well—envied Thistle, I guess there was always this worry that he was just a conceited hunk. One of those young sexpots that Mom talked about. And I thought the world of Dennis. I mean, in spite of all those things I said about him, he was totally, completely wonderful in my eyes.

Then *why wasn't I happy?* Why was I so sure that as of that *second*, when she took him into her, my life had come to an end? I actually felt like something inside me died. I mean that literally.

She was groaning and asking if it was good; and he was talking in this breathy voice, whimpering and asking if she could really *feel* him and she kept saying yes, she could feel him.

There was no missing the climax. He didn't say anything, but his shoulders and arms and back were one mass of tense muscle, and his whole body shook in three or four huge spasms. Then, after a moment, as he relaxed he came out with this *amazing* groan. To judge from the expression on his face, he'd just found out for himself that 'pussy's popular for a reason,' just like Dad said.

Then it was all "Ouch!" and "No, baby, *stop*, wait" and so on. I guess it really was his first time ever. So he was hung, and hurt poor Thistle (poor Thistle! Gimme a break) when he tried to pull free. Anyway, they lay in a heap for a while until his knot let him loose. I sat there thinking these cranky thoughts like how could any boy get hung up in a pussy that was familiar with Oak's organ. At least I kept my trap shut.

Thistle was pleased as can be. And as for Dennis, well, I could tell Dennis was really happy. No, that's not the right word. When we were together, it wasn't just that I loved being with him—I loved his playful mood, his reckless sense of fun. He liked my company, too. I knew that. And it made me happy. But, well, I'd never seen him like *this*. This was different. Why I even hung around I'll never know. Watching guys have sex was usually a kick for me, like I've said. But this wasn't any kick. I just about chewed my hands off at the wrists, watching them. But I couldn't force myself to leave.

Thistle was talking low but I could tell that she was talking about doing it again, between all the lickings and yanking on big handfuls of pelt, when there was that faint squeal and Dennis's ears popped up and he said he had to go, had to go, had to go, had to go, right away. And to Thistle's astonishment, after a couple of quick licks between his own legs, he jumped to his feet. It's hard to run and pull on pants at the same time, but Dennis gave it his best shot, hopping along in strange postures. When he scampered off he was still buttoning his fly, and carrying his shirt over his arm.

"His people," I explained, smoothly. "They called him. He had to go. He doesn't have a choice, it seems. You just better hope they don't ever call him when he's hung. He'd sooner rip his own cock right out of his body, balls and all, than wait even a minute." I was enjoying feeling superior.

Thistle was making a show of ignoring me while she was toweling off her twat with her tongue, but she was a little put out, I could see.

Then, as she was pulling on her shorts, she noticed something.

"Oh, look," she said, brightening. "Hops. Lots of them. Great." And she went over to one of a bunch of vine things and pulled off two or three of these gadgets like papery pinecones and started to munch on them.

I asked her what on earth she was doing, and she started to give me this song and dance about how Mom had taught her and Firefly how to eat different things, to keep from getting pregnant.

"You're kidding. You mean *that's* what you meant when you said Bolt wasn't going to make you pregnant no matter how often he—"

She swallowed and said, "Exactly". So prim.

"What do those things taste like?"

"Here," she said, "try one".

I could see possibilities for chewing on a plant that would keep a guy from knocking up a date, and said so, but Thistle laughed and said something mean about hardly expecting *me* to worry about that, which hurt my feelings. And anyhow, that's not how it worked, she said. "Mom says, if guys eat this stuff their dicks fall off and they grow breasts," she said.

At exactly the moment I got the news about my dick falling off I bit down on the hops. Oooh, was it bitter! Yrff! *Blfhh!* Ugh! What girls have to go through!

"Do these hops-things work for dogs, too?" I asked, when I caught my breath enough to spit the thing out.

"I suppose," she said, catching on. "But what makes you think I don't want his cubs?"

Well, I was one screwed-up mess and not getting much better. On the way home, I could have strangled Thistle. She couldn't shut up about how divine Dennis was, or Sir Denali as she called him. He was so *cute*, he was like a wolf in all the *best* ways but he was so *refeened* and so *handsome* and so *gallant* and so *sexy* and his fur was so fine and his markings so elegant and his *sweet* white face, he was just *precious*. She'd never *seen* eyes like his, that color—they just ate you alive. And his *gorgeous* plume of a tail. And (getting back to basics) when she felt his knot inside her, she just about died from sheer joy, knowing his manhood was flowing into her, no wolf had ever blah, blah, blah, not even Bolt, who was *masculine* and *strong* of course and knew how to make a girl happy, but all he could think about was two things—his last orgasm and his next one. And so on and so forth.

Of course, all this was music to my ears. And Bolt's—talk about confused. Now, *there* was one wolf who would have gladly rubbed out a certain blue-eyed dog if he knew how to find him. Something I couldn't even bear to think about. I certainly would never tell a 'rock' like Bolt that I even knew Dennis.

Dennis, Dennis, Dennis. Crush on Dennis? What did that even mean? And if I was in love with him, love is sure a funny thing. I guess what I wanted most of all was for that beautiful, dear, sweet boy to be happy. And it was honey in the comb that he and Thistle were making each other happy, since I love Thistle, too.

Which didn't keep me from feeling like throwing up every time I even thought about them together.

In fact, I was so stupid. I admit it. Lame, truly lame. I kept going back to the place where Dennis and I used to play. I kept telling myself it was because it was such a pretty spot. I kept telling myself I didn't even expect to see him. I don't know what I'd have done if I *did* meet him. Sometimes I saw him and Thistle a ways off. Playing, roughhousing. Sometimes all that was visible in the tall grass was his unmistakable tail. And when I couldn't see them for a while, I knew what they were doing.

Well, maybe two weeks after Thistle and Dennis started their daily rolls in the grass, maybe three, I was lying in some weeds on the other side of the bushes from the stream and crying softly to myself and chewing on my wrists and eating dirt, and there was this sneeze. Right in my ear, almost.

I must have jumped ten feet in the air. With a screech. And then I landed very awkwardly. So suave, the whole thing. I was busy trying to pretend that it was all on purpose, so it was a moment or two before I even saw who it was.

It was like a dog, with a red coat, this great plume of a tail, and the most adorable black gloves and socks. A fox! The first fox I'd ever seen, up close anyway. A boy, or a guy in any case, and he seemed very anxious.

"Mister?" he said, blinking. "I'm real sorry. Are—are you all right?" A kid's voice, or so it seemed. Young, uncertain-sounding. He was stammering, and I could see him actually shaking. "I didn't (swallow) m-mean to startle you—Thorn—?"

"Who are you?" I asked, trying to smooth my fur. It came out a little gruffer than I meant. "And how come you know my name?"

"Well, um, I'm, um, my n-name is Tick. I mean, that's what, um, what they all call me, my litter-mates and Mom and all. So I guess it's my n-name. And, well, I know your name b-because, um, don't, um, don't be mad—" he was sort of backing off a step, still shaking, "I kept seeing you and—and—that other wolf? Dennis—? Kept seeing you two playing, and I heard your names. I figured out how you were meeting here regular, and I, well, I, um, liked watching you guys. You're so—well, I mean, I was, um, just watching, honest, just watching. I'm sorry. I'm sorry. I—I didn't mean any harm."

He was kind of bowing, his chin on his wrists, his butt in the air. A sinewy little thing, about the same size as Thistle. Delicate. I decided he must be very young.

"And that girl-wolf, Thistle—? She's—oh, she's *so* pretty. I saw that you weren't playing with Dennis any more, and I was wondering. And then, a f-few days ago I was just here, resting in the shade, and you came and lay down. And talking to yourself and all. And the n-next day too. You seemed all cut up about something. Was—was that cute bitch, er, was she your, um, g-girlfriend?"

I got to looking at him. Pointy little face, like all foxes I guess, but something sweet about him. Just a kid, I decided again. Tight little body. And those black gloves, with such dainty hands and feet. He was pretty. I re-

131

member thinking that, and thinking it was a strange thing to think. The look on his face was the strangest mixture of fear and gentleness. Before I knew what was happening, I was getting these funny feelings, like I had to *protect* him, or something like that. Me, a wolf, protecting a fox kit? Imagine that.

"Please, I'm sorry, I really am. I—I'm a little afraid, I guess," he said, backing off another step, and still trembling, but maybe not as much. "I know I maybe shouldn't be butting in like this. I, well, actually, I kept coming to look for you, because, well—"

His voice trailed off and I could hardly make out the end of the sentence. "—because I thought you might be lonely."

There was something endearing about this kid, but I was busy with my own thoughts and I couldn't help a big sigh. "Yeah, you got that right, Tick. —Is that *really* your name?" (He assured me it was.) "I'm lonely, all right. Look, c'mon, sit down, and *please* stop shaking. No, not here, let's go in by the pool. It's nicer. And more private."

I hadn't any idea why I said that. Maybe I was embarrassed. I was a sorry excuse for a wolf, palling around with dogs and foxes. From bad to worse.

In any case, we talked a little. He wasn't as young as he seemed at first. In fact he was actually a couple of years older than me, but being so much smaller and slighter than a wolf, and so light-voiced, I'd taken him for a youngster. And he seemed kind of nice. Shy. Friendly. Funny, even. It was a relief having someone to talk to. Someone neutral. He listened patiently while I told him about being so crestfallen when, after I introduced my friend Dennis to my own favorite sister, I had this feeling that I'd lost him, and so on.

Next day, I went back to the same place, and I admit it, I was kind of hoping I'd bump into Tick.

The fox and I lay under the bushes and talked. I was still feeling too busted up to think about playing. It was like I was sick with something. So we just talked. That day, and some days after that. Sometimes we didn't do much talking. It wasn't at all long before the kit lost his nervousness about what I'd do, and we'd lie there with our heads together. And I guess we snuggled some. I don't know who started it.

After maybe two weeks of this, mostly just being together and talking sometimes, Tick startled me by nipping my ear and saying something like "Hey, old sock, I bet you can't catch me," and tearing off through the grass. Without even thinking I took off after him. Of course, I could catch him. No problem! It was fun. And Tick seemed to be having a lot of fun, too.

What a difference from a few days before, when he'd been shaking like a cornered rabbit. And when I couldn't think about anything except how hollowed-out I felt.

When it came to rassling, I pretty much had my way with the Tickster, being heavier and stronger. We'd roll around and roll around and then he'd get loose (with my help) and zip off, with me right behind him until I jumped him again.

The exercise and play were wonderful for my mood. And Tick was really a wonderful guy to be with. So far from being sly, like foxes are supposed to be, he was kind of stupidly trusting and open.

He was also, I decided, not merely wiry and small, but sort of scrawny, and one day, when we were lying in a panting heap after a lot of dashing around and tackling and rassling, I asked him if he still lived with his mom and dad, since he hadn't said anything at all about having a wife and kits of his own.

He said he'd never met his father. He had four litter-mates, but his mom had made them all go away about a year before.

"Just made us clear out," he said. "I guess it's standard. The two boys had their own families already. And now my sisters both do."

"Do you *have* a home? I mean, uh, where do you live? In a tree or something?"

He laughed. "Oh, I have a home. Not in a tree. Under a tree. Big old tree. Well, a burrow. Nice, too. But it's just me."

I muttered sympathetically but Tick wasn't having any of it. He kept saying he was okay, and so on, that was just the way it was. But at least that explained why his shorts were so raggedy, and he had a sort of uncared-for look. But he insisted he was okay, could fend for himself.

"Hey, listen, little friend," I said, "all this roughhousing. It's got to be hard on your clothes, and I don't mean to say anything personal, but—they aren't in the greatest shape already. You ought to take off your shorts when we're playing rough."

It was purely sympathetic on my part. You have to believe me, there was nothing clever about it. I swear I didn't have feelings for Tick. He was just a funny, friendly little guy who was fun to talk to and play with. Especially since I always won.

When I said he ought to take off his shorts, he pulled back his head and looked at me and just blinked. He looked very sweet. Puzzled and sweet. There was something about his look that really made me feel all soft inside. A hankering to protect him, again.

"Okay-y-y—," he said. Hesitantly, I thought. "If you say so—I mean if

133

it's okay with you. I guess you're right. But you'll have to let me up."

I stood up, and Tick slowly got upright himself and, never taking his eyes off me, almost like he was afraid I'd jump him when he was defenseless, slowly undid his shorts and pulled them down, bending over to step out of them, and straightened back up again, holding his ragged duds in his hand.

I couldn't take my eyes off *him*, either. Without his shorts he was—different somehow. I don't mean he was naked, that hardly was a surprise. No: he was naked *and*. It was confusing. I had no idea what the 'and' was, but there was a lot of it. His fur, for one thing. The reds and creams and blacks sheathed his body so elegantly, his cheek-tufts were so boyish, the black-lined ears so smart. I actually got sort of embarrassed, I mean, to think that I'd been rolling around with the tight little figure that was now standing there with such an endearing mixture of uneasiness and natural—natural—*beauty*.

"Well, um—," he said, still as a statue and clutching his ratty shorts, as if holding on to them was some kind of protection. "I was thinking—Thorn—c'mon, fair is fair. I feel kind of funny—I mean—you, um, you take off yours, too, okay?"

"You sure don't *look* funny," I just about growled. "You look—yeah, well, never mind, sure, you're right, I guess," I said, and started to undo my own pants.

"Wait!" Tick said, in his light little voice. "Let me."

I was *really* startled by that, but, I don't know, it somehow came across as a fine idea even if it didn't actually make any sense.

Tick stepped up to me, slowly, and I could see he was trembling, not as bad as the day we met, but he was definitely shaking. He had both hands free. I didn't see where he'd dropped his shorts.

It was simple enough. He just undid the buttons and pulled the zipper down. Then he put his arms around my trunk, his hands in the small of my back. He was going after my tail-tab, but at the same time he was lightly holding our trunks together. As he unbuttoned my tail-tab, he slipped his hands under my pants and down over my buns, which would have made my shorts fall off except that his hands on my butt was clamping our bodies together. He was craning up and licking my face. Well, we'd often enough done *that*. But there was something different this time. We weren't wrestling and goofing off. We were standing up, he was naked, and he was holding me quietly against his body and—well—I guess I put my arms around him. It felt wonderful. Tender. Protective.

When I felt his hand slip into my shorts between my legs, I was ready to be shocked and outraged except that I'd never felt *anything* like the thrill of it.

"Thorn," he said in a breathy voice I hardly recognized, "if you don't want this, tell me to stop. I'll stop if you tell me. I swear I will. Please—"

"No," I croaked, "wait, stop, I mean, *don't* stop, oh Tick, wait, let me get out of these—"

He loosened his grip slightly and I struggled out of my shorts. As I bent over, Tick took my head in his hands and licked my ears and around my muzzle. By the time I stood back up, my black prick was right there for anyone to see. All of it. I don't know whether I was more embarrassed or thrilled. Plenty of both, for sure. And why I didn't just juice, when Tick's hand closed around my spike, I'll never know. It was incredible. If I'd ever felt a thrill anything like that, I couldn't remember when or where. He was licking my chest, and had a hand on my butt.

I guess the simplest way of putting it is that I finally understood what Thistle saw in Dennis. Completely understood. And understood what was going on between Mom and Dad. When I was with bitches it was fun but it seemed like after I came there was always this thing going on in my head about "What am I doing here? Why am I doing this?" Not now. Now everything felt perfect. It was confusing, because for once I felt I knew exactly what I was doing, but at the same time I had no idea what I was doing.

My head fell back and I moaned and I didn't care where I was. The feelings all over my body were so intense I could hardly breathe. I honestly thought I was dying. Every stroke of his tongue on my face and neck and chest felt more wonderful than the last. Every press and pull on my hugely ready sex.

"Thorn," he said, softly, between licks. "Thorn. Fuck me."

"What?" The word came out like a kind of cough.

"Fuck me," he said again, in his light, young voice.

"Tick—please—don't—" I was so embarrassed. "What—I can't—let's maybe, um, like, lie down over there in those bushes—?"

"Okay," he said. Softly, like I'd heard Thistle and Firefly talking to their boyfriends. "But you've got to let go of me first."

With a jolt I realized I had a hand between his legs. Well, actually I was holding his cock, as hard as a stick of wood, and had my other arm around his waist.

"Oh, I'm sorry, I guess you don't like that—?" I mumbled, embarrassed.

"Thorn, c'mon, no, I like it just *fine*. I mean, it's just that we can do it even better lying down. And we can't fuck standing up."

We picked up our shorts and headed for a patch of bushes at the edge of a little grove on the hillside. Tick led the way, and I was looking at his slim waist and narrow, red back and plume of a tail. His little buns were hardly visible under his tail.

My thoughts were a real jumble. 'Sex' and 'Tick'? Stupid. But at the same time I could tell I *wanted* that fox. And he'd *said* 'fuck,' hadn't he? But *fuck*? A guy? Can two *guys* fuck? Maybe he meant something else. Like what Briar told me he did with one of his girlfriends. Lick each other between the legs at the same time. We could do that, I guessed, though I'd never imagined doing it with a *guy*. But Briar had assured me that if you did that long enough you could come. I wondered if maybe that's what Tick was really talking about.

I was fascinated and kind of scared at the same time. I knew that my head had just about fallen off my neck when he'd taken my sex in his hand. (What did that mean? What was it doing out of its sheath in the first place?) It was sort of like that first time that Clover had put a hand between my legs, only more intense. Why I hadn't sprayed the contents of my balls all over his chest on the spot, I don't know. I swear, it felt more like an orgasm than any orgasm I'd had before.

By now we were lying down, Tick on top of me. I told myself that that definitely meant I'd misunderstood him. But I didn't care *what* he'd been talking about. This was wonderful. Everything about it. The weight of his body. His fur, his delicious red fur, not as soft as a wolf's fur, nothing (whimper) like Dennis' fine and lush pelt. But every move, every touch, every lick, every murmured word, all of it was *wonderful*.

It was just like sex, too. I mean, the main difference between what Tick and I were doing and what I'd done with Clover and the rest was the amazing excitement I was feeling the whole time.

He was holding me tight when he said it again, right into my ear, so soft and sweet.

"Fuck me," he said.

Happy as I was just to be intertwined with that hard little fur-body, I became quarrelsome.

"Naw," I said, taking his ears and pulling his head back so I could look at him. "Come off it, Tick. That's nonsense. We can't do that. We're both guys. Maybe something else, I don't know what you'd call it—"

Not just his hand between my legs, but some licking he did, down there, just about made my tail fall off, and I was wondering more than ever if maybe we could just lick each other until—

"No, wolf-boy" he said, with the sweetest, most serious look you ever saw. "*Fuck*-cking. I want you to put *this* in me. My tail-hole," he said into my ear, now. "It's as smooth as any bitch you've ever had."

Oh, oh, oh. So *that* was it. Now I remembered Thistle's little accident with her novice boyfriend. And she did say he'd dropped his load, too. So it was certainly, well, practical, even if it was, um…

All these thoughts made me embarrassed and excited at the same time. It wasn't just the feel of his body on mine, or even of his hand between my legs; I'd never felt so crazy in my whole life, in fact, and now it was me doing the shaking when I said something like, "Well, okay, um, do I just, uh, stick it into you, or what?"

No, not exactly, there was this one technical problem, according to Tick. It would be solved if we could find a ripe persimmon. And that was no problem for Tick, who knew this part of the woods better than I did.

A minute or two later, no more, Tick was back with the persimmon. The sight of his naked form slipping through the bushes into our little clearing is a memory as fresh as yesterday. Slim, graceful, upright. Not to say erect. In all his maleness, maybe the slimness of his long waist made his hard-on look big, he stood there for a long moment, a walking dream of red and black and creamy white, looking down at me, lying there.

"You're beautiful," he said, slowly sinking to his knees next to me.

I just snorted. *Beautiful?* This kid didn't know what he was talking about. 'Beautiful' was a fox named Tick. I'd never seen anything or anybody as lovely as that boy, standing over me.

Well, the fox was right. Not the 'beautiful' part. The fucking part. Every delicious, thrilling, exciting sensation up to that point was nothing compared to the feeling of joining our bodies. I'd never heard anything like the little noises in his throat as we coupled. And his body was so tensed and tight. Of course, right away I was afraid—horrified—that I'd hurt him, but he hissed into my ear not to worry. He said it had nothing to do with pain. But his voice sounded real odd. And he was holding my fur so tight I thought he was going to pull it out by the handful.

I wanted it to last for ever. And then *my* whole body went hard, before I just about exploded.

My goodness. *Oh* my goodness. It was so beautiful. Well, even before I came—the most intense feeling I'd ever had—I was *flying*. Whatever we were doing, it was much more thrilling than sex. Oh, my oh my oh my.

Then, once I juiced, I honestly couldn't tell whether I was dead or alive.

When I came to—I wasn't really unconscious, but it felt like it, a little—Tick was lying so still that for a second I wondered if *he* was still alive.

I wanted it never to end. I wanted to lie on top of that little body, I wanted to be tangled up with that little body, I wanted to be right up to the *balls* as far inside that little body as I could go, for ever and ever and ever.

"Was it okay, wolf?" he asked, eventually, his light-sounding voice more back to normal.

I whimpered something about yes, it was okay. It was the most okay I'd ever been. But he'd been so tense. Still clamping him in my arms, I licked his cheek.

"Tick—tell me the truth. Did I hurt you?"

"No," he said. Real quiet. Looking into my eyes. "No. No—you're—pretty big, that's all." He licked my muzzle. "But there's nothing wrong with that. Mmm. Bigger than ever, feels like. Oh-h-h, man! You wolf-boys. That's some knot—"

I sort of moved my pelvis, like I was going to pull out. "Feel it?"

"*Arhgh! Feel* it?" he grated through his teeth, and he quickly grabbed my butt with his hands. Like Blackfoot.

I wasn't really going to pull out—I hardly could, even if I wanted to—which I didn't. But I loved the feeling of him holding me to him.

"A-h-h!" he said, more softly this time. "Yeah, take it easy—*easy*—big boy, yeah, oh, *yeah!*"

When I got unhung, I really was curious to know if the little guy had gotten anything out of it, but was embarrassed to ask. First, I wasn't just talking: I really was worried I'd hurt him. And beyond that, I couldn't imagine what it would feel like, having a hard-on inside my tail-hole. As great as I felt from the moment my hard-on followed the persimmon skin into his body, I wasn't sure it had been nice for Tick at all. Never mind being anything like what *I'd* felt. Or what a bitch feels when she's with a boy. (They do seem to enjoy it. And what was that that Mom had said to Thistle, about the best part of marriage?) But—my fox certainly *seemed* every bit as involved as any girl I'd ever plugged. Well, that's not saying much, and in fact it went beyond that. He was making all kinds of noises and shaking and grabbing handfuls of my hair and skin. And he was so excited or something that he was actually drawing *blood*, chewing on me. I didn't exactly notice, being too busy with the feelings crashing over my body. And now as we lay together he was all kind of dreamy and completely relaxed. It was hard to believe it was the same body that a few minutes earlier had been hard as a tree-trunk.

I don't know how long we lay like that. Getting off of Tick and putting on my clothes was one of the hardest things I've ever done. As I got dressed I watched him lying there, his rangy red and cream body all stretched out and relaxed-looking.

And he was watching me.

"You'll come back?" he asked, as I finished. His voice was soft, and anxious. It broke my heart. There was such sweetness and tenderness.

"Tick—!" I dropped to my knees next to him on the ground and put my hand on his chest. "Don't even think such things." I leaned down and licked his face. "I'll be back," I said, and licked his ears. "I'll be back. And next time I see you, I want you to do me a favor. Promise?"

"What favor?"

"I want—well—I want you to—to, um screw me."

He didn't answer, but the slow smile that spread over his sweet face was all the answer I needed.

"Run along, wolf-boy," he said. "You'll be late."

Of course, I hadn't even gotten home yet when I began to worry. What had I done? What if I didn't like it? What if it was *horrible*? What if Tick was just different from me? What if he was born knowing how to take guys, or he'd learned? Maybe foxes were like that. The idea that two guys could, well, he said it, he actually said it—*fuck*—the idea that two guys could *fuck* had never occurred to me. I couldn't believe that I'd gone and asked *him* to do that. I mean, it was weird enough, going to put my pizzle into a guy's tail-hole. At least until I found out what it felt like. But being—*fucked*—myself, having a guy juice into my guts, whoa, that was beyond weird. It was scary, that's what it was.

Except I was walking on air. Every time I thought of the little guy I got this ridiculous warm tingly feeling all over. And every time I thought about our little, well, sport I shivered with pleasure. Not just the part when I was inside him. The whole thing. Every lick. Every squeeze. The feel of his fur, the feel of his fingers in my fur. I'd never had these lingering feelings after sex with a bitch. Like I already said, after sex mainly I wondered what I was doing there.

I must have set a new standard for squirrelly behavior. By bedtime Thistle asked me what was going on. I mean, I guess everyone noticed I was being goofy but only Thistle asked. I couldn't tell her, not right away. Not even Thistle. But I was desperate for Tick. All I could think about was Tick.

I didn't sleep much that night. Mainly I was so excited about seeing Tick the next day. And thinking over every detail of our—our—well, okay, our sex. It was sex, no doubt about it. And at the same time I was worrying about what I'd gotten myself into.

When I was actually with Tick everything was different. I was too busy feeling wonderful to worry. Even about what it would feel like when he, well, used me like a bitch. All I could think about was how pretty and sweet my fox was. Well, he is. He can't help being just gorgeous, and as for being sweet, that's his way.

It was courtship. We spent the whole afternoon hardly saying a word. When we met we put our arms around one another and fooled around and cuddled and licked, just standing there. Time stood still. After a while, Tick took my clothes off. By the time I was wearing nothing but fur I'd been out of my sheath for so long I'd forgotten I was showing hard. I just put my head back and let him do delicious things to me as long as he felt like it. Finally I pulled myself together enough to take off his clothes—if you call those rags "clothes"—and after some more smooching on our feet we lay down and continued hugging and licking and squeezing.

Tick could have cashed in his chips any time. I mean, I'd promised him my tail-hole, after all, and I doubted he'd forgotten. After we'd been fooling around for I don't know how long, he brought it up. He asked me if I really thought I wanted it. I said I did. He kept asking me. Over and over. It was actually clever of him, I think. I admit I wouldn't have minded a repeat of my skull-popping exploration under *his* tail, but the more he talked about giving him what I'd promised him, the better the idea sounded. At first I was mainly curious (and a little scared) about what it would feel like. Then, with our sex-play and his questions and everything, it wasn't curiosity any more. Still less, fear. It was a need. A craving. I had to have that fox inside my body. I didn't know why. I just had to.

Well, it was an education. Mainly I learned why Tick was so forward about getting me to couple with him in the first place.

And who would have guessed the little scrawn had so much strength in him! He just about cracked my ribs.

I wondered if what bitches got out of sex was anything like that.

As exhausted as he was, Tick could still tease me.

"Did I hurt you?" he asked, with a lick. Just like I'd asked him. I wondered if I'd had the same expression he had. Probably.

"No," I said.

"That's a lie."

"Well, maybe a little."

"Another lie. It was agony. Level with me, pup. You've never felt pain like that in your life."

"Well—okay, okay, you're right. I guess it did hurt," I said. "But only at first. Then—then—weird. It got wonderful. It *is* wonderful. It still is. It was more wonderful when you were, um, fucking. But it still is, just lying here."

Words were useless. I wanted his whole body inside mine. I wanted it to last forever. I'd never felt anything like the way I felt when I realized he was coming—totally thrilled, and at the same time alarmed and anxious because it meant it was ending.

"So you lied, too, when you said it didn't hurt."

"No," he said. "It didn't hurt yesterday. It doesn't have to hurt." I must have looked very puzzled. "You can get used to it."

I really couldn't imagine 'getting used' to that. Tick had been right. Agony was the word for it. If I'd had any idea what it would feel like, I'd never have let him do it. But I was right, too. Somehow it changed, changed into something totally different. Totally beautiful.

"*Used to* pain like that?"

"No. No pain. It just—gets easier. With practice. Even being fucked by a big boy like you." He grinned. "Take you as easy as pussy does. Would you, um, like to find out for yourself?"

What a question. I'd always wondered what bitches got out of sex. I mean, really got out of it. Apart from pleasing a guy they wanted to please. Having kids. Oh, it was obvious there was *something* going on. Take Mom: she was doing a bunch more than 'pleasing' Dad. But bitches didn't go around like Wasp, and for that matter Oak and Bristlecone and Bolt and the rest. Trying to couple with everything that had a fly, I mean. It wasn't any mystery to me why guys were so keen on the whole thing, and it seemed logical that the bitches just didn't get the same charge out of it, or else they'd be doing more what the boys were doing.

Well, who knows about that. All I can say is that if bitches feel anything like *this* boy does, they get a *lot* out of it. More than I could have ever guessed.

"Yeah," I said. "I would. I can use all the practice I can get. How about tomorrow?"

"How about today?"

It made me laugh. I couldn't believe I could find anything that intense funny, but I did. For a moment. Then all I could think about was what it felt like the first time I went into his tail-hole. We lay and talked and nuzzled for I don't know how long. It was so pleasant just being together with him, but it got even more pleasant when he started feeling between my legs.

"Want to do a repeat of yesterday?" he asked, between licks.

"Oh, I don't know about me," I said, grinning. "But I think my cock does."

"Well, ask your cock to make it last a little longer, this time."

I confess I was almost afraid. Yesterday's, um, sport—fun—well, okay, yesterday's *fuck*—had been so intense that I was afraid that a repeat would be an anticlimax.

I needn't have worried.

In the first place my whole body was still full to overflowing with beautiful feelings, put there, five or six inches at a time, by Tick's manhood. And if I had any worries left about whether fucking a boy was a good idea, they vanished for ever as I slipped into Tick's body. No anticlimax, that! I couldn't hardly believe it. And the orgasm was so shattering that I thought my cock had disintegrated. I mean literally.

Well, it hadn't of course, and we lay together for a long time without saying anything, and then lay together for a long time and talked, but mostly were just *there*. I was in a daze, but Tick seemed more puppyish than ever. He was almost frisky. Where he got the energy from was a mystery. I didn't worry much about that, though, I was too busy just wondering at how cute he was and how intense my sensations had been and how much—I think it was the first time I thought those actual words—how much I loved him.

I guess there were a couple of things I was unhappy about. Contradictory things, too. I felt guilty, afraid—no, not 'afraid' I was *sure* that if anybody found out, we'd be in big trouble. It wasn't done, hanging around with a fox. And I was sure that what we were doing was dirty. Real dirty. On the other hand, I realized with something like dread that I couldn't get enough of this guy. And I just hated this business of sneaking off together for sex. Guilty sex. I wanted to be with him twenty-four hours a day. Not just to fuck. You can't fuck twenty-four hours a day, not even Bolt could do anything like that, and I was no Bolt. The sex was fantastic, actually, unlike anything with the bitches, but it wasn't the only thing.

Oh, and guess what? Tick was right. After we'd been doing it for a while, it wasn't hardly painful at all. And one day it was total bliss from the first delicious push to the last groan. (And Tick wasn't going stiff as a board when he took me, any more, either. So I knew I *had* hurt him. I still haven't forgiven myself for that. He tries to shush me, but it really bothers me.)

Well, all that changed. Overnight. There was this huge storm and it rained like blazes for a whole day, and more. As soon as it was dry enough I went out to look for Tick. I was really anxious. And not just because I missed playing with him and the wonderful sex I'd become addicted to. Since we met, the day hadn't gone by without some kind of meeting with the kid, and I was really twisted up with frustration.

I found him, a whole day later, looking bedraggled and woebegone and kind of dazed. His fur was muddy and still wet. One of his eyes was swollen almost shut, and there was a cut on his head.

"I got flooded out," he said. He sounded weak. No, exhausted. "I suppose I'm lucky to be alive. It was dry and safe down there, until the creek rose." He shook his head and looked down at his grubby pelt. "Getting out of a burrow full of water in pitch blackness isn't as easy as you'd think. And then, outside, it was more of the same. Nothing but water." He closed his eyes and groaned.

"What happened to your stuff?"

"Ex-stuff. I don't know where. Under mud, I guess. All I have is what I'm wearing."

'Wearing' was generous. Ragged scraps of wet and muddy unbelted shorts that hung so far below his belly-button you could see the mouth of his sheath poking out of the waistband.

"C'mon, Tick," I said. I was surprised at my own masterfulness. "My mom'll fix you up!"

(Maybe it wasn't so masterful after all.)

Well, at home it was all a little tense. No wondering at that. More than a little surprise all around that I showed up with this *fox*. But they were as much sympathetic as suspicious, even Dad, and Tick was endearing. I could tell that Dad was having a hard time thinking of what to say, though, and Little Briar was kind of highty-mighty. A fox, after all. But Mom and the girls were all cooing with concern.

It wasn't long before Thistle got me aside and demanded to know what was going on.

"He's *beautiful!*" she whispered. "Is he beautiful? Yes or no."

"Yes," I said, unhappily. "He is."

"Does he like you?"

"Yes."

"*Really* like you?"

"What do you mean?"

"I mean—" she pressed her muzzle against my ear, "I mean, *do you fuck?*"

Before I realized what a shocking thing she'd said, I sighed "Oh, uh, yeah. Oh, *yeah*." I didn't exactly *say* it; it was more like a whimper.

"Who's the girl?"

"*What?*"

"I mean, one of you is the boy and the other one is the girl, right?"

"*Thiss*-sull! It, er, it doesn't *work* that way. We both, I mean—"

"Oh! Well! Huh. Imagine that! Which do you like best?"

"Listen, you little busybody. I like *both* best, okay?"

"Doesn't it *hurt?*"

"No. Not at all. Not any more."

"Are you happy?"

I just looked at her, all bright eyes and eagerness, before giving her ears a lick or two.

"Yes," I finally said. "Yes, I'm happy. I never knew I *could* be happy like this. That there even was such a thing. Yeah, you might say I'm happy. —What about you and Dennis? Who plays the boy?"

"Oh, shut up. Since you ask, Dennis and I are just fine. And guess what! I'm pregnant!"

"With him?"

"Oh, Thorn! Really! Couldn't hardly be anyone else! Unless I've been sleep-walking."

Thistle seemed to be as happy as I felt, but it was awkward for her because she couldn't really live with Dennis. In fact, although he was still very friendly, he made clear he didn't want to play house anyway. Not that he even could. But he said, in so many words, that the pups were hers, not his.

She was very happy anyway, and so I was happy for her. Besides, I never really stopped caring for Dennis, and having him as a kind of brother-in-law wasn't at all bad.

But that was a bit in the future, still, and I had so much more on my mind at the moment.

As we talked, the two of us were looking over at the fox, me just about suffocating with affection. He was chatting with Mom and Dad, and I could tell from Dad's expression that he was actually trying to be friendly.

Something about Tick inspired protectiveness in the female members of my family. Much the way he inspired it in me, I suppose, and maybe for the same reasons. He seemed so young, and his delicate features and so on made him seem like a kid. A kid who wasn't ever far from tears. I of course knew how tough and strong he was. And *all* man, where it counted. In fact, his maleness acted on me like some kind of drug, a drug which seemed to be equally potent whether it was passing out of his tail-hole, or into mine, or just from the contact of our bodies, sheath to sheath, muzzle to muzzle. I think the girls were picking up on something—a kind virility, maybe, that was intriguing because it was un-wolf-like. And of course Tick was just plain pretty, with his rich coat colors and delicate features.

Thistle was for all practical purposes married, if she was right about what was in her belly, and besides, she knew the score. But she actually *flirted* with Tick. Firefly had inherited Bolt's favors, so to say, but she was still specially sweet on Teal. But she was flirting with Tick, too. It was so cute. He flirted back, but was deft about avoiding situations where actual sex might be thinkable. Not that Firefly would stoop to having sex with a fox, I thought. But you never know.

One night in bed I told him it was all right with me if he screwed Firefly; but he just grinned and said if it was all right with me he'd leave that sort of thing to Bolt and Teal and the rest.

"Well, look," he pointed out, reasonably, "if Firefly really turned me on, or something, it might make sense to take my chances with your Dad's reaction. Not to mention Teal's and all those other boys you told me about. Even though all of them would love any excuse at all to rip my nuts off. One at a time. It'd be a totally stupid risk. But that's hormones for you. I know a thing or two about hormones." There was a trace of a smile on his sweet face. "Maybe I can confess. When I came on to you—? I knew it was a risk, too. A big one. I figured the chances were about five to one that you'd try to kill me. And if you tried, you'd succeed. But I didn't care. I just didn't care. *This* wanted *that*—" (Both of our cocks were hard and out of the sheath.) "—and it wouldn't take no for an answer."

Long pause, and a lick on my cheek and a whispered endearment or two and, a while later, the muffled sounds of two boys losing their juices.

We couldn't actually screw while we were at home, but Tick used that as an excuse to show me—teach me—about all the neat things two guys can do together with tongues and hands.

The menfolk, well, what can I say? My brother soon stopped even pretending to be polite. He constantly called attention to Tick's small size. Teased him about his name. Sneered at anyone who lived in a hole in the ground. I don't think the girls meant to stir up Briar, but he told Tick to his face he'd kill him if he ever screwed one of our sisters. Mostly he talked about him in front of him like he wasn't even there. You get the picture. Generally unpleasant.

You never know how much your parents know, I guess. And vice-versa. In any case, Tick hadn't been staying with us for a week when Dad came in on Tick and me in the morning, to tell me something I think. We had to sleep in the same bed in any case, but when Dad came in the room that morning we were spooning—on our sides, my arms around my fox, his back to my chest and his butt in my lap. It was warm, there weren't any covers, and of course we were naked. But I wasn't *into* anything, honest, I was just lying there, nestling in his fur. In fact we both were more asleep than awake. But I guess it looked pretty intimate.

Dad stood there for a second, with this flame in his eyes.

"Holy *shit!*" he practically spat, and slammed the door.

Tick made a miserable-sounding noise and started trembling, and tried to get out of bed, but I held him tight.

"I don't think he likes me," Tick said, in a discouraged voice.

I sighed and thought for a bit, pretty upset myself. But I kept my arms around him. "No. You're right. I guess you have a lot against you. Specially now. Dad *seemed* to be managing the idea that I'd have a fox for a friend. He might even have understood if you were a girl. He's made some pretty raunchy remarks about vixens, after all. Who knows. Maybe he was talking from experience, maybe he was just, well, saying stuff, the way guys do. But now—"

I was feeling pretty stressed. I wanted Dad's approval more than almost anything. For Tick, I mean. It was against the odds, I knew, but I hoped Tick might—somehow. Ha. 'Approval'. I'd be lucky if he didn't kill Tick. I'd be lucky if he didn't kill *me*. The look in his eye just now was really dreadful.

Tick said something sort of touching about how sometimes not even *having* a father, like him, was a plus.

After Dad doped out what was really going on, his attitude toward Tick was hostile, but he wouldn't violate the basic laws of hospitality. And besides, he had to contend with Mom's attitude, which was the opposite of his. Plus the little complication that Tick wasn't just some pervert doing dirty, unthinkable things in the bushes, he was my friend, my—even Dad could figure *that* much out—my lover.

I think that's what was going through his mind when he managed to get me alone a few days after he found me with my arms around Tick. We just sat there in silence for a minute or two, Dad looking angry. When he spoke, though, his voice was softer than his expression. He put an arm around my shoulder and put his muzzle against my neck and said, into my pelt, sort of sad-sounding, "Where do I go to get my refund, fur-face? My favorite daughter's boyfriend—well, husband, now—wears a *collar*. And my Thorn, my sweet Thorn, is—" He stopped. Sighed, started and stopped again. "Screwing a fox," he finally said. Not angrily. I glanced nervously at him. His expression was sad, almost stricken. "And not just that. He's—well, I guess I could see—maybe—if you were horny enough—I've been pretty horny a few times in my life—but *wanting* to screw a guy…"

He took my muzzle and turned my face to his, fixing me with this strange expression, angry and anxious at the same time. "Look, it's your dick, son, what you do with it is your own business, I guess, and they say a tailhole has more 'pull' than pussy. I wouldn't know. But I just want *you* know that's some garbage you're sticking it into. A—a bitch-boy. Your scummy friend in there. A guy who lets himself get fucked is total garbage. Doesn't deserve to be alive." He glanced toward the house with this incredible sneering look on his face. "Good thing that nutless wonder you're using for pussy is only a fox," he said. "No one bothers holding anything against a fox. Not even *that*."

He paused, but there was something on his mind I could tell.

"That little shit," he said, shaking his head. "That little *shit*! Your bitch-boy. He was actually showing hard when you were putting it to him. Unbelievable! The pervert! The nutless little pervert! He was actually *hard* while you were *fucking* him!"

My jaw dropped. "Wha—?"

"When I came in on you a couple of days ago. You were plowing the little shit's asshole, and he was showing *hard*."

Before I could answer—or decide what to answer (or even decide whether there was anything I could say at all, that wouldn't make things worse—such as the honest truth, that I *wasn't* screwing him, we were just lying there, and I didn't even know that he was out of his sheath), Dad shook his head and started swearing softly to himself. The general drift was that it was beyond imagination that anybody, *even* a bitch-boy of the fox persuasion, could be so depraved that he'd actually get a hard-on while being totally degraded.

Dad's anger and contempt was terrifying, and I was in a panic.

Back in my room, after I stopped thinking I was going to throw up, it did occur to me that it couldn't be quite as easy as Dad made it sound. It just couldn't be. I mean, how *could* there be that much connection between anything else and what a guy's tail-hole had been up to? When Dad explained to me that any guy who was 'used' was permanently (and obviously) disgraced and degraded and nothing but 'garbage,' Tick had already stirred my innermost feelings countless times. In fact only an hour before Dad told me what he thought of Tick, and why, he'd poured juice into me. And since I found everything about tail-hole sex deeply, unbelievably thrilling, it followed that I, too, had to be a nutless bitch-boy pervert little shit. Garbage. Whose cock sprang out of its sheath at the very *idea* of feeling Tick enter his body. As best I could figure, that proved I was totally degraded. But I loved it—*craved* it. So, why couldn't Dad tell I was 'garbage' by now? A nutless bitch-boy? Worse even than Tick—Tick was only a fox, and me—I'd been *penetrated* by a fox. Horrible even to think about. Fucked. Fucked silly. Bad enough! But by a *fox*!

So, like I say, once I collected myself, I decided Dad must have something wrong. Put differently, the only difference between Tick and me was that Dad had seen Tick get fucked. Or thought he had. That was kind of funny, actually. So much for Dad's garbage radar.

Besides, *nutless?* There wasn't a thing wrong with Tick's nuts. No, indeedy. Or anything else, down there. The only wolf I ever knew who was as horny as Tick was Wasp. And I doubt Wasp got pussy anywhere near as often as Tick got ass.

But in fact the harder I thought about it the harder it was to figure out what on Earth Dad was even talking about. Taking my little red friend into me, that way, was the most intensely beautiful feeling I'd ever known. It made me feel *complete* when we were coupled. The only thing equal to it was the thrill in my whole body when Tick was taking me. And Tick never looked handsomer or happier—or more masculine—than when he was full of my nature. I could feel the muscles all over his body. Him groaning, twisting around, begging me to make it last.

And after I came, the look of bliss on his sweet face didn't quite fit with whatever it was Dad seemed to be driving at. Never mind the feelings of bliss in my whole body. 'Degradation'? 'Garbage'? 'Nutless'? What *was* that all about?

Tick didn't complain and tried to pretend he didn't notice Dad's and Briar's attitude, but it really was unpleasant around the place and he was so cowed and unhappy I figured the sooner we got out the better.

Mom had gotten all busy and altered a whole closet-full of clothes to fit Tick. Old stuff that Briar and I had outgrown, practically a lifetime's supply. I'd never seen my fox look so spiffy.

One evening after dinner Mom brought a little pile of clothes into the bedroom for Tick. She held up a pair of shorts.

"Tick, darling, slip these on. See if they fit. They were Dad's but he didn't like the color and I don't think he wore them even once. I have your measurements but I had to guess about the cut. Since you're built so different from Briar Sr—you and your tiny butt."

My fox wasn't wearing much but shorts himself, and fell to stammering and hemming.

"Oh, for goodness sake," said Mom. "I've seen a lot worse than a fox wearing his fur. C'mon, just try these on. They're almost new; it would be a pity if they didn't fit. But I can't fix them if I don't know how they fit."

Tick was doubtful but stepped out of his clothes.

To his embarrassment, and mine, Mother stood there holding the shorts and looking at him with a gaze that was almost a stare.

"You foxes," she said, eventually, with a sigh. "So elegant. And a tailor's delight. Well, here, boy, slip these on."

The fit was perfect. They were dark green, and the color was fantastic against his coat.

Mom clucked approval and moved to leave. She hesitated at the door and then came back into the room and looked at Tick so long he became nervous. But Tick became nervous pretty easily.

"I'm sorry my man is behaving the way he is, Tick," she said, finally. "I don't understand him. Maybe it's just because *I* don't have any trouble thinking of a boy as something you might want to love."

"No, Mom, Dad thinks—"

"Oh, my goodness, Thorn, I know what Dad thinks," she said, with a little laugh. "There aren't even words in the language for what he thinks. Well, he'll just have to live with it. But—Tick—listen to me. Seriously. I love this boy, I don't want anyone to hurt him."

Tick started to tremble. "I love him *too*, Violet," he said. "Aw, I couldn't even—"

He broke off and started to cry. That of course got Mom all motherly and she sat down next to him and was hugging him and petting him. He was pretty upset.

When he was calmer, after a squeeze Mom pulled back a little and looked at Tick. She looked so kindly you'd have thought *he* was her son.

"Listen, you little sweetie," she said, running her hand over his cheek, smoothing his whiskers. Her voice was soft and low. "My man tells me you're Thorn's bitch." I just about fell off the bed. "But I don't believe it. Oh, Thorn's *man* enough, I don't mean that. But you two aren't actually—you don't—"

"No, ma'm," Tick said, sounding unhappy. "No. We don't. Look, Briar came in on us, once. We weren't doing anything. Anything at all. We were just lying here. Honest."

I cleared my throat. "Well, Mom, he's right, Dad didn't actually see us, er, doing anything. But (ahem) actually, we *do*, um, like what Dad says. But not in the house. We go to this place at the far side of the woodlot. There's a sort of cave."

Mom looked surprised. "But what do you boys—use? You can't very well just—I mean, look, 'bitch-boy', okay, but 'boy-pussy'—"

I was so flummoxed by hearing Mom talk like that that I couldn't say anything. "Persimmons," said Tick. "Ripe persimmon skins."

"The very idea!" She laughed with delight. "Oh, my. You poor dears. Sneaking around and hiding and smearing yourselves with *persimmons*. Here, just a minute, I'll be right back."

When she came back she had a small pile of rags with a little bottle lying on it.

"Oil," said Mom, putting the stuff down on the bed. "I'm sure you boys can think of something to do with it. Use the rags to clean yourselves up. And try not to get it on the sheets."

"What the—?"

"Just be quiet about it. Your father'll never get used to the whole idea, but there's nothing to gain by rubbing his nose in it."

After giving Tick another pet, she left, shaking her head and muttering something about persimmons as she closed the door.

Tick and I just looked at each other. He was still red-eyed and obviously downcast.

So dear. Such a mix of timidity and raging hormones. I put my hand between his legs. Under Dad's hand-me-downs I could feel him getting hard; and in a heartbeat or two I caught up with him. I wanted what I had under my hand so badly I could just about taste it. But I'd already had a lesson in the limited privacy we could count on, and as long as we were still at home I didn't dare let my fox into me.

But I was willing to be consoled by what both Mom and (after all) Dad expected me to do.

"Well?" I said.

"Well?" he answered. A hint of a smile. "I'm your bitch-boy. Hop to it, big stuff." He slipped out of the trousers and lay back on the bed, thighs spread, tail between his legs wrapped over his privates, and looked at me with his black-rimmed eyes. And then, in his light, young voice, he said—so quiet and sweet and dear—just like that first time: "Fuck me."

Tick and I had licked each other off just an hour or two earlier, but you'd never know it from what had come out of his pants when he slipped them off. Hunh! The very *idea* that a guy would be sexually *aroused* by total degradation! What a pervert! Pathetic little bitch-boy! A walking obscenity! Nutless garbage!

Well, if having a guy's cock under your tail is a shame and a disgrace, I'm afraid the next half hour didn't do Tick's reputation any favors. I was inspired, or my prick was. I couldn't believe how much better oil is than persimmons. This was *really* pussy. (Only better.) Unbelievable. Once I was inside him—and realized I hadn't lost my load in the process, despite my brains turning to soup—I spent quite a while shaming and degrading my fox-boy, six different ways from breakfast. Doing it like horses, for example. We'd never done that before. Tick reached back between his legs and took my nuts. I had no trouble understanding why Briar's ears had been plastered against his skull when I watched Willow do the same thing to him a while ago. It felt incredible, but I had to make Tick stop, because I didn't want to juice, yet, and only a little more of that kind of thing and he was going to drain me.

From beginning to end, it was fantastic. Utterly and completely fantastic.

While I was juicing, Tick whimpered and shook so violently, and so much stuff had come out of him, I thought I'd made him ejaculate. (Now what would Dad think of *that?* Like Mom said, there probably aren't words in the language.)

But Tick said he hadn't come, and it was clear he was right, once I tried something. Something new. Well, I mean, Tick had taught me that there was more to sex than hugging and screwing, and after my first-ever oil-slick fuck I just had this sudden impulse—we were still hung—this impulse to raise my chest off of my fox's and bend down and take him in my mouth. It was a risky thing to do, I guess—if Dad had come in on us like that, it would have been all over.

But it was worth it. It was something wonderful. I have to think it was good for Tick. I mean, he was jerking around so hard I was afraid he'd sprain my cock. And I'm surprised both my ears are still attached. It only took a moment, too, so I'm guess he was pretty excited even before I started working on him. *And* I just about drowned. Whatever Dad's opinion, there wasn't a thing wrong with my fox-boy's nuts. No, indeed. Such a little dear. So passionate. So *male.*

So male. I don't know exactly what Mom was thinking, of course, when she was sort of staring at Tick, when he took off his clothes, but she sometimes said little things about him, like how he was such a rugged little stud. That's what she said. 'Stud.' Go figure. To Dad, Tick was my 'pussy-boy' (one of the politer things he called him). To Mom he was a 'stud'.

Not too far away from the house there was a place where we could camp out while we worked on something more substantial, and we moved there. Mom I knew was genuinely sorry to see Tick go, but she was too busy with Briar's plans for settling down with Willow, and Firefly's pregnancy—Teal, after all—to pay too much attention. The men didn't say a word, not even to me. Thistle took me aside for whispered conversations in which she said lots of nice things about Tick and said stuff like Tick and I were so pretty together and it was a crime that two of the nicest men she knew weren't interested in girls.

I had to chuckle a little. 'Men!' Tick was a dear, a complete dear, but to me he still seemed like a randy teen-ager, all hormones and fidgets and hard little muscles. Basically a walking erection drowning in its own juice. *Male* as a creature can be, sure, but hardly a *man*. And I didn't feel a scrap more 'manly' myself.

Dad was sort of on a tear. He wouldn't have Thistle's pups in the house, no sir, no way, but Tick and I suggested the shallow cave not far away, the one we slipped off to to do degrading, shameful, and disgusting things to one another's bodies with cheerful enthusiasm. Mom and Thistle checked it out and said it would do—not much more than a shelter, really, but Thistle was happy. There were only two anyhow, in that first litter, a boy and a girl. They were really beautiful, and nice kids too; and I guess Mom was working on Dad, because eventually he hinted that it wasn't really necessary for Thistle to be 'stuck out there', and the lot of them moved back home. Which Mom used as an excuse to put off having a litter of her own. And knowing what I know now, I'm sure Dad didn't mind, either.

Dennis turned out to be little bit of a jerk. Well, maybe dogs are just like that, or maybe it was his upbringing, growing up in that combination jail and whorehouse. But he didn't take any interest in his kids at all, and was even a little snotty to Thistle while she was nursing and not interested in sex with him. Still, he came by just about every day, even if his notion of conversation was to talk about the terrific bitches he'd been mated to. 'Mated' my ass. That wasn't *mating*. Tick and I are *mated*. And Firefly and Teal.

But I'll give him this: the moment Thistle was ready for him, he was ready for her. He'd visit her twice or three times a day, and she never lost her appetite for what he had to give her. Dennis's standoffishness had its uses. Thistle refreshed her memory of what came out of Bolt's sheath a few times. Bolt was no Wasp, buzzing around other guys' wives, but like Mom predicted—I *think* that's what she was predicting—he never really stopped thinking with his balls. Or maybe he just never really got over losing Thistle. But it had its weird side. He as much as told my brother that he got some sort of special charge out of laying her, now that she was 'some dog's pussy'.

And Thistle actually had a bit of a fling with a boy named Dock. I doubt *that* was spite. Dock was one handsome piece of wolf, about the most beautiful boy I ever saw, actually. Even so, I was a little surprised, since he was awfully young. Just a kid. I mean, he was just barely starting out laying *Firefly's* girls. And not her first litter, either. That's young. Still, something about Thistle made him burn a hole in his pants, and, well, as for differences in age, there's always Mom and Dad for comparison.

Thistle was sort of funny. I sometimes wonder if she didn't inherit a wild streak from Mom. (I had to grow up some before I even realized Mom *had* a wild streak.) Thistle told me that beautiful boys had their uses, but being a husband wasn't one of them. I think she was talking about Dock and Dennis at the same time. And yet—get this—when she talked about those guys, she sounded *motherly*. I never heard her sound 'motherly' about Bolt, though. Oh, she liked him. She never said 'no,' when he came sniffing around. But motherly—?

Anyway, once she found out what kind of father Dennis was, Thistle kept the litters to a minimum, but wasn't above teasing Dennis about how just maybe she was carrying this boy Dock's kids. (I don't think she told him about her occasional visits from Bolt. It would be too easy for Dennis to figure out that every time she was humped by Bolt it was sort of like an obscene gesture.) But as far as I know, Dennis was the actual father of all her litters. And you'd have to see those kids to believe them, they were just beautiful. I think Thistle was disappointed that none of them had blue eyes. I was too, I guess. But they were beautiful cubs, beautiful youngsters, beautiful adults. "Too pretty," people said. Whatever that means. Anyway, especially for 'too pretty' kids, their cubs always grew up to be affable and affectionate and playful. Almost goofy. Not having blue eyes was a plus in the end, I suppose, since it helped them pass as wolves. That was funny, too: everybody *knew* about their squalid background, but they passed anyway. Because they were so pretty.

'Too pretty'—now, that's Tick. From the black tips of his ears to the tip of his great bush of a tail. And there he was, looking me in the face, licking me awake.

"Morning, bitch-boy," he said, with a lewd twinkle. "You awake?"

"Bitch-boy yourself," I said, sleepily. But not too sleepy to feel a certain, well, change happening in my body. "It's *my* turn." Big yawn, big stretch, reaching over to take hold of his furry nut-bag. "You had your ride yesterday."

"In the morning, maybe. I have this memory of a big, bad wolf having his way with a helpless little fox, later on."

"In your dreams."

"Oh, it was a dream, all right, but I wasn't asleep. Who could sleep through *this*?"

"Take your hand off that. No, you weren't asleep. Just about tore my throat out, you got so worked up. But it was charity, pure charity. Besides, you love it."

"So do you," he replied with the cutest little grin. "Unless you've lied to me about a thousand times. Anyway, I can take only so much charity from a big boy like you, before I can stop being able to walk normally."

"Who wants to walk normally?" I gave him a little pelvic bump.

"Don't try to change the subject, baby. C'mon. Say the magic words." He was licking around my muzzle and making slow, copulatory moves.

I grinned at him, sleepily. "Fuck me," I murmured, filtered through a yawn and a stretch.

"I'll think about it."

"Oh, fuck yourself, you mangy cock-tease!"

"That was nice and bedroomy. Oh, *yeah*, and what do we have down here? Oh, yeah! Oh, *nice!* What a waste."

"No waste. It's yours any time. Like in about five seconds, if you don't get busy with that peg. —Ya done sweet-talked me into it; now where's the action, hot stuff?"

All this while we roll around, mussing each other's fur and nipping and licking and gnarring and whimpering.

What a way to start the day.

André "Badger" Blaireau

Awakening

Transformation is not only for the young. Grown-ups sometimes need it just as much as budding teenagers, and this is encouraging. We are creatures who change, which means that while we don' t necessarily always become better than we are, there is at least a chance that we will.

This is the only story in this volume which includes a human and this contrast exposes and enhances the feral nature of the animal, making the anthropomorphism of another character not just a consequence of the furry genre, but a necessary element of the plot.

DANCING LIFE

Uncle Oakie

I don't know if this will ever be found. I doubt it'll ever be read. So, why did I write it and leave it here? I didn't do it to explain my actions or to justify myself. It's because this account of a failed ending to a failed life is a kind of key for me. It's the key to a prison that you helped build and that I've hidden in for thirty-some years. But, by writing this, the bars of my cell have turned to smoke and I'm ready to finally begin living. So, if you're interested, read on—or don't. It won't make any difference to me one way or the other; I'm finally free.

I've always been a square peg in a world of round holes. Maybe it's because I think too much. Always analyzing, measuring, weighing what I thought others would think before deciding how I felt about something. Long conversations in my head held in a split second. Have you ever been at a hiring fair or something and seen a company that you were really interested in? They are there to meet people with your skills, with your background; but you hesitate to approach their representative because a little voice in your head tells you that you're not good enough and that they'll never be interested in you? Well, not me. I have an entire conversation in my head. In my mind I approach the booth and talk to the rep. He goes through the motions of talking to me and then dismisses me out of hand as not even worthy of serious consideration. I feel the pain of rejection as I stand there deciding whether or not to walk up and present my resume. Real pain. I feel anger at the man. Real anger. So, I don't approach his booth and I glare at him as I pass by. He will never know why I mutter 'Dickhead!' as I walk past.

It seems like my reactions to the world are more about what happens in my head than about what is really there. I react rather than experience. I think rather than feel.

Let's make this quick; for the those reasons and others, I have kept to myself as much as I could. At least I have since I realized that you wouldn't have any use for the real me.

When I was twelve, an older neighbor boy learned 'something neat' at summer camp and shared his discoveries with me when he got home. Together we explored our changing bodies. This episode and others taught me things about my body but also about fear. I didn't know how to deal with the feelings I had for him or the things I felt when I saw other boys in the showers after gym or at he pool. I just knew that they didn't feel that way and I was terrified that they would find out that I was different.

My friend and I jerked ourselves and each other off many times that summer and into the school year, but that ended when I spent more time being afraid that the guy playing with my cock might think that I was queer than I did enjoying the sensations of an enthusiastic handjob. I thought a lot—not always clearly. Fear was stronger than reason and was impossible to silence even then.

High school was a hell populated by one: me. I did what I decided I had to do to keep me from standing out too much. This included going out with the occasional girl that was lonely enough to accept. I was willing to accept that I was not interested in dating but no more than that.

As an adult, my career was one failure after another. My internal conversations quickly led me to despise my bosses and coworkers. This led to a shitty attitude and things spiraled down from there. Marriage? Yeah, I got married. I would stand out if I didn't and besides I thought it would make me just like everyone else. Just conform and the fear will go away. Well, let's just say that a marriage is very hard when you don't let yourself be vulnerable, when you keep your wife at arm's reach. Sex was something I did out of guilt for ignoring her needs rather than out of desire. Fantasy allowed me to function and my own hand was my release when I got horny. With everything filtered through racing thoughts, intimacy can't exist and a marriage without intimacy is a sham.

I guess I left out military service, shrinks and meds for depression, several brief sidetracks from the ordinary to explore being an artist (bad), an actor (worse) and a year spent discovering my spirit in a sweat lodge (actually helped for a time). I said I was going to make this quick.

So, where'd that leave me? Easy. It left me with my car parked at the end of a dirt road in the middle of the sticks, hiking to nowhere in particular. The keys were still in the ignition; I didn't plan on coming back. The only destination I had was the 9mm pistol shoved into my belt.

With nowhere to go, I just followed where my feet led me. It seemed like a good plan. I would just wander until I found somewhere that looked like a good place to die, or until I just got too tired to keep going. Either way I was beyond caring.

I've wondered since then if it was really an accident that I ended up where I did. I mean, is it possible that some hidden little corner of my mind remembered that this place was here? Could one little voice lost in a crowd of voices all wailing in despair have made me choose this particular dirt road over another? To wander south from the car rather than east? Those voices have mostly faded to a whisper so I will probably never know. Somehow I don't care. Things worked out like they did and that's good enough for me.

I didn't know why I stopped at first. It took several seconds to realize that there was a fence in front of me and that I couldn't go any farther. While I wondered whether it would be easier to turn north or south or to just eat a bullet where I stood, I noticed a weathered sign hanging on the fence. It'd been used for target practice so many times that it was almost impossible to read but I finally made out that I was at the outer boundary of an unsettled morph reservation. For just an instant, interest burned a tiny hole in the depression.

I had seen morphs of course; anyone who lives on the wrong side of the tracks probably has. I had seen Lenny, the dogmorph who swept and mopped at the Kroger's down the block from my house, a hundred times even if I had never spoken to him. Hell, I no longer even really noticed the grubby dogman and others like him. Shambling forms that looked half man and half some other animal doing menial tasks around town were an oddity but not the reason to stop and stare that they used to be. When I did think about it, their furred faces and hands and the muzzles protruding from under almost human eyes looked rather odd. But I never found them as repulsive as most people seemed to.

But those were the domestics. The 'settled' morphs.

Only morphs who agreed to be settled were allowed to live around humans. The 'safe' ones. The ones who knew their place and had made the sacrifice to prove it. The rest were kept on reservations where they could live out their isolated lives in primitive but humane conditions. Since only a few morphs volunteered for 'settling', most people rarely saw a morph let alone laid eyes on a 'wild' one. I couldn't blame those who chose the reservations for refusing 'settling'. Who in their right mind would volunteer to have their balls cut off and an aggression inhibitor put in their head? Dogs mostly, some horses and a very few cats. The same kinds of animals whose lives had been tied to humans for ages. I had never seen another species although I knew they existed. Even photos of wild morphs were few and far between. I saw one of a hyenamorph in a National Geographic when I was a kid but they didn't show them at all anymore. The government tended to frown on attention being focused on 'the unfortunate results of the irresponsible excesses of a previous generation'. It was common knowledge that there was an organized effort to eliminate the morphs by encouraging negative population growth through incentives like extra welfare for morphs with no offspring and reduced benefits with each birth.

Is it strange that I'd never really thought about these creatures as more than an oddity? I mean, I hadn't even known about the Morph Rights movement; almost no one reported it. Like I said before, I knew Larry down at Kroger's; but I had never really thought about him before. Not as a person. Hell, I'd been discouraged from thinking of them as people. Churches denounced them. Hate groups found new targets and forgot all about the Jews and the blacks and the faggots for a while. Governments banned further research and made it just short of a crime for morphs to reproduce. The morphs that could relocate did it; those that couldn't lived on the fringes, mopping up broken pickle jars at Kroger's or spent their lives trying not to freeze or roast or starve on a rez in the middle of nowhere. Laws made it a felony for real people to have sex with a morph. Society persecuted those that did it anyway—it was viewed as something of a combination of child molester and sheep fucker. Federal lands set aside as nature preserves were put to use as reservations and the rest of the world, for the most part, tried to pretend that they didn't exist.

I walked along the fence, my fingers brushing rust from the chain links as I waded through the weeds and brush till I found what I guessed would be there. I tore my shirt and got a minor scratch on my shoulder wriggling through the hole in the fence but didn't notice. I had a goal now besides killing myself. Somewhere in my mind I'd decided that I was going to see a wild morph before I died. Once I was inside the fence I just picked a direction at random. I figured that if I walked long enough I would run into a road or something.

I was right. I found something.

It wasn't a road. It was a tall stand of cattails and beyond them a small lake. And in that lake: the cougar.

I guess I should apologize in advance for what follows. Not because I wrote it, but because you're probably not going to like it. I didn't write to offend you but I know you'll be offended. You see, for the first time that I could remember, I felt; just felt. There was no room for thought or analysis. My brain was not in the loop. Everything went from my eyes straight to my gut… my chest… my balls… You can't imagine what that was like.

I heard the splashing from a distance. Crouching in the dry, sun-bleached grass I reached back to check the pistol in my belt. Don't ask me why I was checking for protection when my whole reason for going out there was to die—instinct, I guess. Anyway, it wasn't there. It must have fallen out when I crawled through the fence or something; I never did find the damn thing. Deciding that it didn't matter, I started a painfully slow advance on the lake; working to keep the rushes between the splashes and me. It seemed to take forever before I reached the first of the tall, green fronds. Dry grass gave way to sticky, black mud as I worked my way through the cattails until I could see that I was at the far edge of the rushes and knelt down. I parted the fronds so that I might see what was in the lake.

The cougar…

I saw him and was instantly changed. The image bypassed my eyes and brain and stopped time. It consumed me. I didn't think. I couldn't think. I felt—truly felt. No filters. No analysis. Just him as I gazed upon a crystalline sun suspended over this pond. My eyes didn't see the droplets flung from the wet fur of his head to hang suspended around him–a million diamonds reflecting sunlight to form a halo. My eyes didn't see this; my stomach saw it and it clenched tight. My fingers didn't touch the soft, thick, wet, tawny fur of this magnificent creature; but my heart did and it stopped beating. It was not my nose that smelled wet fur and an underlying musk that was many things but most of all male. My lungs filled with it and I stopped breathing. I couldn't take all of him in. Muscles running like the swells of a slow moving river under fur the color of desert sand and sugar. Blunted muzzle, so alien to me yet so perfect on him, jutting from under eyes of purest gold. White furred sheath small and tight, low between muscled thighs caused my scrotum to tighten and pull my balls upwards; almost as if to retract them into my body out of reverence for this creature that somehow defined what it was to be male.

Like a dropped wineglass, the moment shattered. The water suspended about his head resumed its arc to fall back into the lake. His lithe arms stretched for the sky, his back arched to its limits as he embraced the sensual play of sun and water on his body. His closed eyes and a deep rumbling in his chest expressed his pleasure as I watched. Hidden… Spying on him and feeling lessened by that invasion, but unable to look away. He really was a combination of cougar and human. I had seen cougars in the zoos when real animals were still used in those places. He had that same coloration, tawny brown above and white at his muzzle, throat and belly. His skin (pelt?) had that same loose look; like velvet draped casually over a frame that merely suggested his power and grace. His round ears were low on the sides of his skull and turned this way and that. I tried to breathe softer. I watched his movements, marveling at the majestic economy. Every motion was just so and no more, each effortless and natural. He stood upright on two legs much like my own rather than a cat's. They disappeared at mid thigh into the water but he didn't seem to have an animal's legs; not a beast's with the joints oddly placed, making them look like they had too many bends. His hands ended in fingers like mine, thicker and shorter perhaps, and furred of course, but definitely not paws. And there, swimming behind him, skimming the surface of the water and then diving beneath it, was his tail.

I don't know how long I watched him. Certainly it wasn't long but it felt like the sun should have set before the moment ended. Then something happened that almost caused me to jump from my hiding-place and flee as fast and as far as I could. The cougar spoke. Without looking my way. He didn't indicate in any way other than his words that he was aware of my presence but I understood that he knew exactly where I was and that he had known from the beginning.

"You are very loud." His nose wrinkled. "And you smell bad."

He turned away from me and bent over at the waist, dipping his hands into the water. There revealed as his tail flicked this way and that was the scrotum that had been hidden before. Much farther back than a man's and the twin globes looked more like golf balls than eggs in the soft white sac. He brought his cupped hands up and splashed more water over his head and shoulders, continuing his bathing.

I got the message. I don't know how I understood. Maybe because I didn't think about it. I was still locked in the novelty of feeling. He had turned his back on me. He had made himself vulnerable showing me that he didn't consider me to be a threat. Maybe I should have been insulted by this, but I didn't think about it, I just understood. He exposed his maleness to me showing me that he was dominant here and that I was not even considered worthy of a challenge. Again I wasn't offended. I don't know how I understood these things as clearly as I had his words. It just felt right.

There wasn't any reason to keep hiding, so I stood up and moved out of the reeds. Black mud caked my soaked pants. Shirt filthy and full of burrs, hair tangled, I stood before him. That single step took more effort than anything I had ever done before. It wasn't fear that held me, though I did fear him. It was shame. I was ashamed to be seen by this magnificent creature.

As I stood there at the water's edge he turned and stared at me. I noticed his rounded ears now pointed at me and that his pink, leathery nose flared slightly with each breath he took but otherwise he was as motionless as I. His eyes, now more brown than gold but with brighter flecks of yellow in them, stared into my own and if he blinked I didn't notice. Finally I couldn't handle his stare any longer and looked down to where his legs disappeared beneath the surface.

"I am sorry. I didn't mean to intrude."

"Yes you did. You tried to stalk me for a hand's breadth of the sky before reaching your hiding place."

Panic gripped my chest and blood pounded in my ears as I tensed to leap for the reeds behind me, hoping for a head start as I fled.

"Do not try to run."

I barely saw him start to move before his hand was at my throat, needle sharp points pricking my skin telling me that his fingers were more unlike my own than I had thought. My already wet pants got wetter with the splash he raised, and warmth flowed from my crotch down my thighs. His nose wrinkled again and his eyes flicked with disgust. Then he released me and, as smoothly as he had lunged, retreated to his earlier position in the deeper water, once again staring at me as he stood motionless.

"I am faster and stronger than you. And, as you have seen, if I mean you harm then you are already dead. Or should I say deader?"

I didn't understand what he meant by that, but I definitely understood the rest of it all too well. I noticed then that I had pissed my pants when he grabbed me and felt his look of disgust like a knife twisting in my guts. I didn't know why, but I would have rather had him tear my throat out than endure that look. Besides, I had lost the instrument I had brought with me to do what I had driven out to the woods to do. If he was to be the pistol's replacement so be it. I raised my chin and stared him in the eye and took a step toward him.

"Then kill me if that's what you're going to do. But don't try to play with me like a mouse."

I wish I could make you feel how I felt when an arced eyebrow, a loosening of muscles in his shoulders and a subtle flick of his tail told me that disgust had been replaced with acknowledgment. I was not offal. I was not prey. I was not much of anything in his eyes, but I now existed to him as an individual rather than as just an oddity or object of curiosity.

Once again he turned his back to me and this time waded toward a bright patch of sand that sloped up to a grassy hill. Once again I understood silent signals I wasn't even aware of perceiving and I followed.

On the bank he walked around me several times. Actually it was more as if he flowed around me. Now and then a furred finger would pluck at a bit of fabric or toy with a button or wind a strand of hair and then move on. Finally he stopped and stood perfectly still, facing me. He was close enough that I could feel the warmth radiating from his body, smell the wet muskiness of his fur, feel his breath puffing lightly upon my face. After a while, he grimaced and uttered a chuffing cough.

"I am sorry, but you really do stink. Stink of cities and of iron and, somehow, of death."

I noticed that he didn't mention the stink of sweat or piss or fear. These were natural smells. Maybe not pleasant, they were part of his world. Not taking my eyes from his, my hands lifted and freed the first button of my shirt. The rest followed one after the other with me hardly being aware of it as the shirt fell to the ground. I don't remember kicking off my shoes and socks or of unbuckling and removing my piss and mud soaked trousers. I do remember the shame I felt as I hesitated before pulling down my boxers and tossing them on the wet sand. It wasn't that being naked that made me hesitate. It was that I did not want to be naked before him. It felt like hanging a school kid's latest drawing next to a Rembrandt. I can remember his eyes and the reflection of my face in them. He never blinked. His gaze never left mine. Then I was naked.

I managed to wrench my eyes from his and waded out into the water. I stopped at nearly the same place as where he had been when I first saw him and squatted until I was submerged. My fingers reached down to clench handfuls of sand as I felt the pond around me like the birth-waters of the womb. I felt the water lifting and pulling my hair with playful tugs. I felt it enter my ears with that bubbling tickle till suddenly it carried each sound to me with its rich, muffled voice. I opened my mouth to it and shivered when my ass relaxed a moment to let in the merest touch of cool water. Finally, I couldn't remain and I uncoiled and broke through the surface and into sunlight in another shower of sparkling diamonds. This time of my own creation.

Bending over I reached down and pulled up handful after handful of sand and rubbed it into my skin and hair. I scrubbed the abrasive grit onto myself until my skin burned and tingled. I submerged again and again until I had rinsed all of the sand from my body and hair and then continued splashing handfuls of water over my head just because it felt so good to do it. Finished at last, I waded back onto the sandy strand of beach and stood again before the cougar. My bathing must have taken longer than I thought because his fur was rapidly drying, turning a lighter shade of gold where the sun sucked the water from his coat.

The cougar whurffed quietly, almost inaudibly, and sniffed.

"No city. No poison. But still you smell of death."

I wasn't aware that I was going to say it until the words had already left my mouth.

"You are beautiful."

His response was as simply elegant as he was.

"Yes."

I blushed when I realized what I had just said. I wondered what was happening to me.

He turned and walked away from me, speaking without turning his head or otherwise acknowledging me.

"Come. I will lay in the sun and sand in wet fur itches."

Maybe I should have been pissed that he was tossing commands at me but I didn't even think of it. My inner critics were too shocked to voice their complaints. I did notice that he had explained his reason for the command. I took it as an improvement over his earlier evaluation of me.

When I reached the top of the bank I found him already spread out on the grass looking as if he had been partially melted and poured there. He seemed to have no bones, just a loose pool of molten copper baking in he sun. I approached until the tip of his tail twitched and the stiff whiskers on his muzzle fanned very slightly. I moved back a step and sat. Never in my life had I been naked outdoors. I wriggled as the grass under me alternately tickled and stabbed; it was hard to get comfortable. Finally I lay out on my back, slightly propped on one elbow so that I could sneak glimpses of him out of the corner of my eye.

I heard him move and peeked again and saw that he had shifted and was staring at me. Deciding that sneaking furtive glances after we had watched each other bathe was silly, I rolled onto my side and stared back.

It wasn't long before I realized that he was looking mostly at my crotch. I fought an automatic urge to cover myself. I had been fighting hard not to look at his groin. I was curious about the differences that I had seen when he washed. I was too embarrassed to look now that he was so close. Yet, he didn't try at all to hide the fact that he was very interested in what was between my legs. The cold water of the lake had done a number on my cock. I could feel it contracted and my scrotum tight. How small I must have seemed to him.

"Your penis is strange," he said, and then he went on to tell me what he found strange about it. He discussed my most private parts as openly and easily as if he was talking about the color of my eyes or the length of my hair.

"It is one of the few places that you have fur," he said, "you have no sheath. It does not seem to have a bone like the canid's. Does it get larger when you are aroused? The tip is almost like that of a horse. Does it flare?"

Since he seemed so comfortable with the subject, I finally let myself look at his genitals. We had a dog for a short time when I was a boy. I saw his sheath many times as he hiked his leg to piss or as he lay in the living room unabashedly licking himself (the licking was the 'immoral' behavior that had driven my mother to send him to the pound to be put to sleep.) The dog's sheath had been a long, furry tube running from his balls to where I guessed his navel to be. It was attached to his body by a thin strip of skin. The cougar's wasn't like that. It was only a little over an inch or two long and started between his thighs and ended where the base of the cock would be on a man. Either his cock was very short or most of it was pulled back inside his body until he got hard. The sheath was covered in white fur and had a small opening at the tip where just a hint of moist pink was visible. In spite of myself, I wondered what the cock inside it looked like.

As I stared, I tried to answer his questions and to ignore the blush that made my ears grow warm.

"Uhm... Men usually have hair on their heads and faces, but that gets shaved off, under their arms and at their groin. I don't know why. I don't know what you mean about it not having a bone. Do... uh... canids have bones in their penises?" I suddenly thought of Lenny and blushed harder. "Humans don't have sheaths. We're born with a fold of skin that covers the head but that is usually surgically removed shortly after birth. What else..."

I had lost track of his questions and was trying to remember what all he had asked when my body answered one of his remaining questions for me. The warmth of the sun, the novelty of being nude outdoors, looking at him and the talk about penises had caused my own to waken and begin to stir.

"Ah, I see that it does get larger. Lengthening then erecting as it fills with blood. Yes, definitely more like an equine than a canine or feline. Without the sheath, though, and certainly not on the same scale as an equimorph. Why do you remove your facial fur? And how can a people claim on the one hand to be civilized and superior and on the other butcher the genitals of their own young?"

I looked down at my lap to see my penis grown about half-hard. Luckily it did not seem inclined to go beyond that point. I thought hard about cold water, slamming car doors, and dead puppies and tried not to die of embarrassment.

"Uhm... I don't know."

"You become agitated. How strange. We will discuss something else. Why do you smell of death?"

I shook my head as my mind struggled to shift gears.

"I don't understand. What do you mean 'I smell of death'?"

"I see that you do not lie. You do not smell the air that surrounds you." His eyes closed to near slits and his nose flared as he breathed in deeply. "You smell like an animal that is soon to die of disease or injury yet I sense no injury and smell no disease."

I began to understand.

"Maybe it is because I came out here to kill myself." I said.

"How strange. Is this self-destruction common among humans?"

I don't know what kind of response I expected from him. More disgust? Concern? Shock maybe? Whatever I expected, it wasn't his matter of fact acceptance and clinical curiosity.

"What? Uhm... No, it's rare. It's a disease of the mind. Tends to be self-correcting; recover or die."

He seemed truly puzzled by this but didn't seem to doubt in the least what I was telling him.

"You appear healthy. You are not old or weak. Your muscles are layered in fat that tells me you have some rank in your society. Tell me why a male not of the lowest rank would choose to die."

Damn! What a question. When I tried to think of how to explain it to him I realized that I couldn't really explain it to myself. I didn't figure that he would accept excuses so I tried. I honestly tried. But he didn't understand and I gave up.

We were silent for some time before he spoke again.

"Why did you come here? Why did you leave your home to do what you came to do? Why did you leave your car? Why did you enter the reservation? Why did you spy on me? None of these things helped you to die, so why were they important enough to you to keep you from your stated task? These things do not make sense to me."

"I couldn't do this at home," I said, "I didn't want to die in that empty, sterile place. The idea of doing it outdoors in the woods or something just felt right. I don't know why I left the car. Maybe I just wanted to leave the world I hate so much and be surrounded by nature. I got curious when I found the fence. It was something I wasn't expecting and I decided that I wanted to see a wild fur before I died. When I saw you... you were so... so... I... I don't know. I just stayed."

I cringed when I realized that I'd used the slang term for moprhs like he was an attraction in a zoo or something. I expected him to be angry with me. I lowered my head waiting to see what he would do and only lifted it again when I realized that he wasn't going to do anything. I looked back into his eyes. His next words were definitely not those of some zoo animal.

"Ah. These words I understand. You finally make noises that have meaning. You seek out life in your quest for death."

"No, you don't understand. I just came here to die. To make it all end. All of it."

His response was in a low growl.

"I do not misunderstand, human," when he said it, 'human' seemed more of an insult than 'wild fur' had been, "I smell the truth of my words on you or I would not have spoken them. I see in you that you hunt two different animals. But, every hunter knows that you must choose one member from the herd. Hunt only it or you will catch nothing in the end but an empty belly."

I looked at the ground, shoulders slumped.

"I just want to die."

Always the predator, he would not give up.

"You are not dead. You are not helpless. If you wished to be dead you would be. Would have been. You smell of death. Maybe because you do not know what it is to live."

I lifted my head and got angry, "Then what have I been doing for the last thirty-three years?"

"Surviving," he said, "they are not the same thing. You have made it from one day to the next, but have taken no joy from them. Maybe you should learn to live before you die."

I sat there huddled into myself. Nothing left to say. I was too emotionally drained. The events of the last few hours had been too much for me. I felt like I'd fallen into a river and was being carried by it, bouncing from one rock to the next.

I heard him move but didn't even have the energy to look up. I could hear him approach me. The feel of warm paws on my shoulders was not entirely unexpected. Their gentleness was.

He didn't speak as strong fingers dug into the muscles of my shoulders and neck, kneading and rubbing. He had rough, leathery pads on his palms and under his fingers; the fur between them was soft and silky. He seemed to sense when and how hard to press, his hands pulling away a tension that I had carried for so long that I wasn't even aware of it until it started to fade.

It occurred to me that I shouldn't be letting this happen. I was out in the middle of a morph rez, sitting naked, with my back pressed into the belly fur of another male of another species while he gave me the best massage of my whole damn life. It occurred to me, but I didn't care about you enough just then to stop it. I couldn't bring myself to do much of anything but sit there. I was trapped between worlds. I had no reason to live. I didn't have the strength to die. I couldn't seem to care about anything else.

I became aware of a new sensation going through me. Not a sound, not a feeling. Neither. Both. I realized that the cougar was purring. The vibrations moved over me and through me. His hands worked lower and his chin rested on my shoulder. I marveled at the smell of him, the feel of his breath in my hair and behind my ear before I realized that he was speaking to me in a low voice that barely carried above his purr.

"I admire you, hunter. I do not know many who could survive for so long as injured as you are. What matter if the injury is to limb, entrails or spirit. You have shown great strength and courage to come so far and even then to continue to seek life as you plan to die. I have decided to help you on your hunt. But you must choose the prey. Do we hunt Life or Death, you and I? If Death is to be the prey then I will give you what you came here to find. I will end your life for you. But, I would rather help you look for Life. What say you, Sutah?"

His words crashed down on me like a hammer. I collapsed under them. I was helpless against the sobs that came without warning and tore me apart. Never had anyone said anything like that to me. He saw! This creature who had known me only minutes saw how hard each day was. Saw what a struggle it was just to get out of bed, to do the simplest thing when all you wanted was an end to everything. He saw and, in his seeing, I saw my own strength. I was not a loser. I was not a weakling. I had accomplished more just by not taking my own life than most did in a lifetime.

I don't know how long I cried before I was finally able to get the sobbing under control. The cougar had his arms wrapped tightly around me, his chin still on my shoulder. I wanted those arms around me and never wanted them to leave and was ashamed.

"You feel. The dead do not feel. It is pain. But even pain can be a good thing, Sutah."

In spite of myself I reveled in the feel of his fur, his strength surrounding me. His chin nestled deeper into the crook of my neck, his nose brushing the rim of my ear.

"What does 'sutah' mean?"

"It is my people's word for 'strong.'"

I felt something warm, wet and rough run slowly up my neck to tug at the lobe of my ear. At the same time his hands began to roam over my chest and belly. The sensations were so exquisite that it was a moment before I realized what they meant and jerked forward to try and escape his grasp.

I was surprised by how easy it was. His arms fell away and I stumbled from his embrace, turning to face him.

I wiped the light trail of his saliva from my neck, "What the fuck! What the hell are you doing?"

Is it possible for a feline to have a 'hang dog' expression? If so then the cougar wore one that day. He looked at me with eyes full of regret, but somehow I realized that it was not regret for having embraced me in that way but for something else entirely. He made no move to come after me. He just sat there watching me before answering.

"I had hoped that you would hunt Life. I sought to dance Life with you."

"Dance Life with me? What do you... oh... Oh, my god! We're both male! We aren't even the same species. How could you even think that I could... oh, my god..."

I stared at him, seeing that perfect form, that grace, that power, that awe inspiring beauty and masculinity; and I knew how he could think that I would. I didn't want to admit, most of all to myself, that I wanted him. I wanted him! More than anything wanted him to want me. It was forbidden. It was disgusting. It was against the law. It was immoral. But I wanted him. I pictured in my mind the expressions of everyone I saw looking at me—knowing that I was a pervert. I felt disgust at myself. And there he sat watching me watching him. I wanted him and he knew it.

I thought about you. You who had sat in judgment of my life to that point. You were there when I didn't try out for a part in the play because you might humiliate me if I was less than perfect. You were there when I didn't smile back at the young man at the coffee shop who smiled so beautifully. You filled me with fear. Fear that I was wrong about what his smile meant. Fear of the million things I pictured happening if I admitted to myself what I truly desired. You were there the first time I made love. You were there measuring my performance even though it was her first time too. It was fear of you that made my first time with her rather than with the one I wanted it to be with. You wouldn't even let me admit to myself that I wanted him. You have always been there. I've always been afraid of what you would think of me. Trying to make you think well of me has always been more important than even me thinking well of myself. That is why I wrote this.

Maybe it was because the whole situation was so surreal. Maybe it was because I was emptier than I'd ever been in my life. For whatever reason, I still feared you but there was more. I hated you! I wanted to strike at you, to hurt you.

Rather than let you make guesses about me I will tell you exactly what I did. You can brand me as a filthy pervert. Call me sick or insane. Call the police. Call my family. I don't give a shit. I don't care anymore. Read on. Read about my crimes against man, against God, against nature.

He didn't raise his voice. His words barely reaching me.

"I did not want the world to lose something beautiful. I smelled your desire. Did you not smell mine?"

I have thought of myself as many things, but beautiful has never been one of them so it took awhile for me to realize that he was talking about me. Strong? Beautiful? Me? I started to wonder which of us was actually mentally unbalanced. Smelled my desire? What desire? I knew what desire. I could lie to you. I could lie to myself. I could lie to the cougar's ears. But when my very body betrayed me to his nose what good were lies?

I looked at him. Forced myself to see him, eyes moving slowly over his body. His head was flatter than my own. His muzzle was short and seemed to flow from his face rather than jutting forth like a dog's. It was flat on top and rounding at the sides where his quivering whiskers waved in the slight breeze. His nose quivered with his breathing and I knew that it was reading things about me that I didn't even know my body was telling him. His brown fur faded to a luscious creamy white around his lips. The tip of one fang was visible on the left side. His shoulders were rounded and broad, flowing into the powerful arms that had been wrapped around me moments before. I saw that the white fur of his chest ran under and down the insides of each arm. I saw the tips of his claws, almost invisible retracted as they were, at the tip of each finger. His belly was a sheet of flat muscle and I saw where my back had left an imprint in the fur there. His legs were spread and I allowed myself to stare at his crotch, the sheath a little thicker than before, the opening more pronounced. His tail was draped over his thigh; mostly still, only the very tip flicking now and then.

I felt a stirring in myself. In my gut… in my chest… between my legs. I panicked and almost ran; instead I made myself take a deep breath instead and crouched where I was.

I closed my eyes and tilted my head back and inhaled slowly through my nose. I tried to wake up a sense that had all but died since man climbed down from the trees. I smelled the dusty musk of him. The hint of wet fur. The animal smell of him. I allowed myself to experience the different, the feral, the forbidden.

With my eyes still closed I leaned forward. I crawled toward him blindly, extending one hand until my fingers touched the fur of his chest. I felt the silken softness of his pelt. I pressed into the unyielding muscle beneath. I slowly trailed my palm down his belly, feeling the fur flow like water between my fingers. I felt the vibrations as the cougar started purring again.

I didn't jump as the tip of my mostly limp cock brushed across the fur of his leg and immediately began twitching and growing.

Eyes still closed, I turned my head and leaned to place it against his chest, letting the purr fill me. Finally I opened my eyes and looked up at him and surrendered. I looked at him with fear, with desire, with pride that something so beautiful could want me. I slipped my arm around his chest and held tightly as I closed my eyes again and let myself disappear into him. I didn't flinch when his arms once again wrapped around me.

I felt his breath in my hair as he lowered his muzzle and inhaled deeply, taking in my scent. I lifted my head and looked at him. Raising my hand, I hesitantly pressed it against the side of his muzzle, stroking his cheek. Soft fur and stiff whiskers alive under my palm. His mouth opened slightly and I breathed his breath deep into my lungs as his mouth slowly moved toward mine, finally pressing my moist lips against his furred ones. Our mouths ground together as we exchanged breath in an ardent kiss that grew in passion by the second. I felt his tongue, like wet sandpaper, dance lightly across my lips as he tasted me, and then slip between them to dance with my tongue. I squeezed him as tightly as I could; I fed urgently on his lips and teeth and tongue. My fingers gripped the fur at the nape of his neck. His answering embrace forced the air from my lungs.

His fangs pressed my lips, pinching them almost painfully against my teeth. His stiff whiskers scratched my cheeks. I felt the tips of his claws scraping the flesh of my scalp and back and reveled in the sensation. His purrs became interspersed with chuffing growls of approval and desire as our mouths continued to devour each other hungrily. I groaned my need, locked away and denied for so long, into his muzzle. The cougar snarled and I felt his teeth close on my throat as his tongue lapped roughly at my neck until the skin there burned and sang. I jumped when I felt a feathery light touch tickling up my side and knew that his tail had joined us.

Like so many others, I had always assumed that when two men joined together in a sexual union that one took the male role and the other the female. There was nothing female about the cougar. To the contrary, he was more male than anything I had ever imagined; but I didn't feel female with him. I felt my own masculinity more fiercely than at any time in my life. My blood sang with the knowledge that I was male. The fact that I knew what I was making him feel excited me. Knowing that he knew exactly what his ministrations were doing to me inflamed me. That fundamental understanding of the other that I could never communicate to a woman made doing things that I had previously only thought of in a female context a celebration of my manhood.

I gathered my legs under me and, with my shoulder planted against his chest, drove forward pushing him back onto the grass, me atop him. My mouth chewed on the tuft of fur under his chin. He growled happily and wrapped his arms tighter about me as he began gnawing on my shoulder. His sharp teeth hurt but felt wonderful. I ground myself into his belly, feeling my cock drive through his fur. I swear that I could feel each hair as it passed over my manhood and brushed my scrotum. I experienced every touch and lick in ways never dreamed. My whole body was a single nerve alive and hungry for each new sensation. I felt something warm running across my thigh leaving trails of wetness behind it and knew that his animal penis had begun erecting. I shuddered in pleasure.

He growled playfully and rolled us over, pinning me beneath him. I felt his wet cock twitch as he rubbed it purposefully up and down my thigh and realized that he found the feel of my smooth skin as exquisite as I did his fur. Smiling up at him, I lifted my head and licked at one of his delightful fangs.

I was taken by surprise when he suddenly snarled and batted my head with an open fist hard enough to make my ears ring. I was trying to figure out what was happening when he leapt to the side and stood facing me in a crouch. His fingers flexed and his tail twitched. The first two inches of his pink erection poked from his sheath and bobbed back and forth as he growled his challenge at me and at the same time smiled. I understood then what was happening and rolled to my feet facing him. Yelling a wordless, feral sound at the top of my lungs I rushed at him and drove my shoulder into his stomach.

He braced himself and took my rush easily. Wrapping his arms around my waist, he used my momentum to lift and flip me until I was held upside down. My back against his chest, his wet cock rubbing my neck. Again he chuffed happily and I felt his wonderfully rough tongue part the cheeks of my ass and run its way up, across my asshole and finally lap off the underside of my balls. Helpless, I shuddered in his arms and barely avoided being taken by surprise again when he tossed me from him. I managed to land in a ball and roll to my feet without more than a bruise or two and crouched, panting at him. His snarl was as horrifying as it was beautiful as he launched himself effortlessly at me. I tried to brace myself but might as well have been a leaf for all that I was able to stop him. His weight on me drove the air from my lungs and, while I was helpless on the ground, he lapped repeatedly at my nipples. I'd never thought of my nipples as sexual before then. His sandpaper tongue brought them pleasure, then pain, and finally through pain into ecstasy. I swear that I had an orgasm without cumming. My whole body shook. My world contracted to the feeling of that tongue and fur on my chest. I couldn't breathe.

Then he was gone.

I struggled back to my feet and staggered a minute before facing him again. I was scratched and bruised. Blood from a split lip dripped down my chin. My ears rang and my chest heaved as I struggled to get enough air. Across from me he stood ready. He was fresh and untouched. He had barely exerted himself and I was already at my limit. There was no way that I could defeat him. Did that make me feel defeated? No! I understood. This was not a fight for victory. It was a celebration. A celebration of our power. Of our bodies. Of our spirits. Muscle and sweat and blood. I threw my head back and with a roar of elation I attacked him with every ounce of my being. He had shown me that I couldn't hurt him and had freed me to unleash everything feral that was in me. There was no need to hold back I thundered at him. His roar echoed mine and we met again and again in a battle that was as much prayer and sex as it was violence. Finally I had nothing left to give to the battle.

He sensed this and stopped. I lay on my back in the grass. His body sprawled half on top of me and his deep, rumbling purr made me wish that I too could purr and show him my contentment. I had never been as sore or as tired or as deeply at peace. I began to recover while he stroked me lightly here and there, soothing or stimulating as the impulse took him. His tongue cleaned the blood from my minor wounds. I felt his tail twine about my thigh like a snake and tickle playfully under my balls. His tongue moved over my body, joining his paws in a marriage of textures that soon had me trembling. Through this I lay still, letting him do as he would. Trusting him, welcoming all that he did. I felt his weight leave me but didn't open my eyes. His hands, fur like the touch of a silken cloud, tickling and exciting. His tongue was like raspy fire at once so soft and abrasive. His touches opened doors for me and it was as if I entered my body for the first time; living in my body rather than riding it like a puppeteer guiding a marionette.

He must have known that the roughness of his tongue would be too much on my most sensitive flesh. When he lifted me to settle between my thighs, he left off his licking and contented himself with rubbing his hands over my chest and belly as my legs settled around his hips. He continued to stroke me as he began to rock between my knees. My eyes were still closed so I didn't know what he intended and cried out, arching my back, as just the very tip of my cock flowed into the fur of his belly. His hands pushed me down, holding me in place as he settled into a regular rocking that permitted only my glans the barest contact with his fur. That light touch made me yearn for more but no matter how I tried to push myself deeper, he held me in place. I was helpless under him. I thought that my cock would explode if it got any harder. Yet, with each slow stroke of luxurious fur, my painfully hard erection expanded even more. His tail reentered the game and began tickling my feet with the same light, controlled stokes. I kicked and fought to escape his torturous assault, but his tail remained wrapped around my calf, the tip continuing to brush up and down the sole of my foot.

My head was thrashing back and forth. I felt as if I was at the point of no return half a dozen times. Each time praying that I would cum and find the release that his controlled restraint denied me. Each time I found that instead I only became even more aroused at a new plateau. The cougar purred and growled the whole time above me. I opened my eyes and looked at him and saw the pleasure he derived from seeing me in such ecstasy. Suddenly I knew what I wanted. What I needed. Not him and me. Us. Not two. One.

He was unprepared when, instead of trying to thrust into him, I used my locked ankles to pull him to me. I squeezed until I felt his sheath press against me. He looked down, his eyes searching mine, to see if I was sure. A look of understanding smoothed his features and he resumed rocking over me. This time it was his moist, fiery penis that rubbed oh so lightly against me, riding up and down the crack of my ass and over my tightly crinkled hole.

If I had thought that his fur rubbing my cock had been torture I was wrong. That was nothing to the need that he inflicted on me then. Every time his cock passed over my hole, adding to the wetness building between my cheeks, I opened to him and tried to pull him inside me. The heat radiated by his cock was incredible and I could feel that he was built very differently than me. My ass tingled and itched with need. He braced his arms behind my knees and with each slow, controlled thrust of his hips he pushed them a little farther back toward my head. Our bodies were not the same. Things did not match up in a way that made coupling easy. It was not a spontaneous act or one of domination. We were partners working

175

together to make a joining possible.

By the time my knees were pressed almost to my ears my anus was no longer tightly crinkled. Teased by the tip of his cock brushing it again and again and wetted by the cougar's copious emissions, it was now a bright pink ring of desire aching to be filled. The cougar shifted and I felt his knees grip my hips. I was incoherent with fearful anticipation and ground my teeth to keep from crying out as he leaned over me and I felt him slide slowly closer until the tip pressed lightly at the rim of my virginity.

He entered me in one quick thrust. My teeth clamped down on his shoulder as he snarled above me. The very narrow tip of his cock entered me easily, parting my flesh and making way for the cone shaped shaft that followed. It got wider and wider toward the base forcing me open. I was beyond stretched by the time his sheath was pushed back and he was buried inside me, twitching as he filled me in new and unbelievable ways. It was more than having a male's cock in my ass. It was the feeling of being joined with him, of having given myself to him as wholly and as utterly as I was capable of. It stung. It burned. I felt at the very edge of being torn apart. The tears that flowed down my cheeks were not tears of pain but of joy.

I felt his cock jerking as he trembled atop me, struggling to hold still while I grew used to being filled this way. I couldn't wait. I was hunger. I was need. This was not a time for making love. I was in heat and it was time to mate. Even though he was in me, I felt as if I was mating him as surely as I was being mated. I bucked against him and growled into the fur and flesh still clamped in my teeth. He understood and began thrusting. His hips were a blur as he jabbed into me with short rapid thrusts, growling and chuffing. I felt a strange sensation every time the end of his cock plowed in and out of me. His eyes closed to slits as he struggled to push all of his maleness into me and then even more. I felt his cock passing over my prostate so quickly it was more like a vibrator than a stroking. My cock was finally buried fully in his fur and the stimulation devoured me until I could only hang onto him and whimper.

It was only a couple of minutes before the growling, heaving cougar on me snarled and clamped his jaws on my throat and roared as he plunged deeply and quivered. His cock spasmed as it began releasing his feline seed into me. His body temperature must have been higher than mine because I felt the warmth of his ejaculate filling me with every jerk of his cock. His cum was rushing into me. I was being bred! My own orgasm wracked me as my cock pumped jet after jet of semen into his fur making it slimy, and wet and urging even more from me. I ground myself into him as desperately as he ground himself into me. His jaws about my throat. His breath panting damp and hot against me. His cock spewing his essence into me. His fur drinking my seed. His arms holding me. His weight pinning me. My pulse throbbing. My head spinning. We came. We came and came until neither of us had anything to give the other.

He pulled himself from me rather quickly, causing me to wince as I felt that strange roughness pull through my well-used opening. Releasing my legs, he allowed them to stretch out again and pulled himself up beside me. Reaching out an arm, he pulled me until I rolled over and my head rested on his still heaving chest. His hammering heart slowed to a quiet counterpoint to his contented purr as I stared at the wet, matted pool of my sperm in his fur. Believe that, as I fell asleep on him, his arm around me, his semen seeping from my pleasantly sore anus, I was not thinking of you and what you would think.

I awoke slowly, taking in the world piece by piece. The fact that I was outdoors. The feel of air and sun against naked skin. The feel of warm fur under me. An ache deep inside me. The wonderful sting of a no longer virgin ass. I opened my eyes to look upon my strange lover. The tawny landscape of his body spread out before me. The perfection of his pelt marred only where my semen had been allowed to dry in his fur. Even in sleep his muscles were defined and beautiful under his hide. I smiled when I saw that even now his tail was not quiet and that it twitched at the tip, knocking white fluff from a dandelion. Finally I raised myself from his chest and stretched, much like a cat, enjoying the pull of muscle and tendon. The cougar opened his eyes and I smiled at him as I leaned down and softly licked his muzzle.

We touched and stroked each other awhile, neither of us speaking, before rising and heading down to the water to clean ourselves. The cool water not only cleaned, but revived and soon we were splashing each other playfully. Eventually we tired of this and climbed the bank back to our grassy knoll. There we stretched out in the evening sun. I retreated to the shade after a few minutes to reduce the sunburn that I was sure to have the next day. Propping myself against the trunk of a tree I watched him basking in the warmth. How effortlessly he seemed to be able to let everything go and experience the moment to its fullest. Quiet, content, I watched how the oranges and pinks and purples of the deepening sunset changed the color of his fur.

When the sun was only a glowing wash of muted pastels across the sky I moved from under the tree to rejoin him. He seemed so content, so peaceful, lying there on his belly. Even his overactive tail seemed finally to be at rest. I reached out a hand and stroked it down his back, entranced all over again by the feel of his fur under my touch. I turned and knelt beside him and my other hand joined the first in stroking and then kneading the cougar as he drowsed. I was delighted to find that, just like a house cat, the scruff of his neck was loose and very pleasant to massage. I kneaded the muscles under his pelt and without realizing it I softly drifted into the moment. Hands and fur. Skin and muscle. Slowly I worked my way down his back. I was in no hurry. Every inch of him was a new vista to be explored and cherished. An almost inaudible purr and quiet moans were the only indication he gave that he enjoyed the attention he was receiving. When I reached the base of his tail I discovered another similarity between him and a house cat. My thumbs dug into his spine where his tail began and, like I had flipped a switch, it jerked up and his hips raised off the ground. He actually mewled. I couldn't help teasing him a bit, pushing that magic button several times when he didn't expect it before I continued on. His haunches were a glory to explore and I spent much time kneading and stroking and caressing them. Eventually I reached his toes and helped him roll over so that I could begin slow journey back up.

I massaged the insides of his legs and his belly, always coming close to but never quite touching his balls or sheath. For a long while he remained still but I could see his jaws clench and his ears flatten against his head as he struggled not to react. I allowed my fingertips to brush the silken fur at the opening of his sheath as lightly as I could and was rewarded when he twitched beneath me, and whined quietly. Emboldened, I stroked all around his groin but always managed to avoid it until I saw the moist, pink tip of his feline cock poke forth to glisten in the moonlight. Now I dragged my fingers up the underside of his tail, trailing them lightly over his anus. Even this excited me. To touch him there. Both intimate and forbidden. I began to understand how he could have used his tongue on my ass as he had earlier, though I wasn't yet ready to consider doing the same. I lifted his balls as my fingers trailed around them and finally stroked them up his short, but delightfully full sheath. I was intoxicated. I seemed to instinctively know how to pleasure him. In doing so I brought myself unimaginable joy. Every time he shuddered or growled or writhed under me my cock bounced in response and my heart hammered with excitement.

I watched, mesmerized, as his maleness protruded farther and farther from his sheath, turning from pink to red. It began swelling and pulsing under my touch. I saw that he was indeed a cat down there, though of human dimensions. This did not surprise me. I had read that big cats had relatively small penises but knew that what had plumbed the depths of my admittedly inexperienced ass had been many things but not small. I saw a band of small, rough knobs almost like the blunted teeth of a rasp encircling the upper third of his cone-shaped penis. These must be what had produced that odd pulling sensation when he fucked me. It struck me again how comfortable I was with that thought, 'he fucked me'. Comfortable, hell. It was arousing and liberating. As I continued to play with my feline lover, his cock continued to twitch and jerk. A droplet of fluid seeped from the tip, a single pearl trembling in the light of its sister, the moon.

He had pleasured me with fur and rough tongue—with power and control. Now I would show him that my species had a few delights of its own. Bending over him, I pulled his sheath down as far as I could, exposing as much of him as possible. I licked slowly and firmly up its length until I gathered that sacred drop on my tongue. My head exploded when the taste of that offering filled me. I didn't hear his roars as my mouth lowered onto his maleness taking him fully. I didn't gag when the narrow tip of his penis opened my throat and provided passage for more of his cock, but his barbs proved to be too stimulating for much of that activity. Pulling back slightly, I held my mouth on him and used my tongue to stroke the underside of his bestial shaft while the feral musk of his crotch filled my head. Lapping quickly then slowly, lightly then with all the force I could muster, I breathed into his belly, my lips locked tightly around him. When I started to pull back he bucked his hips, trying to make his cock follow. Now it was my turn to hold him. I rested my legs on his thighs and curled around until my cheek lay on his belly. I stared down the length of him with the tip still trapped in my mouth. I lathered it with butterfly-light strokes of my tongue and then bobbed my head down to take him to the sheath. I reached a hand between his legs and began to tickle and scratch at the underside of his tail and over his tailhole.

The suddenness of his orgasm took me by surprise but I managed to ride my bucking lover, never allowing his cock to escape my hungry mouth. His seed burned as it jetted into me. His roars deafened me. The claws of his hands and feet ripped free huge clods of soil as he thrust and quivered and continued to pulse his essence into me. Even when there was no more to be had I suckled at him. Still my tongue laved over him, my lips drew him in. My fingers pulled and squeezed and urged him on. I couldn't have stopped even if he had used his claws to pull me away. I rubbed his slick organ over my lips and cheeks, smearing him over my face and with a groan took him yet again. My cock ground into his thigh as I devoured him, slurping and sucking, groaning and grunting.

Twice more he gifted me with his semen. Twice more his roars filled the night and startled sleeping birds into flight. Twice more he cried out to the moon, "We are alive!" and, in my heart, my roars joined his. Twice more I urged him to heights I had only dreamed of. Finally we were sated. Finally I stretched out atop him and thrust my tongue into his muzzle allowing him to taste of our Dance.

It was not my cock, but the cougar that reminded me that I had not cum, so intent had I been on draining him totally. I felt his hand close around my turgid shaft and groaned into his mouth. Sitting up and rolling me off of him he rolled over and rose to his hands and knees. His tail lifted revealing that most guarded portal. He looked at me over his shoulder, not just offering himself but telling me that his need was as intense as my own.

He had been slow with me, preparing me, getting me ready. I was too far gone to be slow with him. I was beyond thought. The fur of his hips clenched tightly in my fists, his tail pressed against my chest, the precum gathered at the tip of my own maleness was all the preparation he got before I plunged into him. I could not stop until my groin was pressed tightly against him. Our combined screams reached the heavens. Immediately I pulled out to the brink and plunged into him again... and again. I was not making love. We were mating. I bred him desperately. I took him and he took me. My blunt nails clawed at him as my hips pounded into his flesh. His head whipped from side to side as he pushed back onto me demanding even more. The sounds of flesh hammering flesh. The sucking sound of his violated orifice as I pulled out to slam back again. Heaving breath. Coughing roars, moans, whimpers, panting. Sweat flowing down my back and chest. Fur sticking to my chest and belly as I fell forward over him and locked my arms around him, pulling him back onto me as I heaved once and again and again and then stayed deep inside him as the floodgates opened and my balls gave up my seed. Short jabbing thrusts each ending in another surge of semen to fill him. Panting and dizzy I rested on his strong, broad back before pulling myself from him with a wet, sucking pop.

Realizing how violent had been my assault on him I started to apologize and then saw the satiated look of utter contentment on his face. He remained where he was, ass in the air, head resting on folded arms. A tiny trickle of cum dribbled from his still open hole. His eyes were half lidded and glazed. Even his whiskers hung limp and relaxed. I became aware of a strange yet familiar odor and looked down at myself. Even that morning I would have been horrified and disgusted by the sight of the slight stain on my cock and pubic hair. Now I saw it only as the natural result of our impassioned mating. Unpleasant but easily taken care of and no cause for distress. I rested a bit, letting the night air cool my burning flesh. I enjoyed the feeling of salty sweat drying on my body. I smiled as the cougar's ass slowly settled in stages until he lay flat and sound asleep. Then I returned to the lake and washed myself for the third time.

That night I slept in a cougar's arms under the stars.

The following day I walked with him to his home where I stayed for many weeks. I left my clothes lying there on that strand of beach where they had fallen. They stank. They stank not of cities and iron, but of fear… and of you. I won't try to lie to you and say that I didn't have qualms and attacks of guilt after my experiences that night and the many nights that followed. Dances shared with my feline lover and with others. I did. Eventually though, I learned to live for how I felt rather than how I thought you would feel. Eventually I fell in love. I have been mated to a wonderful coyote for several years now. He thinks the world of me and I love him with all of my heart. I am happier than I ever thought anyone could be. But he has seen that a shadow still lingers. I no longer let you guide my life, but I have been haunted by the fear of what would happen if you truly did find out about me and who I have become. That last vestige of fear is all that remains of my prison.

So, now you see why I write this. I have feared what would happen should you discover me and I choose to live with that fear no longer. There is no need for you to discover me because I have revealed myself to you. I don't write this so that you can judge me; I seek neither your approval nor your censure. I write this because I now see that you are the bars to my cell. You are the shadow. And with this key I can say to you… Goodbye. I can now walk through you to the coyote waiting for me. Waiting to Dance Life.

Man's Men

Unfashionable though it may be, the stereotype of the 'manly man' has a solid basis in reality. The sensitive 'man of the eighties' and the open-minded 'man of the nineties' have been joined by the metrosexual 'man of the twenty-first century' and any depiction of old-school masculinity is typically met with derision and contempt as if it were some arcane parody.

And yet many males remain old-fashioned. They boast and mask their emotions behind tough bluster and this is ordinary. It is therefore refreshing, on occasion, to read fiction that portrays such much-neglected personalities.

"A Helping Hand the Morning After" is an interesting story, not just because of the mood it evokes—the core excitement of a long road trip with a good buddy—but also because it shows, without any ulterior intentions, 'ordinary guys'. The fact that they're gay and engage in sex somehow doesn't enter into it; they're as comfortable with their sexuality as the typical straight college jock is with his.

A Helping Hand
the Morning After

Stormcatcher

Rollins groaned as he felt himself coming to, eyes blinking open groggily as the car bounced hard enough from a pothole to rouse him. He gritted his teeth as the hangover-accompanied headache seemed to wait until he was more conscious, then pounced on his brain like a rabid dog, making the space behind his eyes feel like a hippopotamus was sitting on it. His mane was mussed over and unkempt, his mouth felt like he'd been gargling socks, and he noted that part of his vision was skewed with some weird red color that alarmed him, at first... until he realized that it was just his red-tinted aviator goggles that had slipped down to cover one of his eyes. He grunted and shoved the covered lens up and off his eye, only to see a flash of movement from his peripheral vision. The sun visor on the passenger's side of the car was flipped up abruptly, flooding the young lion's face with light and making him yell in pain as he jerked his hands up to block out the blinding glare.

"GAAAAH!" he roared. He slapped the visor back down, then jerked his goggles down over his eyes once more to filter out some of the painful light, his vision now all red but the infrared tint added to the lenses helping to ease the pain a little. He snarled softly, teeth bared, and abruptly swung the back of his fist up and around to thwack the beefy right shoulder of the driver and his trip companion, a burly-looking minotaur. "You sum'bitch. Dammit, Kal, why do ya have to be such an evil bastard? Oww, my fuckin' head!" He groaned and dropped his face forward into his hands, rubbing his temples with his fingers, trying to stroke the pain away.

The bull snickered deeply, both big hands on the wheel and a tight, wry, smarmy smirk across his face. "Wakey, wakey, sleeping beauty!" he snort-ed, grinning sideways to the cat. "Sleep well, I trust? God knows, you sure put away enough last night to knock a normal fella out for a good three weeks."

The lion snorted softly as he opened one side of his trenchcoat, his brows furrowed in pain and growing annoyance as he thrust a hand into the inner lining pocket, searching for something. "Depends on if said 'normal fella' has an asshole of a trip partner to harass him," the feline grumbled. "Crank your voice down a couple notches, will ya? My damn head feels like it's gonna explode." He lowered his glaring gaze down to peer into the pocket as he tugged it outwards. "Where the hell are my smokes?"

Kal glanced at him, then shook his horned head grimly as his grin faded. "Rolly, not to sound like your pop, but I think that between what all you smoked and drank last night, you got enough shit floating around in your system to qualify for a detox clinic. Besides, I think Traci swiped the last one from you just before we left, this morning."

"Say what?" the lion snarled, jerking his irritated face around to look back at the bull. "Awww, maaaaan! Oughta pull that lil' mousie girl's tail till it's permanently straight, for that…"

The minotaur laughed. "Bud, you don't know the meaning of the phrase 'permanently straight'. You had enough boytoy and girl groupies clambering to get into your pants this weekend to damn near put you into rock star status."

"Stop jerkin' my chain," the lion mumbled. "And if we're anywhere near a convenience store, your shaggy ass better pull in so I can get me some cancer sticks." He sat up and blinked, then yawned toothily and scanned the scenery. Mostly desert as far as his eyes could see, the landscape and horizon broken only by cacti, the occasional road marker or billboard, and a bright blue sky filled with streaming sunlight. "Where are we, anyway?"

"Oh, 'bout thirty miles outta Tecumseh," Kal rumbled.

Rollins' brow perked. "Thirty miles? Damn, that's… " He ignored his hammering head to do some quick calculations, and he frowned. "That's gotta be a good three hundred miles out from the flats. Either you were hauling some serious ass, or… " Another thought slowly dawned on him, and he swallowed, rubbing his dry throat. "Shit. I must've really… " His green eyes widened behind his goggles, and he let out another, deeper groan of realization.

Kalek smirked again, even wider than before. The sound of him trying to suppress a roll of thundering laughter came out sounding like he was blowing snot.

The lion sighed, laying his head back against the headrest of his seat as the modified GTO tooled down the road, engine rumbling coolly. "Okay.

Damage control report time… " he muttered. "What happened?"

Kal glanced at him again, and then reached a muscled arm behind and around his seat, carefully balancing motions between reaching back with one hand and keeping hold of the wheel with the other. His thick fingers found and rummaged inside a paper bag that was sitting there, and he tugged out a tall black aluminum can with a stylized blue "M" on it, dropping it onto the lion's lap. "Maybe you better start swigging on that. Help flush your system so you can appreciate the dirt I'm about to lay on you."

Rollins stared dumbly at the can as he held it up and scrutinized it. "Monster. Lo-carb." He panned his gaze over to the bull, frowning. "My fave. You bought me my favorite drink, without me smacking you upside the head to get you to do it." He realized what that must mean, and he rumbled to the bull even as he popped the can open and lifted it to his lips, "Is it too late to take back my question?"

Kalek licked his lips slowly, the look on his face one of relish, as though he were about to tuck into a good dinner that he'd been waiting hours for. "Should I begin the sordid tale before, or after you started your little shake dance on top of the bar, clad only in a pair of boots and a G-string bikini?"

The lion coughed as some of the energy drink fluid nearly went up his nose, and he thumped his chest briskly as he shuddered. "Tell me you're kidding. I mean it. Lie to me if you have to."

"I think it was 'Danger Daize' that was up onstage when Mina pulled you up onstage with her, and she proceeded to pretend to give you a blow-job while a couple hundred screaming listeners cheered her on. But then, she always did think you were kinda cute. I'm guessing that you went back-stage after that last gig of theirs we saw in Toronto to do more than just give her flowers."

Rolly rolled his eyes and sighed, looking out the window of his side of the car as he shook his dark brown locks of mane firmly. "Mina's a sweet gal. And she's quite taken. She's screwing Donnelly, her lead guitarist, and has been since before the band got big, just in case you forgot," he scoffed, smacking the bull's heavy thigh with his palm playfully.

"Uhhh… yeah," Kal grunted, his muzzle twisting a bit in a grimace of disbelief as he rumbled, "And he's as bi as you are, if memory also serves… and, I do believe he introduced Mina to you after he picked you up in a gay bar last time they came downtown."

The feline scowled a bit and muttered through his fingers as he stroked his own mouth a little. "Fine. So they're both cute as hell, and they have an open relationship. And if you do both the folks in a couple when they're both present, it isn't like you're cheat—" He shifted in his seat, feeling suddenly fidgety, and he heard the soft crackle of something coming from his groin under his jeans. He frowned starkly down at himself and muttered, "There's something in my pants."

"Oh, no shit!" the bull laughed. "I think that something is the reason for most of last night's mayhem."

"I'm serious," the lion rumbled, unbuckling his belt so he could slip his hand into his groin. He rummaged around his cock with slowly moving fingers, grasping a few objects that were thin and papery. He pulled them out, and looked at them dully. "Hunh. Five-dollar bill and a phone number..." He squinted his eyes at the name scribbled above the digits, and had trouble making it out. "Damn, it's smudged. Kinda looks like...'Jamie'? 'Jumi'? Who the hell?" he muttered. He looked over at the bull. "Should I be very afraid, very insulted that he or she only slipped me a five-spot, or just nauseous?"

Kal shrugged and rumbled, "Can't say that the name rings a bell... but then, you'n me met a lotta folks, this weekend. Burning Man's huge, y'know. Besides, I was probably too busy taking blackmail pictures."

"Ooh. Speaking of photographs..." the lion grimaced, grunting softly as he felt something flat and slick against his ass. He pulled out a Polaroid snapshot, then stared at it, eyes widening. "Whoa. Dang, I'm sorry I was so drunk that I don't remember this."

"Eh?" Kalek murmured, glancing at the photo. "Gimme that." He grabbed the pic out of the lion's fingers, then held it closer, glancing at the thick black penis in it that looked vaguely equine. It was big enough to require two hands to hold it, one of the hands looking suspiciously like one of the lion's as thick bubbles of cum dappled the length, getting smeared onto the glistening shaft. "Oh, yeah! I remember this guy. Big ol' stallion, had you jerk him off on top of the bar during your little dance. Audience loved it."

"What?" Rollins gaped, staring at the bull with open mouth. "I jerked off a horse in front of a full house?"

The bull shrugged. "I don't recall anyone complaining. If I recall, the security guard on duty was too busy assbanging that little pink-punk haired Chihuahua chick. Been awhile since I've heard a gal cuss like that in Spanish."

"Sounds like it was quite the family moment," Rollins muttered, as he felt something else besides the natural equipment shifting in his underwear. He felt the slick plastic of a condom wrapper against his fingers, and sure enough, he pulled one out of his pants. He turned it over in his palm and sighed. "Ahh. An unopened rubber. At least I tried to use protection."

His bull pal stared at the condom, then down at the lion's crotch. "Holy crap, how much are you hauling down there, this morning?" he grunted. "You got a whole freakin' department store under yer balls. Let me have a turn," he rumbled, as he thrust his big hand over and down into the lion's boxers.

"Hey!" Rollins squawked in protest, his lap wriggling as the bull's thick fingers felt around his cock and gently nudged at his balls. "Cut it out, ya walking hamburger, those are my family jewels you're messing with."

"Yeah, yeah, boo-fuckin'-hoo…" the bull grunted. He kept one hand on the steering wheel as the fingers of his other hand came into contact with something plastic, and he tugged it out carefully. "What have we here?" He peered at the object, which turned out to be a woman's lipstick. Kal snickered, then uncapped it and read the color. "Demented. Looks like puke green. It'll go fabulous with your eyes," he grinned, as he tried to smear some of it on the lion's cheek.

Rollins grabbed the lipstick out of the bull's fingers, scowling again. "Kal, you're being a major pain in the ass. And watch the road," he grunted, pointing a fingerclaw out at the concrete as the mildly distracted bull tried to face paint him.

"Nope. 'Major pain in the ass' was probably what I was last night when you and me double-teamed that hot little puma dude in the bathroom," the bull smirked, shoving his hand back down into Rollins' underwear to quest for more items.

The lion gasped as the bull's fingers went to work again, grunting tightly as he murmured, "Ahhn… y-yeah, I think I do remember that part, actually… Thought he was gonna swallow my balls, he was sucking me so hard…" He glanced down at Kal's hand as it felt him up, then he looked over at the bull and rumbled, "How come you didn't get totally shitfaced, last night?" He noted Kalek's fingers slipping a bit on the steering wheel, and he reached over and helped steady it, giving the bull a slightly annoyed glance.

"Quit drinking last year, bud," Kal murmured as he tugged what looked to be a small glass vial full of powder out of the lion's groin. "Saw what Marty's car looked like after he wrapped it and himself around a telephone pole."

"Seriously?" Rolly rumbled, his eyes widening at the bull as he stared at him through the goggles. He let go of the steering wheel as the bull alternated between looking at the road, and studying the object he'd extracted from the lion's underwear. "Aww, wow. Kal, I'm sorry, I didn't know that

that was what happened to him. Hadn't seen him in a few months."

Kal replied, "Hey, you didn't know. I sure miss him, though. We had some fun times together, and he really would've had a blast with us if he'd been with us this weekend."

"Yeah," Rollins murmured quietly. He and the bull didn't speak for a moment, and he glanced over at the vial in the minotaur's palm. "What the hell's that?"

The bull didn't answer, but the way his thick brows were furrowing and the frown on his face didn't reassure the cat much. Kal dropped the vial onto Rollins' trench-coat, and the feline picked it up, peered at it, then took out the stopper and sniffed a bit at the contents. He jumped, then looked startled. He rolled down the window swiftly and chucked the vial out of it, his own face grim as he rolled the window back up again. "Great. Nose candy. That wouldn't have gone over well, if we'd gotten pulled over."

Kal tightened his grip on the wheel with both his hands for a moment, the leather around the steering wheel creaking softly. "Well, given where it was hidden, the cop probably wouldn't have found it unless he gave you a frisking, in which case he probably would've turned you on so much you probably would've offered to suck him off. And it's not like whoever gave that to you is probably gonna be anyone you'll ever see again."

Rollins grunted at his friend's reply, and scowled a bit. "Don't matter. That shit creeps me out. Smoking a joint's one thing, but coke's… mmph! Hey… " he grunted in protest, as Kalek's hand once again wormed their way down into his friend's underwear. "Dammit, will you knock that off?" he protested, his groin starting to wiggle as he gave out an involuntary little moan.

The bull was starting to deliberately stroke his fingers against the lion's foreskin, and when one of his fingers brushed over the feline's glans, it sent a ripple of shuddering pleasure through him that made his cock start to stiffen up a little bit. "Unnh! Okay, now you're starting to rummage the wrong way on purpose," he chuckled, giving the bull a sly grin.

"Says you," Kal rumbled, grinning right back at him as his fingers continued to fondle. Not immediately coming into contact with anything else, the bull managed to keep his grip on the wheel with one hand as his other hand tugged the lion's boxers down, enough to expose the feline's thick brown foreskin and heavy balls. He glanced down at his friend's cock, then smirked and shook his head in wonder as he wrapped his fingers around it and slowly started to stroke. Rollins' thick red glans began to play a gradual and repeated game of 'Peek-A-Boo', exposing itself through the skin like a Cyclops' eye one moment, then receding out of view as the secondary skin slid back over it and threatened to obscure it again, a tiny drop of pre squishing out of the feline's piss slit as the bull worked him. "Geez, lookit, you're starting to horn up again! You're the only guy I know who can still get it up even after a night of hard drinking and partying like the one you had last night, Rolly. I'm frigging envious."

Rollins leaned his head back against the seat and let his mouth hang open a bit, grinding his meat slowly through Kal's fist as he grunted to his friend, "T-... takin' advantage of sweet, innocent lil' me when I'm trying to recoup from a hangover... You mean, mean bull... "

"Hah. 'Innocent'! Another word you don't know the meaning of, bud," Kal smiled, keeping one hand firmly on the wheel as the other diligently masturbated the lion into a firmer state. "Speaking of, how'd that hot-looking little cherry number slinging drinks last night taste? I've never seen a group of folks intermingle a shot-drinking game and cunnilingus like that, before."

"Oh, the blonde vixen?" Rollins chuckled, in spite of his restless member. "I gotta admit, she tasted pretty damn fine—although for a moment, there, I think she had three tongues working her at once, including mine. Lousy logistics, but still fun." He paused, remembering, then chuckled. "We all found out real quick why they nicknamed her 'Squirt', though. And it ain't got anything to do with her being petite."

"I'll take your word for it," Kal rumbled, as he drew a warm thumb-pad several times across Rollins' exposed glans, smearing the pre that had collected there until the lion's cockhead glistened. "I got offers from some mighty cute ladies, last night, but I'm afraid that my tastes'll always lie with the sausage. 'Sides, I couldn't be sure how many of 'em were making those offers because they were legitimately interested in me, or because they were hoping to get their mitts on you."

Rollins gasped loudly as his midsection jerked upwards a bit, and he growled through snarling teeth to his friend, "Yaaah! D-dammit, Kal, you know how sensitive I am when you do that," Then he opened one of his eyes to give his friend a bit of a sharp look. "And cut that kinda thinking out. Jeez, Kalek, you're an absolute stud. Looked in a mirror lately, for proof?" he chuckled. "All that hard muscle of yours is starting to work its way into your brain, if that's honestly what you think."

"Yeah, but I'm not a pretty and popular little leo boy like you, am I?" the bull grinned, winking sideways at him.

The lion snorted, gripping the bull's hand and tightening his own fingers around the minotaur's own thick digits as he tried to get his friend to stroke him a bit faster. "You can pretty much cancel out the 'boy' in that phrase, thank you. I just turned twenty-six, remember? In gay terms, that's pretty much out to pasture."

"Don't even get me started on how much bullshit that is, Rolly. I am a bull. Nobody knows bullshit when he hears it like I do. Besides, you can't fool me, I've known you for too damn long. You had a great time, this weekend, and you needed it." He paused his rubbing to give the lion's firm nine inch cock a wiggling in his fist for emphasis, then he winked at the feline as he rumbled, "C'mon, admit it! You loved it, didn't you? The concert, the booze, the handfuls of folks trying to get you plastered so they could take advantage of you…"

"Mmm… All because of that damned group I'm in. That's all it is," Rollins moaned, closing his eyes again as he stroked Kalek's vein-latticed forearm. "Nobody knew who I was, before that happened, and even now, I get folks asking me about it." He opened his eyes and gave the bull a self-conscious look as he rumbled, "Although if you really think that anyone was trying to get to me through you this weekend, I apologize. Now that I've got total strangers wanting to score with the folks I work with, and trying to get me to fix 'em up, I know how crappy it feels." He rubbed Kal's fingers slowly, his brows creasing in temporary frustration. "Not that I can't identify with 'em, too. I've been praying for Heat to notice me ever since he joined up, and he won't gimme the time of day."

"You for real?" Kal rumbled, pausing his strokes on the lion's cock, for a moment. "Whoa. I knew you'd told me that you kinda had the hots for the mutt, but I didn't know that it went past the physical." He frowned a tad, then glanced at the cat again. "You sure it isn't just a fixation brought on by his pheromone thing? That's pretty powerful stuff, y'know."

Rollins shook his head resolutely. "He hardly uses those, even in the field. He hates 'em. Thinks they make him into a manipulative freak. Damn, I almost wish he would unload on me with 'em, because at least then, I'd have an excuse to jump his ass. I want him to seal that knot of his up my ass so bad, I can't stand it."

Kalek felt the lion's cock throb needfully in his hand as the cat imagined himself getting taken by his teammate, and he smirked as he rumbled to him, "Man, you really do want him bad! Your dick feels like it's got a steel core, the way it's throbbing in my fist."

The lion grunted. "Don't matter. He'll never notice me. Hell, he thinks I'm a total slut. How you like that one?" he chuckled, shaking his head ruefully at his friend. "He's the one who can make folks want to screw him just with his pheromones, and he thinks that I'm the slut. Go figure."

"I dunno if I'd call you a 'slut', exactly, pal, but let's be honest with ourselves—you do love your pussy and cock, don'tcha?" Kal grinned, winking at the lion. "Not that there's anything wrong with that, mind you. But maybe your canine pal has a different mindset, when it comes to relationships. Maybe he wants to settle down with just one guy or gal."

"Guy," Rollins corrected. "He's most definitely roving on routine cock patrol, only."

"Ahh. Well, in that case, maybe you should fix him up with me. I don't have any super powers, but I've been told that I make a pretty mean crème brulée and that I give some damn good back massages," Kalek offered.

"Join the queue line of wistful thinkers like everyone else," Rollins chuckled. "And jeez, keep your eyes on the road! I like you playing with my dick, but I don't want us to have a wreck." Noticing that the bull was inadvertently tooling the car gradually over the centerline of the highway, he gripped the wheel and guided it back into the right lane once more.

Kalek looked forward, then shook his head at his absent-mindedness and pulled the car over onto the shoulder of the road. "Looks like I'm so focused on taking care of business, that I'm not watching my driving."

Rollins cocked his head at the bull, looking mock-angry. "Oh, 'business'? That's how you refer to the act of jerking me off?"

Kalek turned sideways in the seat to face him, his expression intent. "No. I should've called it the 'business of giving you pleasure', because I take it seriously. And speaking of… " He leaned his head and upper body over, gripping Rollins' cock carefully as his tongue lapped up the rivulet of warm pre that was drooling down the side of the cat's foreskin. Rollins shivered and groaned softly, his hand reflexively coming down to nestle itself into the bull's thick head of top-hair. Kalek felt the weight of Rollins' hand on the back of his head and neck, and his own cock stirred firmly in his jeans as he rumbled very lowly, "I think you remember how I like to do it." And with that, he tugged the feline's foreskin back, exposed his friend's glistening cockhead, and engulfed the cat's upper prick in his mouth, swirling his long, thick tongue around the glans as he flicked his tongue tip gently in and out of the lion's foreskin.

The feline gasped hotly as he leaned back in the seat, having to tilt the backrest backward some with the manual lever to give Kal's considerably broad upper body some room. "Unnnh…" he groaned, his eyelids flickering. "Fuck… Kal, are y-you insane? Cop might see us!"

The bull didn't answer, his head and frame slowly engulfing Rollins' cock whole. He pushed his lips down until they nudged firmly against the lion's furry balls, using disciplined breath control to keep it hilted deep. The lion's protests died out quickly in a whimper of delight as his fingers dug into his friend's hair, and a pleased and muffled rumble of response vibrated around the cat's cock, shivering it to the core.

Slowly, Rollins started to ease his hips up and down, his glistening cock sliding in and out of Kalek's warm mouth as he felt the bull's saliva trickling down his shaft. If he could have seen the corners of the bull's mouth, he would've noticed both edges of it quirking upward in a satisfied smirk as the big fellow's head started to bob rhythmically over the lion's crotch. The cat gripped one of the bull's horns and give it a light shake, making his friend snort thickly into his testicle fur, and the lion's form was almost blotted out completely as the bull's profile overshadowed most of his seat. The lion tried to keep his thrusts slow and gradual at first, the bull starting to bob his head up and down a bit less to make the feline pump upward harder with his hips. Rollins knew what the bull was up to, and his body tried to resist—and almost as soon as the thought entered his mind, he felt the bull's thick, firm fingers gripping his thigh in an iron grip so tight it actually hurt a little. The rippling pleasure he felt radiating from his cock was ignored for a moment as needles of pain sang out from his leg and thigh, and he jerked in his seat hard.

"Oww! Dammit, Kal..." he panted softly, the pace of his thrusts picking up a bit as sweat started to congeal on his brow. "O—okay, okay... ! Have it your way, ya ornery fucker..." And with that, he began to hump his balls and lap briskly up against Kal's face, the bull holding his visage hovered and still over the lion's cock as the slippery foreskin slicked in and out of his mouth, glistening dully. The lion's furry sac slapped firmly against Kal's clefted chin as he mated rampantly with his friend's mouth, and the bull's warm breath blasted Rollins' groin on each pass.

"Mmmn... feels so f-fuckin' good..." Rollins moaned, his head lolling a bit on the headrest as his fingers curled into Kal's thick black top-hair. "Jeezus, man, I love it w-when ya... let me use yer mouth as my t—temporary pussy..." His legs and hips pumped faster still, and his words elicited a sharp flick from Kal's ears and a heady groan from the big minotaur's throat. Kalek's thick hand smacked the back portion of Rollins' thigh, wordlessly commanding him to face fuck him harder, and Rollins obeyed, his eyes shut tight and panting openly as the bull's tongue flicked in and out of the lion's foreskin. The bull teased and caressed the lion's slick cockhead with his tongue with all the skill of a five-hundred dollar evening escort, and Rollins found his gonads melting into a tingly sort of butter as they veered him straight toward shooting his load with each smack they made against the bull's lips.

Kal seemed to sense how close Rollins was, and he upped the ante at the last minute by shoving one burly hand up and under the lion's shirt to seize and tug at the feline's nipple ring. He tugged it downward firmly, while at the same time his other hand muscled its way up and under the lion's bouncing testicles until it slid up his friend's posterior cleft, fumbling for his companion's snug pucker. His digit slick with drool, the bull nudged it up against the lion's opening, then burrowed it inside, easing a finger that was easily a good five inches long by itself up until it pressed the lion's inner gland like a joy buzzer. Rollins' head shot back and his teeth bared themselves fiercely, his arms clinging to the bull's head as he felt himself start to climax.

"Nggh... F-Fuck... Gonna... cum... Mmnnh!" The lion jerked his groin firmly upward and buried the bull's face in it as he felt his balls spasm, and he clung to Kalek's frame as thick bursts of warm lion semen burst into the bull's mouth and spackled themselves against the back of the mino-taur's throat. The large bovine swallowed each gout of cum patiently, throat working without spilling a drop as Rollins' head snapped wildly back and forth, a roar of release vibrating the interior of the car as Kalek continued the pressure on the cat's prostrate and on his friend's taut nipple. It took a minute or two for Rollins' testicles to fully empty themselves, and a good four minutes after that for his body to stop jerking in aftershocks of plea-sure from the bull's services. Kalek let go of the lion's strained nipple, but he kept his finger slid firmly up the lion's inner passageway until he was confident that he'd drank every drop of spunk there was to be had. Then he slowly withdrew his finger and slid his head off the lion's cock, with flopped wetly against the feline's abs. The cat's eyes were lidded, and his muzzle hanging open, ragged, panting breaths gasping from his throat as he stared weakly at his friend.

"Mmm. Now that's what I call a fuckin' protein shake," Kal rumbled, glancing out the back window of the car, then out the driver's side window to make sure that there was not indeed a policeman or tourist to be seen.

"Shit," Rollins chuckled softly, as he began to get his wind back. "All the action I got last night, and I'll be damned if being sucked off by you wasn't better than the rest!"

Kalek snorted as he checked his face in the rearview mirror to see if the lion's rampant face-thrusts had bloodied his nose. "You're a bullshit liar, but you're a cute bullshit liar," he smirked. "Although given that I don't do that for just anybody, it damn well better have felt good!"

"Hey, I can't help it if folks don't know that you occasionally like to be the sub, in an oral sense," Rollins chuckled.

"And they better not find out from you, either, 'cause if they do, I'm gonna kick your ass!" the bull rumbled, swinging his gaze from the mirror to the cat, still grinning as he did so. He pointed a burly finger at the feline and waggled it at him in mock menace. "I may not have a bunch of high-powered compadres like you, but that don't mean that I wouldn't be able to get my revenge on ya, somehow."

"Shut up and c'mere," Rollins grinned, quirking a finger at the bull and pointing at his own face.

"What, you wanting round two?" Kalek rumbled, looking surprised and amused. "Forget it, pussycat. I'm already gonna be scraping your aftertaste off my tongue for the next five hou—mmph!" The feline shut his friend up by gripping the back of the bull's burly head and drawing him in close for a warm, deep kiss, sliding his semi-rough tongue into the bull's mouth and caressing Kalek's own tongue and mouth with surprising tenderness. The bull squirmed at first, but then gave into the kiss and returned it, both males with eyes closed. Rollins basked in the warm glow of his friend's total masculinity and musky scent, his tongue tasting just a hint of his own orgasm from moments before. He drew the kiss out for as long as he could, and when it ended, Kalek opened his eyes and gave the lion a shy smirk and a quizzical look. "Well. What was that for, hunh?"

Rollins brought both hands up and cradled the bull's face in them, staring bluntly into the minotaur's dark eyes. "For dragging my ass out of H.Q. and showing me a wonderful time this weekend. I really needed this. You've always known how to get me to loosen up, Kal."

"Goddamn right," the bull grinned, rubbing noses with the feline as he straightened back up and sat back down in the driver's seat, then roared the car to life as he guided the car back onto the road. "And your scraggly ass better not ever forget it, either."

"Hey, why we leaving so soon? I can't let you drive in your current condition!" Rollins laughed, reaching over to fondle the bull's own groin, which was swollen with the erect minotaur cock that was straining at Kalek's jeans.

"Sure ya can. And don't you worry, I plan on letting you repay my little oral kindness when we get to a hotel room, tonight. Meanwhile, we're gonna stop at the next greasy spoon we find, and you're gonna buy me breakfast," the bull said.

"You mean my own grease wasn't filling enough?" Rollins grinned, leaning back in his seat and taking another swig of the energy drink. "Must be more like oriental food. Half an hour later, you'll be hungry for more of it."

Kalek shook his head good-naturedly and slipped on his sunglasses as the car roared down the road. "Hanging around with your group has done made you delusional, bud."

Nerves and Roses

Angst and romance. Hope for connection and fear of rejection, anyone who's been in that stomach-churning stage before a potential relationship can relate to that sense of powerlessness and paranoia.

In "My Place in Your Life" this is taken a little further, the story rather daringly combines some genuinely hot sex with a genuinely engaging relationship tale involving the protagonist's deep uncertainty about his emotional position in a sexual ménage a trois.

Such a combination could easily slip into self-satisfying angst couched amid torrid sex, but the author pulls off a careful balance, that wonderful trick that meakes the difference between pornography and erotica: sex serves character, character serves plot, plot serves emotional journey.

My Place In Your Life

K. M. Hirosaki

Jasper looked at me across the table with his icy blue husky eyes, and the look in them made me feel worse for not feeling better. I shrunk back into my chair and stared down at my hands, folded atop the table. He tilted his head to the side and reached his arm out, taking one of my hands in his. "What's wrong, Shon?" he asked. "Are you upset about something you're not telling me about?"

I lifted my head back up and gazed back into his kind face. "Nothing's wrong," I replied. That was a lie. Well, not really. I suppose the situation needs explaining.

It was a few months back when I first met Jasper. We were both regulars at this all-night snack shop that's on the corner of Rayce and Blossom. I work late, a lot of nights, so I'd usually end up drifting in around midnight or so. The place only has three tables, and it was never crowded at that time of night, so when someone else would stop by to grab a bite to eat, chances are it would be someone you recognized. Jasper was one of these fellows. And it didn't take that many times running into him for me to notice that he was checking me out.

Like I said, Jasper's a husky. He's a very handsome husky at that. He's only three or four years older than I am, but he looks a lot older than that. But he doesn't look older in a way that makes him look 'old', really. He just looks more grown up. It might be that the fur that frames his face is more of a deep, intense gray than an actual black color. Or possibly it's the way that he carries himself so that he comes across as sporty at yet still mature.

Then again, maybe I just look young.

In my own opinion, I'm nothing special to look at. Being a wolf and all, it wouldn't be that difficult for me to get myself toned up, but I'm just lazy about that sort of thing. I'm left with my own share of body fat plus extra, but my shoulders are naturally on the broad side, so that helps a little in making me not look fat. At least not too fat. So I guess I'm not ugly or anything, but I was still surprised that someone like Jasper (who I definitely consider better-looking) would be checking me out.

To make a long story short, Jasper and I started going out. Just casually, mind you—you know, two guys who have an interest in one another hanging out with one another. He was—is—a really sweet guy, and I love him to death. And therein lies the problem.

Jasper and I really clicked, right from the beginning, and it didn't take much time for us each to realize that there was a spark between us. Then Jasper had to lay down the news that he was already taken.

His boyfriend was another husky named Luke. To be fair, Jasper hadn't been keeping secrets from me. It had just never come up. But once he realized that I was interested in him as more than just a friend, he was obligated to mention it.

Actually, he wasn't really obligated to, and so I'm thankful that he did. He and Luke are allowed to see other people outside of their relationship, so long as they let each other know. I could have felt betrayed, but I didn't. Jasper could have just kept all of that from me, but he didn't.

I was given a few days to think about things. Jasper had offered to let me meet Luke first before committing to anything, but I didn't want to. At the time, it was easier to pretend he didn't exist. And so the next time I saw Jasper, I told him that I was okay with the idea of being with him even if he did have someone else. That night, we went back to my place, and he made love to me (and I don't use the term lightly). And the look in those wonderful eyes of his just... spoke to me, and somehow I just knew that he cared about me.

So here I was with Jasper, looking back at him across the table. And I knew he knew me better than to believe me when I said nothing was wrong.

"I can just tell Luke you're not interested, you know," Jasper said, keeping his voice as calm as always.

"But... I don't know. I've never been with two folks at once before." Yes, you heard me right. This was what I was being hesitant about.

"It was just a suggestion. He just thought you might like it. I don't think he was implying anything by it," Jasper replied.

I had to admit it. I found the prospect intriguing, and actually pretty arousing. But I wasn't sure I could bring myself to go through with it. And it wasn't because of Luke, either.

Luke's arguably better-looking than Jasper. They look a lot alike, actually. If you saw them together and didn't know them, you would probably think that Luke was a younger brother and not a lover. He and Jasper were both the same age, but Luke just looked younger; he was the shorter of the two, as well, closer to my own height.

When I first met Luke, I'd been expecting to feel really awkward. I was waiting for the rush of jealousy to start filling me, but it didn't. In fact, Luke and I really got along well right from moment one. Even seeing him together with Jasper, exchanging those little touches that lovers do... it just didn't bother me. I wish for the life of me that it would, but it didn't. I wanted to be upset with Jasper for being with me when there was someone else that he loved, but I couldn't. And it felt odd to me, as I guess you can imagine.

With the three of us together, it felt like being among old friends I'd known for years, even though it had only been a few months. Three friends, inseparable... until the day would end, and I would have to go my way, and Jasper and Luke would go theirs. It was only at those times—when they'd still be together, and I'd just be on my own—that I ever really thought about the two of them as the couple that they were.

"I'm flattered by the proposal, honestly," I said to Jasper. And I meant it.

"I sense a 'but' coming up here," Jasper said.

I swallowed a tiny lump in my throat and tried to think of how to phrase myself. "It's just that... I didn't know that Luke thought of me that way..."

Jasper rubbed his fingertips along my wrist. "Come on, you know that Luke really likes you," he said. "And you mean a lot to me, and he thinks—we think—that it might nice if we could both be close to you."

I was too shocked to respond right away. On more than one level, Jasper had a point. Luke and I were good friends, but I was afraid of getting to know him on his own. I had never even been around him on his own without Jasper, because part of me wouldn't let myself file him under anything besides 'Jasper's boyfriend'.

So, if it was true that Jasper really wanted me to be a part of his life, then it was a good sign that Luke was okay with that.

"I'll do it," I said quietly, nodding my head. Jasper smiled back at me with the same grin he always had when he was happy.

There was a single flicker of doubt as soon as Jasper, Luke and I arrived at their house the next night, but it went away as quickly as it had come. We had gone out, eaten dinner, had a good time, and had now come back to their home. The only difference was that this time, I wouldn't be leaving right away like I always had before.

Luke walked off into the laundry room to take care of a few things he had left undone earlier. Jasper took me with him into the bedroom. As if on autopilot, I sat down on the edge of the bed and folded my legs to the side. Jasper sat down beside me and rubbed his hand at my lap. "Are you sure you want to do this, Shon?" he asked. "If you're not, just say the word."

I shook my head. "No, I do," I replied, turning my head and resting it on his shoulder. I put my arm around his waist and held myself close to him, breathing in his scent. I could tell that he was getting turned on at the prospect of what was imminent, and I didn't blame him. My own pants were certainly feeling a bit tight and confining.

Jasper touched my cheek and turned my head up, leaning down into a kiss. I let him slide his tongue into my mouth, and I sucked on it gently as it moved around. His large, broad hands slid against my back, up under the back of my shirt. My heart beat faster as he touched me, and I wrapped both of my arms around him and pulled myself as close against him as I possibly could, my tongue pressing deep into his mouth. Control and restraint always seemed to go right out the window whenever things started to get heated between me and Jasper.

I felt one of Jasper's hands move down between my thighs before he suddenly drew back away from me. Both of us turned in sync and faced the doorway. There was Luke, leaning against the doorframe, doing a good job of mimicking a stereotypical clothing catalogue pose. In an instant, Luke went from being a friend whom I'd only ever thought of platonically and turned into an object of lust. I had always admitted that he was attractive, but in that moment, his toned canine form was just so striking.

"I leave you two alone for one minute and already you're at it. This should be fun," he said, his grin wide on his face.

Luke's furry tail wagged from side to side as he stood upright and walked softly over toward us, the hard-on in his pants plain to see. I reluctantly let go of Jasper as he stood up to embrace his lover. Jasper pulled Luke into a slow, passionate kiss, just as he had done with me only seconds before. The two huskies rubbed their hands all up and down each other's bodies, and I could see just how well they knew each other in that regard. In a movement that was almost too fluid for me to believe, Jasper pulled Luke's shirt off, and then immediately afterward Luke did the same to Jasper. It was almost like watching synchronized swimming, just a lot sexier.

They closed the gap between themselves again, black and white fur shifting in all directions as they both continued to touch one another all over.

Jasper hooked one arm around Luke's upper back and reached down between their bodies with his other hand. He deftly undid Luke's belt and his zipper, then hooked his fingers inside of the fabric and pushed his lover's pants and underwear off. Luke's legs were thin enough that the pants fell right around his ankles once they were past the widest curve of his hips.

I got a kind of rush I'd never felt before as I saw my friend naked for the first time. His shaft stuck up hard and full, pressed into Jasper's belly-fur. I could hear him moan into the other husky's muzzle as he went and unfastened Jasper's pants in return, fumbling a bit more than Jasper had, but still succeeding in getting them off in a matter of seconds. These two guys were good at making me feel unpracticed and prudish.

I was practically mesmerized as I watched Luke and Jasper. Obviously, I knew that Jasper and Luke had sex, but I'd never actually sat there and pictured it. Now, seeing the two of them like this was turning me on more than I could have imagined. Nude, the look of family resemblance they had was even stronger, and it gave the scene a sort of incestuous edge that I knew wasn't really there, and for some reason, that just made it hotter to watch.

Jasper reached his black-furred hand down and wrapped it around both Luke's shaft and his own, and began to stroke slowly. I was transfixed, my own erection straining against my pants as I watched the man I loved playing with another. So far, the ménage à trois hadn't even technically begun yet, but I was already seeing the wonderfully naughty appeal of it all, up close and personal. As if he were reading my mind, Luke opened one of his eyes and looked sideways at me as he and Jasper continued to kiss. There was a mischievous glimmer in that look that killed the last lingering doubts I'd had about agreeing to do this.

Luke broke off the kiss and pulled back slowly, a tiny strand of saliva stretching out between their mouths briefly before it snapped. He gasped quietly as Jasper kneaded his palm firmly against their slick tips. "Now, honey," Luke said. "Let's not get too carried away in front of Shon, here. It's not fair to just make him watch." He reached down and carefully pried Jasper's hand away, and Jasper gave him a quick lick on the cheek before they both stepped back over to edge of the bed where I sat.

Without warning, Luke put both hands on my shoulders and bent down to kiss me. Instinct made me put up resistance for a fleeting moment, but then I opened my mouth for him, kissing him for the first time. I thought that I could taste Jasper on his tongue, and I whimpered subconsciously as one of Luke's hands ran down my side and down over to the zipper of my pants, wasting no time. He popped the button free and pulled the zipper down, then pushed forward on my shoulder with his other hand.

I lay down on my back, dazed and still, and Luke hovered over me as he reached down into my pants. I let out a moan of contentment as I felt the warm, bristly fur on his fingers, those digits wrapping around my shaft. "Mmmm… I love how warm and hard you are," he whispered into my ear as he slid his hand up and down my length, getting it slick with my fluids.

I felt the bed shift as Jasper lay down beside my head. I turned to look him in eyes and smiled at him. Luke began to bite and nibble gently at my now-exposed neck, causing me to close my eyes and murr happily for a moment before I looked back at Jasper. He was still grinning at me, and he petted me between the ears. "No second thoughts, hon?" he asked.

I looked down at my hard member as Luke jerked it slowly, then back into Jasper's eyes and gave him a teasing grin. "Does it look to you like I'm having second thoughts?" I said.

Jasper chuckled and ruffled my fur. "Then I hope you enjoy this," he said, sitting up. Luke let go of me and pulled my pants off of my legs. I sat up and took my shirt off, tossing it onto the floor. Now, I was naked, and I had a pair of naked huskies kneeling on the bed to either side of me, staring at my body in silence.

After a pause that I couldn't even measure, Luke said, "He really is a lovely young wolf, dear. I can see why you like him."

"True," Jasper said with a grin. "It's not just that, though." My heart fluttered in my chest, and I felt foolish, but being complimented like that, especially in front of Luke, made me feel wonderful. I was being overrun with dual emotions: the raw eroticism of knowing that Jasper was going to share me with his lover, and the warm reassurance that Jasper cared for me on more than just a physical level. It was an unusual mingling of feelings to deal with, but I was too overwhelmed to care.

Luke crawled over and straddled my chest, reaching down to pet my cheek and my ear. The tip of his wet, musky-smelling cock was inches from my chin, and I licked the side of my muzzle on pure reflex. Luke turned and looked to Jasper, who hadn't moved. "Do you mind if I take his mouth for a while?" Luke asked, running his hand over the side of my muzzle. I noticed that Luke was switching back and forth between talking to me, and talking *over* me, as if I wasn't there—as if I were an object. Part of me felt bad for liking that.

"That's really up to him," Jasper replied, petting my other cheek. Luke locked his gaze with me and I went to open my mouth to speak, but he placed a finger down on my lips, silencing me. I just looked up into his eyes and nodded, and without a word, he sidled further up my chest. Slowly, I ran my tongue along the underside of his shaft as it came into reach.

I closed my eyes and moaned quietly as the taste of his warm canine fluids hit my tongue. Once again, the taste was reminiscent of Jasper, but was distinctly its own flavor. I leaned my head forward and took his cock into my snout with total eagerness, letting my tongue work in a spiral as I did. Luke put one of his hands on my shoulder and stroked one of my ears reassuringly with the other while his fluffy tail wagged back and forth, tickling my belly. It spurred me to suck on him harder, and his dull moaning let me know I was doing a good job.

The mattress shifted next to me, letting me know that Jasper had gotten up off the bed. I couldn't see him, Luke's body blocked my view, but I wasn't planning on looking anyway. For the time being, my concentration was fixed on licking and sucking the hot, firm shaft that filled my mouth. Luke was drizzling freely, and I swallowed him down, relishing the taste.

I suddenly pulled off of Luke's throbbing shaft and yelped in surprise. Jasper had just tickled one of my feet, and I heard him laugh at my reaction. Luke patted me on the side and chuckled. I smiled up at him and wrapped my thumb and forefinger around the base of his hard cock, taking it back into my mouth again, and he went back to caressing my ear as I bobbed my head back and forth along his length.

My tail bristled when what must have been Jasper's hand ran along it, up to its base. My own cock quivered and trembled in the air as I anticipated his touch. But it was not to come. Without warning, Jasper slurped his tongue up underneath my balls, lapping at my hole. My whole body tensed up in pleasant shock, and I had to concentrate hard in order to not gasp out in pleasure again or, even worse, accidentally clamp down on the dick in my mouth. Jasper licked in tiny circles at my tight entrance, and I let a small moan out around Luke's shaft.

Jasper put both of his paws on my thighs and pressed his tongue up inside of me. The feeling of it wriggling around, warm and wet, made my still-unattended cock strain with welled-up excitement. Luke started to rock back and forth slightly, slowly fucking in and out of my muzzle. I sucked harder, my mouth forming a loose seal around his moving shaft as I swirled my tongue around it, paying special attention to the tip. For the first time, Luke started to make pitiful noises as I teased his drizzling slit.

Luke firmly grabbed onto the fur between my ears and pulled my head back, his cock sliding out of my mouth with a wet popping sound. He ruffled my whiskers and smiled at me. "Easy, there. You're a bit too good at that. Don't wanna get off quite so soon," he said, before leaning back and brushing the fringe of his tail over my crotch, making me giggle.

My brain suddenly registered something in the tone of Luke's voice, and it made my concentration falter. Luke's voice was just that: Luke's voice. This was one of my best friends, not a lover. I just didn't think of him in that way, and all of a sudden I began to feel really weird about what I was doing.

A instant later, I put the thought out of my mind and stopped caring, as I felt Jasper take hold of my legs and wrap them around his waist as he stood up. He reached out and grabbed onto my cock, causing me to let out an airy sigh of pleasure. Then he sidled up to the bed and positioned his own warm, wet shaft up against my rear. He shifted back and forth, letting it rub in between my furred cheeks, over my spit-dampened hole. A shiver ran up from the base of my spine to my brain as I thought about what it felt like whenever Jasper fucked me, and my body trembled in anticipation.

Luke got off of my chest and laid his head next to mine, his body stretched out in the opposite direction. I could see Jasper now, standing there, looking at me with his loving smile. I nodded to him, and then the other handsome husky put his mouth to mine again, our tongues entwining with the passionate familiarity of long-time lovers. I let out a sharp whimper into Luke's muzzle as I felt Jasper start to bear down on me, the wide head of his plump cock pushing at my entrance, just beginning to spread me open. With a sudden, tiny thrust, Jasper's tip slipped inside of me, but whatever cry I tried to make was muffled by Luke's tongue working around in my mouth.

I moaned out into Luke's muzzle as his boyfriend started to bury his shaft within me. The pain and discomfort were distinct, but Jasper was being careful, like he always was. I would tense up and shudder; he would stop for a few moments before pushing in further. He was fairly thick, and I was tight, with the result being an overwhelming sense of fullness as he penetrated me. Luke wrapped his arms around me, and the feeling of having a warm husky body on either end of me made me tingle sublimely.

Soon, Jasper's length was fully embedded in my tight passage, and he rubbed his hands at my stomach in wide circular motions, intended to soothe me. I wagged my tail between his legs ecstatically, wanting so badly to feel him pounding into me. I knew that he wouldn't, though, because Jasper was just like that. He'd take his time, making sure not to hurt me. I was so far lost to lust and passion, though, that I wasn't sure I'd mind if he did.

The kiss ended as Luke pulled back away from me and stared deep into my eyes with a lascivious gleam. He crawled alongside my body, looking up at Jasper. Jasper reached down and stroked the back of his head, and Luke

204

wagged his tail happily, positioning himself over me on all fours before lowering his head to swirl his tongue around the tip of my shaft. Above my muzzle dangled his nicely-shaped balls, along with his bright pink erection jutting out, framed by the fur of his crotch. I leaned up in order to take his cock back into my mouth, but my body froze as Jasper suddenly pulled out of me and quickly thrust back in.

Jasper's member slamming into me made me emit a yelp that turned into a whimper as Luke suckled down hard on my cock. I had never been so pleasured from both spots at once before, and my mind spun trying to make heads and tails of the mixing sensations. Jasper built up to a steady, gentle lovemaking pace, which somehow felt synchronized with Luke's incredible sucking. For half a second, I wondered if Luke sucked off Jasper more often than the other way around, or if Luke just had more natural talent. Not bothering to dwell on it, I again lifted my head up, and this time succeeded in getting Luke's warm shaft back into my mouth.

My nose pressed up into Luke's furred sac, and my consciousness began to swim in a mess of hormones and pheromones. I slid my tongue all up and down the husky's cock, wrapping my arms up around his lower back to hold my head up. Jasper began to pump in and out me a bit faster as his size loosened me up and made it steadily easier for him. I fixated on just pleasuring Luke with my mouth and tongue in order to distract myself, waiting for the pain and discomfort to fade.

Luke stopped sucking and threw his head back, yipping loudly as he suddenly began to spurt out into my muzzle. His warm, thick fluids shot out in a series of bursts that splattered onto my tongue and slid down to my throat. I did my best to not choke or sputter, and I swallowed it all as he came harder for those few remaining seconds. The strong taste lingered, a light, sticky film still coating the inside of my mouth. Luke's legs wobbled and he almost collapsed on top of me, his head resting lazily in my lap as his chest grew and shrank against my belly with his loud panting.

Now that Luke had stopped sucking on me, and vice versa, all of my attention was riveted on Jasper, taking me as deeply as he could. He would thrust his hips forward fast, then pull back out slowly to his tip, then thrust back in. My breathing was punctuated by his pumping rhythm, and all I could hear for a few moments was my pulse rushing within my head. The room seemed to go dim, and I thought that I was going to faint until I realized that my eyes were just partly closed due to the waves of pleasure crashing through my entire body.

Jasper started to ram into me harder, and I waited for him to hit his climax and fill me with his seed, but he suddenly pulled out of me and stopped. I propped myself up on my elbows and looked to the edge of the bed to see what had happened. Luke's hands were resting on Jasper's hips, and the smaller husky looked up into the taller one's eyes. Jasper gazed back down at him as if there were nothing unusual happening, but I could see his cock twitching even from where I was, and I could tell that he had been very close to finishing himself off inside of me.

"Is something wrong, Luke?" Jasper asked in a whisper, petting him behind one of his ears.

Luke craned his head back and knelt submissively on the bed. "Will you let Shon fuck me, honey?" he asked quietly.

Jasper's eyes met mine. "Would you like that?" he asked me, his hand still absent-mindedly stroking Luke's head and ears.

One look at Luke's face was all that I needed. He had gone from being an in-control dog, getting me to suck him off, to a needy, willing vessel hoping to repay the favor of pleasure back to me. Both huskies looked me expectantly, and I swallowed the breath stuck in my throat and said, "Yes."

Excited, Luke turned to the side and got onto all fours. He wagged his tail at me slowly as I crawled up behind him and brought myself to my knees. He looked back over his shoulder at me with wide eyes as I put both of my hands at his hips. "Don't worry about hurting me," he said, "I just want you to mount me and have your way with me." With that, he lifted his tail up and raised his rump, and I knew that that's how he really wanted it. Truthfully, I wasn't big on hurting folks, but I'd try not to hesitate. I pressed myself up against his hole, and immediately he tried to bear back against me.

I got a firm grip on Luke's hips and pushed as hard as I could, and he yelped in shock as I made it past his clenched ring and fell forward so fast that before I could stop myself my balls smacked against his and I was suddenly completely inside him. His body shook and his head went back with a loud, rumbling moan. "Oh, that's it, Shon," he groaned. "Now take me like I'm your little bitch!" I had never imagined that Luke had this kind of side to him—but being inside him felt so good, and I wanted to make him happy, too, so I began to pound in and out of his rear as hard as I possibly could, relying on a more base canine instinct that I didn't tend to let myself feel. My balls were tense and heavy between my legs, and I knew I wouldn't be able to last very long.

As I rocked back and forth into Luke's nice, tight backside, Jasper stepped up onto the bed. He raised one leg and stepped over Luke's back, standing over him, facing me. His cock stuck out in front of my face, and I didn't even stop to think about anything before I leaned my head forward and slurped him into my muzzle. He made no noise, and only cradled the back of my head gently. I kept my mouth on his shaft and looked up into his face. The situation began to feel wrong again; I was trying use my eyes to convey to Jasper how much I loved him, despite that I was at the same time fucking his boyfriend.

Jasper must have seen the emotions come through on my face, because he stroked my muzzle softly and said, "Everything's okay, dear; don't worry." I closed my eyes and just sucked harder. Luke was panting and shaking all over, his insides clenching and unclenching around my driving cock. It was all too much and I went over the edge, emptying myself into him as I whimpered out around Jasper's long shaft and clamped my muzzle down around him firmly.

Luke's legs gave out on him, and he flopped down onto the mattress, causing it to shake. I had to struggle a bit to keep Jasper's cock in my mouth, so I sucked on him harder, holding him in place with my tongue. Jasper's legs continued to shake after the mattress had stopped, however, and an instant later, I got my second mouthful of husky for the evening. His grip shifted from my head to my shoulders, and he let out a just-audible moan as he spurted again and again into my muzzle.

I licked Jasper's head and shaft clean and then leaned back, smiling up at him. He laughed happily and carefully stepped down off of the bed, then sat down between me and Luke. Luke hadn't gotten back up yet, so he just rolled onto his back, a look of glowing satisfaction on his face. I looked back and forth between him and Jasper and chuckled under my breath as the rush of orgasm slowly faded.

"That was... amazing," Luke muttered, closing his eyes and flitting his tail. "Thanks for finding this one, love," he said as he plopped a hand down on Jasper's thigh.

The twinges of guilt and doubt within me suddenly exploded into full-on intensity. Had I just made a huge mistake? Had I been stupid to think that this was supposed to have been anything emotional? Was I even Luke's friend, or was I just some outlet for kinky sex? And what about Jasper... Jasper and me, Jasper and Luke...

Jasper put his arms around me and dragged me down with him as he lay down. I was on one side of him, and Luke was on the other. I was betting that he felt like a pretty lucky guy, having the two of us. What I was wondering now was if I really should have been there at that moment at all.

I loved Jasper. I really, honestly, truly did. And I could only hope that he loved me back. I liked Luke, but I didn't love him. At least, I didn't love him like I loved Jasper. I couldn't even begin to think of what I might have meant to Luke, and I was pretty sure I didn't want to.

I lost track of time as I lay there in Jasper's arms, with Luke's arms over those. I just wanted to fall asleep and stop thinking. Most of me was happy—ecstatic , even.

But the rest of me knew that I couldn't be content. Not until I knew—once and for all, one way or the other—what I was, and what I meant to two men whose bed I now shared.

To make a long story short, I fell asleep still feeling awkward, woke up still feeling awkward, had breakfast with the two huskies and then went back to my place, all while still feeling awfully, painfully awkward. That, and it's all a bit hard to remember after that point.

I'm not sure I can really explain just what the jumble of emotions in my head was like after that. I don't even know if the right words exist for it. Maybe if they did, my feelings would have been easier to make sense of. As it was, I wasn't so lucky. The simplest way to put it is that I was overrun with confusion and doubt, but that's just *too* simple, really.

There wasn't any progress with my own thoughts until a few weeks later, when Jasper finally said something that pointed me in the right direction.

As with a lot of our meaningful conversations, we'd just finished having sex. I nestled my head down into the pillows as Jasper put one arm around me and stroked between my ears with his other hand. The tall husky snuggled up behind me, and I could feel his sticky, spent cock press up against my back as his erection began to go down. My nostrils twitched a little as I inhaled the scent of sex that was thickly overlaying the air in the room.

Very often, Jasper and I would just lie there after making love with neither of us saying a word for several minutes. This was one of those times. I was content to simply relax and listen to the sounds of him breathing, and the sound of my own heart pounding in my chest as the afterglow slowly took me over. Everything else seemed insignificant when I was in the arms of my lover... or at least, that's how things used to be. Lately, the nagging voice in the back of my brain had been getting louder and louder. And I didn't like what it was trying to tell me.

Jasper prodded me in the back with one of his hands. "You okay, hon?" he asked, and I could hear the concern in his voice. "You're quieter than usual." Apparently, I'd been spacing out as much as I'd thought. The past few times I'd slept with Jasper, I always ended up thinking about the time a few weeks before when we had been joined by Luke.

I liked to think that Jasper really did love me. I wasn't sure, but I honestly did think it. But at the same time, I couldn't help but think that he loved

Luke more, because he'd loved Luke first. Their relationship was still fine, as near as I could tell, and I didn't notice him treating Luke any differently than me. But whenever Luke and I were both around him, there wasn't any kind of 'romantic' tension between any of us. It was like we'd suddenly just become normal friends.

"Do you..." I started, "Do you know what Luke thinks about... you know, the three of us, last month?" I was too embarrassed to actually say it. Heck, I was still in disbelief that I'd actually done it.

Jasper hummed in thought. "I was wondering which one of you two was going to be the first to bring that up," he said. "It's like you've both been pretending it didn't happen."

My attention was suddenly back on the moment. "So he hasn't said anything bad about it, then? He doesn't feel like we overstepped the bounds of our friendship or anything?"

"Not that I know," Jasper replied. "Whenever he mentions you, he talks about you the same way he always does. I think he would have said something if he was bothered, though."

I wasn't sure if that made things better or worse. To not have said anything at all almost said volumes of its own. It was like I wasn't even worth mentioning again. What was I supposed to think? That it was okay for one of my best friends to drag me off to bed, have his fun, and never give me a moment's thought after?

Jasper put his other arm down underneath me and rolled me over to face him, then gave me a gentle kiss. "Please, Shon, don't worry about it," he whispered. "I can talk to him if you like, or..."

"No, no, you don't need to do that," I replied, shushing him. "I'm sure it's fine. I'm just oversensitive to things, I guess." That was probably true. But I didn't want Jasper to be involved in this on my part. I was especially concerned because I still didn't know what Luke really thought of me, not just because of what we had done together, but more because we were essentially sharing a lover.

I was willing to share. I just didn't know about him.

Luckily enough, my fears about Luke and how he thought about me didn't plague me constantly. More to the point, I was still able to be around him and treat him like the friend he was. Sexual tension wasn't a thing with me and Luke.

It probably should have been, though; Luke was still quite an attractive husky, and that boyish demeanor of his, that flowed through all of his aspects, held a different charm than my attraction to Jasper. Some older people try to emulate that charm and fail. Luke didn't even have to try. It was just a part of him.

When I spent time with Luke, that part of him made me feel better. Even though he was the same age as Jasper, it felt like he was my age instead and that helped, somehow, with my being comfortable. If the two of us had met outside of Jasper, I still think we would have become really good friends anyway, and possibly something more. As it was, though, I was still nervous that he only put up with me because Jasper liked me. That was why I'd made the move to spend time with Luke on his own.

So even though the two of us really clicked, I never hung out with just him by himself. It was probably my own subconscious fear that kept that mindset of mine going. But I knew that I had to make an actual effort to get past that and in the process hopefully learn whether or not he and I were actually the 'good friends' that we felt like.

Over the course of a few weeks, I started finding time to get Luke alone so we could spend time together, just the two of us. We'd do lunch, take in movies, and the like—just casual friend stuff—and sure enough, there was no 'weirdness' on his part in how he acted toward me, even out of Jasper's view. That was one fear put aside, which left just the one thing that I was neurotically troubled with: what, if anything, had that one night meant to him?

Luke was sitting beside me on my couch; the two of us had just gone out for a light dinner and returned to my apartment to just hang out. The youthful edge he had was ever apparent in the way that he lounged about. His canine scent was very faint but still always lingering around him, and concentrating on it was reminding me of what it had been like to be with him. I thought about the threesome we'd had and felt those conflicting emotions well up inside me again.

No sooner had I realized how hard I'd gotten than I felt Luke's hand grope me. My neck and back arched backwards as I let out a rumbling sigh at the unexpected sensation. "And just what has *you* all excited at a time like this?" he asked me with a grin.

I didn't know how to answer, and for the most part, I didn't care. I just pressed my hips upward so I'd grind gently up into his palm, the length of my cock stretching out the fabric of my pants, even though I still had no idea why he had suddenly decided to make a move on me. Luke responded by rubbing his palm along the seam of my crotch as he tucked in closer next to me. "If I didn't know any better, I'd think it was *me* that was getting you all turned on, little wolf."

The 'change' was very noticeable. I had noticed it while in bed with Luke before: when it came to sex, his voice was totally different, almost as if he were a different person. I decided to ignore it, though, and just played along with things. "Is it so strange to think I might be attracted to you?" I asked.

Luke leaned in closer, his black and white face brushing up against mine as he licked at the side of my muzzle, his clawed fingertips beginning to pull down my zipper. "Maybe not," he replied quietly as his fingers slipped inside my pants, where he grabbed my shaft through my underwear, milking another gasp out of me. "After all, I remember how good it felt when you sucked me dry that last time."

Hearing Luke talk like that to me was doing a good job of just turning me on even more, and I didn't know why. But I wasn't about to complain, and before I said another word, Luke pulled my boxers out of the way and wrapped his hand around my shaft, pulling it out into the open. The brief touch of the cold air was soon quelled as the rest of his warm-furred hand stroked its way along my length, which was already nice and drippy. "In fact, if I had known you were so good at sucking cock, I would have asked Jasper to let me in on some of the action earlier," Luke continued, his other hand working at undoing his own belt.

I suddenly felt like I was doing something very, very wrong. I didn't know if Jasper would be okay with what Luke and I were about to do. Immediately, I rationalized it to myself by noting that Luke had technically started it. My fingers worked at unbuttoning the top of my pants, and then Luke started to pull them off of me as I removed my shirt. Luke took off his shirt as well, and then pressed his bare chest to mine. Our mouths locked in a deep, slow kiss as the husky started to stroke my hard lupine member again.

"So why has a sexy young wolf like yourself been so shy about making a second move on me, huh?" Luke asked, whispering into my ears as he nipped at them with the tips of his teeth. I couldn't respond, not unless you counted my strained upward thrusting as I tried to bear up into his grip. "It felt really good, you know... having you fuck me like that..."

The mental image of that memory struck me like a flash going off. I remembered how much he'd obviously wanted it. And now, I wanted to him to tell me to do it again.

Luke swung his leg over me and sat in my lap, his tail waving back and forth between my legs. He slapped one of his hands on my shoulder and unzipped his pants with the other, letting his cock slip out against my belly, before leaning in to kiss me on the nose, causing his shaft to ride up through the fur on my stomach. "I really want to have you inside me again, Shon," he said. "But I know I don't deserve that."

His voice had flip-flopped from being dominant to being submissive, and yet he still sat in my lap, grinding his rump down into my crotch. His paws spilled down my sides as he slid down the length of my body, nuzzling his nose down my chest and stomach. He pressed his tongue into my navel and swirled it around, then brought his muzzle down over my cock, breathing warmly on it.

"I guess I just talk too much," Luke said, barely audible. "You should just—" He paused to let his tongue glance at my tip. "—shut me up, shouldn't you?"

Raw carnal instinct took over common sense, and I raised my hips to bring myself closer to his mouth. But Luke kept himself just out of reach, his eyes fixed down between my legs. He followed up and down with my motions, always staying just a scant few inches away. Finally, out of sheer frustration and pent-up horniness, I put both of my hands on the back of his head and held it down, thrusting up to jam my cock into his snout. The husky began to suck away at me without even a moment's hesitation, rolling my shaft around the inside of his warm mouth with long, wet strokes of his strong tongue. When I stopped moving, so did he. He turned his eyes up at me and gave me a certain look, and I finally understood what he was getting at.

Taking the hint, I held his head firmly in my hands and let myself buck up and down into his mouth, and he moaned and whimpered in obvious approval. He slathered his tongue all around as my shaft slid back and forth along it, and each second that went by only spurred me on more. I realized in that moment that this was all part of Luke's little game; it didn't matter if he was being toppish or being bottomy—what he wanted was to be in control, and to have things go his way. This was what he wanted, and right then and there, I wanted it as much as he did.

I left my self-control behind and kept fucking into Luke's muzzle as hard and as fast as I could, and Luke met my pace, sucking and slurping at my cock with a fervor I'd never seen. His cheeks puckered inward with suction, and the saliva oozed around in between my shaft, his tongue, and the walls of his mouth. I wanted to stop, to slow down, to let the feeling last, but I knew Luke had other things in mind. Moaning loudly, I stopped fighting the urge to resist the pleasure that was coursing through my body.

Luke's wet maw made slurping sounds that bordered on the obscene as I took his muzzle, gripping his head just behind the ears. From the way that he was starting to try to bob his head along with my movements, I could tell he wanted me to get off, so I let myself go. Then, just as I started to fire out into his mouth, he tore his head free of my grip and pulled his head back, bolting his eyes shut as he caught my jizz with his face. My fluids splattered all over his cheeks and muzzle, the white gobs standing out where they leaked across the patches of black fur. When my climax finally subsided, the willfully disgraced husky opened his eyes and his mouth spread out into a grin.

"Mmmm… very nice, Shon," he murred out at me. He pulled himself forward and rested his head on my belly, staring up into my eyes, his still-covered face looking very out-of-place for the expression. "I'd ask if that was any good for you, but I think I already know the answer to that," he said, licking his tongue out at the side of his muzzle, slurping a bit of my fluids out of his fur.

I put my hands on Luke's shoulders and pushed him back, slipping down onto the floor between him and the couch. "So now do I get to repay the favor?" I asked wryly, staring him down.

Luke wormed his way back, his hard cock jutting out from the open fly of his jeans. "No, no, no," he said, scooting back further away from me still. "I just need to get your pleasure. I'm beneath you. I don't warrant getting off."

For a second or so, I was confused, until it clicked in my head that this, too, was all part of Luke's little game. He had his role to play, and it was up to me to play along with it. Playfully I pounced forward and I succeeded in pinning the husky down on my carpet. I lay down over the length of his body, trapping his shaft between us. Luke squirmed below me, pretending to try to get away, causing him to smear a few slick, wet streaks through the fur on my underside.

I stuck one of my hands down, dragging my claws up the inside of one of Luke's denim-clad thighs, then wrapped my fingers hard around the base of his shaft, giving it a big squeeze. He closed his eyes and gasped, but did nothing else. He made no effort to move, and was apparently trying to lie perfectly still. I began to stroke my clenched hand along his hard and increasingly slippery shaft, and I could tell that he wasn't going to help me get him off; I was going to have to force it all on my own.

My other hand slipped down inside the opening of Luke's jeans and cupped at his soft-furred balls. A wordless sigh came out from his mouth, and I could feel his tail wagging happily down against the carpet where my bare legs lay stretched out. I rapidly rubbed, stroked, and kneaded his cock, getting him slick and hot as my fingers moved up and down faster and faster, causing friction and spreading around his clear fluids. His eyes stayed closed, fists clenched down at his hips. I leaned in and bit down at the crook of his neck, and succeeded in getting a beautiful, pathetic whimper from him. He was forced to writhe a little, and I could feel his sac begin to tense up.

I jerked Luke off at a frantic pace, nibbling and biting every so often, trying to break his concentration so that he'd lose control and go over the edge. I could feel it working bit by bit, but at my current pace, I was going to end up chafing him and making him sore more than I was going to cause pleasure. Unsure of what to try, I squeezed and tugged on his balls as hard as I felt I could without damaging him, and his eyes bolted open in a kind of shock that I knew he appreciated. He yipped loudly, and soon thereafter my quickly-stroking hand ended up getting covered in his sticky juices, with whatever leftover spillage remained soaking into the fur of our bellies.

Luke was panting, fully spent. His chest heaved and fell down again and I rested atop him, and the smile of contentment that grew on his face made me happy. After lying there a few moments, I rolled off to lie on the floor beside him, taking one of his hands in mine. He turned his head to the side and looked at me with a blank, glassy stare.

"No fair," he mumbled. "You cheated."

I laughed a little. "But you wanted me to win."

"Maybe," he replied. "Maybe not." I returned his cocky, smug smile with a brief tickle to the belly.

For the next minute or so, Luke and I simply lay there, catching out breaths and letting our more conscious thoughts come back to us. And when I could think again, I once more remembered that the man beside me wasn't my lover—he was just Luke, my good friend. And I felt bad about that.

I couldn't let my brain stew over things like I had after the last time we'd been intimate with each other. I sat up and put my hands in my lap. Luke looked up at me curiously and sat up as well. "Is something wrong, hon?" he asked.

I shook my head. "I… don't know," I said. "I mean… this, right here—you and me. Does this mean something? I mean, I know that Jasper and I—"

Luke cut me off. "Wait, wait, wait… hold on," he said, shaking his head. "This isn't about Jasper at all. This is just us."

"I know, but… but what does that mean? What does that make us?"

"What does it make us?" Luke asked, sounding more than a bit confused. "It doesn't make us anything. Not anything we weren't already before." I stared back at him, and he went on. "We're still friends, you know. I hope that's not what you're worried about."

I sighed. "But doesn't—"

"Does it bother me that we can be friends and still have sex? No. And why should it? I really like you, and I *think* you like me and all. What's to keep us from having some fun?"

Part of what Luke said then made a lot of sense. True, the sex *didn't* have to be more than sex. If Luke was okay with that, then I supposed that I could be okay with it, too. I knew I loved Jasper. I liked Luke, but I didn't love him. And he felt the same way. We knew where the lines were between us, and they just happened to allow for a lot of things.

That was when something new dawned on me. It was something that should have dawned long before: what exactly did Luke think about me and Jasper? Did he think that Jasper and I were just friends, like we were to each other? Had Jasper made it clear exactly how 'close' the two of us were?

Or were we even really that close at all? Was everything I felt for Jasper all one-sided, all just in my head? Suddenly, I wasn't very sure if I could answer that.

And I knew that my doubts would only grow and grow until I learned that answer.

The paralyzing guilt, doubt, and moral dilemmas grew after that, which isn't a huge surprise. It made me sad, not just on the surface, but because I'd been so used to the fact that being with Jasper had always allowed me to be able to pretend that he and I were the only two folks in the world. I didn't want to face reality if it meant losing that fantasy. Go me.

It was getting more and more difficult for me to rationalize things to myself. I tried to reconcile the fact that just because Luke was Jasper's lover *first* didn't necessarily entail *first* and *foremost*. That, of course, made me feel bad about Luke, and how I was treating him.

Nothing changed the fact that Luke was youthful, sexy, and fun to be with, and after breaking the ice that first time with the two of us alone, we'd taken to, well, being intimate with one another pretty often, it never failed to be quite pleasurable. I did my best to not let myself find it awkward that I was physically involved with him without being emotionally attached. Sometimes that worked; sometimes it didn't, because I knew that my real connection was with Jasper.

My love for Jasper was unbearable at times. I wanted to believe that things were still nice and perfect between us, despite Luke being in the equation. Except that, well, I wasn't sure I was believing that anymore.

I thought back to being in Jasper's bedroom months before, where everything had clicked, and I knew once and for all how I felt about him. And here was Jasper, with me in that bedroom, like so many times before, looking at me with those lovely blue eyes of his, and I knew at once that my emotions were showing through plainly on my face. He reached out with one his soft, white-furred paws and stroked my cheek gently. "You're worried about something, honey, aren't you?"

I hung my head just a little bit. I wasn't surprised that Jasper was able to read me so well. "I dunno," I replied. "I'm just preoccupied, that's all."

Jasper sighed. "I know you well enough to know that that just means you don't want to tell me," he said, taking his hand back and giving me a disapproving look. I met his gaze back and immediately turned my eyes downward again. He had me, and I knew there was no way to fight it.

"It's just that... I'm worried. About us, y'know?"

This time, Jasper put one hand out onto my shoulder and tipped my chin up with the other so that I was looking him in the eyes. His handsome features looked all the more endearing with the look of genuine, legitimate concern awash on his face. "Shon," he said, "I'm only going to ask one more time for you to tell me what's wrong. After that, I'm just going to take your word for it that things are all right until you tell me otherwise." An ultimatum. A nice one, but still an ultimatum. He didn't want to play this game with me.

I didn't want to play it with him, either. "I'm afraid of losing you," I said, my voice barely a whisper. "You mean so much to me, and I want you to be happy, but..."

One of his fingers traced its way along the side of my lupine muzzle, not sensually, but reassuringly. "But what, dear? Tell me what's on your mind."

I took a deep breath and swallowed, collecting my thoughts, focusing them, and trying to figure out what to say. "I'm afraid," I said again, "that my place in your life is only going to cause problems further down the line."

Jasper put both of his arms around my back and pulled me close to him. I rested my head against his chest and I breathed hard and fast, almost panicking as I waited to hear what he had to say. "Oh, honey," he said, petting the fur between my ears, "you don't need to worry. We've been over this before."

I looked up at him, and he continued. "Things with Luke and me are fine. He's okay with your being with me like this. And he's promised me that if he has any problems, he'll tell me. So please, don't worry anymore," he said, lifting my head up and giving me a kiss on the side of my snout.

Sure, Luke might not have had problems, per se, but he also didn't know how deeply I felt about Jasper. At least, I was pretty sure he didn't know. I hadn't said anything, and I tried not to let on. That was part of my reason for letting myself have sex with Luke in the first place, I realized then: if I was close to the both of them, maybe Luke wouldn't think that Jasper was as special to me as he truly was.

But for that matter, maybe Jasper wasn't sure if he was special to me, for the exact same reasons.

I pulled myself back up, supporting myself with my forearms and staring into Jasper's face. He smiled at me, and then that smile turned into a confused look. "You okay, Shon? Honestly?" he asked.

I opened my mouth, ready to confess everything right then and there, wanting more than anything to just let Jasper know just how goddamn much he meant to me and how I wanted to spent the rest of my life by his side, interweaving all of his joys and his sadnesses with my own. But when I tried to get the words out, nothing came. I wasn't ready to tell him. Not yet. Not in words. Instead, I leaned forward and put my mouth to his ear and whispered to him. "I want you to have me," I said. A little bit of a double meaning there, and not smoothly delivered at all, but thinking straight wasn't really working.

Jasper rubbed the length of his snout against mine and gave me a chaste little kiss. "Right here, right now, you mean?" he asked with a happy, playful smirk on his canine muzzle. It was good to see that he was still agreeable enough to let me turn an awkward situation into a more pleasant one.

I slipped a hand down and cupped his crotch through his jeans, squeezing nice and hard. "Right here, right now," I parroted back, mirroring his grin and nipping at his neck with my front teeth. He let out a muffled sigh as I grabbed him, and I felt his body react to the touch.

Both of Jasper's hands found their way to my sides, and the husky used his sharp claws to scratch hard enough up and down along my body for it to be felt through my shirt. I tilted my head back as I leaned forward still, staring up into his eyes as I flicked the tip of my tongue out of the front of my mouth. Skipping any pretense and ceremony, I unzipped his fly and plunged my hand into his pants, then quickly pulled his cock out from his boxers and out into the open. Already, he was mostly hard and damned well ready. I winked at him as I rubbed my thumb down over his slit, spreading a droplet of the drizzle that was there down to the ridge of his glans, where I moved my thumb from side to side.

Jasper still just rubbed and scratched my back and sides, his eyes closing partway as he flashed me a smile that seemed to be made of a cross between love and lust—the kind of expression that I, at least, knew I was making for him on my own face. My index finger and thumb formed a circle just below his head as his cock finished swelling to its maximum. I stroked his long, pink shaft slowly and evenly, tickling it with the bristly fur of my wolfish paw. The husky took one of his hands off of my back and unsnapped the button on his jeans to afford himself some more comfort.

"That feels good, doesn't it, hon?" I asked wryly. I knew that Jasper liked it when I'd speak all teasingly to him while we did things to one another. And I got the reaction I wanted, because he just nodded with a light 'rrf', and another sizeable drizzle of pre slid its way down his length. My muzzle went down and I licked my way up his shaft with my tongue tip, teased a few licks at his slit, and pulled back with a loud contented moan to let him know how good I thought he tasted.

Carefully, Jasper took hold of the bottom of my shirt and pulled upward. I lifted my arms up and let him take it off. The husky ran one of his hands through the light gray fur on my chest, then tweaked one of my nipples hard between two of his claws. I responded by squeezing his shaft hard in my full grip, using just enough pressure to milk out some more of that wonderful, slippery fluid without causing him pain. He quickly flung his own shirt up over his head and tossed over the side of the bed.

I leaned forward, poking the tip of my muzzle against the husky's warm, fluffy chest, continuing to stroke him as his cock got more slippery. I found one of his nipples and let my long, wet tongue slurp over it before I slipped it into my mouth and gave it a tender suck. Jasper stroked the back of my head and neck slowly, holding me ever so gently against his chest. My grip on his erection loosened, and I began to run the flat of my palm up and down the underside of his shaft. I could feel Jasper fumble with the catch on my pants with one hand, so I angled myself to the side in order to allow him more room. His hands spilled down the back of my head and neck over and over again, and I bit down on the nipple between my teeth. Jasper let out a sharp, hissing gasp as his entire body tensed up, freezing his movements.

After I released my bite on his hard, sensitive nipple, Jasper succeeded in getting my pants open, and I closed my eyes as I felt his hand slip down and cup my warm, swelling member. His fingers wormed around independently of one another, sending pulses of pleasure through me and coaxing my length up into his hold. When he had me at full hardness, he let go, put his hands up on my shoulders and pushed me back into an upright position. "We need to get these off of you, wolfy," he said to me as he pushed back further, forcing me onto my back. I looked up into his face as he gazed down at me, his fingers hooking the inside of the waist of my pants.

With a fluid motion, he pulled my pants all the way off, leaving my stiff cock still trapped in my underwear. Next, he squirmed and got himself out of his own jeans, leaving it so that we mirrored each other, wearing nothing but boxers. He slipped his boxers off as he stretched his body out to lean over me, letting me take in the sight of his handsome naked form, alternating between staring into his wonderful face, and staring down at his dripping cock, its pink shape standing out against the white fur of his belly. Jasper wasn't so well-endowed that it was frightening or anything, but he was pleasantly above average in size.

Jasper lowered himself down and kissed me, our muzzles locking deeply, my frustrated passion flaring up all throughout my being. He pawed and rubbed at my sides, our bodies wriggling together, my slick cock sliding back and forth against his. I let out a longing whimper as he broke off our kiss far too soon, and he slid himself back. He crawled back over the mattress, pulling my shorts off as he went. They caught on one of my hindclaws, but with a quick flick, the husky got them free and threw them aside. He gave my foot a tiny tickle and drew himself forward again, bringing his head up between my legs. He looked up in my eyes, winked once, then gripped the base of my cock between his fingers, holding it still as he slid his muzzle down onto my length.

My head went back and I took a loud, deep breath as my senses took a second or so to catch up with themselves. Jasper moved his flexible canine tongue around slowly and carefully, getting my cock all wet with saliva. His tongue worked in repeated spiraling motions around my shaft, and he suckled on me without any real rush as he went. He was methodical, calculated, relaxed; he was careful not to overstimulate me, and his leisurely attentions gave the impression that he could go on doing this all day and be content just with that. I lay still, doing nothing except for letting out the occasional quiet moan, and I just let myself bask and revel in the sensation of having Jasper tend to me with his mouth.

The pleasure had made me almost numb to everything else, and so when Jasper finally pulled his muzzle up off of me, it took me a few moments for me to realize he had stopped. I propped myself up on the tips of my elbows and looked down at him. He was leaning forward on his hands, looking up and down over the length of my body. One of his hands grabbed at my furry sack for a split second, then rested on the inside of my thigh. "Roll over onto your stomach, honey," he said. I did as I was told right away, my tail wagging slowly behind me.

I heard Jasper fish through his nightstand drawer for a few seconds. I then heard the sound of the cap of a bottle of lube being popped off, and I released a deep breath I hadn't realized I'd been holding. One of Jasper's fingertips pressed up underneath my tail, the cold sensation of the lube sending a chill up my spine. The fur along my back stood on end for a moment, and I did my best to relax myself. No sooner had I thought that than I felt one of Jasper's slippery digits slip up inside of me, causing a jolt of minor discomfort as he spread my ring open. That slick finger twisted back and forth as he probed it in and out, getting me nice and lubed up on the inside before he added a second finger to the first. I bit down on the comforter until the stretching sensation passed, then I allowed myself to enjoy the feeling of his fingers moving around inside of me.

"Do you think you're ready?" Jasper asked, leaving his fingers in place in case I might still be too tight.

I lifted my head up from the mattress and nodded. "I think so," I answered, and my tail wagged all on its own. Looking back over my shoulder, I saw Jasper stroke his hardness up with some more lube, and so I lay back forward, spreading my legs just a little more. His fingers withdrew, and he held me spread open with one hand on my rump as he leaned stretched out over me. The tip of his cock prodded up under my tail, his hands gripping my shoulders. He petted me softly on the back of my head a few times, and then I felt him begin to press in. The head slipped in easily, and then I shifted slightly as his shaft began to sink in behind it.

A dull moan rumbled out of my half-open muzzle at the feeling of Jasper's canine member entering me. He kept on petting me, trying to relax and soothe me as he worked his way deeper with short, tiny thrusts. I let out a *yip* as a twinge of split-second pain hit as his cock moved inside me at a somewhat odd angle. Jasper pulled back an inch or so and held still. I simply nodded and tried to raise my rear a bit, to let him know that I was still ready to take the rest of him. He gave my shoulder a squeeze and bore down into me again, and I treated my husky to a pleasure-filled moan as I felt him push deeper.

He was lodged almost the entire way within me. "How's that?" he asked, kissing the tip of one of my ears.

I pressed my body against the mattress and lifted my hips a little, forcing the last part of his shaft to sink the rest of its way inside of me. "How's *that?*" I asked right back, my voice not even fully in my throat, as my body was still adjusting to having him inside me. The warm breath from Jasper's quiet laughter tickled my ears, and he lay over me for a while, unmoving, letting me acclimate.

A space of echoing heartbeats later, Jasper began to pull out. His cock was warm and slick, and moved with progressive ease as his hips cycled up and down. He held onto my upper arms as he built up a comfortable lovemaking rhythm. I closed my eyes and nestled my face down into the pillows, muffling my breathing as I let all of my senses focus on my body and Jasper's. The scent of our warm bodies tingled in my nose, and pheromones conveying raw sexuality hit at something far more primal and indescribable.

For that moment, the only thing I was aware of was him and me. And in that moment, I could do nothing but hope that the same held true for Jasper... that for that one moment, I might be the only thing on his mind... that for that one moment, the only thing important to him was me.

My wandering thoughts suddenly lashed back into reality as his cock hit firmly at my prostate, and I squeaked out a happy, pleasure-laden whimper. His thrusts were still long, full, and slow, and so I did my best to move my own hips back to meet his as he took me so lovingly. My body trembled all over as it tried to make sense of the conflicting sensations of intense physical pleasure and pure psychological contentedness. I stopped caring, though; I just wanted it all to last.

Jasper pulled himself closer to my body, kissing the back of my head, simultaneously allowing him to penetrate deeper into my now not-so-tight hole. I tried raising my rear up high to meet him and I mustered up all the concentration I could to speak. "Fuck me harder," I said, sounding almost like I were begging. And in a sense, I was. But he responded by upping his pace, his cock pumping into me a little bit faster and a little bit harder.

I moaned at the feeling, both mental and physical, and he must have taken that sound as a good sign, because he kicked his pace up yet another notch. It was wonderful, having him thrust into me, my body bucking up into his, my cock rubbing against the bedding. Jasper's claws dug into the skin on my arms, and I could tell that he was using a good amount of restraint to keep himself from giving in to the call of lust. But I wanted him to—I wanted to feel him slamming into me, to feel his cock pound into me again and again as he was taken over by that raw drive that blocked out everything except for the desire to mate with me.

Like he had read my mind or something, he suddenly began to fuck into my rear harder than I could recall him ever doing before. His claws curled inwards into my shoulders, and I could smell faintly that he had drawn blood. His thick canine shaft pounded into me over and over, and I couldn't tell if I was moaning out Jasper's name, or just unintelligible sounds. The rhythm of his movements grew more and more unsteady as he took me harder, and my body spasmed and clenched around his member as it drove back and forth.

With a slight grunt as his only warning, Jasper hit his climax. He didn't stop, however, and I could feel his sticky juices spurt out onto the back of my balls, in the cleft of my rump, and the outside of my hole as he kept thrusting while he came. His breath was ragged, and I felt his heart thudding in his chest as he collapsed onto my back, the shaft of his messy, spent cock resting in between my cheeks. I curled my tail to one side as I caught my breath, my pulse racing as my body tried to readjust to the sudden lack of sensations spilling through it.

Jasper kissed me on the cheek, petting down my sides repeatedly. He then stuck one of his hands underneath my chest, then rolled over so we were both on our sides. His head angled up over my shoulder and he stared down at the bed-sheets, and then at my still-hard cock. "You didn't get off yet," he said, making it a plain observation. It was a fair one to have made; sometimes I would get off just by having him fuck me, certain things (that I could never put my finger on) were just right.

My heartbeat wavered as my pulse changed yet again, because Jasper reached down and squeezed my shaft hard in his hand and began to stroke me frantically. I craned my head backwards into the crook of Jasper's neck and bowed my spine back as my body writhed. He didn't let up, though; he slipped his hand down between my legs, scooping up some of his own spent juices onto his fingers, and then used them on my cock as he jerked me off.

His fingers slipped along my length with incredible speed, holding me practically paralyzed as he toyed with me in his grasp. My muzzle gaped open as I did my best to gasp for air between whimpers and moans and yelps. With the combination of my juices and his, he was able to bear down hard on my shaft and still stroke quickly, causing a massive amount of friction. I held my eyes shut and waited for release to hit me.

Not long after, it did. My orgasm hit my body full-on, and I shouted wordlessly as the head of my cock erupted. The first spurt splattered onto Jasper's paw, and then he gripped me down at my base. The rest of my seed fired out hard, clear off the edge of the bed as he held my cock in place while I emptied myself. I was dizzy, and the room spun for several endless seconds before I was able to lie still on my back without feeling like I would fall somewhere.

I lay there with Jasper, his arms around me, holding me close. It was a position we'd been in many times before, but that didn't detract from it making me feel wonderful to be with him like I was. The minutes went on, and I basked wantonly in the afterglow, knowing that it was going to end, but just enjoying it like it would last forever anyway. Jasper slid his claws along my chest and prodded the back of my head with his snout, and I breathed easy with a big smile of contentment. This was how I wanted things to always be.

The red light of the digital clock on Jasper's nightstand reminded me of the unfortunate fact that Luke was going to be home sometime soon, probably in an hour or so. I rolled over in Jasper's strong arms and gave him a kiss on the nose. "We should probably get cleaned up and stuff, before... you know..."

Jasper kissed me back, this time on the mouth. "Maybe," he said. "We don't have to, if you want to just lie here or something," he offered.

I could feel the tears well up behind my eyes, but they didn't start to flow just yet. "But, I mean... what about Luke?" I asked.

"What about him?" Jasper asked. "It's not like he doesn't know that we do this."

I shook my head. Why did this have to be so fucking difficult for me? "No, that's not it... I..."

Jasper tilted his head. "Are you embarrassed about being seen like this or something?" He sounded curious.

Now I really did want to cry, but I didn't let myself. "No, you're not getting it!" I blurted out, almost yelling and immediately regretting it. "It's like... it's like what we're doing is wrong!"

This time, Jasper was the one to look upset. "Wrong? Whatever do you think is 'wrong' about any of this?" His feelings sounded hurt.

"It's just..." A few tears had pooled at the bottoms of my eyes now. "I don't want to pull away from you, but I don't want to hurt Luke, either, because he's my friend, too, and everything with the three of us is..." I wanted to scream or something, because I knew that I was just babbling and couldn't just speak my mind. What I felt about everything seemed so simple and so complicated all at the same time... Finally, I got frustrated enough to break through any hesitation. "Do you love me?" I asked Jasper, one of my paws down at his hip.

Jasper ran his fingers over one of my ears and sighed. "I'm a little hurt that you'd even think you had to ask that, honey," he said softly. "You should know that I do."

I was crying now. It was light and soundless, and I don't know if it was because of happiness or despair, but I was crying. "But what about Luke? Isn't he..."

"My boyfriend?" Jasper finished for me. "Yes. And I love him. Is there a rule somewhere that says I can't love more than one person?" he asked, trying to make it sound like a joke.

I shook my head. "No, but..."

Jasper cut me off again. "Look, I love you," he said, "and I want you to know how much I mean that." I stared back into his face, the tears still silently running down over my cheeks. "And just because I love you doesn't mean that I have to love Luke any less, or vice-versa. That's just how it is."

I believed him, and not just because I wanted to believe him, or because what he said made sense. As much as our situation didn't make sense, I still believed him, and I hugged him closer to me. "I hope you don't have a problem with that," Jasper asked me, sounding like his typical self.

"I don't, no," I replied, kissing him on the lips. I knew now that our weird little relationship was workable, but there was one very important matter still left. "But does Luke have a problem with it?" I asked.

Jasper's eyes turned a shade more serious. "I hope not," he replied. "I'd like to think that he understands how things are between you and me."

I pulled away a bit, to give myself more room to breathe and more room to get a look at his face. "Well, have you told him that you love me?" I asked.

"No," he replied, and he sounded ashamed of that. "And I should, I know." He went quiet after that. I knew that whatever he was feeling at that moment must have been too strange and too awkward to put into words, so I didn't push for them. I just held him gently and then sat up on the edge of the bed, gathering my clothes from the floor.

I think Jasper got nervous at seeing me get ready to leave. "I'm not going to hide this from him, Shon," he said.

"I know, hon," I replied. "But until Luke knows exactly what the two of us entail, I'd rather he not have to see us like this."

Jasper sat up naked on the bed, watching me as I got dressed. "I take it you're not going to hang around, then?"

I shook my head. "No. I'd rather give you guys time to yourselves. You'll probably need a lot of time to get things explained right and…" I trailed off. There was nothing I could say about that particular subject that Jasper didn't already know. And he responded just by nodding.

"On the chance that Luke… doesn't respond well," I said, "just… don't spare his happiness for mine, okay? He was here first, after all."

Jasper nodded again. I think, for the first time, I was seeing him afraid, in self-doubt. But I knew that he'd find a way to bring himself to do the right thing. He'd talk to Luke, and then we'd all see how things went from there.

I turned and walked out of Jasper's apartment and began my way home.

Four days later, my friend Dijit and I were out having a round of drinks together at a small bar that we'd both recently started going together again. Except my little foxy friend wasn't being very talkative tonight. I didn't know if it was because he was bothered by something, or if it was because I was a lousy conversation partner on account of my being so spaced out.

I still hadn't heard back from Jasper... or Luke. I had to assume that Jasper had at least had his little 'talk' with him. But in the meantime, I had been in the dark.

I was concerned, granted. But four days wasn't such a long time as to be *too* worried. Maybe Jasper and Luke still needed time to sort things out. Maybe they needed time to reassess their relationship with each other in order to see if that could accommodate for me or not. Or maybe Luke had just been completely unwilling to accept the idea that Jasper could love someone else. I had no idea.

And I wish I did know, but that would have to come later, I figured. I was still confused, doubtful, and worried about the two of them, just like I had always been the entire time I had known them both. And just like that entire time, I was still wondering, more than anything else, if my love for Jasper was something that could be returned freely.

I was still wondering. The difference now was that I wasn't completely hopeless to the prospect that the answer might be 'yes'.

Misunderstanding

"No Free Rides" is a rather unique yiff story, based on a challenge that the author had received, where he was asked to come up with a story in which someone actually managed to rape himself.

Homophobia and fear on one side, unintended sexual allusions and intimidation in a spirit of utter cluelessness on the other, this story makes the reader cringe and weep and giggle.

Tragedy and arousal are hard to mix without slipping into the realm of sadism, and this dark piece manages to retain a rather upbeat core—because at the heart of the matter, neither of the characters bears the other any ill will. Rape without malice—now there's a brain-teaser.

No Free Rides

Uncle Oakie

Michael cursed to himself yet again and rubbed his paw vigorously on the windshield, trying to create a clear spot on the steamed-up glass. When he could finally see again, he was rewarded with the monotonous swipe of the wiper blades and the staccato beat of fat raindrops on the glass. The headlights revealed a dark stretch of empty, black road in the middle of wet, empty countryside indistinguishable from the previous hundred miles of wet, empty countryside.

"Damn! I hate the rain. Wet fur itches so much." he grumbled to himself, "Why can't somebody come up with some conditioner or something that'll keep fur from itching every time it gets damp? Why the hell wouldn't a service station somewhere that must get ten meters of rain a year not have a cover over the damn pumps? And no full service so that some other chump can get his fur soaked while I stayed nice and dry in the car! Argh!"

Michael reached under his vest to scratch enthusiastically at the deep gray fur on his chest and side. Finally relieving the worst of the itching, he reached forward to adjust the blower on the car's heater hoping to force enough airflow from the ancient thing to dry his fur. He looked up and, growling, rubbed his paw on the windshield again where it had already fogged up for the umpteenth time in as many minutes. The clear spot revealed… a plane landing in the middle of the road! No, a car stopped by the road with flashers blinking and… someone walking in front of it!

Balding tires made a pitiful attempt at squealing as the car fishtailed and the driver swerved to avoid hitting the guy. Too smooth rubber surrendered to wet blacktop and hustled the vehicle through the bushes and into a ditch. Michael's head banged the steering wheel as the engine chugged twice and died. The dim, misaligned headlights lit only wet branches, fresh dirt and a surprisingly beautiful swirls of stars that the dazed wolf slowly realized were only in his head.

Kent had been trudging down the side of the road away from a car that had died amidst some very strange whining and a gout of oily-smelling steam that he guessed would prove to be very expensive; especially whenever whoever he found to tow the disloyal machine realized that he was stranded out in the middle of nowhere. He had gone barely a hundred yards when he was startled by headlights moving up behind him and had turned to flag down the car. Once he realized that the driver didn't see him and that he was directly in the path of the battered vehicle, he barely had time to leap into the ditch beside the road; landing, of course, in the biggest puddle in his field of vision and turning an ankle in the process. Even as he was flying in the air and landing in a truly impressive splash he heard the crash as the car hit the bushes on the other side of the road. As he pulled himself from the mud, the car's engine coughed and went silent.

Shaking the mud from himself as best he could, Kent worked his way up the muddy slope and limped across the road to the opposite ditch where he could see taillights glowing up at the rain. He reached the car and looked in to see a large wolf just leaning back from the steering wheel and rubbing at a bloody spot on his forehead. He tapped on the window and stepped back as the door opened and the wolf climbed out.

"Are you okay?" two concerned voices echoed each other.

Kent chuckled in spite of himself, "Yes, I'm fine. Just a little startled and a bit muddy. Okay, make that scared shitless and very muddy, but otherwise unhurt. But how about you? That cut on your head looks nasty."

Michael pulled his hand away and looked at the blood. He touched at the wound and looked at his paw again then smiled. "I'm alright. Head-wounds just bleed a lot. This is nothing. Looks like the old bitch has had it though."

Kent felt his heart climb into his throat, "There is someone else in the car? Ohmygod! We have to do something. I'll go get help! Wait here and see if you can flag someone down."

He was startled when the wolf tilted back his muzzle and howled. It was a moment before he realized that the bloody, wet-furred lupine was laughing. When the wolf was able to speak again tears had joined the blood and rain dripping down his muzzle.

"No, there's no one in the car. The 'old bitch' I meant is this rusted hunk of baling wire and prayers that, until a minute ago, passed for a car. There's no way I can get this back on the road."

The wolf walked to the front of the car, reached under the bumper and heaved. The front of the car lifted a little bit but nowhere near enough to put the rear tires on the road where they could get purchase and pull the car to safety.

Kent examined the situation for a moment and tapped his lower lip. "Get in and see if the 'old bitch' will turn over for you. I have an idea." He stepped into the bushes and disappeared from sight.

Michael had little hope of anything less than a tow truck getting the car back on the road, but figured it wouldn't hurt anything to try the… uhmm… Come to think of it, he had no idea of the species of the person he had almost run over. Between the shock and the dark and what was truly a phenomenal amount of mud, he had never noticed. Anyway, it couldn't hurt to try the whatever's idea. He climbed back in and turned the key, expecting nothing. He was surprised when the engine not only started but settled down into a steady purr that actually sounded healthier than it had in months. Maybe something had been knocked right in the accident. He sat behind the wheel for a couple of minutes before his almost victim returned with what looked for all the world like a wooden fencepost over his shoulder. To his surprise, it turned out to be a wooden fencepost.

"I noticed the trunk of that fallen tree just a couple feet in front of your bumper," said something barely recognizable as a deer, "I thought that a lever might be able to raise the front end enough. This looks like farm country so I hunted along the edge of a field till I found a relatively sound post and was able to wriggle it loose. Get back in, put it in reverse and, when I yell, hit it."

Michael had barely gotten into position when he felt the front end come up and just managed to stomp on the gas pedal when a very strained yell came to hit the gas. He felt the tires slip, squeal and finally grab the road. He almost bumped his head on the wheel again as the car jerked backwards and he finally found himself back on asphalt. When the car had come to a stop, he reached over and opened the passenger door, tossing handfuls of crap into the back seat. He was almost finished when the other guy reached the door and leaned his head inside.

"Any chance you could give me a lift to the nearest town? That was my car right back there that caused this whole mess. She died on me and I'd just started hiking to wherever."

"Sure. It's the least I can do for almost turning you into road-kill. Just let me finish clearing away some of this mess." He used the opportunity to take a better look at the guy he had almost killed. In the glow of the ceiling light he saw that the buck was a little small for a white-tail, probably a mule deer but that was hard to tell under all the mud. He admired the lean form in quick glances and couldn't help noticing where the rain glued wet jeans to the deer's crotch. It looked like the little deer might have some moose blood in him if the size of that package was any indication. Such thoughts popped like a soap bubble when he saw the gold wedding band flash in the light. Oh well, it was a nice fantasy; the wolf doubted that he was ready for any action outside his own head just yet anyway. He quickly finished transferring the refuse of a road trip to the back seat and waved the deer inside.

Kent climbed into the car with a little trepidation. While coming around the car, he had seen where the rain had washed mud from the rear bumper revealing a rainbow flag sticker and a similar one beside it in blue and white with a red heart on a black field in one corner. He understood the former but wasn't sure about the latter. He thought that it had something to do with sadomasochism but couldn't be positive. The thought of getting into a car on a deserted road with a wolf who looked to be very strong (he had seen how the wolf's chest and arms bulged when he tried to lift the car) and not only a homosexual but quite possibly into violent sex scared him more than a little. He looked around and realized that this was the only car he had seen in nearly an hour and decided that he had little choice.

"Thanks. I wasn't looking forward to walking all night in the rain only to get fucked by the first mechanic I managed to find." Kent winced when he realized the possible implications of what he had just said and wondered whether he should try to rephrase it or just let it go.

Michael noted his unexpected passenger's nervousness and could smell the hint of fear pheromones rising from the deer. When he saw the buck wince and replayed what had just been said, he realized that the deer had probably seen his bumper stickers and was experiencing the all too familiar reaction of the homo-ignorant. How to talk to a homosexual without offending them or, worse yet, making them think you may be one of that kind too. He suppressed a grin and did his best to help the deer relax.

"I'm Michael Lasher, by the way. Nice to meet you."

"Kent Reed. Thanks again."

"Hey, that was some pretty quick thinking with that post and trunk. Even with the lever you must be pretty strong—especially between the ears. If it wasn't for you, I'd still be sitting there cussing out this pitiful excuse for a car."

"If it wasn't for me, you would never have ended up in that ditch in the first place. But thanks. I make a living out of problem-solving so it just came naturally to me. No big deal."

"Well, I'm still impressed. What is it that you do for a living?" Michael asked and tried to settle into the drive. The smell of a warm, wet, rather sexy male sitting next to him was heady and he needed the conversation to distract him before Mr. Happy woke up and made a wet, itchy crotch even more uncomfortable.

"Well, it's hard to define unless you're in the field too. I work with computers and networks. I'm a troubleshooter—that is, equal parts programmer, administrator, technician and babysitter. Kind of a jack-of-all-trades-master-of-none for the twenty-first century."

The miles began to disappear under the wheels of the car as the two settled into a conversation. The deer was impressed by some of the pointed questions the wolf asked. If it wasn't for the situation and the personal questions that popped up now and then, he would have almost thought it was a tech interview by a prospective employer. As it was, he had a hard time keeping his mind on the questions as he continually tried to read the body language of the wolf and searched every question for innuendo. He had never been comfortable around homosexuals, or 'gays' as they called themselves, and found it impossible to keep the knowledge that he was sitting next to one from being foremost in his thoughts. When Michael reached down to fiddle with the heater controls Kent almost jerked out of the seat when the hand brushed his knee.

After about twenty minutes Michael noticed a rest stop coming up, slowed and pulled into it. Before Kent could panic he announced, "I need to take a leak and think we could both use the opportunity to clean up a bit. Wet fur is bad enough but, if this mud dries in it, I'll end up scratching myself into a dandy case of mange."

Even though Michael could tell from the way Kent shifted from foot to foot that the buck really needed to piss, he had finished his business and returned to the car before Kent headed in himself.

While the deer was inside, the wolf took the opportunity to find his cell phone under the mess in the back seat and make a couple of calls. One of the things he did was find out where the next major town was and make arrangements to have the deer's car towed there.

He started to call his boyfriend to let him know what had happened when he remembered that he wouldn't be there. Anton was gone. Had been gone. Anton had abandoned him for that femmy, slut ferret. Damn! It had been four months! When would memories of the breakup quit blindsiding him like this?

Eventually the buck returned to the car looking much cleaner, if no drier and no more relaxed. The wolf slipped his cell phone into his vest's inner pocket just as the deer climbed back into the car.

Michael tried to start a meaningless conversation to pass the time and after a while the deer began responding, but seemed even more distracted than before. The smell of fear was so strong that Michael had to crack a window. He didn't think that the buck could be that nervous about riding next to a gay guy and decided that it was none of his business unless Kent decided to talk about it on his own. He did discover that the ring was from a marriage that had ended over a year past. He guessed that Kent just wasn't ready to let go of things yet and so kept wearing it. Considering that Michael still hoped to see his ex every time he came home to his apartment, he could relate.

With most of the mud gone, Michael got a better look at his passenger. The buck was even hotter than he would have guessed. He wasn't heavily muscled, but had the body of a dancer rather than a twink's boy build. Definitely a grown man—exactly what the wolf liked. The cinnamon fur darkened to an espresso brown along the backs of his arms with frothy cream-colored fur on the undersides. He reminded the wolf of a hot cappuccino; Michael loved the taste of hot cappuccino in his mouth.

Dammit! He had to stop thinking that way. The tightening in the crotch of his jeans only made the wet itching even worse. Besides, the buck was straight and all Michael was likely to get out of such thoughts was blue-balls. He tried to finish his clandestine examination without thoughts of what it would be like to be cuffed to those antlers while the buck rutted his ass. Definitely a mule deer rather than a white-tail. Michael wondered why the species was called that and immediately thought about what had been hinted at beneath wet jeans plastered to the buck's thighs. Dammit!

For his part, Kent was trying hard not to piss himself. Once the wolf's fur had dried a bit he had noticed that Michael had many scars on his head and muzzle. The cut on his forehead would soon be indistinguishable from a dozen others on his face and his muscle-corded arms. The wolf wore faded jeans, heavy black leather boots and belt, both with heavy silver chains on them. He also wore a black leather vest with a bulge on the left side of his chest. It was the bulge that scared the deer most of all; he was certain that he had seen the wolf quickly slip a gun under there when he had gotten back to the car. Maybe it had been there all the time and was just for protection. Maybe it had been pulled out from wherever it had been hidden just for him. Just as he decided to jump and run, the car started moving and he was trapped.

The wolf's fur was mostly dry by the time they approached the outskirts of the town that was his immediate destination. Mostly dry, that is, except for where the blower couldn't reach. The damp fur matting his crotch was driving him mad and he continually reached down to scratch or shift his package, trying to make himself comfortable. He was glad when he saw the auto yard he had arranged to have the deer's car towed too; soon he would be at a hotel and able to scratch to his heart's content. It was about five AM when he pulled into the dark lot. The place should open in about an hour and the deer should be able to take care of things from here.

Kent could see the lights of town not far away and then looked around at the dark, empty lot with rusting hulks of cars blocking the view from the road. He looked at the wolf, who was smiling at him with one paw under that vest and the other kneading his crotch, and knew that he was in serious trouble.

"Uh… What are we doing here? I need to get to a phone and make arrangements to get my car towed." The door handle was only inches from Kent's hand. Could he open the door and roll out of the way faster than the wolf could pull out his gun and bring it to bear? He didn't think so. He didn't think that he could even move anymore. He had to try. He didn't want to be raped. He didn't want to die. His fingers closed on the cold, metal handle.

"No. You won't need to do that," said Michael.

The wolf was so totally distracted by the itching that seemed to have gotten worse now that the town and a hotel and comfort were so close that he didn't even notice that the deer seemed on the verge of panic. He was about to explain about the calls he had made on the cell phone when the deer reached down to open his door and started to get out. He dug under his vest so that he could offer Kent his phone but the deer already had one foot on the ground and seemed eager to leave.

Michael remembered what he had forgotten to ask for back at the rest area, "Wait! There's something I need from you before you go."

Kent's heart stopped beating as he paused with one foot outside the door and looked at the gay wolf sitting there massaging his groin and reaching for the gun. He realized then that he was willing to do whatever he had to do to survive. He didn't want to die. His decision made, he pulled his foot back inside the car and closed the door.

The wolf said, "Before you go… "

Kent interrupted, hoping to take some kind of control before the gun actually made its appearance, "No. Please. Just let me. I've known this was going to happen from before I even got in the car. I know what you need from me."

Michael was confused when a hand tentatively closed on his wrist and slowly pulled it out from under his vest. He was shocked when the other one slid his paw away from his itchy crotch and replaced it. What the hell was happening? Fuck it! He knew what was happening and wasn't about to resist. He wriggled in the seat as the deer's hand began to explore his crotch. He hadn't allowed anyone to touch him there since his sinuous brown lover had left four months earlier. It was time and he was ready, more than ready; he was eager. The first button of his 501's popped open and he wondered why the deer was doing this. He was straight, wasn't he? Or was this the reason his marriage had ended? The second button gave way and he no longer cared. He growled happily and looked down as one by one the buttons popped and his sheath was exposed. He remembered the bumper sticker on his older brother's van back in high school: Gas, grass or ass... no one rides for free.

Kent took a deep breath and paused a moment as the fullness of the wolf's crotch became visible to him. His heart hammered in his chest and his stomach churned with what must surely be disgust. It had to be disgust. Didn't it? He couldn't believe that he had gotten himself into this position. He couldn't think about it. If he let himself think then he would not be able to hold back the panic. If he panicked he was probably going to die right here. Oh gods! He didn't want to do this. He couldn't do this. He had to do this.

Between the folded-back fly of the wolf's jeans he saw the thick, heavy, creamy-furred sheath crawling up a hard, rippling belly. He saw a small swelling at the base of the furry tube and gulped. He had forgotten that they had knots. Farther down between the wolf's thighs he saw two large testicles rolling in a downy soft sack. He was almost hypnotized by their slow dance in the lupine scrotum. They were easier to look at than the pole of flesh, even hidden as it was now. He sat there as the smell of the wolfen groin was picked up and wafted through the interior of the car until his nose was full of the smell of wet fur, sweat and the almost overpowering scent of very male muskiness. It was as if the very essence of being male was carried in that smell. Slowly, almost of its own volition, he watched as his hand reached out and closed around the wolf's sex.

The tube of flesh almost burned Kent's paw as, for the first time, he touched a cock that wasn't his own. Inside the sheath of soft fur he felt a thin hardness; much thinner than he had expected and much harder. It felt like a thick pencil except near the base where it swelled into a soft ping-pong ball. He didn't notice the wolf's paws clenching at the vinyl seat of the car, nails digging gouges in the ancient upholstery. He failed to note as the wolf began to pant but heard the tiniest growl escape the well-toothed maw. Taking the growl for an order, he forced his other hand to reach down and cup the lupine balls as he began to gently squeeze and lightly stroke the wolf's cock in its sheath. As he stroked he felt the first twitches from the hardness in his hand and almost whimpered as the shaft thickened.

Michael was totally taken aback by the aggressive approach of the deer. He'd been positive that the deer was a homophobe. Obviously the nervousness had just been Kent trying to decide when and if he would make his move on the wolf. He had even admitted that he had decided that this was going to happen before he even got into the car. Kent had only been divorced for a year; he must be inexperienced. Suddenly the reek of fear made sense. It was kind of tacky for the buck to act without asking but that could be forgiven. Three years with his dominant lover had taught him obedience to someone else's desire. It was how he liked it. He growled as he felt the soft warmth of a hand close around his cock. It had been so long since he had felt an intimate touch.

Kent trembled as he continued to stroke up and down on the wolf's rapidly thickening sheath. He had never touched another male but knew the things that felt good on those few occasions that he had been able to convince his wife to touch him there. He was going to do his best to get this over with as quickly as possible and hoped that the wolf wouldn't demand too much from him. He let his fingers grip the penis behind the hardening bulb at its base and squeezed rhythmically, startled when he felt the wolfen hips thrust once in response. His other hand continued to roll the large testicles gently, marveling in spite of himself at the delicate softness of the fur covering the ballsac. As his fingers slid further up the sheath they encountered something small and hard in the fur near the opening. He looked closer and saw a small gold hoop piercing the lip and winced at the thought of how getting that must have felt.

The buck silently prayed that his captor would be satisfied with a paw job and let him go. With this new incentive he intensified his efforts as he manipulated the wolf's sex. Remembering the hip thrust, he concentrated more effort behind the knot of the cock and carefully began pulling down on the balls. It seemed to be working and soon he got his first glimpse of the cock itself as it thickened and lengthened while the sheath began to pull back of it own accord.

The red cock was smooth and wet and actually looked a little like his own but without the half's' curve of a deer penis. The knot in his hand was something new and it was growing faster. He could feel it pulse in his palm and he hoped that the wolf would cum soon and that this would be over.

Michael growled in earnest as his knot was kneaded and stroked; he felt the fullness in his balls growing as they were pulled down and away from his body, causing an exquisite tension. As the ache intensified, his cock grew even more sensitive. He could feel the pulsing ripples of pleasure rising through his shaft and his knot almost hurt with need as it began to fill the confines of his sheath. The buck's fingers gripped him behind the knot and hit that magic spot. In spite of himself, the wolf's hips bucked off the seat as he thrust his cock forward, unable to resist the instinct to tie. He felt his sheath pull back with a sharp pain that barely fell short of a torn sheath, and popped free. Warm moist air from the heater, hard callused pads on the deer's fingers and the soft fur of the palm suddenly caressed his exquisitely sensitive cock all at once. He hoped that the buck would permit him the pleasure of exploring the deer's body afterwards. He wanted to return some of the pleasure that he was being given when Kent was finished.

Anton had discouraged Michael from being vocal during sex, except to beg. But this wasn't Anton and Michael didn't feel like begging. He snarled with pleasure and lifted a paw to gently cup the back of the buck's head and softly raked his nails through the rich fur in the well behind his unexpected lover's ear. "Oh yeah! That's it baby! You got it. There... yes... right... there!"

Kent felt a tiny thrill when he realized that the wolf was responding with passion to his ministrations. What had been pink and slick was now purple and mottled. Delicate veins snaked over the knobby surface of the cock and clear drops of fluid dripped steadily now from the blunt triangular tip, wetting the fur of his hand. The wolf's cock had transformed from a slick pencil under his fingers and he now saw a thick pole of heavily veined, purple flesh. The wolf's organ was almost too thick to wrap his fingers completely around and was at least six inches long before it swelled into a knot nearly the size of a baseball; behind that, a couple more inches of thinner shaft disappeared into the contracted sheath.

The buck flinched when the wolf laid a heavy paw on his head. Michael was going to force him to do more. When the wolf had snarled at him and thrust his turgid cock free of the sheath it had scared him, but also given him a tiny sense of power. For an instant, he had almost been able to believe that the wolf was as much at his mercy as the other way around. That feeling died when he felt the paw clawing at the back of his head. He stared down at what he held in his hand and wondered if he could do what was expected of him. He leaned toward the engorged cock and muffled a whimper, already stifling a gag. The smell of the wolf's sex was overpowering. He could see individual pulses force tiny jets of watery pre from the winking tip. Closing his eyes and bracing himself, he slowly extended his tongue to the wolf and the taste filled his mouth.

A deer's tongue evolved to strip leaves and buds from branches that were loath to give up what they had worked so hard to grow. The long, dexterous and extremely strong instrument easily reached all the way around the wolf's shaft and completed almost half of a second circuit before Kent's nose was pressed against the wet knot and the gold ring in the wolf's sheath dug into his cheek. Precum leaked down the cock and coated Kent's tongue with its musky saltiness while the wolf panted and growled over him. He looked up the washboard stomach at his captor as the wolf's head jerked back and started to thrash back and forth. He felt the lupine shudder and heard growls turn to whimpers of pleasure.

"Oh fuck! Ohfuckohfuckohfuck!" Michael couldn't believe the feelings when the deer wrapped his tongue around his cock. He was a little angry that Kent had taken things this far without ever once asking if it was okay with Michael, but the habit of obedience was too strong for him to resist this incredible assault on his long-neglected cock.

Kent had been afraid that the taste of cock would make him puke but realized that it was not horrible; mostly salty but endurable. The feel of having another male's cock under his tongue was a different story, but he was trying hard to do what he had to do without thinking about it. But he couldn't help thinking about it. Couldn't stop thinking about how it was hard and soft at the same time. The texture of its slick surface under his tongue. The way it twitched when he hit an especially sensitive spot. He began extending and retracting his tongue, causing it to snake up and down the lupine cock. His other hand began to rhythmically pull on and release the wolf's balls. The tiny flame of power started to flicker its way back to life. He had been totally helpless a second ago and now he was controlling the powerful predator that had taken him prisoner. He was the one making the wolf shudder and moan. He didn't notice that his own sheath had become uncomfortably tight.

Anton's otter tongue had been very talented and Michael had loved the little laps and licks fluttering like butterflies all over him, but that didn't prepare him for the sensations of the deer's long, powerful tongue gripping him in a sinuous, tight embrace as it literally milked his balls of their juice. He felt strong fingers yanking on his balls making them ache with a wonderful pain that only served to intensify his need. His head whipped back and forth as the deer's wet nose panted hot breath across his fully engorged knot. His back arched as he felt himself being carried closer and closer to a release that seemed to flee at almost the same pace. Always closer but never quite to the brink. So long! Too long! Oh fuck! He needed to cum so badly! The wolf's nails raked across chest, clawing at his fur violently enough to knock the ancient and bulky phone from his pocket. Please, he thought, not like Anton... *Don't leave me on the edge. Let me cum. Please!*

"Lick it. You... unh... are good, buck! So good... uh... uh... uhnh... Suck my cock!" he panted. The close air of the car was rich with the smell of desire and sex. The lingering traces of fear that reached his nose were weak and little more than a memory.

Kent's back was starting to ache, sharp jabs of pain shooting up his spine from leaning over the lust-enraged wolf. Being very careful not to startle or anger him, the buck worked his way to the floor until he knelt with one knee on either side of Michael's leg. The wolf shifted to give him room as he continued to growl and order Kent to do the awful deed he had been praying to avoid. He leaned forward and pulled back at the same time on the wolf's cock until it was pointed at his face. He didn't notice that leaning forward pressed his cock against the lupine's denim clad leg, intent only on preparing himself for what he had to do next.

Opening his muzzle he lowered his head and felt a hard, wet, twitching cock slide into his mouth. Oh god! He had a cock in his mouth! A male was shooting his precum into his mouth! He was staring at a male's crotch watching a penis disappearing between his lips! He was smelling a male's sex musk, staring at droplets of precum slowly soaking into belly fur! His fingers held another male's balls and were making him jerk and twitch and whimper! What was happening to him? He closed his eyes and lowered his muzzle the rest of the way until his lips pressed against a stone-hard knot and the tip of Michael's cock spurted pre directly against the back of his throat. He almost gagged as he lifted his muzzle and lowered it again, extending his tongue around the shaft on the down-stroke and retracting it as he pulled back. His world disappeared into the steady motion of head moving up and down over someone else's sex. Tongue back and forth over a cock. Hard penis grinding unknowingly against another male's leg.

Michael couldn't help himself. He grabbed the rack of antlers scraping so wonderfully on his belly and chest in both hands. He pulled down with his hands and pushed up with his hips. It had been so long since he had been buried fully in someone's muzzle. Too long, and the buck was far too skilled to be a beginner. The wolf could feel the hardness rubbing on his shin and shuddered.

"Take it... take my cock! Eat it, buck! Oh... god... Fuck... Fuck... Ohh..."

Kent found that he had to rest his arm across the wolf's thighs to try and keep the cock in his mouth from going too deep as the wolf began humping himself against the deer's muzzle. It took a moment for him to realize that the gun had fallen from his captor's pocket. Another to realize that the gun half resting on his outstretched arm was actually an ancient cellular phone about eight times the size of the ones they sold now. A split-second more to realize that he didn't care. His lips began to feel sore as the huge knot pressed them against his teeth. Precum ran steadily down the wolf's shaft and still the buck's cheeks began filling with the stuff until he swallowed another male's seed. He hardly noticed the taste as the cock in his mouth began swelling even more and jerked against his tongue. His tongue worked harder and faster on the slippery shaft as he heard the wolf snarling and snapping at thin air over him. He didn't notice the feel of rough fabric against sensitive flesh as his own hips continued to rock against the wolf's leg.

His wife had always lain passive when he used his muzzle (or anything else for that matter) on her. Thin lips pressed tightly together, his wife had always endured such attempts to pleasure her and then confessed her 'sinful' participation to her priest as soon as she could afterwards. Sex was missionary position, preferably when she was most likely to be fertile. Anything else was sinful and 'her wifely obligations'—the price to be paid for the gift of children. When five years had gone by with no quickening of her womb she had left him. While he had used tongue and paw and penis on her, trying to elicit some pleasurable response, he had often wondered what it would be like to be with an enthusiastic partner.

He had begun this thinking that his life depended on it. He knew now that he was not being forced but continued anyway, part of him couldn't help reacting to the vocal, thrashing responses of his unasked-for partner. He was filled with a sense of power, of control and because of that, couldn't help feeling a bit of the pleasure he was giving the wolf. Part of him couldn't help just desperately wanting to give pleasure. To know that he could do it.

Michael could feel his impending climax building at the base of his spine. His balls tried to pull up into his groin. A pressure grew behind his knot, promising release and ecstasy. He tried to warn the buck that he was about to cum but couldn't form the words, only snarls and grunts.

When the wolf's fingers gripped his rack and pulled him back Kent couldn't give up that control and resisted. He sucked hungrily and madly at the now twitching organ in his mouth, snorting around the fleshy pole until the first scalding jets of thick lupine semen splashed into his mouth and began to trickle down his throat.

Suddenly he realized what was happening, what he was doing, and jerked his head back, pulling his mouth off the fountaining cock. Several jets of sticky whiteness hit his nose and muzzle, coating his face in the heavy ejaculate of the twitching, whimpering wolf.

Michael came to himself slowly, feeling his breathing and heartbeat ease their frantic pace. Watching as the flashing stars in his eyes slowly faded. When he could move again, he lifted his head from the seat and looked down at the deer on the floor with his cum dripping off the buck's face with thick plops. The deer just sat there without moving, quiet and seemingly as dazed as Michael felt. He shifted his leg back to his side of the car and saw a spreading wet spot at the buck's crotch and marveled again at the size of the bulge there.

"Thank you. That was wonderful and I had no idea how much I needed it," he said.

The buck sat quietly on the floor for several minutes before raising his cum-wet muzzle, "I should go now."

"I wouldn't mind sharing a cup of coffee with you, but I understand how it goes. Don't worry. I'm not one of those that insist on a cuddle afterwards, no matter how sweet it can be. But you may want to clean yourself up a bit first before talking the mechanics." he leaned forward and ran his finger through a strand of cum hanging from the deer's nose.

Kent stared at what Michael had wiped from his muzzle uncomprehendingly for a moment. Then he looked down at the cum-stain spreading at his own crotch and began to sob uncontrollably. He fell to the floor of the car in a huddled mass of misery.

The wolf just sat stunned for a moment and then reached down to pull the deer up and into his arms where he hugged and rocked him, trying his best to sooth Kent's near-hysterical sobbing; wondering what had happened. It took a long time for the wracking sobs of the deer to quiet and longer still to get the full story from him. To learn how and why the deer had thought at first that he was being raped. And how, even worse to the deer, he had finished knowing it was because he wanted to. To learn that it was the deer's first time with a male and certainly not the magical moment anyone's first time deserved to be. It took a long while for Michael to explain why he had not resisted. How he had felt helpless under the ministrations of the deer. For a very long while both sat quietly in the car in an empty parking lot. Once he'd gotten the tears under control, Kent couldn't bear to be touched any longer.

By the time the repair shop opened, Kent had made himself presentable and his hysteria was restricted to a certain wildness in his eyes. He saw the tow truck bringing his car onto the lot and made ready to leave Michael's car. He stood outside the open door and looked in at the quiet wolf, wondering if either of them was going to be okay, "Michael, I don't want you to blame yourself. What happened was my fault. I should be apologizing to you for taking advantage of you that way. Yes, it has me pretty messed up right now. But, maybe I need to be messed up. I learned some things about myself that are going to take some work to deal with, but now at least I know they're there."

Michael looked at the deer and nodded. After a moment he pulled out his wallet and extracted two cards and handed them to the deer, "Here, take these. One is my card. If you ever need to talk or anything please don't hesitate to call me. The other is the business card of a very good therapist who is helping me deal with some pretty heavy shit I'm learning about myself."

Kent looked at both cards and put them in his wallet, "Before I go, there is something I'm curious about. When I tried to leave the first time you stopped me and said that there was something you needed from me first. What was it?"

The wolf chuckled sardonically, "You're not going to believe this but I represent the owners of a small startup in Toronto and I'm on a recruiting trip looking for someone to manage their system. That's my job. You sounded good and I was going to ask for your card so that I could contact you professionally." He looked around at the car and at himself, "I usually fly and rent a car. My business clothes are in the trunk."

The deer shook his head with the irony and smiled softly before closing the door and walking away. He didn't look as he heard the engine start and the car drive out of the lot. He stood watching the sun rise on a new day—knowing that he was not the same man he had been the day before but not knowing who he had become.

Michael sat on the bed in his hotel room. Another room in another city on yet another business trip. So many nights spent alone in strange rooms in strange places. He decided that it didn't much matter where you were alone if there was no one special to return to. He sighed and sat and thought about that strange night during a similar trip several months ago when he and a stranded deer unwittingly took advantage of each other. He wondered what had happened to Kent. The confused deer had never called Michael or the therapist. He hoped the beautiful buck had found someone to help him deal with the events of that night.

The dejected wolf abandoned his gloomy thoughts to go and answer a knock on the door. He opened it and stared blankly at the person on the other side. The mule deer at the door smiled at him.

"Hello, Michael."

"Hello, Kent."

"I hope you don't mind, but I convinced your office to tell me where you were recruiting and the front desk gave me the room number."

"No, I don't mind. How have you been?"

"I've been fine. Learning a lot about myself. Learning who I am and what it means to be happy."

The wolf noticed for the first time the faded 501's hugging the deer's ass and the t-shirt with a wave of pride colors embroidered on it. He saw the gold hoops hanging from the deer's right ear and smiled. "And what kind of things have you learned?"

The deer smiled back and moved into the room. He flowed into the wolf's arms, kicking the door closed behind him, "Let me show you."

Don't let me die a virgin…

When folks are in peril, they sometimes do peculiar things. Passions that are usually kept under control may burrow their way to the surface with a vengeance; unspoken desires may find a voice.

Not always is this a sweet, touching thing. The uglier side of one's personality may suddenly be exposed in the face of imminent danger, and some very poor decisions can be made.

"Preventing Hypothermia" explores these issues with few reservations. The author shows his dedication to the story, rather than the characters' egos, by allowing them to display some very unflattering personality traits.

Preventing Hypothermia

Stormcatcher

Devin rubbed his fingerpads over the frosted-up windows of the Hummer as it plowed its way steadily onward through the snow, staring down with understandable trepidation at the thick blanket of white that was piled high over the ground. It seemed like it was a vast ocean churning just a foot or two below the bottom of the passenger side window, and when he looked from it up to the huge gray expanse of sky overhead, it was almost difficult to tell where one ended and the other began. There weren't really any trees around to mark the boundaries between horizon and ground; in a place like Alaska, one got more used to seeing glaciers instead. The mournful sound of the wind whistling around the vehicle was like a vengeful spirit searching for the slightest chink in the armor of the Hummer so it could tear its way inside to the two occupants perched on the front seat.

The huge bulk of the ram morph sitting in the driver's seat had a facial expression even more grim than that of his fox passenger. Randall Kleghorn was a towering fellow, roughly seven feet tall including the apex of his curled horns—and his broad, muscled body was a testament to a male that was no stranger to making tough decisions, working hard, and enduring harsh frozen temperatures. The petroleum mining facility where he and Devin worked was part of a large chain of such institutions, and he had been in his current position as lead foreman for well over fifteen years. It usually took a lot to get the ovine rattled, and although the fox had never seen the ram become completely unglued, he had only seen the ram's current facial expression twice before—and both times involved a serious

245

problem that could have affected himself and everyone else at the plant.

The ram's steely gray eyes were narrowed and his brows deeply furrowed as he hunched over the large steering wheel, his face staring intently ahead at the unrelenting whiteness trying to obstruct the vehicle's way. His mouth was turned slightly downward in a dire frown, and the coarse hairs of his blonde and gray-peppered beard twitched along with his face's muscle spasms as they strained from his consternation. His ears flicked nervously near his thick, curved horns as they listened to the grinding of the snow against the inner rims of the tire wells, and he didn't like the way that his huge booted foot felt on the accelerator. He'd been gradually giving it more gas as they had left town, and they'd made good progress, at first—but the snow never stopped falling, and the way it was lashing over the windshield was making it harder to see. They had ridden mostly in silence, each knowing what a risk the voyage had been, to begin with… but because the snow wasn't letting up as supplies had started to get low, and since the small town of Tyson was only seven miles away, he'd figured that if he and Devin got an early enough start, they'd be back well before sundown. Neither of them had counted on the blizzard actually picking up steam as the day had worn on.

The vulpine swallowed nervously, his green eyes wide as he turned carefully around on the seat and cast a worried glance into the back of the Hummer, where supplies were stacked so high that he literally couldn't see out of the narrow window in the back. He sighed, snorted a little, and shook his head, turning back around to face gloomily and resolutely forward once more. "Well. Guess we don't have to worry about the beer getting warm, anyway," he muttered to his boss, his joke half-hearted.

The ram grunted back and shook his head slowly, his expression growing only more agitated—and for a wild panicked second, the fox worried that his supervisor was going to belt him one across the muzzle for being flippant in the face of a bad situation. To his relief, however, Randall only sighed and cranked the defrost settings up to their highest level as he rumbled deeply, "Damn it, if this just don't beat all… I've been the top foreman at this base for the last nine years, Dev, and I ain't never seen it come down like this. Never. This one's a record-breaker, for sure."

Devin nodded, his big pointed ears quirking. He frowned and furrowed his own brows a little, looking down into his lap in self-chastisement. "Yeah… and it probably didn't help that I just had to stop in at Sturdyk's and see if they got anything good in. A good book sure ain't gonna do much good if we end up frozen solid."

This time, the ram did turn to look over at him, glowering just a little.

"Don't even. If anyone takes the blame if something happens, Dev, it'll be me. I'm the boss, remember? I'm supposed to know what the risks are and prepare for them ahead of time." He shook his head angrily and turned back to concentrate on the road that really didn't seem to be there, thanks to all the snow. "Besides, you weren't in there but about twenty minutes. No sense in you apologizin' for bein' literate."

Devin glanced sideways at the huge ovine, then shrugged a little bit and nodded once. He rested his right forearm against the doorframe next to the window and drummed his fingerclaws quietly against the padding, his own sharp ears starting to realize just how hard the motor was working to continue onwards through the snow. His throat felt as dry as a desert, and he had to swallow several times before he could get his question out without sounding like he was croaking it. "So. Level with me, Kleg," he murmured, turning to his boss again. "How worried should I be?"

Randall didn't answer him for a moment or two, but finally, he gripped the wheel tight enough in his fingers to almost make his knuckles turn white as he rumbled to him in a low voice, "Depends on the Hummer. I've taken this thing through mud bogs and rivers where the water level was literally up to the hood, and it barely slowed down… but this is different. This shit's like trying to make it slog through a swimming pool fulla oatmeal."

The fox's heart lurched in his chest, upon hearing that, but he was grateful that the ram didn't try to avoid the seriousness of the situation. He nodded nervously, then watched the road for a minute before he asked, "How far you reckon we are from the camp?"

"That's the good news," the ram replied. "Odometer says we've come a good four miles, so we're a little over halfway there. But if the engine dies, we're pretty much fucked. I figure that snow's about waist deep, by now, and there ain't no way we'd be able to make it through that kind of drift with a three-mile walk. The wind chill out there's gotta be in the negative double-digits, from the sound of it."

The Hummer went on for another twenty minutes or so, the fox and ram totally silent the whole time, as though afraid that even speaking might slow the already-burdened vehicle down. But then the crunching of the snow under the tires both seemed to intensify and slow down, and the ram's brows shot upward in alarm as he heard the transmission in the engine begin to grind. The vehicle's progress halted, and the dim halo of the headlights faltered on the snowbank in front of the Hummer as the motor promptly died.

For a few terse moments, the very air seemed to freeze around the pair.

247

Kleg stared resolutely forward, trying to keep his expression neutral—but he couldn't stop a sharp twinge of fear that ripped through his nervous system and manifested itself in the form of a jerk in the right side of his muzzle. Devin sat bolt upright in his seat, his expression stark and his eyes almost comically wide. It might've been enough to make the ram laugh, under different circumstances, but Kleg immediately recognized the panic slowly starting to seep into the vulpine's features, mingled with a millstone of guilt from the jinx he believed he'd brought upon himself and his boss just from talking about the potential danger. The fox's thick, bushy tail fluffed heavily outward, and it seemed to Devin that he could feel every hair on it as they spiked outwards sharply in fear.

Randall finally snapped out of his own trance, and brought Devin back down to earth with him sharply by growling out his exasperation loudly. "God... dammit!" he swore, hastily pumping the gas and flicking the ignition key off, then taking his foot off the gas and trying to turn it on again. "C'mon, Bessie, sugar, don't do this t'me... I needja to be my sturdy bulldyke of a workhorse..." He didn't get any results from his efforts other than the headlights dying, which made his heart sink. That meant that the battery was probably dead, or so depleted that it would need a good thirty minutes to replenish itself, and of course, there weren't any other friendly motorists with jumper cables happening to pass by. He gritted his teeth and pounded the steering wheel with a meaty fist almost hard enough to knock it out of its adjusted setting, and he clenched his eyes tightly shut and lowered his head, hoping wildly that Devin wouldn't be able to hear the thundering of his heartbeat. Fear and anger rushed through his nervous system and spread an icy chill all over his body; a chill that he knew would most likely become literal and potentially fatal swiftly now that the heater was out.

Devin didn't say anything. The ram could hear the fox taking deep breaths that started deep within the fox's body, and it didn't take long for his sharp ears to pick up the tiny wheezing sound that often accompanied an individual whose breath was on the verge of going into hyperventilation.

The ram opened his eyes and stared gravely at the fox, then reached a big hand over to take the mike of the CB radio into his big palm. He switched the unit on and noted with a great measure of relief that the pale green light on the frequency display lit up as it should, and he furrowed his brows intently as he fiddled with the tuning controls, static crackling across the speaker with tinny sharpness. "There's still a chance," he rumbled to the fox as he lifted the mike to his lips, hoping that his words would calm his worker down somewhat. "Thank heaven I always put a fresh battery in this radio once a month whether it needs it or not. I dunno if the guys'll be able to pick up our signal in all this wind, but it's worth a shot."

Randall found the channel that he thought was the least filled with static, and he started to transmit. "This is Big Horn calling the Fortress of Solitude... Big Horn to Solitude, do you copy? Over."

He and Devin listened breathlessly, and there were a few crackles, but no response. Devin stared outside with accumulating dread as the light began to fade from the sky, and night began to fall. It had to be close to four in the afternoon, and at this time of the year, night came calling horribly early.

The ram looked worried as he waited, then tried again. "I said, this is Big Horn calling Solitude, Big Horn to Solitude, can you read me? Guys? Dammit, stop jerking off to bad internet porn and pick up, damn yer hides!"

Only the static from the radio broke the silence in the cab of the vehicle, but even then, the fear shared by the two males seemed to have a palpable life of its own.

Randall gripped the mike in both hands as if he were about to kiss it passionately. "Davis!" he roared into it, the boom of his voice feeling as though it made the whole vehicle shake. Devin jumped in his seat, but held his breath, not even wanting his breathing to interrupt the ram's task. "Henshaw! I swear, if I get back there somehow and find out that you guys been stoning it up in the goddamn rec room again, I'm gonna fuckin' string ya all up by your innards..."

Nothing. The static continued to buzz softly, not even an occasional spike scratching from the speakers to break the monotony.

The ram slowly released the send button, and he felt a weariness overtake him that made him want to rest his forehead on the steering wheel and doze off. It came not only from the mind-numbing surplus of fear, but also from his frantic analysis of how to handle Devin. It was clear to him that the fox was on the edge, and if he didn't choose his words very carefully, he knew that Devin might literally go into hysterics.

Slowly, he switched off the CB, then looked over at the fox grimly. Devin's eyes were locked onto the ram's face, and they seemed to be far too bright. There was a twitching to them, a sort of glassiness that made the ram worry even more. Kleg cleared his throat softly, then rumbled lowly to the vulpine, "Okay, Dev. I'm not gonna lie to you, we're in pretty deep shit. The guys can't get our signal in this wind, but we got one more chance at reachin' 'em—but I'm gonna need you to work with me, so take a couple of deep breaths or whatever you need to do... then tell me when you're ready. Okay?"

Devin barely nodded, but that was better than nothing. The fox balled his gloved hands into fists, then closed his eyes and did as instructed, taking several deep breaths and exhaling them slowly. It calmed his-heart rate down a bit, and when he re-opened his eyes, they seemed a bit less crazed.

"R-... Right. I'm sorry. I almost kinda lost it, for a minute, there," he murmured apologetically to the ram, his ears drooping a bit.

"And I don't blame you. But like I said, let's not give up yet," the ram rumbled. He pointed to a large metal box that was attached to the back of the fox's seat, nearly obscured by the supplies piled up in the cargo area of the vehicle. "There's a flare gun in the emergency kit in that box, behind you. You're smaller than me, so I need you to see if you can clamber back there and get it out for me. Think you got enough room to maneuver?"

Devin craned his head and neck back to follow the direction of the ram's finger, and he nodded. "Yeah, I think so. Gonna be a tight squeeze, but I reckon I'll manage." He got up and eased himself over the backrest of the seat, then handed the ram a few of the smaller supply items that had been placed on top of the kit. He opened the box carefully, then blinked as he stared down at the goods inside, grunting softly with the weight of the gun as he carefully hefted it out of the box with both hands and handed it to his boss. "Holy shit, this fucker's heavy... whaddya use to fire it, cannon rounds?" he murmured, scratching his head a bit as he nodded at the large gun. "I didn't know they made flare guns that big."

"Yeah, this one's a doozy, all right," the ram agreed, his brows furrowed deeply as he checked the gun over and made sure that it was properly loaded and in good working order. "It's bigger than average because it's got a longer range to it—see how long the barrel is?" he rumbled, tapping the extended tube near the gun's firing port. "This fucker's Everest expedition worthy. The flare effect's got a range of roughly twelve miles, and it's got a heavy report to make it more audible. Sounds like an M-80, when it goes off in mid-air." He looked back at the emergency kit again, then pointed at it once more. "There should be a pair of safety goggles in there, too. Hand 'em to me, willya, please? And gimmee two more rounds for the gun."

Devin nodded, opened the box again, and rummaged around until he found the goggles and rounds in question, handing them over to the ram as sudden surprise registered on his face when he realized what his employer was proposing to do. "Waitasec... Kleg, you're not gonna go out there to shoot that thing, are you?"

The ram gave the fox a look that made it clear that he couldn't believe the fox would even ask such a dumb question. He pulled on an extra pair of Thinsulate gloves over his fingers before pulling on a pair of thicker woolen mitts over those as he rumbled, "What the hell am I supposed to do, Dev, hang it out the window? It's gotta be aimed at just the right trajectory, or the guys back at the base might not see it. And no offense, pard, but the way that wind's kicking up out there, I'm not sure you'd even be able to walk in it."

The fox snorted, and Kleg was actually glad to see a bit of indignation on his friend's face as the vulpine started to pull his coat more tightly around himself. "Geez, Kleg, I ain't that much of a lightweight!" he muttered. "Besides, it's gotta be a good thirty to forty below, out there. I'm worried yer gonna get frostbite."

"Trust me, I ain't gonna be out there long enough for that to happen, if I got anything to say about it," he grunted. The ram slipped the goggles down onto his face, adjusted his tuque, then nodded at the emergency kit once more. "You'll find an assload of those pocket warmer packs in that kit, too, way down near the bottom. I'm gonna probably need every slap-ass one of 'em, so unwrap 'em all and have them at the ready for me. I'm gonna need ya to help me stuff the fuckers up under my shirt, into my dungarees... everywhere."

Devin gave the ram an odd expression, upon hearing Kleg's words, but he nodded obediently and again rummaged inside the emergency kit, finding the packets and throwing handfuls of them over the seat and into the front, then he climbed back into the passenger's seat and begin to rip the packets open carefully but as briskly as he could. He gave the ram a worried sideways glance, then asked, "So—level with me. If the guys see your flare shot, how long you think we got, and how long do you think it'll take 'em?" he asked.

Randall shrugged. "Well... the Super Cat's the only thing we got on the base that I think can handle this kind of snow volume, and because it's so big and slow, it might take 'em a little over an hour. Right now, the snow's above our tires, but it ain't up to our hood, yet, so as long as the cab's still visible, they should be able to see us. If it piles up onto the hood, though..." He paused, then glanced sideways at the fox as though not sure if he should go on.

Devin took a deep breath, then nodded. "Go on. Spit it out, Kleg, I can handle it."

The ram sighed, then nodded and rubbed his forehead a bit as he murmured deeply, "If it comes up over the windows, we're pretty much fucked. We'd freeze if we tried staying in here, and unless the guys were within our line of sight and they spotted us coming toward 'em, we'd never make it on foot."

Devin stared blankly at him, but then sighed a little as he sat up onto his knees and poked his upper body and one of his hands behind the seat and rummaged around a little bit, coming back up and around with a bottle of whiskey in his grip. He waggled the bottle at him as he began to fiddle with the cap, murmuring to the ram, "Wanna join me in a before-doom nightcap, then? If there's a chance we might freeze to death, we might as well go out with grins on our faces."

The ram gave him a look of horror, and promptly snatched the bottle out of the fox's grip and stuffed it back behind the seat. "Are you nuts?" he growled. "You can't drink booze in a blizzard! It dehydrates you faster, and thins your blood, and that makes it tough for you feel your extremities starting to freeze. That's just askin' for hypothermia to set in. You want me carryin' yer frozen corpse back to Tressa and tellin' her why yer fox pride fell off?" he snorted, a smirk with just a touch of uneasiness to it settling onto his features.

Devin's face looked surprised, then immediately chagrined as his ears drooped a little bit and his shoulders slumped. "I'm not normally much of a drinker, anyway, but given what's going on, I… I dunno, I guess I just figured 'what the hell', y'know?" he sighed. He sat down firmly and propped an elbow onto the door ledge again as he stared miserably out at the snow, the view slowly clouding over with ice crystals all around the edges. "I gotta say, though, I dunno if Tressa would be all that distressed, to hear something like that. Won't matter much one way or the other, come next month. Ironic as hell, if you ask me."

"Hunh?" Randall frowned, cocking his head sharply in confusion at the fox's words. "What're you talkin' about, Dev?"

Devin turned and gave him another surprised look, one brow arched. "You didn't know? None of the other guys told you?"

The ram grunted and spread his big hands, obviously not having a clue. "Told me what?" he demanded.

"Shit!" the fox murmured, looking dazed. "I guess for once, they've actually been keeping it under their hats. Given how fast gossip normally flies around our ranks, I'm honestly shocked." He shrugged and pulled one leg up to rest the edge of his booted ankle onto the seat, then he propped his muzzle onto his knee as he clasped his hands around his limb. "Me and Tressa are splitting up, Kleg. The divorce oughta be finalized in another week and a half, or so."

The fox's words gave Randall enough of a shock to make him pause as he tightened his coat and scarf around his neck, the ovine's shaggy brows lifting in surprise as he regarded Devin solemnly. "Yer shittin' me!" he rumbled, his bearded maw hanging open for a few moments. His jaw worked up and down for a moment as he tried to find something comforting to say, but the situation at hand and his own stress kept the words from coming. "Damn, Dev, I'm truly sorry to hear that. I always figured you two to be pretty solid, together."

Devin finally swiveled his head enough on his knee so that he could look at his boss, and he shrugged a little. "Why apologize?" he murmured. "Ain't like it's your fault, Kleg, unless you're one of the guys that's been fooling around with her, which I seriously doubt. You always were more tightly-laced than the other fellas."

The ram's muzzle dropped open even wider than before. "You think she's cheating on you?" he gasped. "That why you're splitting up with her?"

Devin shook his head wearily. "I know she's cheating on me. I can smell it in her scent, I can tell by the way she acts when I'm around, I can tell by how jittery and jumpy she is all the time." He shrugged a little bit, then he gave the bull a look mixed with guilt and sadness as he said, "She can't even look me in the eyes anymore, Kleg. I try to have a conversation to her, and it's like she don't even wanna participate. I know it's the guilt she's feeling that's making her act that way, and what really hurts my heart is how much misery it's causing her. She hates the idea of betraying me, but she's too afraid to admit that she's doing it, because she doesn't want me to be angry at her."

Randall stared at Devin thoughtfully, as though he were trying to read the fox's face to see if his friend was lying to him. It was really more than the ram wanted to believe. Tressa had always seemed to be so sweet and trusting, and she had gravitated toward the ovine as a surrogate father figure, just as he had looked upon her as a daughter of sorts. He really didn't want to imagine her having sex with anyone that wasn't her husband, but he also knew that the remote nature of their collective home had taken its toll on others before in negative ways, and perhaps she was no exception. The isolation and gloomy surroundings had a way of making even the most grounded and thoughtful individuals act in ways totally uncharacteristic of their normal behavior.

He reached over and laid a firm hand onto Devin's shoulder. "Tell you what. Let's hit the 'pause' button on this here conversation for just a moment, till after I shoot off this flare. But I want us to talk about this soon's I get back, because I'm gonna be shaking pretty hard and I'll need something to take my mind off the cold. You keep unwrapping those packs, and I'll be back in a sec. 'Kay?"

Devin nodded, his face worried but resolute as he sat down and continued to open the pocket warmer packets. "You got it, boss-ram. Be careful out there, hear?"

Kleg nodded, then adjusted his coat collar to make sure that there wasn't any of his pelt exposed, and made sure he had a good, firm grip on the flare gun. He tucked the two extra rounds into his coat pockets, then took hold of the driver's side door latch with thickly-gloved fingers. He turned back to Devin, his words a bit muffled by his scarf as he tugged it up and over his muzzle as best he could. "Brace yourself. Gonna try to close the door as fast as I can."

Devin nodded again, then closed his eyes and gritted his teeth as the ram opened his door, and the wind attacked the temporary opening, sweeping into the cab and chilling it harshly as the ram's bulky form struggled to get out. He managed to nearly tumble into the snow bank just below the door of the cab, then slammed the door shut with Devin's assistance. Suddenly awash in an ocean of snow, the ram instantly felt the solid bite of the cold on the bit of his cheekruffs that were exposed, and he stared at the front of the nearly hemmed-in vehicle, trudging forward a few feet to stand in front of it. It was an effort, and even with his strong physique, he felt his muscles protesting in the wind.

Inside the cab, Devin tried not to watch Kleg too closely, diligently working to get the pocket warmers unwrapped as fast as he could—but try though he did, he inevitably latched his worried gaze onto the ram's hulking figure, a vague outline of black and grey surrounded by wind and snow on all sides. He saw the ovine fumble with the gun, then carefully raise his arms up over his head, limbs angled slightly forward. There was the flashing light of discharge from the gun and the sound of the flare being fired, and a thick puff of smoke was visible for perhaps a split second before it vanished in the wind. Devin straightened up in his seat, keenly worried as he saw the ram hunch over as though shot, himself—but then he realized what the ovine was up to from Kleg's elbow movements, as the ram was apparently re-loading the gun's chamber. The fox jumped sharply in his seat and let out a yip of surprise as the sound of a considerable explosion went off some distance overhead, and there was a brief but noticeable flash of light that reminded him a bit of lightening. The effect was mildly bolstering, and Devin realized that Kleg was right—that sound and light would be visible for miles around, and he figured that everyone at the mining facility should have seen it. Slowly at first, he resumed unwrapping the packets as Kleg fired off the second round, reloaded, then fired the last one. The hunched-over form then made his way quickly back to the driver's side, and the fox scrambled to help him open the door, then reared back as Randall hauled his shivering form inside and slammed the door shut again.

"Kleg, ya did it!" Devin beamed, his face excited as he immediately went into action, grabbing up the packets that he'd unwrapped and starting to stuff them down the front of the ram's coat, worriedly checking the ovine's face to see if it was discolored. There was a dark pinkish-redness on the ram's upper cheekruffs, but there was no sign of ice accumulation. The fox slid two packs into place on both spots, and the ram's shivering gloves came up to hold them there, the ram's eyes closed and teeth chattering as the flare gun dropped to the floor, forgotten. "Damn, but they'll hear and see those for sure, I just about fell outta my seat, the noise was so loud! Are you okay? You feel numb or tingly, anywhere?" he asked anxiously, continuing to push the packs down the ram's shirt and tugging his friend's shoulders forward a bit so he could do so for the ovine's back.

"F-fuckin' freezin'..." Kleg shivered, stating the obvious. "Nuh-not... f-feeling anything n-numb yet, though." He reached forward and grabbed one of the fox's handpaws, causing Devin to jump again as one of his eyes peeped open and stared firmly at the vulpine. "K-... keep talkin' to me. Don't lemme f-fall asleep."

"I won't, boss-ram, don't worry. You just sit tight, and bounce around a little. That'll keep your blood circulating and keep you awake," Devin advised, diligently continuing to work. The ram nodded and complied with the fox's idea, his large frame starting to jiggle and bounce in place as the motion helped the warmth packets drop lower inside his coat and shirt. The manufactured packets began to do their job, the artificial heat from them slowly seeping into the ram's pelt and skin, then into his body, steadily downplaying the coldness that was wrapped around him. So intense were his movements that Devin's own smaller frame began to jiggle and bounce on the ram's lap, and in spite of the situation, the fox couldn't help but smirk. "Geez, big fella, you go! Picking our talk up where we left off, I bet that Tressa'd give anything to be in my boots, right now. Ridin' your lap like this would probably be enough to get her pussy good n' moist."

The fox couldn't have chosen a better set of words to snap the ram awake if he'd tried. Both his eyes opened and fixed a baleful glare on the fox, even as his shaggy eyebrows shivered tiny snowflakes all over his cheeks. "Guh—goddamn, Dev, d-don't be s-such a p... pervert. T-Tressa's your wife. And she's g-gonna stay your wife till the d... divorce is final, and even if shuh... she offered, I c-couldn't do it. Holy shit, Devin, she's luh... like a daughter t'me. I couldn't f... fuck her any more than I could fuck yu... you!"

Devin's gloved hands were busily rubbing the ram's face carefully, the fox having run out of heat packets at last but noting with some relief that they appeared to be doing their job quite efficiently. Kleg's broad shoulders had slowed down their shivering, and the ram's facial features seemed to be more alert as he watched the fox, the steady bouncing movements under Devin's rump starting to feel less frantic and more methodical as the ram's muscles relaxed a bit. The fox chuckled at the ram's words and gave him a playful wink as he rubbed the ram's sides and chest briskly, giving him a knowing wink. "Hey, now, boss, careful what you say. I might surprise you with how willing I might be, for that. I mean, shit, that's pretty much what I've been practicing with those magic holes over at the Fantasia Parlor, y'know? A guy's gotta hone his talents!" he snickered.

The ram actually stopped bouncing, upon hearing that, his voice now nearly back to normal and his speech no longer so slurred by cold-induced stuttering. "The Fantasia?" he gaped, narrowing his eyes a little at the vulpine. "What the h… hell were you doing hanging around in a place like that? That joint don't exactly draw in it's sh… share of the ladies."

Devin stopped, as well, a look of surprise but also of delighted triumph showing on his features as he jammed a fingerclaw toward his boss and rumbled, "Ahhh, so you do know what it is. Sounds like I ain't been the only one hangin' around, down there!" he laughed. "So c'mon, spill the details. Or were ya too busy spillin' somethin' else?" he grinned, as he began to sweep some of the cold packet wrappers from the seat onto the floorboard to get them out of the way. He climbed off the ram's lap just long enough to get the long Thermos canister that had some leftover coffee in it from town. He straddled the ram's lap again, then unscrewed the top of the canister, making the ram drink some of the lukewarm brew inside.

Randall grimaced at the taste of the stuff, but drank it anyway, his scowl still firmly in place as he looked back at the fox. "Oh, get off it, Dev, I wouldn't go near that place with a politician's dick. That flophouse is so nasty, I'd be too afraid to touch any of the doorknobs in it for fear of getting some kinda STD," he snapped.

"Awwww, c'mon," Devin laughed, fully enjoying his boss's discomfort more than he'd been prepared to realize. "It ain't all that bad! I've bumped into one or two of our own guys drifting around the place, although I'm sure that we mutually pretended that it didn't happen later, if you follow me," he rumbled with a shrug. "Hell, for all I know, it might even be one of the guys that's nailing Tressa now, or maybe one of'em that offered, but got turned down."

The ram stared at the fox with a look of slack-jawed disbelief and shock for a few moments, but his brows were firmly furrowed in disapproval, and

Devin could tell that his friend was quite unsettled by his words. "Waaaait a minute... Wait just a goddamn minute," he rumbled. "So, you ain't jokin'... are ya? All that horseflap you just fed me about how much you love Tressa, and how sorry you are that the two of you ain't been able to work your marital problems out with each other... and now yer basically admittin' to me that you been cheatin' on her the whole time, too, and with other guys, no less!" He shook his head in dazed, unpleased wonder at the fox and murmured, "Holy shit, Dev, what the hell is wrong with you? You think two wrongs make a right?"

Devin peered back at his boss, his own ears perking sharply as just a hint of indignation entered his tone. "Whaddya mean 'horseflap'? I do love Tressa! And I'm honestly sorry that her and me couldn't work things out, yeah, but that don't mean that I'm gonna let my own needs get left by the wayside while she's getting boned by my co-workers. And jeez, what's with the holy crusade?" he snorted, giving the ram the once-over with mild disdain etched into his features. "So I stuck my dick through a hole in a wall a couple times and got it sucked off by somebody I didn't know, and maybe I been toyin' around with other guys and feeling what it's like to have a cock up my ass. Big fuckin' deal. Ain't nothin' wrong with doing somethin' like that, given how limited our options are, around here. Yer makin' it sound like I committed some kinda federal crime."

Randall frowned darkly at the fox and shook his head in disgust. "How the fuck am I supposed to react, Devin? I can only take your word that everything you've said is true, but either way, my views toward two folks that I've always admired and cared about has just changed for the worse. And here I thought I knew you two so well, too." He shook his head in shocked amazement, his eyes staring forward starkly for a moment as he seethed a little. "Damn, whatever happened to the Tressa I used to know? Does she know about your little secret?"

The fox grunted. "What's so secretive about it?" he demanded. "I told you before, Dev, it's a biological function. Simple as that! It's a need of the male body, just like breathin' and shittin'. All the guys do it, we just don't talk about it out loud," he shrugged. "C'mon, Kleg, let's face it. If they built a brothel up here tomorrow, do you honestly think that all the customers would be only single guys?"

Kleg grunted as he shifted position a bit, the topic of conversation and his own revulsion at it making him acutely aware of Devin's weight on his lap, and made him consider pushing the vulpine off of him—but the temperature inside the cab was still considerably cold, and he could see Devin himself start to shiver in the wake of it—and body heat was body heat, whether the ram liked it or not. So he settled for digging his hands deep into his coat pockets as the packets on his cheekruffs slipped off, the ram continuing to attempt to justify his offended air to the fox. "I'm not talking about other single guys. I'm talking about you," the ram rumbled, pointing at him. "If cheating on each other is your and her way of dealing with marital problems, then why the hell did you two get hitched in the first place, hunh? Why not just ditch the whole 'marriage' thing and have an open relationship? You know, one of them polycarbo... polygamut..." He furrowed his brows as he tried to recall the correct pronunciation of the word, and finally gave up and rumbled with a grunt, "...you know, that... 'controlled, multi-partner' thing."

Devin laughed. "You mean 'polyamorous'. And that wouldn't have worked at all. Tressa's not bisexual, and I'm not so sure she'd be too keen on the idea of watching me and another guy go at it, even if she thought the other guy was hot." He rested his chin on his knee again and smirked a little, then said aloud to no one in particular, "kinda too bad, when you think about it. I suck dick pretty damn good, if I do say so, m'self."

"Aw, fuck, Devin, don't make me puke!" Kleg shuddered, his face looking as though someone had just shoved a rotten piece of fish under it. "Spare me the details, willya? I don't know what kind of shit you and her have been doing behind each other's backs, and I don't wanna know. I'm just disappointed as hell with you both," the ram muttered, reaching behind his own seat to snag a bottle of water from the mini-cooler. The cooler had no ice in it because given the weather, it didn't need any—but the cold inside the vehicle had taken its toll, and most of the liquid inside the bottle was nearly frozen. The ram had to settle for crunching the plastic of the bottle enough to force the remaining water to the surface, straining to squeeze it out of the mouth of the bottle and into his needy throat.

"Oh, now you're being a hypocrite," Devin snorted. "Seriously, Kleg, you mean to tell me that you never let anyone else get you off? C'mon, admit it—you can only jerk yourself off so many times before it gets boring. You've never gone up to The Fantasia and just let yourself get sucked off even once?"

"Yes!" Randall growled at him, face squinched up in annoyance as he crinkled the upper portion of the bottle brutally with his hand. "Yes, I have, if we're gonna be balls-out honest with each other. Are you satisfied, now? I found a hole, stuck my dick through it, got a mighty enthusiastic blowjob from somebody on the other side, and came down their throat till my balls damn near ached. Happy?"

"Matter of fact, I'm not," Devin snapped, giving the ram a bit of a disgruntled look right back even as he said, "It shoulda been me on the other side of that wall, getting a mouthful of that big crank of yours. I bet I could suck you off a hell of a lot better than anyone else there could."

Randall's eyes widened a little both in realization and discomfort as he realized what the fox was inferring, and he looked at the fox with narrowed, suspicious eyes. "Whaddya mean by my 'big crank'? How do you know how big I am? You sayin' you been checkin' me out, before?"

Devin rolled his eyes, his face completely unashamed. He snorted softly. "C'mon, Kleg, if a guy's got as much as you do between his legs, even straight guys are gonna take a look. We got communal showers, remember? All the guys have checked out yer meat, at one time or another, and if they don't come away from it shakin' their heads in envy, then they're wishin' that you'd stretch their asses around it good n' hard."

The fox stared at the ram with keen eyes that almost seemed to glint, and in spite of himself, Randall shuddered inside his coat a little when he saw the look that was in them, and his quivering had little to do at that moment with the cold. There was a frostiness and lustful look to them that made his friend look totally different to the ram, and he found that he suddenly realized how truly uncomfortable he was growing with the entire situation. A can of worms had been opened that Devin was not going to allow the ram to close, and the big ovine found himself seriously contemplating getting out of the cab of the Hummer and taking his chances with the elements again. When the fox spoke at last, his words were low but quite clear.

"Y'know… back when Tressa and me were still good together, Kleg, I could plant my knot up that hot little bitch's cunt two times in one night, and she'd still scream for more. I used to know and cherish what a hot lay she was, and now that she's getting her action elsewhere, I'll be damned if I'm gonna sit out on the sidelines. And now that I've had some male on male experience, I'm pretty sure I could give her some decent competition as far as getting another guy off goes." He gave the ram a once-over, his gaze lingering on Randall's groin noticeably and deliberately, and he didn't have to say anything else with his mouth to let the ram know what he was thinking. His eyes did all the talking, as did the handpaw that lazily began to rub his own groin.

The ovine tried his best to keep his eyes from watching what the fox's handpaw was up to, and he only barely managed to do so. Finally, the ram swallowed hard and turned his head to face out the drivers' side window, which was already opaque with snow and ice. "I do believe that you n' me are done talkin' till our rescuers get here, if they get here—and maybe even for a good while after that."

"Oh, fuck that shit," Devin growled, his muzzle wrinkling in agitation as the hackles rose on the back of his neckruff. "You just admitted to me that you got sucked off at the Fantasia at least once before, yourself, so knock of the 'holier than thou' act, Kleg. And get real while yer at it, willya? There's a damn good chance that we're gonna freeze to death in this heap. Here. Today. In less than an hour." He licked his muzzle off again, then gave the ram a hopeful but stern look. "This might be the last time to fuck that either one of us ever gets again, and I know I can make you cum, Kleg. I wanna feel what it's like to have your nuts pinned up against my ass while you're spurtin' your load up my fuckhole."

He sat up on his knees and unzipped his coat, then lowered a hand to grip his cock through his pants, putting himself on display for his boss. In spite of the cold, all the talking he'd done about sex had made his shaft start to stiffen, and it made for a decent handful as he waggled it gently in his pants with his hand. "See this?" he rumbled. "You got me hard just thinking about it. I'm as hard as all those other times when I was sleeping at the barracks after work, by myself, Tressa either on duty or probably out getting her sweet pussy plowed by some lucky bastard... and I'd sit there and play with myself, thinking about having that monster cock of yours sliding down my throat n' tasting your fuck lube."

Kleg found the taste of bile rising in his throat at the vulpine's words, and he screwed up his features even as he tried to use the positions of his hands in his pockets from hiding the very slight stirring in his groin that came as a result of the fox's musk. "Devin, you are one sick little fucker, and I think the cold must be startin' to get to your brain." He licked his muzzle reflexively, then lowered his own voice as he gave the fox a glare that he hoped could curdle milk. "Let's get one thing straight, right now: you ain't doin' nothin' sexual to me, or vice-fuckin'-versa. You're gonna wait till the rescue shows up, then you're gonna get your ass back to Tressa and the two of you are either gonna work all this shit out between the both of ya—or I'll see to it that you both get shipped outta here. Given what we're payin' you, I won't have any trouble finding an engineer to replace ya with. I don't need some kinda swingin' married couple causing problems among the ranks of my other workers."

"Problems?" Devin snarled, pulling his muzzle flaps back to expose his teeth to his boss. "Holy flyin' shit, Kleg, you oughtta be payin' us extra for keeping morale up, far as I'm concerned! And I hate to say it, but this time, you ain't gonna be the one givin' the orders." His eyes glinted again as he grabbed the ram's right hand and placed it squarely on the fox's crotch, the vulpine grinding his firm erection against his boss's fingers as he snarled into the ram's face, "You feel that? Well, you're gonna suck my nice hard meat, and you're gonna put that big beautiful dick of yours straight up my ass, and you're gonna fuck me till you blow your wad—'cause if you don't, I'm gonna tell the rest of the crew that you did, anyway. Tell 'em that this cold situation made ya snap and start talking crazy, and that you used yer authority to bully me into havin' sex with you."

Randall felt cold icicles of horror start to creep up his spine, once more in a way that had nothing to do with the cold. His eyes widened a bit even as his brows furrowed downwards, and he tried to keep his voice under control as he rumbled to the fox, "Sorta like what yer doin', right now?" he shook his head, realizing that what the vulpine had said really was coming to pass. Devin's eyes weren't focused, and it seemed to the ram that he could feel the fox's pulse racing through his fingers as he was made to fondle the vulpine's erection through Devin's pants. The icy, chilly glaze in Devin's orbs showed several emotions and states of being all at once—panic, lust, frenzied adrenaline—but not rationality.

The ram felt what could have been a lump of stone in his throat, and he swallowed hard as his thick fingers massaged Devin's groin. The pair locked eyes, and a sort of mutual, bitter understanding silently arose between the two of them, as frigid as the wind was outside.

"So," Kleg finally muttered, breaking the silence at last. "This is how yer gonna let it go down, then. You're willing to toss away your marriage, our friendship... drag me down with you and make me feel like a dirty slut, just like you and your wife... all because you're bitter for her cheatin' on you, and the only way you feel like you can get the final word is by getting my dick up your ass. That about cover it?"

Devin's eyes narrowed a bit at the ram, even as he nodded. "Oh, so you're gonna trash our friendship because of this, hunh? Well, if that's the way you want things to be, bud. But that's pretty dramatic n' petty for a guy that I go so far back with." He lowered a shivering hand to clamp it warmly against Randall's own groin, his gloved fingers stroking slowly back and forth over the ram's own firming erection. "Besides—from what I'm feelin' down here, your mouth's the only part of you that's protesting."

Randall's mind felt numb, even as his cock stiffened uncomfortably under his dungarees and Devin's hand. He pressed his head firmly back against the headrest of his seat and gave the fox a look that was smoldering with a mingling of anger, distaste, and distantly below those, lust. "Fine. Let's get this over with, then," he grunted, as he unzipped his coat to give himself more maneuvering room.

"Don't take your coat off," Devin growled softly, his hand lifting off the ram's groin long enough to press the ram against the seat. "There's only one part of you I gotta expose to do this, and I reckon it's only fair that if anyone does any stripping, it'll be me. Won't be the first time, now, will it?" he grumbled bitterly, as he slid out of his own coat and lay it aside on the seat.

"I pity ya both," Randall sneered. "It's a sad thing, what's happened to the two of you."

"Peachy," Devin snarled softly right back. "I'm sure that she'll have something equally dramatic to say, if I decide to tell her about what you 'n me are about to do. So I reckon you better shut your pie hole and make sure that I enjoy this." He leaned forward, his face and muzzle right next to the ram's as he slide his hand around to massage the back of Randall's neck, before gripping it firmly. He gave the ovine's neck and head a light shake and growled to him in a low voice, "Let's us start off by makin' this corruption complete. Kiss me. Make it nice n' cold."

Kleg's eyes closed, squinching shut a bit as he angled his head only slightly, preparing himself to receive the fox's kiss—but he didn't open his mouth. Devin moved his muzzle in and prodded it against the ram's lips, his own tongue sliding out of his mouth and nudging his boss there, lapping slowly over Randall's maw. The ram's ears twitched under his tuque as he heard the sound of Devin's fly being unzipped, then he felt the fox's erect cock being pressed firmly into his right hand, the vulpine's fingers sealing the ram's gloved hand around his firm length. Seven and a half inches of vein-latticed vulpine prick quivered in midair as Devin rubbed Randall's hand and fingers all over his member, then made the ram give his full, hefty, white-furred balls a fondle and a warm squeeze. This made the fox gasp against the ram's face, and he panted softly against Kleg's neck as he hunched his prick slowly in the ram's palm, wincing just a bit from the sensitivity of the cotton gloves against his member.

"You're not makin' with the tongue action, boss-ram," the fox said to the ram with a low, accusatory growl. "C'mon, now. We're both about to die. Don'tcha wanna go out with a 'bang', literally?" He gave the ram's head another light shimmy with his hand, and he snarled even lower, his tone hard and businesslike. "Let's try that again. And put some effort into it, this time."

Randall's face grimaced even more tightly for a moment, and the ram had to fight the urge to squeeze the fox's cock hard enough to cause the vulpine immense pain. Grudgingly, eyes still closed, he opened his lips partway, and Devin slid his tongue into the ram's mouth, lapping insistently at the ram's own tongue. The ovine gave the fox's tongue a few half-hearted laps in return, and he could feel Devin's breath on his face as the vulpine tried to arouse the ram into matching the fox's fervor. He could feel how hard Kleg's own cock was, and the fox felt some pre trickling from his piss slit as the ram's fingers stroked his length.

Devin took off his own gloves, then moved his hand down to smear his fingers firmly against his glans, daubing up some of his natural vulpine lubricant. He spread this warmly onto Kleg's lips, and although the ram let out a muffled grunt of protest, the scent of Devin's liquid arousal hit the ram's nostrils like an out-of-control truck. The salty taste spread over the ovine's tongue, and he pressed his mouth fully against Devin's, his tongue sliding deep into the fox's maw as the fox suddenly found himself having to cling to the ram's shoulders for support from the enthusiasm of the kiss. A small spurt of his pre spackled against the ram's flannel shirt as they gripped at each other, and a muffled growl of pure lust burbled into Kleghorn's throat as Devin writhed lewdly against his employer. The fox spread his legs further apart still as the ram's hand fondled underneath and beyond his balls, two fingers sliding up to see how tight the vulpine's posterior cleft was, and the fox began to paw at the ram's zipper, finally having to pull his head back and away from the kiss as he panted breathlessly at the ovine.

"Damn…!" he breathed. "That's more fuckin' like it, boss ram," he panted. His other hand worked with deft skill as he unbuckled the ram's belt, then began to unzip the ram's pants, his own tongue lolling just barely out the side of his muzzle as a look of concentration crossed his features. "Your turn, now. Show me what I want."

Randall opened his eyes and stared balefully at the fox, his own chest breathing a bit heavily from the kiss that he hadn't wanted to give—but the smell of Devin's pre had been intoxicating, and the ram knew that there was no point in turning back now. Feeling as dirty on the inside as he felt cold on the outside, he reached a hand below the seat and gripped the seat adjustment lever, sliding it back so that there was more room for the fox. There wasn't much clearance because of the supplies heaped up behind him, but he now had enough room to stretch his legs and frame out somewhat, making it easier for Devin to get to his midsection.

Devin gripped Randall's thick, strong fingers, then made the ram claw at the waistline of the vulpine's boxer shorts until he had little choice but to tug them downwards, the fox groaning softly as he felt his stiff red length flop forward into the ram's palm, a little bit of pre spilling from his piss hole and dribbling onto the cold vinyl of the front seat, where it began to crystallize slowly. Kleg questioned the wisdom of the fox exposing his lower body in such a manner in such oppressive cold, but he didn't bother voicing his concerns. The vulpine managed to get the ram's pants unzipped, then had to pause and take his own boots off so he could fully remove his own pants and underwear, shivering with what could have been either cold or excitement as he did so. Now clad only in his coat, shirt, and double-thick wool stockings, he straightened up and peered expectantly at the ram's tented boxers.

The ram gripped his length and pulled it out of his pants, then grunted as he repeated the movement to pull out his huge testicles. His dangling gray sacs seemed big enough to fill a good portion of a dinner plate as they flopped onto his lap, his member at a full twelve inches as it waggled uncertainly in the frigid air. A little over two and a half inches thick at the hilt, the black girth of it made it seem a bit less like a penis and a bit more like a small club, accentuated by the round bulbous knob that jutted firmly above it all.

Devin's eyes widened at the sheer size of the ram's penis, the fox's facial expression looking as though he was taking a tour of the inside of a bank vault and was given an invitation to roll bodily in the money. His knot bobbled above his fur-covered testicles as he pressed his pink length up against the ram's stiff member and gripped both penises warmly with his black-furred hands. His own prick was already leaking enough pre for his fingers to smooth over his own cock and a good portion of the ram's, although the ovine's girth made holding on to both members a tricky affair. The fox gave his own balls a squeeze and winced a little as his enthusiasm shot a mild bolt of pain through his spine, but it had the effect he'd intended, as another small gout of pre spurted up into his cupped palm, letting him rub the natural lube warmly down the top side of Randall's huge meat. The ram shuddered in response and groaned softly, closing his eyes and gripping Devin's midsection firmly with both hands, thick fingers digging into the fox's rump as the vulpine eagerly returned the grinding motions, both firm erections buried against their own pelts. Devin gripped one smaller hand and arm around Kleg's shoulder and neck and hugged himself tightly against his boss, his own eyes closing for a moment as his whole body shivered in a way that had nothing to do with the cold. "Awwww, yeaaaah, boss-ram... yer feelin' how hard you got me, don'tcha?" he murmured lowly, sucking air through his teeth in a low hiss. "That goddamn dick of yours is a fuckin' work of art. Thing's big enough to turn any married guy into a flamin', ass-wigglin' lil' twinkie-queer."

Randall snorted at that, his frozen breath pluming against Devin's fur as the fox tugged himself away from the ram's chest and glanced over his shoulder to see if he had enough clearance to lower his upper body. He managed to slip his legs and knees carefully off Randall's lap so he could sit his knees on the floorboard, both his knees and feet feeling the mild shock of melted ice water from the ram's boots seeping into his socks and fur—but the sight of the ram's cock jutting like a fleshy tower toward him at face level pushed any thoughts of discomfort out of his mind in a flash. Ears and whiskers twitching, he grasped Randall's black cock reverently with both hands and closed his eyes, leaning the ram's fuck flesh against his face and nuzzling his features all over it as he panted softly in utter desire. The musky smell of his boss's arousal, perspiration, and an extremely faded taint of urine created by recycled beer filled his nostrils and made his own cock throb dully against the seat as he leaned against it.

Kleg leaned back and tried to relax, his eyes sliding shut as he attempted to will his erection back down into a more flaccid state—but the sight of Devin making his adoration of the ram's cock so obvious didn't stop his piss slit from leaking pre all over Devin's rubbing nose and whiskers. The fox lapped his tongue slowly all over the ovine's huge glans, making it glisten slightly with drool and making the ram gasp thickly as Kleg's fingers came down firmly onto the fox's neckruff and clamped onto it hard. The fox shuddered and paused for a moment, wondering if the sullen ram had suddenly decided to get himself out of this situation by snapping the vulpine's neck—but after the ram didn't do anything else for a few moments, he gave the ram's shaft a swift but thorough washing with his tongue, covering it from hilt to piss slit and back again with his eager drool. He relaxed his worries when his actions made Randall lay his head back against the headrest of his seat and moan thickly, the hairs of the ram's beard quivering as a deep exhale made plumes of frost brush over Devin's face. He massaged his drool carefully over Randall's huge balls and said lowly, "Yeah, boss... that's what I wanted to hear, that sweet moanin' coming from your throat. Gonna be making you do plenty more of that, too, soon as I get this monster dick lubed up good n' proper and then make you put that milk in my back door."

With that, he carefully lowered his face over Randall's cock, holding it steady with both hands as his nose angled completely downwards, his maw opening to carefully take the upper portion of the huge black shaft into his head. Taking a deep breath of his own, he lowered his muzzle down inch by inch on the ram's cock as he felt the huge knob nudge inexorably toward the back of his throat, his warm tongue doing its best to keep the ovine's pre dribbling constantly. By the time he reached his gag point, he realized that there was still a good two or three inches of cock flesh inside his fingers, and even with his eyes closed, he knew that it might be impossible for him to engulf Randall's cock completely; his jaw would be screaming for mercy in less than five minutes. He cursed inwardly, but then his perked ears heard Randall groan once more, the ram's fingers lightly clutching the back of his head and obviously not wanting him to stop. This made him feel an odd twinge of pride, and he couldn't help but wonder what Tressa would think if she could only see him now, on his knees between his boss's legs and servicing him like an eager whore.

Carefully, he withdrew his muzzle until only that small doorknob of a cock remained, then he moved his mouth back down again, fingers and thumbs squeezing the base of Randall's cock warmly as he began to suck him off in earnest. The soft, wet sounds of cocksucking began to echo softly in the cab, nearly drowned out by the fierce winds outside—but not even the fearsome cold could make the penises of either male start to wilt. The fox now knew that he had the ram right where he wanted him, and the feeling gave him a sense of power and control that aroused his own member so much that it seemed to be radiating a heat of its own. The steadily leaking rivulet of vulpine pre oozed slowly down his shaft and onto his knot and balls only to spatter soundlessly onto the floorboards. Devin's fingers stroked his engorged cock in time with his head's movements on Randall's cock, and he pulled a shivering hand back and around to his ass cleft, seeking out his pucker and lubricating it with as much of his own pre as his harried balls could possibly muster.

Randall panted raggedly as he gripped Devin's bobbing head with both hands, easing his midsection slightly upwards with each downward movement of the fox's muzzle. His eyes were closed and his face somber in a look of stern concentration, shaggy brows furrowed and his goatee hair quirking firmly as low grunts and gasps of pleasure edged from his throat. "Y... you're... good," he admitted grudgingly, teeth clenching sporadically as he slid his cock slowly in and out of the fox's muzzle. "M... must've been getting m... more practice at the Fantasia than ya let on... You must really be wantin' their 'Premium Slut' m... membership card..."

Devin gasped for breath as he slid his muzzle off Randall's cock long enough to take a few desperate breaths, his jaw aching dully at the strain that it had undergone in the last few minutes. The fox's face was utterly consumed by lust, and his eyes shone as he substituted his black-furred hands for his mouth, his fur bristling at the smell of his boss's pre. "Like the way I'm chowin' down on this big fucker, don'tcha?" he snarled. "Course ya do. I could make a goddamn monk beg me to suck him off, after he got a feel of my mouth technique."

The fox shivered as he thumped the ram's cock up against his face and felt a thick runner of drool and pre slide down against the side of his muzzle, looking up at the ram as he continued to stroke him with one hand. "How many ladies you made scream for more with this thing, Kleg? Couple dozen?" He cocked his head and wrapped his tongue around the ram's length as best he could, licking his way up the towering black shaft before licking his boss's personal salt off his lips and murmured, "Kinda too bad y'feel about Tressa the way you do... I'd pay good money to hide in my bedroom closet and watch you fill up her hot little pussy with as much of this monster as she could handle. I bet she'd be so cranked up that she wouldn't even notice me jackin' my load all over the both of ya till it hit her face."

Randall lifted his head and glowered darkly at the fox, his disposition as cheery as a thundercloud. "If you wanna make me lose that erection you're worshipping so hard, you just keep right on saying things like that," he warned.

Devin rolled his eyes and shrugged as he carefully edged out from under the steering wheel and pulled his knees up off the wet floorboards to carefully clamber his way back up into the ram's lap. He half-turned and adjusted the steering wheel behind himself, using its width as a makeshift backrest as he straddled his legs and feet on either side of the ram's beefy waist. He slid himself slightly up onto the steering wheel and rested the soles of his stocking feet up onto Randall's torso carefully. He gripped the big ram's cock with his hand just below the glans, and guided the pulsing black knob up until it was firmly nudged against his tailhole, and he lay his head back against the top of the steering wheel as he perked his ears sharply at the sound of the heavy knob squishing softly against his quivering pucker. "It's funny, in a pathetic kinda way, Kleg. Here I am, trying to give you a bit of bliss before we both kick off, and all you can do is whine and try to ruin the moment by reminding me about my poor lil' slutbag of a wife. I never would've figured you to be such a masochist."

The ram answered nonverbally, lifting one of his middle fingers to display it rudely and plainly in the fox's face. The fox shook his head and sighed, closing his eyes again and ignoring the ovine's gesture as he savored the feel of his boss's cockhead massaging firmly against his tailhole. It was an interesting contrast of sensations: the warmth of the fox's tailhole pressed up against the ram's glans contrasted sharply with the cold air that made Kleg's heavy balls shiver and want to draw up slightly.

Kleg stared down at the fox's snug-looking puckered orifice, and he couldn't help but snicker a little. "You think I'm a masochist... I can't wait to see what kinda face you make if you're honestly dumb enough to try shoving every inch of my crank up your ass. There ain't no way you're gonna get that thing all the way up there, and both our cocks are prolly gonna freeze and fall off while you try."

"Wanna bet?" Devin snarled, his ears lying back just a bit more as he nearly growled in anticipation at the obvious challenge. "I bought Tressa a big ol' foot-long dildo ta keep her occupied on the nights I was workin' late, and she ain't used it in a long time on account of her getting the real thing from the other guys... so I been toyin' around with it, some. I can take that stiff fucker almost all the way up my shitter, and if your big slab of fuckpole feels as good as that fake 'un does, then I'm gonna have you splatterin' yer gunk up inside me in no time."

"Bullshit..." Randall murmured, his eyes lidding almost at the same time as his teeth gritted together, savoring the feel of the fox's tight muscle ring caressing and kissing his cockhead, the smaller vulpine taking several deep breaths as he willed his anus to relax enough to admit the ram's glans inside of himself. Slowly, he bore his weight carefully down onto Kleg's cock as it popped somewhat abruptly past the fox's natural resistance, making him let out a sharp yip of initial discomfort until more of the ram slid slowly up into his snug passage. A low, shivering sigh then whispered from his muzzle as he made his orifice slowly devour the ram's black length, more runny strands of pre and drool spattering the ovine's huge balls and the floorboards.

"S-so big..." Devin groaned. "Shit...! Guh... gimmee it, boss-ram... I gotta have it all!"

Randall gasped, using his thick arms and strong fingers to help keep the fox from lowering himself too abruptly, both as a sign of feeble resistance and as an effort to keep the fox's body from impacting against the ram's huge balls too abruptly. "Unnnhh... !" he gasped tightly, air seething through his teeth. "F-fuck, yer tight... so snug it's almost hurtin' my crank..." he groaned.

Devin gasped louder and draped his head back until it was laying backwards over the top of the steering wheel as his hands scrabbled for purchase on the lower half of it, his fingers curling around the underside of the wheel and locking into place as his stretched anal ring took in almost all of the ram's thick cock. Thick droplets of sweat ran down the vulpine's face as he fought against Randall's efforts to keep the entry gradual, and his ears lay low against his head as he gritted his teeth and strained downwards. He knew that it was going to be a battle of wills to see if he could actually make the ram shoot his load up into him, but now that he'd come this far, he was confident that he could surmount the ram's moral compunctions completely. "Fuck that fuckhole," he panted up to Kleg in a seething voice, his eyes narrowed to slits as he savored the feel of the ram's meaty cockhead slowly delving up into him. "I ain't... g-getting outta this truck t-till I got yer cum up my ass, boss-ram."

Once his length was buried up into Devin as much as it was able, Randall's heavy head and upper body thumped back against his seat as his mouth gaped open, and a gutteral moan eased out of his throat as he lavished in the feel of the fox's warm insides all around him. He kept himself hilted inside the fox's body for a few minutes, noting with a bit of grim satisfaction that Devin was shivering noticeably from the cold. He gripped the fox's thighs hard and began to withdraw slowly, the wet squish of his throbbing prick audible in the quiet of the cab of the Hummer. Devin's arm muscles ached in silent protest as the fox tried to make the ram take him forcefully, but even with adrenaline pumping through his system, he was no match for the ram's strength, and his position gave him the disadvantage. The ram pondered leaving himself impaled inside the fox until the vulpine either passed out from the cold or relented and told the ram that they could stop, but the idea of the vulpine possibly expiring with the ram still inside of him made for a most unappealing mental image, indeed. And despite his anger and resentment, there was still a part of the ram's subconscious that didn't want Devin to die, even though he was repelled by the fox's conduct. Best to get this all over with, then try to put it behind him as they pondered the much more important matters of survival and rescue.

There seemed to be just enough room between the ram's midsection and his positioning on the steering wheel to allow the fox enough maneuverability to move with Randall's thrusts. Light plumes of steam began to rise from the ram's cock as he slid it into and out of Devin's taut tailhole, the mixture of pre and drool wetter than before as he primed the needy fox's ass ring. Randall's forehead started to sweat liberally, thick droplets of his perspiration splashing onto Devin's lush rusty-red pelt and white chestruff as he rocked the fox's body onto his erection again and again. His eyes were narrowed into slits as he watched Devin's face, his own midsection hunching firmly up into him and reveling in the pure sleaziness of the moment even as his subconscious mind screamed at him and berated him for doing something so immoral with someone still bound by a marriage. He wondered idly how his team from the camp would react when they found himself and the fox frozen solid together in their lewd positioning, permanently joined at the groin and pucker in an eternal embrace of utter lust.

Something bobbled fiercely just below his narrowed line of vision, and as he lowered his gaze to see what it was, he realized that it was Devin's cockhead. Fully engorged and so strained with blood that the tapered tip of it looked almost purple, it hunched and bucked in time with the ram's thrusts, aching to be buried in the snug vagina of a wife who wasn't there.

Devin was in ecstasy, his head still draped back over the top of the steering wheel as he rode his boss's cock slowly. He slapped his hands forward and onto the ram's shoulders, clinging to him as he tried to grind his pelvis up and down on the ram's cock even faster, but Kleg wouldn't allow such. The fox snarled his frustrations aloud, his eyes opening narrowly as he panted raggedly, studying the ram's face and gaze carefully, and as he realized where the ram's eyes were looking, a cruel smirk spread itself across his features.

"You... l-likin' that f... fox cock, Kleg?" he grunted, breath heaving through his nostrils and mouth as his anal ring slid smoothly up and down the ram's black prong. "Looks tasty, d... don't it?" He lowered a hand to close his fingers around the hilt of his shaft, waggling it derisively at the ram. "Suck it," he commanded.

"No," the ram snarled, his voice low and steadfast as he promptly ceased his thrusting. "Bad enough that I'm doin' this, and you ain't usin' my throat as your cum dumpster."

Devin's neckruff puffed outward and his muzzle wrinkled in fury, the fox baring his teeth up at the ram as he strained a bit to reach over and pick up the Thermos off the seat beside him. "Goddammit, Kleg, you're gonna suck my dick, and you're gonna swallow my load... or so help me, I'll chuck this here Thermos through the window and we'll both freeze even faster. Now get to it. And keep fuckin' me!"

Randall stared at the fox with open-mouthed disbelief. "You've gone fuckin' batshit, haven't you?" he grunted, starting to resume his thrusts in and out of the fox's snug anal passageway once more. He shook his head in dazed wonder, a good bit of the bliss he'd been feeling from the fox's inner walls caressing his length now gone from the sheer lunacy of Devin's words. Nevertheless, he didn't try to see if the fox was bluffing, his head lowering toward the vulpine's shaft and his nostrils filling with the arousal scent of the vulpine's pre as Devin smeared a runny trail of it over the ram's sniffer.

Moving his rubbery lips with care, he drew the fox's glans into his mouth and started to suck it, tongue whipping all over the fox's pulsing cockhead as a few thick spurts of pre rewarded his efforts by spattering against the back of the ram's throat. His thrusts fell out of synch for a moment as he lowered his maw further still down onto Devin's cock, and after letting out a gasp that sounded like he was having an asthma attack, the fox helped him by arching his back on the steering wheel and pushing his groin firmly upwards into the ram's warm oral embrace, the fox's dark fingers releasing the bottom of the steering wheel and latching onto the base of Kleg's curled horns on either side, clinging to them for dear life. Kleg felt Devin's anal ring rise a bit higher off of his cock as the vulpine hastened to fuck the ram's mouth, and he purposefully moved his lips a little higher as his head used shorter movements to bobble around the fox's shaft, hoping to coax him up and off of the ovine's prick.

"Ohhh! Ohh, you f-fuckin'... bastard," Devin gasped. "Tryin' to... c-coax my ring off yer dick with that mouth, hunh? Well, it... nngh... it ain't gonna work!" He felt his ring releasing more of the ram's cock as his midsection thrust upwards in the opposite direction, the fox being unable to allow his cock to resist the lure of Randall's warm tongue and maw. But then he remembered his goal and he again pushed himself carefully but firmly downward once more as Randall bucked his hips upwards, a muffled grunt of frustration edging out from around his mouth full of Devin's cock. Once again, a rhythm developed, and Devin found himself lost in the glory of the most glorious—and up to that point, only—simulated sandwich-fucking he'd ever had. Randall wasn't overly skilled at sucking cock, having not had a lot of practice, and the occasional light grazing of one of his teeth against Devin's cock flesh was mildly jarring—but the ram did have plenty of experience with ass fucking, and the feel of his huge girth filling the fox's rear hole full made any other discomforts mild by comparison.

Randall bobbed his head on Devin's cock at a faster pace, the taste of the fox's spurting personal lube filling the back of his throat and running warmly all over his tongue as the vulpine's snug anal ring once again milked his cock steadily toward shooting his load. He slipped his fingers over the Devin's balls and gave them a squeeze as they jutted up and down with the fox's groin movements, and as his large glans prodded firmly and repeatedly against the vulpine's prostrate, he felt Devin's knot begin to swell. The ram took a deep breath and closed his eyes tight, ignoring the twinge of pain in his back as he swallowed as much of Devin's shaft as he could, his tongue flicking rapidly all over the underside of the aroused vulpine's cock. Devin let out a strained, prolonged grunt through his gritted teeth that drew out into a yowl of release as his fingers gripped onto the ram's skull tightly, and his body jerked hard as Randall slid two beefy fingers over the vulpine's swollen knot, squeezing it as thick ropes of fox semen splattered all over the inside of his mouth and down his throat.

The ram was unable to make a sound as Devin's shaft stayed buried in his maw, but the fox's climax made the snug ring stroking Kleg's cock clench and convulse tightly, causing the ovine to shudder hard in the need for his own impending release. The biting cold, the stress of being coerced into a sexual situation against his will, and the sheer intensity of the horrible day had taken its toll on the older male, and now all he wanted was for it all to be over. Bolts of pain intermingled with ripples of pleasure assaulted Devin's nervous system, and he continued to shoot his load down the ram's throat as if his testicles were imploding, the firm pumping of his anal ring around Randall's throbbing cock finally pushing the ram over the edge, as well. Heavy gouts of potent ovine semen spattered pointblank against Devin's prostrate gland as the ram hilted himself inside the fox, and only the steel-firm grip of the ram's hands on the fox's thighs kept Devin from bucking himself off of the steering wheel. The fox hunched against Randall's warm, rubbery lips until his climax started to die down, although this took several minutes… and when the eruptions from his piss slit diminished down to sporadic dribblings, he was finally able to pull his head up and try to recover his breath, his chest rising and falling swiftly as he panted raggedly.

"Y-you… sum'bitch… !" he groaned lowly as he gripped Randall's horns firmly, keeping his head down for a moment. "Hunh… had to… fuck with my knot a luh… little, didn'tcha?" he panted, tongue lolling out of the side of his muzzle as he kept himself firmly seated on his boss's still quite hard erection. "F… feels like you shot d-damn near a pint of cream up muh… my fuckhole…" He finally let go of Randall's horns and splayed his arms back against the steering wheel, as Randall slowly withdrew his mouth up and off the fox's shaft. "Admit it, boss ram… You loved havin' me be yer bitch."

Randall belched softly as he also began to recuperate, his lungs working like a giant set of fire bellows as the aftertaste of Devin's cum registered heavily on his tongue and from his throat. He grunted and didn't reply until he felt like he could speak without gasping too much, then he rumbled deeply, "You're a tighter fuck than a virgin trailer park whore, and with only half the moral fiber and attractiveness," he muttered, turning his gaze to the side so he wouldn't have to look at the fox's face directly.

"The world hates a poor loser, Kleg," Devin frowned, giving the ram a shake of his head as he hugged himself with his arms and began to rub his shoulders and sides briskly, the cold inside the cab more potent than ever and rapidly becoming more palpable against his pelt. "I suppose it'd be too much to ask for some post grudge-fuck cuddling, wouldn't it?"

The ram shuddered, then simply slid his hands under Devin's shoulders and lifted him bodily off the steering wheel and messily off of the ram's cock, which slid wetly out of the vulpine's orifice. The fox let out a low yip and whine of protest, but didn't move to stop the ram due to his own fatigue. "Get off of me," the ram muttered. "And get dressed. I don't ever want to see your cock again."

"Your loss," Devin shrugged, giving the ram a look that was a good deal more petulant than he'd meant for it to be. "But you sure sucked it like you were enjoying it." Shivering harder, he managed to get his pants back on, then his boots, his shaking fingers making his efforts more difficult. The ram hoisted his waist off the seat long enough to flop his spent cock and balls back into his pants, then he carefully zipped back up and buckled his belt, blinking listlessly out his window at the bleak world covered with snow outside.

The two sat in silence for what seemed an eternity, but when Kleg glanced at his watch, only about twenty-five minutes had passed. He looked from the watch to the ice-covered windshield, then blinked, his face looking stark and a bit surprised at the same time as a revelation struck him. He sat bolt upright in his seat, and Devin looked over at him, snapping out of his moping a bit. "What?" he murmured, raising a puzzled brow at the ram. "What is it? Do you see something?" He followed the ram's gaze out of the windshield, then began to rub frantically at the glass, growling in frustration. The snow was now up to the hood of the Hummer, and the two could see precious little beyond twenty feet in front of the vehicle. "Damn this fuckin' ice..."

"They're not coming," the ram rumbled quietly.

"What?" the fox asked again, whipping his head around to look at the ram with some irritation. "Whaddya mean?"

"Just what I said. Weren't you listening?" the ram said to the fox with a fatigued, weary sort of patience in his voice. He slowed his words down for the fox's benefit. "I said... 'They're... not... coming.'"

Devin blinked, then snorted at the ram, cocking a brow at him in annoyance as he said, "Kleg, did I bust your nut so hard that I sprained your brain? Of course they're coming. I think there are folks in China that heard those flare bursts, a little while ago. It's just gonna take the guys a bit to plow through all this mess in the Super Cat, that's all. Thing'll only go a top speed of about forty miles an hour, and that's in good weather."

"No. They're not. They didn't see the burst, and it doesn't matter..." the ram breathed, his features looking deeply contemplative. "They're not coming, and it's no big deal—because I can get there on foot."

"Uhhh... " Devin murmured, frowning deeply. "Aren't you the one that told me not even two hours ago that if we tried that, we'd be dead? That's a good three and a half miles in a record-breaking blizzard. Don't go nuts on me, Kleg," he warned, "...not when we're so close to being rescued."

The ram started to adjust his coat and pulled his hat on more tightly, then pulled the Thinsulate gloves back on, stuffed as many of the leftover heat packets into his coat pockets and down his shirt and up his pants legs as he could, and finally tugged the goggles back down over his eyes. "Chance I'll have to take. Besides, I just know that they're not coming, and I owe it to myself to try to make it. And I just realized something else..." he rumbled, as he paused in his preparations to stare at the fox blankly. "I don't have to stay here with you."

Devin sat up in his seat, his muzzle dropping open as though the ram had just slugged him a good one in the gut. "What?" he grunted. "Kleg, you can't just leave me here!"

"Why not?" the ram shrugged. "You're not supposed to cheat on your spouse, either. But you did. And worse yet, you made me an accessory to such, which isn't something that a friend should do to another friend." The ram glanced at the supplies behind the seat, then looked back at the fox and rumbled, "But hey... you should be fine. At least you won't starve, but I hope you like your M.R.E.'s at brick consistency."

"Hey, whoa! Wait a minute!" Devin gasped, his face going terror-stricken now that he realized that the ram was serious in his attempt to make the trek. "Kleg, let's... You're blowing this whole thing way out of proportion, y'know? Look, let's, let's talk this out. I mean, holy shit, I think you're an attractive guy, and I just figured that you wouldn't think that having sex with me was that big a deal—"

"Ahh, but that's just it," the ram interjected, jabbing the fox in the chest with a finger hard enough to make Devin wince and rub the spot he poked. "You didn't ask me to do it. You blackmailed me into doing it. And that's just the way you operate, isn't it?" he asked, staring at the fox in an accusing manner. "Guys like you are so used to doing things the way you want to do them because you think it's more important for you to have fun, and to hell with how the things you do affect the folks around you. It's always all about you, isn't it?"

"Kleg, will you slow down?" Devin gasped, his face both annoyed and fearful at the ram's manner. "It's not like that! If you'd just fucking listen to me for a goddamn minute..."

The ram put his hand out and clamped it around Devin's muzzle, causing the fox to blink a little, then struggle lightly as he placed his hands on the ram's and tried to pry the ovine's fingers off. He went cross-eyed for a moment as he looked fearfully at the thick digits holding his mouth fast, and his ears splayed, looking up at the ram helplessly as Kleg overshadowed him.

Randall leaned down until his goatee was nearly touching the end of Devin's nose, then he murmured to the fox in a voice so low it was almost a whisper, "I need you to answer two questions for me."

He let go of Devin's muzzle, and the fox rubbed himself dazedly, his heart beating fast. He was now on the hot seat with a ram that was clearly on the verge of snapping like a twig, and he had absolutely no way of knowing what the ram was going to do or say. In light of everything that had happened, he decided that the best course of action might be to cooperate—at least until a better opportunity presented itself.

"All right," the fox answered quietly, nervously meeting Kleg's gaze with his own. "Let's hear 'em."

"When you first started cheating on Tressa, what was the first thing you did?" the ram asked.

"What? You mean, who was I with?" the fox asked, puzzled. He scratched his head a little, then shrugged as he finally said quietly, his face perhaps blushing just a little., "I, uhh… I don't think I remember. It was some guy—feline, I think, might've been a lion—but it wasn't anyone that I work with," he quickly added, as though that added legitimacy to his actions. "It was just a mutual blowjob kinda thing, at the Fantasia."

"So, you don't even remember his name," the ram snorted lowly. "Nice. Well, all right, fine, it sounds like you're being honest with me, which I appreciate."

Devin sighed, feeling uncertain inside for the first time in a long time. "What's the second question, Kleg?" he asked, wearily.

The ram looked down at his lap for a moment, then slowly looked over at the fox, his expression somber. "When you said that Tressa was cheating on you," he murmured, "…did that begin before or after your first trip to the Fantasia?"

Devin looked thunderstruck. He stared back at Kleg with his muzzle hanging open and eyes wide for a moment or two, then immediately clapped his mouth shut and flicked his gaze around frantically without moving his head too much, unable to make eye contact with the ram.

"Wh-what?" he stammered. "Aww, c'mon, Kleg, that was ages ago! How am I supposed to remember back that fa…"

"It's a simple answer, Devin. 'Before', or 'after'. Which one is it? Guess, if you have to," the ram broke in, his voice gruff.

"Hell, I don't know!" Devin grunted, his tone flustered and impatient as he threw his hands up a bit, then let them drop back onto the seat. "I... I guess it could've been after, but what's that got to do with—"

"Ah! So you admit it," the ram rumbled, his face wrathful as he pointed at the fox accusingly. "You started cheating on her before she started cheating on you! And here you had me thinking that what you did with me just now was your way of getting back at her." He shook his head angrily, then muttered to the fox as he opened the driver's side door and pushed himself out into the roaring wind, "You really oughtta be ashamed of yourself, Dev."

"But...! But I didn't... You can't just—Hey!" the fox yelled, lunging after the ram as he tried to clasp at Kleg's arm. But the ram had already left, and the fox scrambled out of his own door after the ovine, immediately swept over with freezing cold as he sloughed through the thick snow to chase after the ram. The freezing wind and snow lanced into his face like thousands of tiny needles, and his teeth were chattering within moments, but heated rage burned in his cheekruffs as he tried to confront the ram by standing in front of him, holding up a gloved hand. He had to holler to make himself heard over the wind.

"You wait j-just a goddamn muh-minute! You're p... putting words in m-my muzzle!" he yelled.

"You said it yourself—you cheated on her by going to the Fantasia. You agreed that that was cheating," the ram hollered back. He pointed back at the Hummer and yelled, "Get your ass back in there, Dev, you're gonna freeze to death out here! I have to get back to the base so I can beg your fucking wife's forgiveness for what we did." The ram lowered his head to keep his face out of the wind somewhat, and he slowly started to press his way forward again, teeth gritted against the cold. Devin jumped forward and clung to the ram's arm with both of his own, the look on the fox's face—what the ram could see of it, anyway, looked desperate and pleading.

"But I m-muh... made you do that!" he yelled to the ram. "That was my own f-fault! C-c'mon, K-..Kleg, d-don't do this t-to me... Y-you'll nuh... never make it! I'm alruh... ready gonna luh... lose my wife, I d-don't wuh... wanna lose you, too..."

If the ram heard the fox's words, he didn't give any indication of such, keeping his forward movement constant. Kleg refused to look back at the fox, his eyes squinting through the goggles as they swiftly became ice-crusted, making him have to brush the lenses off periodically with his fingers. The cold seeped in around the heat packs and tried to haunt his joints, but given how much peril he was in, the ram was strangely calm. He somehow knew that he'd make it back, because he had a mission, now—and something very, very humbling to ask Tressa's forgiveness for. And once he'd cleared his conscience, he would pick up the pieces and start over, much like he suspected that she would have to do.

"And hell, who knows…" the ram thought grimly, a bit of a lunatic grin spreading across his features as he trudged steadfastly forward. "Maybe I'll fire Devin for sexual harassment, and I can let Tressa be in the room so she can offer to be my testimonial witness in court."

The ram lost track of almost everything. He could dimly hear Devin screaming from some distance behind him, but the sound soon became indistinguishable from the wind whipping and howling around his body. He continued to plod forward, hoping that he was still following the main road and not veering slowly off-track, and he began to count his steps to keep his mind occupied and give his body something to focus on besides the horrible storm. The heat packs were more or less useless now, vague little pillows barely spreading a lamb's breath of warmth upon his limbs and body as he made his way through the morass of white, and the ram felt his mouth panting hard behind his scarf as the effort of slogging through the thick snow started to take its toll on his circulation.

It took maybe thirty minutes for the ram to start losing feeling in his limbs, even though they were still moving. It was difficult for him to tell how much time had actually passed, and he found to his annoyance that he'd lost place in his step counting and had to pick an arbitrary number close to where he thought he'd left off several times. He was saying the numbers aloud in his head, and although it was difficult for him to be sure, he began to think that his mental pronunciation of some of the numbers was coming out garbled. He rubbed his arms and legs briskly as he walked, praying that the dreaded tingling sensation wouldn't set into them.

After walking a bit further, he suddenly realized that somehow, part of the ground had lifted into the air and was levitating in front of him, a shimmering, glowing snowy mass that seemed a good deal brighter than the snow around him. Kleg swiped the ice from his goggles and peered straight at it in wonder, his maw still open and panting behind his scarf as he wondered what was happening. The patch of ground became brighter still, and the ram stopped in his tracks, now actually having to partially shield his eyes from it.

"Oh, cool! Aliens, come to give me a lift in their UFO," he thought idly to himself, his own rational thought apparently missing in action. The cold and his fatigue were doing a number on his mental acuteness, and he found the whole idea of aliens or whatever this light turned out to be to be ludicrously funny. A dry choking sort of wheeze pushed from his throat as he waved an ice-caked arm at the light, his feeble attempt at laughter, before his face went slack as he realized suddenly what he thought it really was.

"Angels…!" he thought, his mind reeling with the possibility. "Oh, how beautiful… Wonder if they're telepathic… Hey! Can you folks hear me?" he shouted mentally. "How about taking pity on an old ram who's on a soul-burdened mission? Think you gents could give me a lift on those seraphim wings of yours?" And again, he had to choke out a horrible facsimile to a laugh. As though angels would waste their time on the likes of him. He smiled weakly as he tried to make out their form, but saw only the barest flicker of shadow cross over the brilliant whiteness as he watched intently.

Had there been a casual observer, he or she would have seen the ram pitch forward face first into the snow. For Kleg—seconds before the light left him and everything went to black—it felt as though he were flying.

It took the ram a few moments to open his eyes, and once he did, he grunted with pain and closed them tightly again. A strong headache throbbed dully behind his eye sockets, and he tried to lift his hands to rub carefully at his orbs and then promptly wished that he hadn't. His muscles were in as much agony as they would have been the morning after a strenuous weight-training workout. His throat felt dry and thick, and his own words were so dry and crackly-sounding that they made him wince even as he heard them. "Oh… gawd, my fuckin' head…"

In spite of his misery, though, he noted with a huge measure of relief that there was no snow or wind. His surroundings were eerily quiet, and there was something heavy covering his body. Ignoring the pain that shot through his temples temporarily as he raised his head slightly, he saw that he was back in his own room at the mining base, covered with several blankets and quilts. His arms and legs felt tingly and sore, but at least he could feel them, and he dropped his head back onto his pillow with a low sigh of relief. It took his nose a few moments to detect the other scent in the room, right next to the bed. Apparently, he wasn't alone.

The figure next to him shifted, then slowly stood up, leaning up and over to stare down at the ram's exhausted face. The somber, graying visage of Doctor Ernie Mason peered down at him, the husky's pale blue eyes staring unblinkingly down into Kleg's gray ones.

"Welcome back, Kleg," he rumbled lowly, his muzzle turning up just a bit at the edges in a wan smile. "We were all hoping that you'd make it."

The ram grunted, and as Ernie's scent registered more firmly in his mind, he realized that there was something missing—the acrid stink of alcohol. The canine was, for once, apparently stone cold sober.

"Ernie," Kleg muttered weakly, raising a beefy, shivering hand toward the dog. Ernie clasped it carefully and gave his boss and friend a comforting squeeze as the ram murmured, "What happened? Did you guys get the suppl—" Then his eyes flew open, his senses jarring awake as his head jerked off the pillow, the ram ignoring his migraine as he gave the dog a panicked look, the whole nightmarish event flooding his mind all over again. "Devin!"

The husky shook his head firmly. "Kleg, you're still recovering—you can't let yourself get so worked up, and you probably got a humdinger of a headache," He reached over to a small tray sitting on the ram's nightstand, then picked up two capsules of medicine and poured the ram a small cupful of water. Then he supported the back of the ram's head with his hand as he tucked the capsules into the ovine's mouth with the other, then held the cup to the ram's lips so he could swallow the aspirin. After he made sure that Kleg swallowed the capsules, he carefully but insistently laid the ram's head back down onto the pillow as he rumbled lowly, "Devin's still alive, but he's not here."

Kleg let out a sigh of relief that might have shaken the bedcovers, had he been feeling stronger. He nodded acknowledgement at the canine's words even as he rubbed his forehead a little, then murmured lowly to the dog, "We alone?"

Ernie nodded and got up long enough to walk to the door of the ram's bedroom, peering out into the hallway and looking in both directions before closing the door firmly behind himself, coming back over to sit by the ram's side. "Alone enough. The guys are in the mess hall eating dinner, and they know you're alive—but I don't figure that I'm gonna tell 'em that you're awake, yet." He shifted uncomfortably in his seat, then gave the ram an apologetically stern look as he murmured, "There's a few things we need to talk about, though, I'm afraid. We can put it off for awhile till you feel stronger, if you like, but Central's pressing me for report details," he sighed, shrugging a bit as he lowered his head for a moment, then looked back at the ram.

"Mmmn. Thought as much," Kleg mumbled, frowning a bit as his brows furrowed. "Alright, then, first things first. I take it, that wasn't the heavenly host that I saw hovering over me with that bright light, just before I must've collapsed."

The dog raised a brow at the ram, looking puzzled. "Given your state at the time, it might've been," he rumbled, his tone serious. "But more'n likely, it was just the Super Cat's searchlight. You were still standing when the beam hit you the first time, and you collapsed a minute or so after.

Lucky for you two that we saw the flares, and luckier still that we got to you before you froze to death, trying to walk your crazy ass back here," the dog growled softly in admonition. He gave the ram's side a light swat with his palm as he grunted, "Jeezus, Kleg what were you thinkin'? I hope you realize what a completely lucky sumbitch you are that you didn't wind up a quadriplegic, from frostbite."

Kleg nodded, frowning deeply. "I know. I know, it was completely insane and ridiculously foolhardy of me, and I should've known better, yadda, yadda, yadda..." he murmured. He paused and looked down over his covered body, then slowly looked back over to the dog. "But I, uhh... take it, I still got everything."

Ernie gave him a stern look and nodded. "You fared a damn sight better than Devin did, that's for sure—and he's lucky that he only lost two fingers and part of his foot."

The ram shuddered, and although the memory of what transpired was again fully in his brain, he was sincere when he murmured lowly, "I'm sorry to hear that."

"Yeah, well... fuck that for now, he'll live. And we gotta think of what to say to Corporate so they'll shut the hell up and drop this," the dog growled, and there was an undercurrent in his tone that made the ram look at him curiously, keenly aware that the canine hadn't told him the whole story, yet. Ernie picked up his clipboard with his writing tablet on it, then placed his pen to the paper, his pale eyes staring at Kleg expectantly. "What's it gonna be, chief? You were there, and this's gonna need your signature on it before it'll stick."

The ram sighed, his eyes rolling in his head and making him wince slightly as the headache flared up for just a second. The words rolled dully off his tongue like they'd done on paper and on his monitor screen countless times before, when he didn't need to tell his superiors the entire truth— lest undesirable fallout occur. "The Hummer stalled and died, and Devin and I got a little panicky because we couldn't agree on a course of action. I couldn't reach you guys on the radio, and decided to use the flare gun... and then decided to chance making it on foot while Dev was supposed to stay with the supplies. We got into a pretty big argument over that, and he was against the idea of me trying to go it alone... and my guess is that you guys found him not too far behind me, trying to catch up with me in spite of my order for him to stay put. Am I right?"

Ernie nodded, his face concentrating as his hand moved swiftly to take the ram's words down in shorthand. He paused for only a second and darted his gaze over to the ram, then continued writing, muttering lowly,

"That's what the official version's gonna say, yeah…" He wrote some more, both males quiet for a moment, until the dog paused again and murmured to the ram, "and I take it, that the reason for Devin's voluntary termination would be 'personal', mostly due to his divorce?"

The ram frowned, but nodded slowly, his eyes silently asking the dog a million questions even as his mouth uttered only one. "Ahh. So, I take it, they went ahead with that, then…" He sighed, then eyed the pitcher of water on his nightstand. "Can I have some more of that, Ern?"

"You bet," the dog nodded, putting his clipboard aside as he poured the ram another cupful, then held it to the ram's lips and helped him drink. "Need to keep plenty of fluid in your system, now that you're outta shock." He made sure the ram finished the water, then offered to pour him a re-fill, which the ram declined with a shake of his head. The canine sat back down, but didn't pick the clipboard back up. He crossed one leg over his other knee and clasped his hands around his knee as he fixed the ram with his own look of thinly-veiled curiosity. "Alright. So, we got the official version taken care of… Now I'm wondering if you might be willing to run through the rest of it with me, if you feel cozy with such. And bear in mind, it'll stay confidential—but there are some things in their divorce paperwork that you might have to sign later anyway, so some of the details will probably be legit."

Kleg shrugged. "What's to tell, Ernie?" he rumbled. "Devin mentioned in the Hummer that he and Tressa had been having problems, and it'd been the first I'd heard of it. He said that they were thinking about splitting up, and apparently, they did."

The dog nodded. "We all know that," he replied, as he leaned closer to the ram and lowered his voice, both brows furrowing ominously. "What I'd like to fucking know is why Devin saw fit to leave Tressa every cent of his severance and pension, except for ten thousand dollars—and maybe while we're at it, you might consider lettin' me have a peep at that letter he left for you," he murmured, reaching sideways to open the ram's nightstand drawer. He pulled out an envelope that had what was apparently a fairly thick letter in it, with the ram's name on the outside. The dog dropped it onto the nightstand next to the pitcher, and the sound of it hitting the wood was heavy enough to be audible. The dog's eyes shone with morbid curiosity at the letter, then kept their glint of eagerness intact as they slowly panned over to the ram's face.

Kleg looked surprised, staring at the letter as though it were from a long-lost relative he never knew he'd had. He stared blankly back at Ernie, his slack jaw finally shutting and his features going solemn after a few minutes. The dog frowned a little, but got the jist of the ram's silent answer.

"Eh. Fine, be that way. Guess it really ain't none of my business, but you can't blame a fella for trying," he muttered, one brow furrowing a bit in a half scowl before his face returned to neutral and he picked up his clipboard and started to write again, pretending to be engrossed in the report.

Kleg stared sullenly at the envelope, then back at the ram, another detail nagging at his subconscious. "Ernie," he rumbled, "...when you say that Devin left Tressa all of his severance and pension, 'bout how much was that?"

The dog's writing hand paused, and he frowned tightly, not looking back at the ram for a moment, as if debating on whether or not to answer—but finally, he did. "Don't remember the exact figure, but I wanna say it was somewhere to the tune of about fifty thousand dollars, I guess." His hand went back to scribbling nonchalantly, even as Kleg whistled softly.

"And he left her every cent of that except for ten K?" Kleg murmured, looking surprised.

"Well, given that he's been workin' for this company since he was damn near nineteen years old, it ain't that much of a surprise, is it?" the dog grunted, putting down his clipboard long enough to lay it aside and lift a bottle of what looked like whiskey up from the floor to the ram's nightstand, placing it on the tray next to the water pitcher and looking at it morosely. "That's a mighty long time to tuck back paycheck change, given Dev's age, so that figure sounds about right."

Kleg looked at the bottle, then back at the doctor. "Ernie, I appreciate your lookin' after me, don't get me wrong..." he murmured lowly, "...but I couldn't help but notice that you ain't blitzed."

"How perceptive of you," the dog muttered, giving the ram's side a playful shove that contrasted with the dog's grim facial expression. "Might be partly because I been looking after your gristly old ass, off and on for the last two weeks, so I ain't had time to drink. You reckon?" he murmured, giving one of the ram's horns a tug.

The ram looked back at the dog, and the two stared at each other thoughtfully for what felt like a long while. Finally, the ram murmured, "There anything else you haven't told me yet, Ernie?"

The dog rubbed the back of his neck a little bit, then eased his chair to sit as close to the ram as possible, his head leaning over so that the ram wouldn't have to strain himself. He licked his muzzle a bit, then rumbled quietly, "Randall... I've seen some males change over time, but I'm here to tell ya... I ain't never seen no one act the way Devin MacIntyre did when he came to from his frostbite surgery. It was like somethin' in him was broke, and it didn't have nothin' to do with his lost limbs. What the devil happened between you two, out in that storm?"

Randall thought very hard at that moment, and for a few seconds, he debated telling the dog everything. But even as he opened his mouth to speak, the thought of the dog spilling the beans on his next bender made him reconsider, and he heard himself say lowly, "I... I made a mistake, Ern. A couple mistakes. I said and did some things I shouldn't have, and that's why Devin and I had words."

The dog fixed the ram with a stare that let Kleg know that the canine didn't believe his words for a minute, but he simply nodded once and murmured, "Did ya, now. Hmmm. I wonder..."

The ram looked away from the canine for a few moments, staring up into space absently as the canine scratched one of his ears with the pen he was writing with. Finally, he shrugged, then picked up the clipboard and opened it to the final page of writing, pointing down to a line near the bottom of the page. "Anyhoo... I suppose that this is all water under the bridge, now, or it will be, once you put yer John Hancock on this here line so I can fax it to central. This oughtta shut 'em up, hopefully." He held the board still for the ram as Kleg nodded and took the pen, and then signed his name on the line indicated. The dog checked the signature, then nodded, heading for the door. He put his hand on the knob, then rumbled over to the ovine, "you hungry?"

The ram thought about it, then wrinkled his muzzle a bit and shook his head. "Not really."

"Well, tough," the dog said gruffly, frowning a bit. "I'm sendin' one of the boys down here in another hour or so with some grub, and if you don't eat it, I'm gonna fuckin' feed it to you intravenously," he warned. Then he pointed to the whiskey bottle on the nightstand and said in an authoritative tone, "Oh, and by the way—I better not see you swigging outta that bottle, either. It is strictly for medicinal purposes, only," he growled, winking at the ovine.

Kleg's eyes quivered. He couldn't bring his mouth to move, but his facial expression showed the canine his gratitude. Ernie smiled at him a little, then opened the door and was about to step out into the hallway when the ram called after him. "Hey! Ernie?"

The dog paused, then poked his head back into the room. "What?"

Randall paused, then asked the dog hesitantly, "This is gonna sound really stupid, but... do you believe in that old sayin' 'What goes around, comes around'?"

Ernie paused, his face grave. He waited a few moments, and the door creaked in his grasp before he nodded once, firmly. "Matter of fact, I do."

"Why?" Kleg asked.

The dog didn't hesitate. "'Cause sometimes, I have to."

They stared at each other a bit longer, two old males temporarily pondering on the unspoken. Finally, the dog held the clipboard aloft. "I'm gonna go send this report, then I plan to get heinously and inappropriately drunk," he announced. "But if you need me or any of the guys, just buzz us on the intercom. And after you get a bite to eat, you need to try walkin'. Your legs'll be mighty wobbly, but you should be okay if you take it slow."

"I'll do that," the ram nodded. "Thanks for keepin' me alive, Ern."

"My job," the dog grinned. Then he closed the door behind him and headed down the hall.

Kleg stared over at the letter for a long time. He reached out to touch it, fingerhooves scraping lightly across the paper. He lifted it slowly up to his face, then set it onto his chest, his hand still gripping it, fingers shaking a little. His mouth set in a firm line, and although he told himself that he needed to read it, a part of him didn't want to.

He leaned his head back onto the pillow and closed his eyes, slipping the arm that was holding the letter under the covers with him so he could lay it on his chest. His headache had waned, and sleep overtook him mercifully and more easily than he could have hoped for.

Bad Boys

Stories don't have to be about good people doing good things in bad conditions. It is rather daring, not to mention risky, for an author to present a story about someone doing bad things. The reader's moral judgment of the author is a great risk, not to mention his enjoyment of the story.

In "Bad Timing," the author makes a clear choice by daring to show his protagonist's flaws, without feeling the need to let him overcome them. And the result, as we shall see, is less than justifiable...

Bad Timing

Timbo

Confusion: As I opened my eyes, the bright orb above me pierced my retinas with searing pain. I noted that I once again was on a cold tile floor, my chest nestled up against the hard ceramic tub. I rolled onto my side, letting a little bit of the nasty stickiness in my mouth spill onto the ground. My mane dragged on the ground, collecting the mix of fluids beside me. Hunched over, staring at the puddle of drool and sweat, I attempted to remember what, or who, I did the previous night.

Realization: It's not that I especially liked the disorientation at the end of a trip. I had tried to forget the downfalls by drinking near the end, but I ended up hammered, waking up in a blur. Had I really gone as far as I thought I did with Mike? My body wasn't sore, and that unmistakable taste wasn't sloshed into my mouth. I forced myself up at that point, using the wall as stabilization as my lower joints finally kicked into order. Horizontal became vertical, allowing my mind to make sense of the room. The door was halfway open, the television seemingly on too loud. I curled my claws along the wall and threw myself toward the doorway.

Remembering: I could smell him. I could smell that wolfish musk. I must not have failed my objective, but something was registering wrong. How down and out must he have been for us to go as far as at least a kiss? Our confrontation in the restaurant the night before had ended in some extreme words between us. I was surprised he even decided to show up to the room afterwards. As I stumbled out of the bathroom and into the glowing room, the television's tubes flickered light off of a single white sheet of paper on the bed. I focused my vision to read it, but I had known already what it would say.

"Damn it."

"Drinks, anyone?" The waitress, a lioness, turned and strutted around to in front of where the wolf and I were lying down on our beach towels. She shook her rear, allowing her hula skirt to dance around and entice our eyes, but only Mike's followed. It really irritated me that such a blatant display of sexuality by a woman would be allowed at a family friendly hotel. Her disgusting actions worked perfectly on my friend however. Mike sat up and waved at to the lioness, scratching his black chest fur and somehow brightening his dark gray wolf eyes to kick in his own charm.

"I'll take vodka on the rocks," the wolf chirped, his paws gently sliding up behind his head to show off more of his stacked upper body. "And my feline friend here," he trailed off, allowing me to answer. The lioness was busy try to write something down as she gazed at Mike, no concern directed toward what I might want to order.

"Just a coke, please." I shook my head as I spoke, my words a mere mumble as I simply stared in amazement at the ridiculous interaction between man and woman. The lioness was indeed very attractive and would have turned heads anywhere she went. But the fact that she was flirting with Mike to get him to order a drink made my blood boil. I was about to say something to push her along when I was interrupted.

"You think I could see your ID, cutie?" Even her question required *by law* was somehow slanted sexually with a mere pet's name. Her tone was dripping with seduction, and Mike didn't help the situation any when he smiled.

"Babe, my ID is up in my room. If you want, we can go up there together and get it after you're off." His devilish grin and thick charm overwhelmed me. I plopped back down on my towel and tried to ignore the situation.

"Well, let me go get those drinks for you guys." As she turned and began to walk away, her head crooked to the side and she said plainly, "I'm off at five by the way."

Mike cupped his paws around his muzzle as she rounded the pool, heading off in the distance. "Bring a friend!"

I sighed loudly. "Does being in Hawaii give you the ticket to flirt with every girl here?" I sneered as I stared into the cloudless sky above. It was a beautiful day on the island of Oahu, but somehow even the perfect weather and amazing view of the ocean in front of me couldn't make me feel any less uncomfortable with Mike's constant propositioning.

Mike spun around and stared at me. "You're single... I'm single. There's plenty of hot ass around here that should be taken advantage of."

"Hot ass, huh?" The lioness that had served us earlier stood there, staring down at Mike with a long glare.

I chuckled as I watched Mike's mind backpedal to come up with a smooth way out of the situation. I couldn't help but feel he was getting what he deserved for treating this trip as a sex venture. The whole reason we were in Hawaii was for my mother's wedding, which had already gone off without a hitch. While my mother and new step-father had dashed off to Maui for their honeymoon, Mike, his parents, and I were all staying in the same hotel to make flying back to California an easier arrangement. We had a few extra days before our return flight however, so Mike and I were spending our last remaining time relaxing. While he was staring at whatever skinny piece of ass walked by, I was looking for the other guys.

Mike didn't know I was gay. He kept trying to get me to 'hook up' with every female cat that walked by with a tight ass or big breasts. The truth, however, was that I was checking him out. Mike and I had known each other for years through school, but had really grown stronger as teammates. We had just graduated from Mission Viejo, the best high school team in the nation, but only he had decided to play college ball. I might have been a linebacker, but I wasn't interested in the stereotype any longer. One scholarship to UC Berkley later and Mike was on his way to the stars, but the quarterback and I hadn't grown apart at all. His mother had been the bridesmaid at my mother's wedding.

Even though we had been friends for a long time, I never could take my eyes off of him. It didn't help that Mike was stacked all around from constant working out and playing ball. But, he was always truthful and a caring individual. You could confide anything in him and he wouldn't overreact. Combine his amazing personality and his gorgeous body, and you had a mean, lean, womanizing machine. I wouldn't go so far to say that I was *after* him, but as I sat there and watched him attempt a recovery from his failed conquest, I dreamed of holding him in my arms as my boyfriend.

I must have been considerably out of it because Mike threw a couple of ice cubes at my head. My sight came back into focus as I rubbed the back of my head and growled. "What the fuck was that for?"

The wolf glared at me awkwardly. "You were just staring at me. I said your name like four times. The waitress even made a comment."

I wiped a bit of water from my brow where the ice cubes had struck and sunk back into my chair. "Sorry, I was daydreaming."

"Dreaming of that lion and you in bed, I hope." Mike laughed and looked away, browsing the pool for more slutty women.

I scoffed and put my sunglasses back on, trying to use the sun's warmth to calm my irritation. "Sometimes I wonder, Mike, if all you care about with these girls is to fuck them and leave them." The phrase I was tossing around in my head came out as a mutter before I realized I had said it.

"You know what Jared?" Mike's head flew around to stare back at me. He didn't sound too annoyed at my comment. "That waitress, the lion, and her friend are going to meet us at that steak house down the road at seven tonight." He slapped his paws together as he spoke. "They're single, we're single, and you haven't had any *fun* all week. We're going to have a good time tonight." The wolf lay back down on his beach chair and continued to browse around at more of his potential prey.

I shook my head and sighed, resigning to my fate. "Whatever."

"Come on buddy, we're just meeting up. Why are you always so hung up on these things?" Mike's smile was soothing, but it wasn't helping my anxiety at all.

"I don't want to hook up with just some random girl, dude." Sighing, I continued the stroll down the path from our hotel to the neighboring tourist shopping mall. Contained within the open-air mall was a steak house where we were meeting to two girls. The waitress didn't seem like the kind of deep-thinking woman I would have preferred to share time with. If I was going to actually put up with a date with a female, I would want her to have at least some substance. Unfortunately as we spotted the two cats, a lion and panther, I could already tell they weren't the brightest duo.

They were standing outside the busy restaurant. Neither Mike nor I had been there before, but the bellhop had recommended it as the best place on that side of Oahu for steak. A large neon lit sign out front screamed 'Chuck's Steak House' in the dim light of the sunset. Some of the well-sized establishment's windows glowed in the light, and as the smell of grill pierced my nostrils, my eyes danced around, browsing for guys. I saw a number of middle-aged men with their families, but quickly grew bored when I realized my own possible opportunities were next to nothing. Every guy here appeared to be married or partnered to some skinny, hardly-dressed woman trying to fit into the temptation-filled sexual fantasy of the islands. When Mike and I finally drew near our dates, I finally took a good look at them and discovered they were no different.

Outfitted in long flowing skirts, the Hawaiian print-clad pair stood out with the bright exuberance and stupidity that only two young and shallow cats could display. Colorful leis and flowers adorned their upper bodies, bounded below by obnoxiously vivid bikinis. They were already deep in conversation about how Mike and I were 'late'. I suppose being there after them, although we were early according to our meeting time, construed us as 'inconsiderate jerks' as they so eloquently put it. My eyes had already wandered away to some of the more beefy men before Mike jabbed me in the side.

"Excuse my counterpart here ladies," he danced around vocally as he poured on the charm. I was half ready to just tell him they'd sleep with him anyway, but the lioness drew near.

Her eyes widened and focused intently on my brow, seemingly examining every crevice for imperfection. "Your friend doesn't talk much, does he Mike?" Her tone was filled with bitchiness, so I couldn't resist the strong reply.

"I generally let others make fools of themselves, rather than comment," I hissed. I tried to sound a little humorous, but it didn't work. The panther was already hanging onto Mike and it was apparent I was stuck with my own species. Well, I had to admit she was at least the pinnacle of fashion and had a nice body, albeit lacking in brains.

The wolf laughed at something the panther mused and then abruptly spun around. His paws pointed around as he introduced the group. "Ladies, this is Jared. Nice guy. A little cynical but very romantic." My insides felt like dropping to the ground as the wolf called me romantic. If only Mike had known how romantic I had dreamed of being with him. "Jared, this is Kelly." A sickness enveloped me as his deep gray eyes fell on the panther with total adoration. He turned and motioned to the lioness. "And this is Macy. Kind, charming, and fucking hilarious." I held my tongue from noting she hadn't made me laugh yet. I gave the lioness another look as she turned, leading in front of me as Mike urged us inside.

The restaurant was well lit but completely packed with others. Every bench in the waiting area was fully in use and there were many standing around, attempting to remain in their family clusters. Beyond the sign in desk was the standard steak house joint, complete with all wood tables and tall-backed booths. Scurrying around were at least a dozen waiters carrying out orders and dropping off large plates of artery-clogging goodness. My mouth watered and my mind wandered to thoughts of sharing a plate of steak and shrimp with Mike, just the two of us.

"I already made the reservation," the wolf hollered over the noisy bustling of people around us. Almost immediately we were being guided by someone taking us to our seat. I let my ears take in the noise, something I had grown to miss, being in calm and peace for the last four days. As we headed over to a table in a much quieter area and sat down, my eyes gazed around the room and found a few more adorable men, but they were plainly with families on vacation. While disappointed, I tried to keep my hopes up but then noticed the vivid discussion of 'ugly outfits' going on between the two females next to us. I turned again and stared off into space.

Mike began small talk with *both* felines as my mind wandered to the more important fact at hand: I had been in Hawaii for four days but had not approached any guys. At home I would have been a lot more open and willing to approach someone I thought might be gay, but with the wedding and my family and best friend not knowing of my other life, it was very hard to break away and feel safe on the prowl. Even with my feline heritage, my size made it impossible to really sneak around without being noticed. I wasn't entirely that large, but I wasn't the skinny jock that picks up all of the hot cheerleaders.

There was really only one guy that I had my sights on then. The biggest problem I had to overcome with Mike was coming out to him. The timing needed to be perfect so I could arrange for both of us to be sufficiently hammered to push any physical interaction along. I wasn't planning on *raping* Mike. I was just going to try and allow him to explore something he might not have thought about with me.

The alcohol, and possibly the GHB I picked up, would help him open up to the new experience.

At some point Mike had ordered drinks. I drew on the Mai Tai in front of me as I began daydreaming about how I would have loved to just take that big wolf right there in the restaurant. My eyes drooped down to the table below, and I zoned out the commotion of the restaurant. Boredom was setting in and I really was not interested in the lioness next to me. However, she jabbed me in the side at some point where I was supposed to enter into their conversation.

I swung my head back to glare at the lioness. "Excuse me?"

Her face glowed with pure anger. "Did you hear what I said?"

I scoffed and took another sip of my Mai Tai. "Honestly, no I didn't. I was too busy staring off into space." I filled the table with sparks of anger and irritation, something the wolf noticed immediately and attempted to contain.

"Hey man, chill out." He turned himself back toward the ladies. "He's just been a little out of it, that's all. Right lion?" The forcefulness in his speech pushed me over the edge.

The Mai Tai was no match for my anger as I slammed it down. I rocketed out of the bench, pulling down the Hawaiian shirt I was wearing and brushing back my mane while the burn of the alcohol wrenched throughout my chest. "Yeah. Sure. I'll be right back." Hissing as I spun on a dime,

I strolled off quickly toward the restroom. I already needed a break from this madness. My patience had been broken finally by my supposed ally and it had quickly become apparent that I wouldn't be comfortable at the table. With my eyes focused on the sanctuary that was the men's room, the restaurant flew by in a blur. I shoved my paw out to grasp the handle and flung the door open.

A gray paw grabbed the door behind me. "We need to talk."

"You ever think that's maybe not what I want?" the lion hissed. Jared leaned back against the wall and stared fiercely into the wolf's eyes.

"What the fuck Jared?" the wolf spat back, his curse reverberating around the bathroom. The silence while Mike pondered his thoughts began to dig into Jared's heart. Doubt became outright fear and terror of the subject that was about to be discussed. His mind raced as fast as his heart to come up with one good outcome but it could not.

Am I really ready to tell him this?

Mike threw his paws up in frustration and paced around the room. Opening and closing a stall door, he murmured, "if it isn't someone like Macy that you want, then what is it?" His glance shifted back to the cat, his eyes full of a mixture of anger and confusion. It was an evil look that burrowed straight into the lion's heart, filling it with dread.

Jared sighed and stared back, trying to convey meaning through his look rather than speech. His jaw was seemingly wired shut from his own confused fear and doubt. The lion felt the back of his mouth fill with sickness. His gut wrenched with fear as he hesitated, the uncertainty of his best friend's reaction filling his mind.

Would he hate me? Will he give me a hug and say it's alright? What if he's waiting to hear I'm gay for the go ahead to be with me? No. Damn it! He's too straight to care. He'll be pissed off and confused, but I'm stuck in a corner now.

Jared's thoughts were slammed into the wall as Mike nearly broke a stall door with the sheer force of his throwing it shut. The wolf stood staring at the door as it flew back and forth, each time hitting the latch a little softer. His head jerked around to the lion and gave the cat a mean stare, the same evil look from earlier remaining.

"Damn it! Is it other guys?" The question hung, stale, in air that was already filled with enough tension to start a war. The lion could hardly keep his eyes on the wolf's angry glare, but he dared not look away. It was becoming a mind game, Jared knew, and breaking focus would result in a lost opportunity. It was the time to do it. It was time to tell the wolf how he really felt and stop dodging around something so important to him. Still, the lion could not speak it. Every muscle-fiber in his face clamped that muzzle shut, fright still coursing through the lion's veins, preventing him from doing anything but the simple nod he gave to the wolf.

Once again, the wolf took the initiative. "That's what it is, huh?" His reactions, while starting to grow calmer, were still tainting the air thicker with accusation.

Jared didn't know how to react calmly in that kind of environment. He was fighting back tears. He was thinking how much he just wanted to say how he felt. The lion even opened up his muzzle to just say 'yes, and I want you'. But something else in his mind took over.

A sinister tone emitted from the lion's muzzle, "You're just one smart-ass canine, aren't you?" The statement was filled with harsh sarcasm and it tore through the cloud of shit in the air like the razor on the lion's leg the night before.

"So you're gay..." the wolf tripped out of his muzzle in a growl. "Great. Do you know how fucking stupid this is going to make me look?"

Screams of rage flew through the confused lion's head. He shouted, "You know what Mike? *Fuck you!*" The insult removed any remaining sanity as it echoed against the tiled walls. The wolf began to look noticeably dejected as the lion continued. "Now because you have a gay best friend, you're going to look like a fool? To who? Your team? Your family? Your possible fuck buddies out there?" The cat snorted and slammed his paw into the wall. He turned and looked at the paw before doing it again. The pain offset the mental anguish and made the lion's whole world real again, something he had grown accustomed to doing to himself. With the throbbing of his paw to guide him forward, he stepped closer to his much larger 'friend' and smirked. "Don't worry about that, buddy. No one's going to find out that your best friend is *tainted* with homosexuality."

Mike looked visibly destroyed. His eyes fell to the ground, and his body slumped against the frame of a nearby stall. "Come on, Jared," the wolf muttered, "it's not like that."

"Then how is it Mike? Do you even give a shit about how I feel?" Jared screamed down at the wolf, his fury penetrating any last bit of understanding he might have had for the wolf.

Mike raised his head up, his eyes wide and filled with confusion. "Dude, you know I do. But... but, this just doesn't make any sense."

"No, Mike. It does. You were just too fucking ignorant to see that maybe for two seconds I wasn't interested in your sluts." Jared's voice was growing calmer, but he panted strongly in between sentences and growled after he finished. He waited, watching as the wolf tried to comprehend the entire situation. The lion almost laughed at the pathetic response of the lupine as his patience waned. He stared down at the slouched wolf and scoffed at his lack of a reply.

You know what Mike? I'll save you the trouble.

The lion turned around with a sharp hiss from his muzzle. "You wouldn't understand. You have no idea what it's like to live a lie or to have what you want more than anything in the world dangling in front of you constantly." He stared at the door and shook his head as he stepped toward it. His muzzle barely moved as he muttered, "fuck it. I wouldn't want to shatter your precious ego anyway."

It didn't occur to Jared that while Mike had looked dejected and beaten, he was one hell of a strong wolf when he was angry. Two large gray paws clamped down on the lion's shoulders and threw him forward with ferocious velocity. The lion tumbled across the room and slammed into the sink fixtures. His forehead bounced off of the faucet, allowing a steady stream of blood to escape from the new wound. As Jared collapsed into a heap, Mike stumbled a few steps away and grabbed the door handle. He ripped the exit open and slid out into the bright restaurant, never sparing a glance over to the broken feline.

"So I guess tonight is off then Mike?"

I stared at the wolf disgustedly as I opened my hotel door. "What the fuck are you doing here Mike? Didn't I make myself clear?" My glare contained thick anger and distaste, something I tried to convey to the arrogant wolf. Playing hard-to-get could be done but was always difficult in delicate situations like this. Anger was clouding my seduction, and the wolf wasn't going to help with his current attitude. But, he was back. The wolf was here and I could finally take advantage of that.

"Hey! You listen here Jared," he started aggressively, but quickly faded back, his words hitting the ground with a solid thud. He sighed as his paw moved onto the frame, supporting his bulky body as he leaned forward with a sulk. "I don't think you understood me at the restaurant."

"I think I did. I think I understood your arrogance perfectly." The words snapped out before I could realize the severity. I couldn't directly see his eyes but I felt his dejected look burrowing into my feet. "Come inside so the neighbors don't hear this." My paw swept around and offered him access to the single-bedded room. As he deftly stepped inside, my eyes still caught and gawked at his natural athletic nature. (*Still always the quarterback.*) The comment barely escaped being shifted out of my clasped muzzle unintentionally. I was literally preying on my best friend, but it felt great.

The lupine took a seat in one of the crappy recliners in the corner. I closed the door behind me, collecting what I might say. I was severely pissed off from earlier, but part of me just wanted to forgive him. He was alone, with me, in my room. He felt guilty, and there was alcohol to be consumed and drugs to be toyed with. Tonight would be the night. But first I needed to mend our situation.

"So, did you come up here to rough me up some more?" I muttered, stepping over to the bed. I made sure to brush the small bandage on my forehead guarding the wound from earlier.

Mike slapped his paw on the small desk next to him, rattling some change on its surface. "I'm such a moron Jared. You were just in my face and I didn't know how to react, you know?" His words flew out hastily and with a piercing purity only someone who was truly sorry could replicate. I nodded, letting him continue. He sighed, uttering, "You know I would never want to hurt you, but I was cornered. I was stuck. My best friend, who I thought was one of the straightest guys I knew, ends up coming out to me in a bathroom of a restaurant."

I frowned. The timing had been terrible, and although I intended to use my sexuality against him, I hadn't planned on being in a bathroom. I also hadn't planned on being thrown across the room and cutting my forehead on a faucet, but I could no longer blame the wolf for his actions. "Listen Mike, I understand the conditions were not ideal. I didn't want to bring it up then, but that situation was intense. You weren't very friendly about me being gay."

"I know man..." the wolf trailed off again, obviously filtering through conflicting thoughts. "I guess my whole perception of you just changed. You were just always 'Jared, my best friend.' In the bathroom you became 'Jared, the gay guy.' It was just drastic. It didn't help that you were being such an ass to the girls."

I rose and faked a smile, pulling the other free chair over to wolf's recliner. Sitting down, I placed my paw on his broad shoulder and gave it a firm grip. "Well wolf, I'm still the same old lion. I've always been gay, so it's not like I suddenly changed." I let my paw fall off the wolf's shoulder and run down his arm. "It was hard for me to even accept my sexuality at first. I thought it would change me into something else." I turned and looked out the window, trying to create a more dramatic feel. "But when I finally just said 'Screw it: I'm gay,' I understood that it was a part of me and not something I would develop into." I looked back at him with an easy grin as I shrugged. "It's a big of a part of me as my eye color."

The wolf bought my smile and reciprocated. "Yeah, I think I get that now." His eyes matched my own and for a second I caught a twinkle. Was it something more than just acknowledgement? No. He was still unsure of the whole 'best friend being gay' situation. But knowing that now he was in a more comfortable position emotionally, I figured I could push the situation along.

"I had nothing against those two… *felines*… but I just was tired of window-shopping for something I didn't care to buy, you know what I mean?" The wolf nodded, of course, as I stood again, letting my tail flick near his face. Every bit of charm in my body was coming to the surface, trying to ease the wolf into acceptance.

Mike sat up straight as I headed over to the small bathroom/kitchen combination in the hotel room. "Jared, I'm sorry I put you in that situation." He genuinely felt bad; however I was still going to punish him for his actions.

I shrugged, acting as if I dismissed his ignorance as nothing major. "Hey, it's no big deal. You didn't know." I fumbled around my pocket for the vial of GHB and slipped it out, opening it behind the counter silently. As I grabbed two glasses, I spoke down at the counter. "By the way, you didn't get a chance to play with those girls, did you?"

"No, why?" the wolf responded, baffled.

I tried not to sound too eager when I replied, "Just checking. Want something to drink?"

My left paw clutched the back of the chair Mike was sitting in, grasping hard to prevent us from following forward. I was kneeling down in front of him, straddling his leg, leaning in to continue our kiss. My other paw grabbed the back of the wolf's head, pulling him forward and locking our muzzles. His disapproval was muffled as I turned my head to the side, allowing my tongue to force its way between his lips. I leaned further in, tipping the chair backwards with my paw. As my mind focused on the kiss more and more, I didn't notice the chair begin to slip. Mike's tongue was beginning to explore my own muzzle. As my head pushed harder into the kiss and my weight shifted further forward, the chair's legs gave way and we fell back.

I landed on top of him with a deep thud that reverberated throughout the room. The kiss stopped. The wolf pulled back, staring me in the eyes. We both tried to recover from the sudden jolt, but our reflexes were not in the best of conditions as the chemicals further circulated throughout our veins. Mike was stuck between me and the chair and couldn't move. I held myself a few inches above him, our muzzles still only barely apart as our eyes did the talking. I knew that if I got him drunk this would happen. The drugs were helping I was sure, but those gray eyes stared back at me with a lust I hadn't seen in any man in a long time. After a few more breaths, I drove my lips back down to him and locked him in a long kiss once again.

Maybe I was imagining he was enjoying it. I felt him up a bit as we lay there on the ground, and the wolf wasn't hard. But, he wasn't fighting the kiss at all. And his eyes... It didn't *really* matter to me if he was truly enjoying it or not, because I knew that the stuff I had him on would 'help' him forget what happened tonight. The wolf deserved it. You simply don't assault your best friend when he comes out to you and expect there to be no consequences. Besides, kissing was only the tip of the iceberg for what I had planned. Seeing the wolf enjoy other activities would be a lot more fun.

I was sufficiently startled when Mike shoved me away, breaking our kiss once again. "Hey... Ja... Jared," stuttered the wolf. I had a considerable amount of leverage on him, yet he continued to fight and attempt to speak. "I... I'm not sure if I... I want to do..."

Please, stop.

His face grimaced as I instinctively shoved my paw into his pants, cupping his balls. Mike let out a few short breaths and reopened his eyes, taking a nice long look at my paw in his pants before staring back up into the air.

Mike's cock began to grow. I couldn't see it directly, but the bulge in his pants told all. The wolf began to moan slightly as he rolled his head to the side lazily, letting his body take control from his brain. My paw pulled out and quickly unbuttoned and unzipped his fly, exposing the tip of his cock slightly above his red briefs. I allowed my claws to lightly graze his sleek head, rubbing the natural lubrication around in my paw. I stood quickly, removing the chair beneath us. The drugs, atmosphere, adrenaline, and my own lust came together all at once as I stared down at my lupine prey. I kicked the chair across the room and dove back down onto my waiting toy, ignoring the crash of the chair slamming into the wall.

The wolf quickly turned his head back to face me and stared in fear. "Come... come on Jared," the wolf whimpered. I bathed in his dread, licking my paw clean as I kneeled down slowly to nuzzle his crotch. Mike mumbled a few more incoherent phrases, which I ignored.

Am I even awake?

I slipped my tongue out and buried my muzzle into his briefs, taking in the wolf's scent of pure masculinity. "No!" Mike cried out, trying to buck me off in the process. His denial only turned my lust into anger. I tried to calmly push his hips back down but he once again tried to force me off. "This can't be…" the wolf stammered on.

I threw my right paw up and wrapped it around his neck, slamming the back of his head onto the ground again. Using my left paw to force his shoulders back down, I slowly moved forward to place my whole body on his, pinning him. "You listen, fucker," I snapped. "You threw me around in the bathroom and you expected to come up here and have a civil fucking discussion?" I was screaming down at him, my rage uncontrollable. "Fuck you, Mike! You hear me yet?"

No, Jared. No. Please.

I picked him up by his neck and slammed his head back down again, sending a loud bang throughout the room. "You're getting off lucky tonight," I muttered, "lucky because you're going to forget this whole god damn thing." I slapped him on the side of the muzzle with force and then stood, watching his convulsing body as he howled in pain and shame. "Get up and get on the bed before I start *really* hurting you."

I laughed as the wolf rose slowly and climbed on to the bed. Mike seemed already worn out as he flopped facedown. The drugs were most likely kicking in, probably making him feel sick and dizzy. As I stood there, staring at the wheezing wolf, I realized the situation, position, and timing were perfect. I would finally be able to take what had always been held right in front of me, just out of grasp.

Fuck, what is he planning…?

I kneeled down beside him on the bed and ran my claw from his ankle, gently guiding it up to his waist. I quickly grabbed the wolf and flipped him onto his back with all of my might as my other paw flew up and grabbed him by the neck again.

It's like gravity is keeping me down right now. I can't get off of the bed.

My free paw pulled down his pants and briefs in one move, dropping them at his ankles.

Mike let out a short breath as the air-conditioned air caught his bits. His whole shaft was exposed, completely hard, teasing me. I leaned down, still holding onto his neck, and stroked his cock with my long tongue, caressing each vein and wrapping around every crevice.

Whoa man, that feels good. Whoa.

My tongue slipped down below his ballsac, wrapping around it and coating his short fur with a good deal of saliva. I slowly let off of Mike's neck, drawing that paw down to rub his chest fur affectionately as my muzzle buried itself below the wolf's balls. I licked quickly at his tailhole, massaging his balls and thick cock with my free paws.

Mike suddenly thrust his pelvis up, trying to throw me off again. I vaulted up on top of the wolf and bent down, seizing his neck again with a great deal of force. As I shoved the back of his head back into the bed, I whispered quietly into his ear. "What did I tell you about fighting back?

Come on man! I shouldn't be doing this.

"Do you think I care how you feel right now? You didn't show *me* any care when I came out to you earlier." I reached down beside the bed and felt around for my backpack, pulling out some thick nylon rope. "Yeah, you apologized. I don't give a fuck! If you want to fight this, I'm tying you down."

With my weight on top of him and the full effects of the GHB kicking in, the wolf's attempts to move around failed miserably. I tied his forepaws together with a tight knot, attaching the pair to the headboard of the bed. I slid off of Mike toward the end of the bed and held his rear paws high in the air, proudly displaying his tailhole once again. I dove back in, driving my tongue deep into the wolf's hole, allowing enough saliva to drip from my muzzle to his entry point.

Ahhh, so warm. Oh god damn, lick that some more.

Mike's breaths became short and heated. He seemed to enjoy the rimming, or it might have been the drugs. Either way, I pulled my tongue out and gave his balls one more quick lick before sitting up to pull my shirt and pants off.

My own cock stood long and tall, ready to plunge into the wolf's now slick hole. I spit a bit on my paw, rubbing it around with my own pre to lube up my cock a bit. Mike's eyes widened with terror as he saw my cock hanging over him. I rubbed my balls as I leaned back down, grabbing his rear paws again to hold them high in the air. I shifted forward a bit, letting my cock head rub gently on the wolf's tailhole.

Oh god that's hot! Too hot! Keep that away! Get away with that thing!

I smiled as Mike's eyes darted around the room but his muzzle stayed shut. "Just to make sure you don't make too much noise for our neighbors," I mumbled as I grabbed the bed sheet beneath us and ripped it out. I reached forward again and grabbed his muzzle. "Open," I commanded. Mike's eyes closed as his muzzle opened, allowing me to shove enough sheets into his muzzle to gag him. I chuckled, sliding back down as I rubbed his headfur and gently spoke my praise. "Good boy."

His tailhole was decently easy to slide into for a virgin. My paws gripped his ankles as I gently pushed all of the way in, allowing his hole to expand and take my full length. I was slightly too long to have Mike take me all the way at first, but as I started to move in and out and Mike began to scream into the sheets, I got farther and farther into him. My motions became fluid and consistent, the rhythm of our mating flowing through me and drawing me nearer and nearer to filling the wolf's entry with lion seed. I had already been close to shooting from earlier, ordering Mike around and such, so I tried holding back my climax as I rowed into him. I was nice enough to reach down and fondle his cock and balls a bit, but it didn't silence his pained cries.

I thought I had used a sufficient amount of saliva as lubrication for the wolf's tailhole, but as I had to shove more and more cloth into the wolf's screaming maw I realized it might actually be hurting him. I was close enough to climax that I continued to hump, however. Mike lay below me, crying and whimpering, making many sounds of pain and only a few sounds of pleasure. He was facing upward, his legs bent in the air to expose his now violated hole. I slammed all the way in suddenly, only being stopped by the bones in the wolf's body at the end of the lupine's tube. I bent down, bringing his muzzle close to Mike's ear, and spoke very softly. "You see what happens when you don't respect the feelings of your friends?"

As I sat back up, Mike's gray eyes cried out for forgiveness as they watched me. Tears streamed steadily out, running down his muzzle and forming a pool on his chest fur. The wolf fidgeted against his restraints weakly, barely fighting to retain any last bit of pride he still had. I saw his cry for help, but I just started laughing. The bastard deserved every bit of this. I felt Mike begin to sob some more, the wolf's tailhole tightening and loosening to each heave of his chest in misery.

"You get turned into a bitch, don't you wolf?" I asked sarcastically. I leaned back, allowing my primal mating urges to retake my consciousness. I pulled back slightly from the wolf and plummeted into him again. As I rowed back and forth, in and out of Mike's ass, I couldn't help but laugh again. "And to think you *asked* me to do this. You *begged* me to have my way with you." I noticed the hole was becoming slicker as the contents of the wolf's opening began to leak.

Jared, I think I'm bleeding. No no no… Here it comes again. Jared…

The sight of red made me growl and pound even harder in and out of the wolf. Mike stopped fighting and just took it, apparently trying to block out the imagery of the scene by closing his eyes.

I neared climax. My rhythm was fast and furious, and I could see Mike's cock was once again becoming hard. I growled again, and my vision became encased in red as my only purpose in life became mating with the 'bitch' below me. As juices finally began to build, as the urge to shoot grew and shrank, I opened my muzzle wide and roared as loud as I could. My lower body tensed all at once, and I shoved my lion cock all of the way into the wolf, completely filling Mike with seed.

Fuck! Please! It hurts! Gahhh! It feels good too! Fuck, fuck, fuck, fuck!

I thought I heard Mike moan as I fell forward, continuing to spurt for a few seconds.

I was purring for a moment before I realized what we were lying in. I propped myself up a few inches to realize that I was lying in wolf seed. Mike had climaxed as well, but passed out in the process and lay there motionless. I smiled as I finally pulled out, watching the rush of fluids escape the wolf's bleeding and wide-open hole. I snickered at the scene, seeing Mike tied and gagged by the bed-sheets with his cock hanging lazily to the side, cum from both of us all over the place. I wished I had a camera to capture this moment forever, but I realized it wasn't something I was going to forget anytime soon.

I picked my feline body up to remove the gag and unbind the wolf. I slowly moved about the room, cleaning up as much of the mess as I could with a few of the hotel towels. I tried to tidy up the room to make it appear as if nothing had happened. I didn't really consider what I did rape... Mike asked for it. And Mike wouldn't remember by himself, but I needed to make sure the wolf would not be aided in anyway. As my system calmed down, the alcohol I had drunk finally caught up with me. I felt myself heave, and I rushed into the bathroom.

I stumbled through the bathroom's door and collapsed on the ground. Lying there, puking into the porcelain god, I wished I could fall asleep with the wolf in my arms.

Fuck... why am I naked?

Jared—

I don't know what happened last night. I woke up... naked... feeling like shit and you're keeled over in the bathroom... naked. I know we drank last night and shit but not what happened after. I tried waking you up but you're too fucked up still on whatever you did. I'm headed back to my room now, but call me when you wake up. I want to know what the <u>fuck</u> happened to me.

−Mike

The lion finally took a seat on the bed the note had been resting on. He lay down, sliding up into a more comfortable position. His shoulder knocked a damp hotel towel off of the bed. When he looked down to see it stained brown, a grin formed on his muzzle, his memory of the night before clear as day.

"Oh, I'll call you alright." The lion's grin grew enormously. "And I'll tell you that you stared right at this ceiling as you asked me to 'have my way.' You'll never know what really happened, but that's my little secret." The feline sighed, and with a chuckle sat up to pick up the room phone. He dialed the number, and as it rang he hissed, "Maybe then you'll learn to listen and respect the feelings of your friends."

The Quickie

Sometimes we just don't feel like reading a work that will
engage our mind and challenge our fixed perceptions.
Sometimes we just want some pleasant fiction to amuse us,
or arouse.

A well-written quickie can, by dint of its intensity, leave a
far deeper mark on us than a long, carefully-constructed
tale. Quickies (I love that letter q!) offer a space in which a
writer can cram as much juicy goodness as he likes, degrees
of richness that would be numbing and even nauseating if
they were kept up in long fiction.

Here follow some such quickies, having no greater ambition
than a moment's delight—for reader and protagonist alike.
They show that even in the space of a very small number of
words there is room for a wealth of character and sensation.

Pretty In Pink

Kohai

O ne of the things I remember most about that night was the anticipation. I could hear them through the door of the hotel bathroom while I was getting dressed. The loud laughter of young men who'd been drinking, beer cans being crumpled up and tossed out, ice shifting as one of them grabs another from the cooler, guys pounding each other on the back and telling each other how fucking awesome this is gonna be.

I reached into the pocket of my jeans, which were hanging over the shower rod, and fished out the card with my orders on it.

Kohai,

I have a job for you tomorrow night. I've got some money on a college football team, and their rivals, the Wildcats, are coming into town for a game this weekend. I tipped them off that there's a pretty, willing young lady at the end of the hall of the hotel they'll be staying at.

I want you to show up there, dress pretty for the boys, and keep them up all night. I know you can come up with all sorts of ways to keep horny young men entertained. They've been told they're only allowed to fuck her in the ass, since she doesn't want to get pregnant, but beyond that they can use her any way they wish without even a condom.

Show up at 9:30 that night and get dressed. There will be an outfit for you in the bathroom. At 10:00, the party starts. Be a good boy and make me proud of you.

– M.

I checked my watch. 9:45. I put the card down by the sink and looked myself over in the mirror. I'm a tiger, orange fur striped with black all over my body, fading to a paler white along my chest and belly. I have a slender build and I'm quite short for my species, but I have a taut, toned look to my body, especially along my legs and ass. I reached down and adjusted my sheath, where an inch of pinkish cock peeked out from the fuzzy flesh (it always does that, even when I'm totally soft).

My boss, you see, he never likes making life too easy for me. I can't say too much about him since he likes to keep his business discreet. Suffice it to say he sometimes lends me out to clients and business partners to help close a deal smoothly and on good terms with everyone. I'm not really a whore, since I don't get paid for it. But there's just something about him that always lets him sweet-talk me into doing whatever he wants. *But he's never had me do anything like this before*, I thought, as I examined the outfit I was to wear.

It consisted of a short, pleated pink skirt, a matching tank top that would show a lot of midriff, some knee-length stockings and a set of lacy pink panties. I could have been fooled into thinking they were custom-made for me. They had a very wide-cut hole for my tail to go through, large enough for an eager young man to slip his cock in there without having to go through the trouble of taking them off, and some soft padding in the front to conceal my own sheath and testicles.

Ten minutes until show time. I drew the lacy material up over my legs and pulled it snugly against my crotch. It took me a few tries to figure out which way the skirt went on (it has a front?). The tank top followed, stopping high enough to reveal the curve of my navel and my smooth, taut belly. I looked up at myself in the mirror and smiled. Now don't get me wrong, I'm not into cross-dressing, and I've never been interested in women. But damned if I wasn't a hot little thing. I'll admit, I blushed to see myself like that.

Five minutes. I paced the tiled floor, trying to remember how women walk, how they speak, how they hold themselves. The guys in the hotel room would not be pleased if they found out I was a boy. Straight guys tend to get really worked up about messing around with other guys. If I wasn't really careful, they might freak out and take it out on me.

One minute to curtain. Actors to their places. No time to back out now.

I took a deep breath, made sure my outfit was all in order, and pulled open the door. As soon as I stepped through, the talking and laughter died down. Over a dozen sets of eyes followed me as I stepped into the room, the air hot and thick with the male scent of sweat and the haze of cigarette smoke. The room was full of young men, some in Wildcat jerseys, some in wifebeaters and shorts, some bare-chested. All were in fine shape with well-sculpted muscles and fur slick with sweat in the confined space. The sight and proximity of the strong males caused a stirring within my sheath, which I hoped would remain unnoticed.

A few of the boys whistled and gave cat-calls as I walked to the center of the room, legs stretched to show my calves as I swayed my hips, keeping my tail slightly raised to allow just a hint of what was hidden beneath my skirt. A young German Shepherd with a '38' on his jersey licked his lips and nudged a teammate next to him, murmuring, "Fuck... I'm gonna love this."

His friend, a shirtless black-furred wolf, nodded and reached between his legs to adjust his impressive package. "Fuck yeah, man. I can't wait to get my dick in her." I giggled inwardly. I love how straight guys curse when they're horny.

I looked around the room, trying to decide who to go for first, or who was assertive enough to take the first shot. Excited as they may be, straight guys get all weird about pulling their dicks out in front of each other. Indeed, the majority of them were glancing at each other out of the corners of their eyes, each one hoping someone else would be brave enough to get the ball rolling.

Luckily for them, one such male presented himself. A beefy lion sat at the edge of one of the beds, the only guy in the room not standing. He wore just a plain wifebeater, slightly faded and threadbare, and a pair of tight spandex shorts that looked like they were painted on. He curled his finger toward me and called over, "C'mere, baby," deep honeyed voice that might be found in a soul singer.

That confidence was what attracted me. Y'see, I'm a total sucker for dominant guys. Not just because they're big or strong, but for that confidence they carry that shows they truly own themselves. There was not a doubt in this young man's mind that I was going to go over to him and do whatever he fucking wanted.

I walked over to him, meeting his gaze head-on. He was handsome, with pleasing features and a strong jaw. His mane wasn't quite full yet, indicating he may have been one of the younger players, though if he was, he carried himself with more maturity than most boys his age.

As soon as I was within reach he grabbed my hips and pulled me into his lap. He cupped one hand behind my head and pulled me into a rough kiss. He pushed his tongue right between my lips, delving deep into my mouth. He tasted hot, saliva mingling with mine, along with the sour tang of a beer he had drunk earlier. With his other hand he grabbed my wrist and put it right in his lap, wrapping my fingers around his cock without any hesitation.

I heard several of his teammates groan with envy, seeing this stud work a pretty young thing so easily. I squeezed his cock and he growled into my mouth. I could feel the outline of the swollen flesh right through that spandex. Fuck, he was big. About eight inches long and quite thick as well. I caressed his shaft through the stretchy fabric, feeling veins, straining meat and a well-shaped glans.

His fingers gripped my hair and pulled me back from his mouth. He wiped a strand of saliva off of his lips and said, "Tell me how much you want to suck my cock." He nudged my hand out of the way and pulled down the front of his shorts, his shaft springing free. It was beautiful. He acted like he was the only male in the room. He acted like he was showing all the other guys how a real stud carries himself.

I stared down at its cock, the cumslit bubbling up a small stream of clear juice as I clasped my fingers around the base. I slid down out of his lap, settling to my knees in front of him like a serving girl before her master. I looked up at him and said in my higher feminine voice, "I want to put your cock in my mouth. I want to worship it with my tongue, slide it into my throat and pump until you give me a nice messy load to drink." It was all true.

He quirked his lips into a smile and put a hand on my head, urging me down between his thighs. "Then do it, baby. Show me what a good little cocksucker you are." He had no inhibition and neither did I. I traced my tongue around the swollen head, cleaning that smear of precum away. It was hot and salty in my mouth. His shaft pulsed at the touch, and I parted my lips and slid the head into my muzzle, collaring it just behind the rim of the glans and washing it with my tongue.

The lion gave a groan from deep in his belly and pushed upward with his hips, easing more of his cock into the slick chamber of my mouth. Behind me I heard one of the boys mutter, "Fuckin' A, she's a total slut." Another replied, "Yeah, man, lookit her go. She's goin' down on him like a pro!"

The powerful male put his hands on either side of my head and began to push more forcefully with his hips, working his cock in deeper. Taking a deep breath, I relaxed my throat as he slid his meat down to the balls, his heavy scrotum anointing my chin with sweat, cock seated in my mouth like it belonged there. He smelled so strongly of musk and male that it made my head spin.

He moved just a single hand to the back of my head to guide me, freeing his other hand to reach down my back and hike up my skirt. I shivered as my panty-covered rear was bared to a group of horny young jocks. I prayed that the padding would be enough to conceal my burgeoning erection. I heard several gasps as I hiked my tail off to one side, revealing the tight pucker nestled between the warmth of my taut buttocks. "No need to be shy, fellas," my strong lion told his friends (when did he become my lion?), "She can do two at once. Can't you baby?" I nodded as best I could with a thick cock ploughed into my throat.

I sensed a few moments of hesitation, and worried that they might not take the bait. But then I heard a deep voice say, "Shit, I'll take some a' that if you pussies won't." A male moved in behind me and a pair of clawed, feline hands gripped my thighs, pulling my hips up. There was the shivery sound of a zipper, and seconds later I felt the familiar hardness of a cock pressing insistently between my rumpcheeks. I relaxed myself and pushed back, and he gave a loud moan as his bloated glans slid in. I squeezed on him tight as he submerged himself in me, and I felt his hips tremble at the sensation.

That seemed to be what the rest of them needed. From the corners of my eyes, I saw other young men pulling their cocks out, losing their self-consciousness about being aroused with other straight guys under a wave of erotic anticipation. I heard them murmuring to each other about how bad they needed this, how good it was gonna feel, how many times they were gonna fuck me. They started to close in around me, a small tiger-striped feline in girly clothes, most of them fisting their drippy cocks as they waited their turn.

They didn't have to wait long. The male behind me, a tawny-furred cougar with an amazing physique, didn't plan on holding back. Not when he had all night to use me. He grunted, rutting his hips faster, pumping his cock into my tight ass, grunting through his clenched teeth, "Jesus… f-feels like she's gonna milk my cock off… Ergh… Damn… Feels so good… F-*Fuck!*"

He shoved into me deep, his balls pushed up firm against my ass. I felt his shaft throbbing powerfully within me, unloading the contents of his balls, preparing a sticky-slick mess for the next guy. He began thrusting again a second later, riding out his climax as I drained him for every drop I could get.

The studly lion before me groaned, a deep guttural sound, as he watched his friend shoot off in me. He planted his palm on my forehead and pushed me off of his cock, grabbing hold of the slick meat and fisting it hard. He aimed it right at my face, the bloated cumslit pursed open and ready to discharge its load. "Nnnnfff!" he grunted, biting his lip as the thick cock pulsed and splattered a mess of creamy white over my face. I held my mouth open and he fired his semen haphazardly into it, leaving gooey trails all around my lips and cheeks. He tasted salty and bitter, his seed forming a thick pool on my tongue.

As always happens, the two males' orgasms gradually faded, leaving them with two softening cocks and me with a mess at each end. The lion eased his cock back into my mouth and I gave it a gentle cleaning, nursing out the dregs of his cum. I felt semen dribbling out of my tailhole as the cougar slid out, taking only a moment to wipe his cock off on my ass. He nudged the next boy in line, the German Shepherd I saw before. "She's all yours, man." Seconds later, the dog thrust his cock inside me with a squelch, using his own teammate's semen for lube.

The lion patted my head, fingers ruffling through my hair as he slid out of my mouth, stepping aside for the next male, a Doberman with the physique of a body builder. The lion clapped the newcomer on the shoulder, encouraging him. "Have at her, man. I guarantee you ain't never had a mouth on your cock like hers before."

From there on the night went smoothly. Every time one male finished, another was waiting eagerly for his turn. I was impressed by how horny these young jocks were. One pair, a wolf and a panther, were willing to press their cocks right up against each other so that I could suck them off together, rather than wait their turn. They came within seconds of each other, their dribbling cocks flooding my mouth with cum as I sucked them dry.

Others formed a semi-circle around my head, working as a team as they passed my mouth around amongst each other, offering service to whoever's cock needed it most. As soon as one finished, they pulled me off his shaft to take my turn on the next guy, my mouth still sticky from their teammate's orgasm.

Some became tired after a few climaxes, and I had to coax them into staying, offering an especially skilled cocksuck for those that remained. I had to remind myself that this was a job, and that I needed to keep them going at it all night. Apart from a few half-hearted protests, none of them was willing to give up the chance for just one more orgasm in the body of a warm little tiger bitch.

I have to admit, I was relieved when I saw the sun coming up through the curtains. While a few of the boys had managed to doze off for a few minutes, I had not had a bit of rest all night. I lay my head on the bed and rested for a moment, listening to the soft breathing of a room full of studly males and the birds chirping through the window. Through slitted eyes, I saw the lion rubbing his face, blinking as the first light of dawn filtered through the shades. He growled and clapped his hands together loudly, startling all of his teammates. "Fuck! We stayed up too long. It's almost morning. Okay, all of you assholes get back to your rooms and grab as much sleep as you can before the game."

The others jumped up as he barked the orders, grabbing their clothes as they dashed out of the room. A few were kind enough to pat me on the head and say thanks or squeeze my ass as they departed. The lion was the last to go. Once again he impressed me, pulling me up to my feet and giving me a wet open-mouthed kiss, showing no inhibition against working his tongue into where most of his friends had deposited their semen just hours before. I felt my toes curl as he squeezed my well-used ass, fingers moistened from my cum-stained panties.

After half a minute, he pulled back, leaving me breathless. Fuck me, but he was a good kisser. He smiled down at me and whispered, "Thanks, babe, you were amazing. You kept us up too late, but damned if it wasn't almost worth it. Lemme know if you wanna hook up next time we're in town." He pulled a calling card out of his pocket and slid it down the front of my panties. I had to stifle a whimper as it brushed the head of my cock, which had been leaking precum for hours. I was amazed that it had managed to go unnoticed all night!

He leaned in again to give me a peck on the cheek, then turned and left the room. I knew my boss had it registered until ten AM, and I thought about crashing on one of the beds for a few hours, but I decided not to chance it. I sniffed, the air thick with the stale smell of male sex and cum, with the more distant odors of beer and tobacco mixed in. I snickered to imagine what the cleaning staff would think when they came in.

I went back into the bathroom to shower and change back into my street clothes. After I had cleaned up, I looked at the lion's card. His name was John. I smirked at the irony.

I'll admit, I felt guilty about what I had done. He seemed like a great guy, and I had hurt his chances at winning a game he cared about just because my boss wanted to make money off of his sport. I hated to think that his team would lose because of me. I wanted to make it up to him somehow.

Then I remembered that my boss' team, the Predators, would probably do a quick workout that morning to warm up for the game. Young college boys tend to be very horny first thing in the morning, and I remember hearing that some coaches order their teams not to cum for a few days before a game. They think it makes them play with an edge...

I knew that it would just create trouble with my boss, and that if he found out he'd make me regret it. Still, it just felt like the right thing to do. I got myself a cup of black coffee and headed down to my car to make the drive over toward campus and the Predators' locker room. Offering the services of a pretty little tiger girl to both teams only seemed fair. They might protest a bit, but... I know how to handle straight boys.

The Moment

Genken Hikage

Beads of sweat slid down the wolf's forehead from under his gray headfur. His breath came in slow, ragged gasps as his clenched muscles strained from exertion. His toe-claws dug into the ground; his hand claws dug into flesh as his body heaved steadily. His mind focused on one thing; the feeling. He pushed harder, wanting to feel the power and the sensation.

The body under him writhed and twisted, but the wolf pushed harder. His muscles bunched and he snarled in expectation. Just a bit longer; he was so close. His muscles strained and he panted heavier as the experience overtook him. The large wolf slammed harder into the bear; waiting for that wonderful ecstasy.

The gray canine could feel the sensation welling up inside him; nearly peaking, but he held it back. He wanted to experience the full-blown pleasure of the situation. The bear under him jerked and shuddered, trying to break free, but only added to the feeling and the sensation.

It was the ursine's turn to growl low in his throat; feeling the wolf's thick fur between his fingers as he pushed against the canine, making the wolf groan softly. *Just a little more,* He thought as his toe-claws dug into the ground; feeling his hand-claws start to draw blood. Like the wolf he was caught up in the sensation; the feeling and sweet pain was all that mattered. He felt all of his muscles tighten almost simultaneously.

The bear broke free suddenly, stealing the moment. The bear pivoted and reversed the act; now pushing into the larger wolf's body. The canine gritted his teeth against the pain, but inside, he knew that this was what he really wanted. The wolf moaned as the bear ground against him, the two creatures fighting for supremacy, but neither caring who came out on top. The wolf arched his back and pushed into the bear, trying to bury all of the bear's self into his powerful frame.

The fat bruin strained on top of the muscular wolf, panting against the wolf's hard body. The canid closed his eyes waiting for the moment to reverse this situation. The bear above him panted heavier now, pushing harder against the wolf, but the canine clenched his teeth and rode with it; letting the bear think he would be the victor in their power-struggle. The bear's burly body pressed into the wolf; making him shudder in pleasure.

The moment had arrived.

The wolf pushed against the bear, no longer going with the flow. The gray canid flipped his partner over and landed on top of him; pushing the bear into the ground as he shoved against the larger bruin. The wolf grunted loudly as he felt the familiar sensation, the feeling of near victory. He strained against the heavier bear trying to push himself to the limit. Every muscle in his body tensed up as the bear panted and whimpered below him. The wolf's body surged; this was it!

"Pin!" the referee called out as the bear relaxed under the panting wolf.

The spectators rose from their seats, applauding and cheering at the amazing match they had just witnessed. The glaring lights of the stadium shone down on the white, rope-lined ring as the two creatures slowly stood. The referee lifted the wolf's paw into the air and let the canid revel in his victory.

"We have a winner!" The ferret referee yelled into the megaphone as the audience cheered louder and the bear slowly crawled out of the ring, disappearing into the locker-rooms.

As the wolf stepped down from the ring, a raccoon ran up to him. The raccoon threw the damp towel he was holding around the wolf's neck; using one end to pad the canine's forehead.

"You did great out there, champ," said the coon. "Just remember you've got another match coming up in two days, so don't party too hard tonight."

"Yeah, thanks, mom." The wolf turned away from the chubby raccoon to sign some autographs. "I've got a question, coach," he said when he turned back around.

"What's that, kid?" The raccoon was busy looking over a clipboard as the two walked into the locker room.

"Who was that bear I was fighting tonight?" The wolf slipped off his shorts and stepped into the shower.

"Him?" The coon was still looking over his clipboard. "Oh, I dunno. Just another challenger who wasn't good enough, champ. You afraid you hurt him or something?"

The wolf soaped himself and stroked his sheath slowly, coaxing his pink member from within and thinking of the bear. "No, just curious really."

The coon watched as the wolf pleasured himself in the shower and smiled knowingly. "Yeah I bet you are. Don't stay in there too long or you'll miss all the fun at the after-party."

The gray canid murred softly to himself as precum started to dribble from the tip of his throbbing erection. "I wouldn't miss the after-party if my life depended on it! I'll see you outside, coach."

"Yeah, yeah I get the point. I'm leaving." The raccoon chuckled to himself as he walked out of the locker room, leaving his champ to his fantasies and knowing exactly who they were about. Maybe the wolf would finally find someone else someday, but for now, this was just as good.

THE HUMBLE GIVER

Stormcatcher

Goddamn, but sometimes I hate being the guy in charge.

All day, every day I work, it seems like—nothing but meetings, conference calls, an endless parade of folks poking their heads into my office asking me shit… I can give them an answer to their questions, but I don't always have the time to even consider if my answer is the right one. I'll say whatever I think I need to say to get them the hell outta my face.

And when it's all said and done at the end of the day, how productive do I feel like I've been? Do I feel satisfied with everything I've done and have had to do at quitting time?

You really don't want me to answer that. Not honestly, anyway.

So here I am, yet again, sitting under the big oak tree in my backyard, languishing in the shade.

I still have my business threads on, even the tie. I loosened it, but I didn't even have the strength to take it off. The stifling summer heat isn't helping. It's days like these that I'm thankful for my short pelt, but being a panther means that you're black-furred year 'round. And that sucks, in July.

I stare idly at the knothole in the wooden property-dividing fence in front of me, and know that he'll be coming out any minute, now. I hope so, anyway, and fate gives me a break in the sound of his sliding glass patio door opening. My hand goes to my groin so I can fondle myself as I heave forward and peer through the hole.

He moves silently and with a sense of mingled timidity and a refined air. Tall fella, he is—he's gotta be a good 6'5", and that's not including the tips of his ears—dressed in a navy blue kimono with elegantly stitched lotus blossoms on one side. He's bare-pawed, and the way his gray-furred body moves under the trees of his backyard, he might be a ghost—but the soft smile on his face is too real, and so is the gleam in those stately brown eyes.

I nearly chuckle as I watch him make his way toward the fence. He steps carefully, and almost apologetically, as though regretful that he has to impose his weight upon mother earth. He stoops down from time to time, checking his plants and talking to them in a low, smooth voice, his Japanese flawless. There's something so sweet about his demeanor, making my normally hardened heart go out to him. He loves his greenery, and his plants flourish at his touch. They are his surrogate children, and he has no one else.

I can identify. But thick ledgers and screens full of mail to be answered aren't quite as appealing substitutes as his leafy companions.. Finally, he's there, on the other side of the hole, kneeling slowly and scarcely breathing. I know that he's hoping to find me looking back through the hole at him, and he does. I wink at him and nod, and give a little wave with my hand, and he bows his head to me. He looks down at his own groin, then back into my face, one brow raised in unspoken question as his hand moves to his sash.

I nod, then open my muzzle and point at it, moving my mouth closer. His answering smile is radiant even as he blushes firmly, the coloration on his vulpine face quite cute as he straightens up and opens his robe slowly.

He's hard as a rock, and blushing though he is, he certainly has nothing to be ashamed of. That thick red cock is at least nine inches, and I watch his tapered tip quiver.

I spread my hands against the wood of the fence and press my face and mouth to the hole, receiving him slowly. The warmth of his glans greets my tongue, and I lap his shaft slowly all over as he slides it inch by inch into my head until he's buried deep in my throat. He holds himself there for a few moments, and the low groan burgeoning from his throat is audible even on my side of the fence. I can see him in my mind's eye, his slim black fingers clamped onto the top of the fence, his groin grinding lightly against the knothole. His thick, bushy tail is flicking in pleasure as his trim, toned hips start to move to and fro.

I work for a *Fortune 500* company, and I've got over one hundred folks that I'm overseeing, in one way or another.

I make a six figure salary.

Some days, I'm doing good to find my pants and shoes, much less function as a decent manager.

And right now, my kindhearted and soft-spoken oriental neighbor, the gent who wouldn't hurt a fly… is using my muzzle as his personal vagina.

My own cock is so damn hard, it's a wonder it doesn't rip right through my khakis.

My saliva swirls around his tool and makes it glisten like oil. His prick is leaking so much pre on my tongue that I don't know where my spit ends and his fuck lube begins, and I hear and feel him start to fuck my mouth harder, the gentle gliding motion of before giving way to a more brisk thrusting as his white-furred balls start to bump lightly against the wood.

His breathing is getting harder, his gasps just a little more ragged—and he quickly abandons the soft and subtle technique, his pelvis hunching against the hole hard as I swallow that slick shaft over and over again, a finger and thumb curling around the base of him and squeezing him just a bit for added sensation.

I hear the wood creak firmly under his fingers as he grips it hard, his back arching and head pulling back as he hilts himself in my muzzle, and I glom down around his crank so not a bit of it is exposed to the air other than his knot and balls. He shoots his wad hard, that nozzle spurting thick fox cum down my throat and into my gullet, where it warms my belly. He cries out softly, utterly pleasured, swiftly draining. I wish that his swelling knot was in front of my chin so I could tug on it a little with my fingers. It's my understanding that it hurts a bit, but also prolongs the orgasm.

He withdraws slowly, and I not only didn't spill a drop of his load, but I give his shaft a good polishing on its way out. There's not a drop of cum to be seen on it by the time I'm done, and he rumbles lowly in gratitude on the other side. His tall form kneels, his head bowed and panting as he gets his breath back, lifting his face to smile at me even as he breathes heavily.

His voice is quiet and smooth, a whisper in the trees as he looks excitedly at my own tented groin. "So good... it felt so good!" he murmurs. "I suck you, now, please?"

Another tribute to his tact. He knows that he doesn't have to, but he wants to. I never got that kind of willingness and altruism even from my ex of five years.

I shake my head at his invitation, but hook two fingers on the rim of the knothole to let him know that it's nothing personal. "I'd love that, but I can't. Got a business dinner meeting downtown that I gotta get ready for."

He nods in understanding, although I see the disappointment flicker across his face. He slides two dark fingers up onto mine, rubbing them softly. "You work much too hard," he says softly. His digits linger on mine, and I'm reluctant to pull away. His head jerks up suddenly, those dark eyes of his bright with hope as he smiles a bit, an idea manifested. "I fix you dinner sometime, yes?"

I smile wider, surprised and touched. I nod firmly, and give his fingers a squeeze. "I would like that very much, my friend. We'll do that soon," I rumble, winking to him as I get up and finally move my fingers away.

"Soon," he nods, echoing me. "You have good evening, I hope."

"You too!" I smile, waving to him as he watches me intently. That tail of his is still wagging.

I'm still tired, but at least I feel happier—and so does he.

My day wasn't a total waste, after all.

Sap and Other Juices

To the jaded reader, simple, old-fashioned romance seems shallow and immature. After all, we live in a world where disappointment is our constant companion and where expressions of undying love are considered terribly, almost criminally naïve.

In "Dreams" the author makes an unapologetic plea for the re-emancipation of straight-up romance with no other purpose than to express a love that heeds no warnings and knows no restraint.

The first-person narration and sparse sprinkling of specifics make this an unusual read, but do allow the reader to very easily project their own experiences onto this story—and the events, to many of us, are very recognizable, whether or not ours had as happy an ending as this.

DREAMS

Shaun "Faora" Ryan

It's been my dream for... so long now. A desire so strong I almost exude it. I can barely remember before the dream, nothing before really seems to matter to me much anymore. And, at the moment, nothing around me seems to matter either.

Except him. Just sitting there quietly beside me on our bed, the TV dousing the room with flickering light. He's wrapped one arm loosely around me, his eyes twinkling in the light. I notice as I turn to face him that he's staring at me again... he's done that a lot since... before.

I still wonder sometimes, wonder what I did to deserve it, wonder how we survived as long as we have, and wonder if he loved me just as I did him. Every time I see that smile though, that delight and beauty and caring in his eyes, I know I have my answers. It's still fresh in my mind, the sudden feeling that shot through me the first time I saw him like this, saw him for real. When I could first see him staring at me like that. Because I know, with absolute certainty, that there is complete love behind those eyes.

I'd seen him before, yes... but it was never the same once we were together. It changed from something ethereal to something physical, something tangible. I can reach out and touch him now. I do, sometimes, just to make sure that it wasn't all just a dream, an illusion created from my wanting mind. I'd been with him for so long... but at the same time, he'd not been there...

I could recall how difficult life had been, when we knew that we were together even when we were so far apart. The times before had been very hard, nearly overwhelming us at times. Bitterness would rise in me every time I saw a couple walking down the street together. I would curse the universe for being so unfair, even as I thanked whatever powers there were for what they'd given me.

I could remember it… clear as day. I could remember coming around the final corner at the terminal… and seeing him there, waiting for me. His eyes had lit up as he saw me, a smile threatening to overwhelm his entire face. I'd frozen for a moment, before running right toward him, wrapping my arms around him and holding him tightly. Our first words to each other had been the simplest expressions of our feelings, that is, when we were able to speak. And all I could remember of the hours after that first meeting was that I couldn't let him go…

It seems so long ago now, as he leans in closer to me. I can see his fur shimmering in the light, almost as bright as his eyes. It's truly amazing how no matter how I look at him, no matter what time, or place, he always looks perfect. An exact image of who I want. It wasn't always what I wanted, but being his… he being mine… it changed everything for me. All of it. He became my idea of perfection, and I his.

I lean forward to meet him half way. There's a slight, happy smile tugging at the corner of his muzzle before it fades away from my vision, our lips meeting in a gentle kiss. The simple touch sends a pleasurable chill down my spine as I reach around, wrapping one arm about his waist while gripping his paw with my own. My eyes close as I revel in his warmth, letting him pull me closer. I still find it amazing that before him, I could live without this.

I feel his heavy breathing through his nostrils, the sound almost masking the happy whimper I let slip from myself. If his arms are wonderful, then his kiss is heaven. I lean up into it, deepening the embrace, dancing my tongue with his. One of his arms slips down, gently massaging the base of my tail and further cultivating my pleasure. He leans back, laying down and lifting me up over him so that I lay atop him. I give him a warm, loving smile as I break the kiss, gazing down at his beautiful eyes.

Neither one of us speaks, because neither one of us needs to. Everything I need to know is conveyed through my other senses, seemingly heightened by the mere presence of him right there. The gentle touch of his paw stroking up and down the small of my back, the mischievous twinkle in his eyes, the growing scent of shared desire… it all mingles together inside me. My heartbeat quickens, thudding powerfully in my chest as electric sensations flood my nerves.

I lean down to kiss him again, longing for the touch of his lips against mine once more. I grip him tightly, never wanting to let go, never wanting the moment to come to an end. Some part of me knows that it doesn't have to end yet, allaying my silent fears. I know with absolute certainty that he'll always be there for me, know that my future is right there with me now, safe in my arms.

I run one hand up his side, drawing a smile from his lips. Gently, I let my tongue slide over his upper lip before meeting his own, the two mating deeply as he breathes a loving sigh through his nose. Our lips part once more and leave me to gaze again into his eyes, drinking in every detail of those expressive orbs. We still need not speak, our desires known perfectly to each other as we embrace once more.

I let my hands slide back down to his hips before bringing them slowly back up, lips brushing together again. I catch his shirt as my paws rise, but he does not pull back, does not resist. He breaks the kiss only long enough to let me lift the shirt from over his head, long enough to give me a smile of assent, before his lips are back upon my own. Never in my life have I ever felt such a want, such a desire. Yes, I'd experienced something like it before, with others… but it was all so different now. This is no want born of lustful desire, no sating of primal cravings; this is a true, deep expression of our love.

And I can see it in him, too. As gentle paws tug away inhibiting clothing, I can see it in his face. This is different from everything before for him, as well. It's not the same at anything else that he's done, anyone else he's been with. Now… now there is an empty place that has been filled, a lonely void somewhere in his heart that I have replaced with my love.

He knows that it had been the same for me. He was an intimate part of me, just as I was of him. And it was this moment, now that we were together, that we share ourselves to the deepest level.

He lies back a little beneath me, his eyes skimming over my naked form. I do the same, taking in the myriad details of his body. Never before had I ever found something so wonderful, so pristine and so perfect in all my life. And I know—though I may not always agree—that he felt the same about what he saw in me. Our eyes locked once more with a jolt of energy, a wave of profound peace and warmth flowing through me.

He parts his lips to give me a toothy grin, almost child-like in its intensity. I know he's been waiting just as long as I have for this, and the knowledge that we're finally together brought a like smile to my own face. Cupping his cheek in one hand, I lift his head to mine, touching my forehead to his. His breath comes quicker, the scent of his desire growing still stronger in the room. It begins to take its toll on me, and my own body begins to react faster.

I start to slide down his body slowly, the feeling of me grinding through his fur sending a little ripple of excitement through him. I continue my descent as I smile wider, opening my muzzle and letting my tongue slide over one nipple. A quiet murr of approval rewards my actions before I continued my way downwards, tongue trailing wetly through his fur.

Our combined scents fill the room now, further intoxicating us, deepening the bliss blanketing our minds. All I wanted was him, and now, finally, after all this time... I have him. We're finally together. The world completely fades away from us. My universe narrows down to a single point, to a single person, to a single instant. He is my life, my love and my all, and now is the time to show him.

I lift myself up a little from him to gaze down between his legs with a smile. There it is, the object of my desire. Well... one immediate desire anyway. I look up at him momentarily, meeting his eyes and dragging my tongue slowly across my lips, before lowering myself back down and giving the tip of his malehood a long, gentle lick.

I feel rather than hear the forceful exhalation above me, his warm breath washing down over my head. A quick flick of my gaze back up to him shows that he's closed his eyes, his mouth open in a silent assent to my actions. I smile again, leaning down lower to lick again, this time right at his base. I swirl my tongue around him, slowly working my way higher and higher, right to the tip.

He begins to vocalize his enjoyment now, quiet whimpers and moans coming from above me. They grow slightly in volume as I take his tip into my muzzle, sliding my tongue down the side of the head as I suckle gently at him. I feel his legs spread a little wider, twitching from the feelings emanating from between them. I allow myself a wide smile... I've been waiting for so long for this, and now, here I am.

I want to waste no time anymore; we've wasted more than enough in our time apart. I begin to move again, bobbing slowly back and forth along his malehood, letting my tongue slide back and forth against it. One of my hands comes up, stroking the inside of one thigh gently while the other rubbed ever so softly over his stomach. I wanted greatly to just touch him, stroke him, explore every inch of his body with my paws... but there will be more than enough time for that later. There is still something I need far more than just that simple pleasure.

I feel his arousal grow stronger and stronger, from the subtle twitching of his hips, to the gentle hand on my cheek, to the taste of his preemptory fluids on my tongue. I savor every sensation I am offered, even as I crave still more from him. I pull myself slowly back up and off him, eliciting a whimper of confusion and longing, before I silence it with a deep, passionate kiss.

I wrap my arms around him and hold him tightly, silently letting him know just how much I love him. And it never ceases to send a thrill of joy through me to feel him squeezing me just as tightly, just as lovingly. This sense of closeness, this level of intimacy… it's exactly what had been missing from my life for so long. Having finally found it brings another smile to my lips, and I can't help but kiss him again.

Time seemed to lose all meaning to us. All that matters is his arms around me, and mine around him. I lay my head down on his shoulder with my eyes closed, breathing softly as I feel his heartbeat against my chest, perfectly in time with my own. We finally pull back minutes later, still firmly in each other's arms. I look brightly up into his eyes with a smile, grinning when I see him return it to me just as brightly. His eyes flicker downward for a moment, before coming back up to my face again. I smile wider still, giving a slight nod. I know exactly what he wanted, and he knows that I want it too.

Disengaging from his arms, I slide down and away from him for a moment. It feels strange, being without his warming touch for a moment, but I console myself with what I know will come. I lay myself down slowly; letting him get a nice, long look at my body, smiling inwardly at the effect I know that will have on him. Sure enough I feel his arms encircling my waist, his head snuggling gently into my stomach. He stares up at me almost reverently, almost as if asking me for permission.

I expose myself to him, openly offering him my body. I've waited this long to be taken by him, and a thrill courses through me as I realize that I'm about to give myself completely over to my love. It seems so surreal, that we've been together so long and that this is the first time… and I can barely wait long enough for him to make me his.

Then I feel it, that warm, damp touch of the tip of his shaft, sliding against my legs as he maneuvers himself into position. A shiver runs through me at the touch, my legs instinctively spreading slightly wider. I let out a whimper of my own, a submissive plea for attention, a want to feel him inside me. And gently… so very, very gently, I get my wish.

The head of his member slowly slides inside me, causing me to shiver and let out a slight grunt of approval. He pushes forward again after a moment, slowly moving further and further inside, until we're right against each other, our bodies joined at last. I feel myself becoming warmer, my body practically igniting as he gives a little push against me. I haven't realized that I've been holding my breath, and I release it in the form of a long sigh. Finally, after so long, my dream is coming true.

We lie there for a moment, both of us just reveling in the fresh feelings jolting through our bodies. I catch his eye as I raise one paw, gently caressing his cheek as I nod. He returns the gesture, stroking the back of my hand with his own. I feel him pry my paw from him, feel his gentle squeeze as he starts to pull back from me. I shiver a little for a moment, but it passes as he thrusts slowly back into me.

Never in my life have I felt such pleasure. Through it all is still a lingering pain from his initial penetration but now, overwhelming all else, is a deep sense of completeness, of universal rightness. I feel my love for him deepen in the first few moments, if it could ever do such a thing. And it's that love, that depth of emotion that makes our joining so much more than either of us had ever expected.

His thrusts are slow and steady, pushing him deep inside of me before drawing back, only to thrust inside once again. Unbelievable feelings, near-overwhelming feelings sweep over me, partly through his actions, but more through the gentle care and concern he makes them with. He only wants to do what I want, only wants to make me happy, only wants me to enjoy myself. It's that dedication that brings yet more to it all, makes me love him just that much more.

I feel a sudden warm breath on my neck, followed quickly by the feel of his lips against it. I arch my back with a gentle moan, giving his pulsing member a squeeze as it slides deeper. He's always known how sensitive my neck is... I hear him gasp above me at the sudden tightness around him, permitting myself a smile. He releases a playful growl, giving me a sudden deep thrust that sends my thoughts into complete disarray, washing them away in a blaze of bliss.

I begin to push myself back against him as I feel the waves of pleasure building higher and higher, only fueling my need of him. I squeeze back against him again, my breath coming in short, sharp pants. Above me my love has closed his eyes, lost in concentration as he works to postpone the inevitable. I face a similar struggle myself, my body edging closer and closer to climax.

Then the familiar feeling suddenly tears through my nerves like electricity, flowing through my veins like fire. Together our bodies light up as the waves come crashing down hard around us, drawing sounds of carnal pleasure from both of our muzzles. I cry his name as we bring ourselves together; my love? Hilting himself within me as I feel the rush of his seed exploding inside me. A gush of my own fluids are released, the pressure of my body easing slightly. The world fades away from my awareness as hot pleasure whites out my mind...

Slowly, I come back to myself. Pleasure-overloaded nerves start to respond once more to my instructions, letting me reach up and stroke his cheek gently. Panting, he smiles back at me, a tear of joy sliding down his cheek as he opens his eyes. And it's this moment that lets me know that I truly found my one, my only, and my all...

...It's been my dream for... for so long now. Years have passed since it happened... but even now, as I roll over in our bed, I can see him there. And I know that even though time has passed, our love certainly hasn't. It's a dream realized, a dream lived every day, and a dream I share with him, forever.

Feather and Swdord

No greater literary device has ever been invented than
contrast. No, not just literature—every art that engages
the senses and the emotions has made use of this simple yet
phenomenally powerful device: two opposing sensations,
emotions or ideas are each strengthened by their contrast
with each other.

We are creatures of relative experiences. We compare every
experience to previous ones and to our present state of
mind and therefore, when we are exposed to two contradictory impulses, each of them is made stronger by the
juxtaposition.

In the appropriately-titled "Innocence," a chapter from the
"Maerchentic" series, this is laid bare. Clashing intentions,
desires and motivations make for a powerful, moving story
in which the author sweeps the reader through a great
many of emotions with a patience and control that do the
story justice.

MAERCHENTIC INNOCENCE

K. M. Hirosaki

I f there was anything more pathetically stereotypical than having a crush on the cute foreign exchange student, then Tyler wanted to know what it was. It was bad enough needing to hide the fact that he had a silly spat of puppy love for what was historically one of the most unattainable types of people to want for, and the fact that the object of affections was another guy just helped hammer in the same.

The young mink was in his second year of study at university, and just coming to terms with his own sexuality had long precluded being able to come out to anyone else. Things were already awkward about it; he hoped that none of his friends noticed the sidelong glances at fellow students who caught his eye. Most of the time, he had been able to avoid it, or had at least been able to be furtive about it. But with this new guy suddenly on campus, Tyler was well and truly challenged to be subtle.

He was a linsang, this student-in-question. If Tyler had to guess, he would have figured him for a graduate student, going by the look of his age, but he didn't have the right air about him for it. Also, judging by how often the mink saw him in the campus coffee shop, he had far too much free time to be a grad student, as well. The other problem with the linsang always being in the coffee shop was that Tyler was always in the coffee shop, too.

In fact, they were both in the coffee shop right now. And, like he had been doing all week long, Tyler was staring at the linsang from a few tables over. His brain was running through a few fantasies—innocent fantasies, at least, about being able to share something like his first kiss with someone like that.

The linsang was lovely. His features were pretty, in a way, and he almost looked more like a tomboy in some respects than he looked like an actual male. The mink admired him for having that beautiful striped tail, that ran so long and fluid before joining up against his backside. When the mustelid's eyes reached the linsang's rear, he took a moment or so to stare, and then quickly looked away when he felt his ears and cheeks burning with a blush.

Aside from the tail, the rest of his body was equally wonderful to stare at. He dressed in a way that was sporty and fun, yet conservatively enough so that Tyler couldn't see the spots and patches of darker fur that he knew ran up along the linsang's sides. That was indeed a shame, though it did make trying to picture him naked a bit more interesting. Tyler bit the tip of his tongue at those thoughts; maybe being so prudish and undersexed for so long were finally taking its toll now that he'd accepted the reality that he was gay.

It didn't matter, though, the mink told himself. He could lust after Mr. Linsang from here until graduation and it wouldn't make a lick of difference. Besides, he'd been watching all week, seeing how the girls would gather at tables and gossip about him while tittering childishly. He was obviously a big hit with the ladies, and it was only a matter of time before one of them grabbed his eye and…

Tyler sighed. He hated the feeling of helplessness that came part and parcel with his sexuality. It was especially hard, being at such a young age, where both hormones and peer pressure just made him crave a partner even more. After his shy, distant gawking sessions, he'd invariably spend the next class period or so feeling really down on himself for being reduced to that level. Life was tough when even your fantasy world disappointed you.

For now, though, he got to stare up from his coffee and his notebooks every few minutes, when he was reasonably sure nobody was paying attention. And he could allow himself the fantasy while it lasted. It was better than nothing.

Unfortunately, things looked like they were going to head back to 'nothing' territory then. The linsang that he'd so busily been adoring began to gather up his things to leave. Tyler felt a twinge when he saw that, wanting to whimper inside as he watched as his only pleasant distraction was taken away from him. He tried to hide his look of disappointment behind his paper cup full of coffee, eyes looking out past the rim, not quite willing to give up that last glance.

Perhaps it was a stroke of luck that he didn't, too. The linsang tossed a few things into his bag, grabbed his jacket, and began to walk away, but he had left something behind on the chair next to him. It looked like a carrying case of some sort. Tyler eyed it for a moment, and then stood from his chair.

He felt rather silly, because it was merely a handful of seconds before he thought of how ridiculous this sort of thing was, but he didn't care. He didn't actually expect it to go anywhere, but he'd at least get a chance to have an excuse to make eye contact. Sure, it was sad, and he knew it, but he'd take what he could get.

With the plastic little case in hand, the young mink padded quickly after the departing linsang, his tail trailing behind himself in a blur of dark brown as he tried to catch up. "Excuse me!" he called out, trotting on the ends of his feet as he caught the linsang's attention and slowed down. "I... I think you forgot this!"

There was a flick of the tail as the linsang turned around to face Tyler. Oh, those eyes! He was even prettier up close! He seemed legitimately surprised at the reason for his being flagged down, but that mildly startled expression melted away into one of curiosity as he looked at the mink. Tyler chastised himself inwardly for the wishful thinking that the linsang might be checking him out, but then that gaze went on a second longer than necessary, and was capped off with a little smile, which made the young mink tingle with a blush.

The linsang's eyes then alighted on the little plastic box that Tyler held in his hands. "Oh, thank you!" he said, chirping with relief. The mink smiled at the miniature outburst-like reply. It was a bit exaggerated and effeminate—perhaps there really wasn't a need to think wishfully after all?

"H-here you go," the mink said, holding the case out. The linsang took it, and put it away into his shoulder bag. A few moments passed, and neither of the two young men moved; both of them just sort of stood there awkwardly, as if each were waiting for the other to say something.

"I'm Tyler, by the way." Smooth. Real smooth, that was. Now he needed to think of an excuse for why he bothered to introduce himself after just being polite. He couldn't, though, and then be began to frantically panic, run flush with embarrassment, and kick himself at the same time for being so stupid.

"Tyler," the linsang said back, testing the name out. "Do you know that you're the first student at this school to have had the courage or open-mindedness to say hello to the weird new foreign guy?" His voice had an accent to it that Tyler couldn't place, but his brain was spinning too fast, anyway, at the elation of such kind words! Everything seemed so hackneyed, and so fake, but here it was—happening!

It wasn't the time to be overexcited, though. Not yet. "R-really? Aw, I was just being nice, y'know?" the mustelid replied, reaching up to rub the back of his head a few times.

The linsang shook his head and clucked his tongue. "Doesn't change that you were still first," he said, smiling a smile that Tyler's heart wanted to believe was only for him. Damn, he felt like such a sap, but the thumping in his chest made everything okay. "Say," the linsang continued, his bright smile showing bright teeth, "you seem like a nice and outgoing young fellow. Maybe you can help me make friends here!"

Oh, it was so unreal! An actual conversation with a stupid crush! If the mink's eyes weren't positively glowing and sparkling right then, then—oh, there was just so much to consider! "Oh, I dunno," Tyler replied shyly. "I mean, I'm just…"

"Oh, nonsense!" the linsang said to cut him off, clapping a hand on the mink's shoulder, making him stand bolt upright—physical contact! Tyler's tail could barely keep still. "You can be my first friend here! How's that?"

Tyler swallowed the lump in his throat, and nodded. "Sure!" he squeaked, sounding ten years younger for a second. "I think that that's a…"

"Take me to a party!" the linsang suddenly interjected again. Tyler flinched back in shock from both the exuberance with which he spoke as well as the words themselves. "It's the weekend in a few hours, right? Some of your friends must be having a party!"

The mink's mind raced again. Surely, he wasn't being hit on, was he? The foreign guy just wanted to have someone to help him get to know people so that he'd fit in better… right? "Yeah, I… guess so. I suppose." He wished for all the world that he wasn't so flustered and so dopey.

"Here," the linsang said, clicking his tongue again as he fished a pen out of his pocket. He ripped a scrap of paper out of his shoulder bag, and scrawled something on it. "This is my number. Call me tonight after you're done with class, and we can see about partying together, okay?" Then, with what might have been a wink (but was probably just a blink, Tyler told himself) the linsang turned around and headed for campus proper again.

Tyler stood there for a few moments, just watching in stunned amazement from what had just happened. He yipped a little and hopped onto his toes when the linsang suddenly spun back around and called out, "By the way, my name's Auringer! But you can just call me Auri, okay?"

"This is not a date. This is not a date." Tyler had told himself that all afternoon as he got himself worked up and done up while waiting for this party. Auri had been right, of course, about a party being easy enough to find. The hard part was not thinking too much of it.

Tyler's hope had been that nothing would seem odd about his showing up and hanging out with Auri. And that seemed to be the case; everyone looked like they were taking it as the mink just being a generally nice fellow and helping the new guy meet some folks. And since Auri was 'the new guy', Tyler didn't think that any of his friends found it weird that he'd be spending so much time with him, since he'd been the one to invite the linsang in the first place.

Auri, for his part, looked like he was having a good time. He was so well mannered and polite when speaking to everyone, and the mink's friends seemed to treat him nicely enough in return. Sure, he was kind of strange, but that was to be expected. When he wasn't interacting with the linsang directly, Tyler paid close attention to his movements and mannerisms. He definitely seemed a bit on the... 'swishy' side, but the mink still wasn't going to let himself be convinced just yet.

Moreover, Tyler kept trying to tell himself, there wasn't actually any reason to assume that anything would matter even if Auri did turn out to be gay. There might have been signs, but how much of that was just the mink reading into things too much? He didn't have any real experience to go by, here, and he was left confused and at a loss with his faint hopes.

Every time he started to feel really awful and lonely, though, it seemed like Auri would look up from what he was doing, and head back on over to him. It was like the linsang had a supernatural sense of when he was feeling down. He knew that it was silly to think that, but it was comforting nonetheless. The end result was that his night steadily kept getting better and better, and while Auri seemed to get along well with Tyler's friends, the two of them seemed to just click so well.

"You're not drinking," Auri noted, after a few hours had passed. The linsang himself had been drinking, albeit slowly, but the mink had abstained. He was too afraid of making a fool of himself.

"Yeah, I know," Tyler said, trying to think of something on the fly that sounded believable. "I sorta drank a bit too much last weekend, and my stomach's not too happy with the idea of more just yet." He was a skinny guy. Auri would probably buy it.

The linsang patted him on the shoulder, again making Tyler wonder hopefully. "Sure you don't want just one?" Auri asked. "You seem a bit tense."

Tyler shook his head, and flashed a friendly smile back at Auri's face with all the courage he could muster. "Ah, I'm fine," the mink said. "I kinda wish they had some soda here or something, but it's no big."

Auri nodded. "Okay. You're cuter when you're not nervous, though," he said.

Startled at that, Tyler quickly looked around the room to make sure that none of his friends had heard it. The music was a bit loud, and so it seemed like the comment went unnoticed. The mink's heart pounded with embarrassment, fear, and excitement all at the same time. "Although the look on your face right now is quite cherishable," the linsang added, winking.

There was no doubting or denying anymore. Auri was definitely making a pass at him. Tyler might be a prude, but he knew that much. He tried stammering something out, but Auri silenced him with a fingertip to the lips. "Let's go and try and track you down that soda for you, shall we?"

The linsang's hazel eyes were suddenly the most inviting sight that Tyler had ever seen. He felt like his arm was moving of its own accord as he reached out to brush a few fingers over Auri's wrist, and then he just nodded, silently. The mink followed the linsang's lead out of the room, trying so hard not to giggle at himself at what was going on.

They got out into the dormitory hallway. It was empty. Auri didn't stop, though, and continued to walk. The mink steadily followed, staying just a few steps behind. When they made it past a few more doors without either of them saying anything, Tyler finally spoke up.

"Are... are we really going to find ourselves a soda machine?" he asked, wringing his hands together in nervousness.

"Oh course!" Auri said, looking back over his shoulder, not missing a step. "I'll even buy it for you." His striped tail flicked sharply to the side after he said that, as if it were a waving flag for Tyler's heart to begin beating faster.

A soda machine was found easily enough in the lobby of the dorm. And, sure enough, Auri got out his wallet and purchased the mink a beverage, inelegant as it was. Tyler took it gratefully, and even though his shyness was overwhelming, he made sure to keep eye contact with those beautiful hazel eyes.

There was an awkward silence as they both stood there, Tyler drinking his soda, hovering in front of the machine. Auri was watching him without staring at him, and the mink felt relaxed, but something still nagged at his mind. He took another long sip, wetting his throat before speaking. "How did you know?" he asked.

Auri looked a bit taken aback, but he smiled. "Just a hunch," he replied, before taking another step closer. "Besides, I figured you were cute enough to be worth the risk," he added, voice much quieter.

Tyler paced a little, finishing off the rest of his drink. He clasped his hands behind himself and stretched along his long back. "Um, Auri? Do you mind... not going back to the party, and just coming back with me to my room?" He blinked after he said that, and quickly added, "Not like that, I mean! I just... I want..."

Again, the linsang silenced him with a finger to the lip. "You don't need to over-explain, hon," he said, smiling. "I wouldn't mind at all." He got a soda for himself out of the machine, and Tyler, rather giddily, led the way.

The walk to Tyler's own room was short enough. Campus wasn't too large, and he was walking rather in a hurry. The mink spent most of the walk explaining to Auri how his friends back at the party didn't know about his interest in guys, guessing that the linsang didn't quite understand a desire for secrecy. Besides, time with Auri was time better spent than time watching everyone else drink.

"So, then, your friends don't know that you like me?" Auri asked, as they arrived at the door to Tyler's room. "That's what's making you nervous?"

Tyler opened the door and let Auri in behind him. "I think so," he said. "Also, I think you're..."

When Tyler closed the door behind himself, he turned around to see Auri standing right there in his face. There was half a second's time for the mink to see what was coming as the linsang stared back into his eyes affectionately and leaned forward, bringing their lips together. A soft squeak was all the reaction that Tyler was afforded before he felt that warm, soft touch, and then, with a feeling of warmth radiating from his lips inward, he relaxed and melted.

His ears caught the sound of Auri's humming, which sounded blissfully happy. Tyler understood why almost immediately. So this was kissing. Finally, he knew what it felt like. He hadn't really ever imagined that kissing actually felt tingly or electrical like he'd hear in exaggerated accounts of the experience, but it actually did! The mink could feel his own throat vibrating from the sensations pouring down through his flesh, emanating from the contact point of their lips. Like magic, it was like everything just felt warmer somehow. It was pure exhilaration.

The kiss felt too incredible. Tyler didn't want it to end. Even knowing that he might send the wrong impression of himself to Auri, the mink set his hands at the linsang's hips, and pressed closer. He felt the press of a tongue at his lips, and he parted them, letting it slide into his mouth and play with his own. A moan escaped him, reverberating back into the linsang's muzzle. Auri's hands grabbed at his lower back in return and held him closer.

Tyler only broke the kiss when Auri suddenly grabbed his longer fingers at the mustelid's rear. It made him yip in surprise, and he pulled back away from the kiss on instinct. He could feel himself flushing up again, but even so, it wasn't enough to replace the warm sensation of the linsang's kiss. Already, he missed it greatly. "I'm sorry," Tyler whispered, staring back into Auri's eyes. "Just caught me off guard. I'm okay."

Without another word, Auri pulled the mink back into another kiss, running one of his hands across the chocolate-colored fur of his cheek. Even the touch of the linsang's fingers felt like it was making his fur stand on end, and he craved the sensation already, nuzzling at that hand. Finally, after years of conflicting feelings and emotions that didn't make sense, his biggest fantasy was coming true, and it was better than he ever imagined. He couldn't let it go. It was like a drug.

Auri kept his arms around Tyler's body and started to shuffle over toward the mink's bed. Tyler noticed this, but he dared not break away from the linsang. His head and neck turned and twisted as he tried to keep the kiss as full on as he could, loving the feel of tongues exploring back and forth. The linsang sat down, and suddenly there was a lap for Tyler to fall into. He slid down into it comfortably, hooking his arms over Auri's shoulders, holding him so tightly. Something in the back of his mind told him that his entire world would end if he turned back.

Suddenly, Tyler let out an airy moan. He didn't even know why at first, but after a second, he figured it out—somewhere during the passionate kissing, the mink had gotten very, very hard, and Auri's fingers had slid down and found his erection. So many emotions shot through his mind at that instant, feeling as if they were shooting through his body itself, stringing together endlessly into one. This was the first intimate touch from another he'd ever felt, and it was amazing, but this was someone he had just met today, and not someone special, and yet he was someone special in a totally different way, and what if he came too early, and Auri didn't understand, and...

And that train of thought suddenly came to a crashing halt as he felt a renewing sense of peace coming over him. He pulled away from the kiss again, and looked into the linsang's face, which in turn was smiling back reassuringly. "Don't stop?" the mink uttered quietly, making the request into a question.

Auri said nothing. Those slim fingers of his just went for the catch of the mink's button and zipper, and with an acute skill, managed his pants open easily. Tyler gasped, feeling excited and nervous, and leaned back so that the linsang had more room. Auri's hand dipped down and pulled down the front of the mink's boxers. Forcing his eyes to stay open, Tyler watched as the linsang's fingers wrapped themselves around his shaft, and began to stroke.

Pure bliss wrapped itself around Tyler's senses. Even though he knew that it must have just been his imagination, it felt like Auri's hand was twice as warm as flesh should be. He didn't care that his mind was getting away with itself, though, because it just felt so good! "Oh... oh, Auri... Auri..." Each time that Tyler spoke the linsang's name, he felt the strokes of that hand on his stiff cock get firmer and faster. His jaw dropped open, but before he could make a sound, he heard a gasp come from Auri, instead.

"Oh, my!" the linsang chirped in surprise, staring hard at Tyler's face. The mink looked back, feeling very anxious at that very unexpected reaction. Auri learned closer, and caressed his cheek more firmly. "You... there's something special about you," he said, as if he were inspecting an item of some collection. "What is it, though?"

Tyler shivered, and began to squirm a little in the linsang's lap. "Auri, what's wrong?" he asked, panicked. Before he could get away, though, his struggling was stilled by a kiss to the cheek from Auri. The linsang's lips lingered there, and then began to move. He sort of snuffled against the mink's face, and kissed and licked as if he were tasting it.

"Oh, nothing's wrong at all," Auri whispered, sounding reverent. "I just finally realized what it is about you, Tyler." His arms held the mink tightly, and he started to try to twist around and lay the mustelid down onto his back.

Looking back up into Auri's face, Tyler couldn't bring himself to refuse. His desire far outweighed his fears. And the fact that he might come across as 'easy' or 'slutty' didn't even figure into his decision. He needed this so badly. He needed Auri to have him.

Auri pulled Tyler's arms up. The mink wriggled and helped the linsang to pull his shirt off, before lifting his feet and rump to help strip his pants off as well. Then, slowly, the linsang peeled off his boxers, leaving the young mink totally naked on his bed. One of Auri's hands rode up Tyler's front, from his hip, over his stomach, and up along his chest. The linsang's claws then dragged bluntly back down through his fur as the mink lay there, panting.

"Yes, that's what it is, definitely!" Auri said, hurriedly taking his own shirt off and dropping it off of the bed, letting Tyler see those spots of fur that he'd tried to envision dozens of times before. He lowered himself so that his bare chest was pressed against Tyler's, and the bulge in the fabric of his pants ground down gently against the mink's exposed hardon. Tyler arched upward, desperate for contact and stimulation, groaning quietly. Auri brought his snout up to the mink's cheek again, nuzzling it tenderly while his hands roamed up and down the mustelid's slinky sides. "Oh, Tyler, you have no idea what this is like for me!"

Tyler didn't have an idea; it was true. At the moment, he only knew how things were for *him*, and they were beyond incredible. Auri's face and hands explored him like he was an old lover that he had known for years and years, who knew every square inch of his body intimately. Tyler could hear that the linsang was taking in heavy breaths through his nose as he poked his snout at the mink's jaw-line and throat. Those whiskers tickled, and Tyler would have giggled if it weren't for the raspy, airy breaths caused by the caress of Auri's hands all down along his body.

Auri lifted the upper half of his body back up, and when he looked down into Tyler's face, his eyes were suddenly a different color. Even in the partial darkness of the dimly lit room, Tyler could see that the linsang's eyes were a bizarre blue color that looked to be glowing faintly. He didn't care for the reason, though. All he cared about right now was that Auri was making him feel better than anyone else ever had—Auri was making him feel better than he'd ever felt in his entire life. "Tyler, you're incredible!" the linsang purred. The mink was a bit confused at those words; he hadn't even actually done anything yet, really, to be considered 'incredible' in his own opinion. But the linsang continued. "Do you even know what you feel like to me right now? Oh, it's just beyond words…"

There was a wave of confusion washing over Tyler's mind that was cut short when Auri suddenly darted down, enveloping the tip of the mink's shaft with his lips and tongue. He let out a little cry of pathetic pleasure as his body seized and arched along his spine, watching fixatedly as the linsang began to suck on him. Nothing in his fantasies could have prepared him for the experience of the real thing, and he whined through his happiness as Auri pleasured him with his muzzle.

His world paradoxically seemed to slow down and speed up all at the same time. It was as if the vision of the room spinning around him was lagged in his brain, somehow, while the sensations of the warm, wet mouth around his cock felt sped up unfairly. He wanted to lose control, and just force himself over the edge in order to feel that ultimate pleasure caused by someone else, but just when he thought it, Auri pulled off.

"Oh, Tyler! You're like glass! I can hear it and taste it coming off of you. So perfect and flawless." The linsang licked his teeth and crawled forward some more, in order to kiss the mink on the chin. Tyler wanted to whine, at first, when his shaft was left cold and unattended like that, but everything else about Auri's touch made it all better. His voice drifted back into his ears. "So perfect and flawless," the linsang repeated. "Like a fresh pane of glass." Tyler could see, now, with Auri's face so close to his own again: the linsang's ethereal eyes were pooling with tears at the bottom. And his voice dripped with a sort of bittersweet quality as he cradled the mink's face. "It's like a field of freshly fallen snow. Do you know what I mean, Tyler? That's what you taste like. God, it's just perfect, and I... I..."

The tears fell from the sides of Auri's muzzle, one by one, dropping onto the soft fur of Tyler's cheeks. Where they touched, the mink's skin felt warm and pleasured, like somehow he was receiving an invisible, sensual massage. It scared him. Here was this young man, obviously something 'other', and he was crying. Was this just some strange melodrama played out for his benefit? Was this even maybe just a dream? He had no way to know. But Tyler needed to give himself up. He had come too far to stop himself.

"Oh, please," the mink whimpered. "Auri, I want you so badly." His words carried his truest emotions at that moment. It was almost like he was in pain, waiting on the cusp of something that he knew would be amazing.

Auri closed his eyes and clenched off the last of those slow-running tears. "Such delicious truth to those words," he said adoringly, giving the mink a happy smile as he sniffled once. He started to work himself out of his tight pants, and Tyler watched with a surreal sense of anticipation.

The linsang's shaft was long, but it was thinner than the mink's own. It looked fragile, like the glass that Auri kept mentioning. Before the linsang got his pants off, he reached into his back pocket, and pulled out a tiny packet that Tyler couldn't identify. Auri kept it in his hand as he wormed out of his pants legs, and then he tore it open.

The faint light in the room glimmered off of whatever it was that was coming out of that packet, squeezed out onto Auri's fingertips. When the linsang brought his hand down to his shaft, the mink finally recognized it for what it was: lube. Auri stroked himself slowly a few times, working his pretty cock up with a slippery sheen, and followed it up by placing another tiny dab onto a fingertip before rubbing it gently at the little hole beneath the mink's dangling scrotum.

Tyler gasped and then held his breath as his pulse began to race. This was really it. This was really going to happen, right here, right now. He bravely reached an arm up for Auri, and the linsang took it, pulling himself down atop the mink's body. Tyler could feel the slightly taller linsang trying to position himself as he hunched over him. Their eyes met again, and despite the otherworldliness of the linsang's glowing irises, Tyler felt so at peace with things, even though he knew that something incomprehensible was happening.

There were more tears now, strong than before. "Just one more time, Tyler," Auri whispered to him with both sadness and urgency. "I need to taste your splendid innocence one last time." Before Tyler could react or protest, Auri had their muzzles locked together in a deep passionate kiss. The mink returned it gladly, the linsang's moans mixing and joining with his own. There was the sudden rush of pleasure again as Auri's fingers tugged up at the end of his shaft, serving as a partial distraction when the linsang sharply pushed into him.

The mink's next moan was whimpered and loud, but still not as loud as Auri's. The linsang sounded almost in pain, which Tyler thought felt a little backwards. With a deep breath taken in through his nostrils, Tyler spread his legs further apart, letting Auri fill him with his slippery member with a few fluid thrusts. The linsang's shaft wasn't thick enough to spread his virgin rear to the point of causing pain, but it was long enough that it felt like it was tickling at all of the right places inside of him that he never knew he had.

A heavy chill descended upon the room, as if all of the heat were slowly being drawn out of it. The kiss of cool air on the mink's hot body made him shiver from both cold and pleasure. Auri's lean body arched over his, and droplets of sweat and tears condensed off of his whiskers. The fingers around Tyler's shaft slid up and down, still slick from lube, while the linsang moved his hips back and forth, claiming the young mink's virginity. As Tyler felt the sensation of Auri's length smoothly sliding in and out him, he felt also a bizarre warmth spill all through his body, fighting off the sudden rush of cold from the air.

Auri murmured under his breath as his snout rested against Tyler's neck. "Footprints in the snow. Cracks in the glass." That same stream of babble kept coming, and Tyler didn't understand any of it. In his mind, the words carried no meaning, like they were nothing but sound, both beautiful and agonizing. The linsang kept thrusting, his pace even and careful, as if he somehow knew the limits to which the mink's body would go. There was a sudden sharp upturn at the end of the next thrust, making Tyler squeak from the force of Auri's hips smacking up against his rear, and then the slower rhythm took back over again.

Tyler wrapped his arms up around Auri's shoulders and held on for dear life. He moaned wordlessly, his voice taking on a higher and higher pitch each time the linsang entered him fully. There was so much stimulation, so much pleasure, and so much warmth. Finally, it was too much, and with a cry of delight, the mink's sinewy body writhed and jerked, his passage clenching down around Auri's shaft while his own pulsed hard, getting the fur on the linsang's stomach and hand sticky and matted.

As the feeling of his first orgasm shared with another pierced Tyler's consciousness, Auri immediately burst out into a wailing, shrieking mess of sobs. He knew that they must have been the result of happiness, but it was still the saddest sound that Tyler had ever heard. It made him cling and hug onto Auri even tighter still, wishing and hoping that it would some-how comfort the linsang. In turn, Auri buried his tear-wet face into the crook of the mink's neck.

The linsang stopped thrusting, and began to just grind his hips hard against the curves of Tyler's rear. The mink could feel that Auri was still hard and unspent inside of him, and he must have been desperate for re-lease. There was a soft nip at the side of his throat before Auri leaned back up, breaking the mink's embrace and holding himself up by his hands. Matted lines of fur showed where the run of his tears had been on his now awestruck face. As before, the linsang cupped a hand at Tyler's cheek. "Gave... You gave this to me. Given, not taken," he said to the mink.

"I don't understand," Tyler whispered back, feeling in his own voice that he, too, was on the verge of tears. He didn't understand why.

Auri just shook his head. "Don't you worry, little one," he said, and Tyler felt himself blushing at the term of endearment. "Let's just both enjoy this." The linsang pulled himself out, and put his hands onto Tyler's hips, at-tempting to shift them. The mink got the hint, and he rolled himself onto his stomach.

"Here," Auri said, pulling Tyler's hips up, bringing the mink into a posi-tion where his rump was slightly raised. The linsang leaned down over the mink's back, pressing against his spine, and took one of those stubby ears between his teeth as his shaft began to sink back inside. Tyler whimpered titillation at the feeling the different angle gave, the length of Auri's cock causing entirely different sensations now. The linsang's teeth tugged at his ear before releasing it, and the smooth thrusting began anew.

The tip of Auri's shaft pressed at and tickled Tyler's prostate, making him wriggle beneath the linsang's body as he was worked back to hard-ness. With each movement of Auri's hips, the linsang's breathing, tinged with sadness, faded away into wonderment. His hands wandered along the mink's underside, brushing through the fur on his stomach and chest, seeking out and finding one of his nipples. The soft pinching made Tyler arch along his spine, causing his backside to lift and press back up against Auri's hips.

Suddenly, Auri's head darted back down, and he clamped his jaw down hard at the side of Tyler's neck from behind, like a vampire. The linsang's lips were sheathing his teeth, preventing him from biting into the mink's skin, and Tyler could tell that Auri was struggling to hold back on his act of dominance. Hot breath and a tense whine escaped the seal of those lips as the linsang stopped thrusting, emptying himself into the mink's body. Tyler felt a prickling run through his body, like a pulsing electrical shock, and he collapsed down onto his mattress with Auri on top of him.

Auri let go of the mink's neck and started to pant and rasp. Tyler bit down onto his pillow and squirmed, bearing back against the still-hard shaft inside of him while he wriggled down against his bed sheets, trying to trigger his second orgasm. It took a few moments of grinding against the fabric, but he soon came again, soaking his sheets and his fur.

He was faintly aware of Auri murmuring to himself under his breath as he drifted off to a blissful sleep.

Tyler snapped back awake with the morning, and immediately panicked. He rolled over, and saw Auri lying there, still. So, it hadn't been a dream, after all. He smiled to himself.

At first, he assumed that the linsang was sleeping, judging by the way he was partially curled up. But after a few moments of listening, he could hear that Auri's breathing was too pressured and heated for him to possibly be asleep. It sounded like he was still experiencing a post-orgasmic rush of pleasure. Tyler tapped a few fingers on his shoulder.

Auri turned around and looked at him. His eyes were back to hazel, again, was the first thing that Tyler noticed. "Even your dreams were lovely, you pretty thing," the linsang said, petting the length of the mink's snout once. Tyler fudged a smile; he couldn't remember what he had dreamed about.

They looked back into each other's eyes for what must have been a couple of minutes before the burning question in Tyler's mind finally escaped his lips. "Auri... what are you?"

The linsang closed his eyes as a solemn expression washed over his face. "I can't tell you. It's better if you don't know."

Tyler suddenly felt a heavy pang in his chest. He knew where this was going. As if on cue, Auri opened his eyes back up, and touched his finger to the mink's lips like he did before. "Don't be sad. I couldn't bear to taste your sadness in the wake of your happiness."

"You keep saying things like that," Tyler asked, gently pulling Auri's hand down away from his mouth. "You say it like I should have any idea of what you're talking about."

Auri shook his head, and clicked his tongue once. "I'm sorry," he said. "I've been… this way for a long time. It's hard to remember what it was like, being otherwise—being like you."

Tyler's mouth opened again to ask another question, but Auri spoke first. "I know what you're going to ask," he said. "But I can't tell you that, either. And you have no idea how much it hurts me that that's the case."

The linsang paused a moment while the mink was silent, and then he went on. "It hurts me. I haven't been able to say that in the longest time. Probably longer than it's been since I felt the way I felt last night with you."

Nothing was making sense. Tyler wanted to cry, but he held back. "I'm never going to see you again, am I?" he said.

Auri nodded lightly. "No," he answered. "You don't deserve the danger I'd bring." Tyler felt the tears begin then.

"Listen," Auri said, holding the mink by the shoulder. "There's a difference between gratification and enjoyment… between doing what one has to do and what one wants to do. Last night, for me, was like… like gluttony. I could have stopped myself, but I didn't, because I didn't want to.

"Innocence… that's something that I'd forgotten the taste and feel of, Tyler. I won't soon forget it again." There was a hint of a smile on Auri's face, but it didn't win out against the solemnity

Tyler went to interject. "But I wanted you to!" he choked out. "I…"

"Shhh," Auri hushed, stroking the mink's cheek affectionately—almost lovingly. "I know you did. And believe me that I don't take it for granted." He closed his eyes. "But you deserve to be able to give your innocence to someone better than me." When his eyes opened again, they were back to the radiant blue from the night before.

"What's going to happen now?" Tyler asked, staring back into those eyes. "I'm scared."

Auri ran his fingers up to the mink's temples, and pressed in softly, letting a warm feeling pass through his body. "You won't be," the linsang whispered, and those were the last words that the mink heard before he felt the sudden compulsion to sleep come over him.

When Tyler woke up, he found his cheeks damp from tears, and wondered what possible reason he could have had for crying.

Afterword

FANG Volume 2, also available from Bad Dog Books, was first released as the curiously-named "FANG Volume H05" around Halloween 2005. The theme of gay erotica is continued in this volume, with a slant toward horror.

Stormcatcher returns, showcasing the melancholy sensibilities he displayed in "Preventing Hypothermia", as do Whyte Yoté, Kyell Gold and K. M. Hirosaki; the latter contributes "The Fox and the Unspeakable Horror", a raucous and scandalous parody of Lovecraftian horror.

Two submissions from your humble editor also grace the pages, one of which covers the roadside adventures of the spry young hustler Owen Zelazny and the cocky thug-dog Q. I. Malloy from the brilliant yet lamentably, as yet, unfinished "Maranatha".

Finally, four stories from Ben Goodridge round out the volume, one of which never-before-published. These "Arcanum Arcanorum" stories so impressed this humble editor that, during the unfortunate episode in early 2006 when a variety of carpal tunnel syndrome cast a shadow of doom over FANG's future, when Ben Goodridge applied for a job as managing editor to ensure its continuation, the decision to hire him was an easy one.

Ben's editorial prowess will go on display in the forthcoming FANG Volume 4, the first non-erotic entry in the FANG line, focusing on the genre Science Fiction.

As always, FANG is on the lookout for new talent. If you're interested in trying your luck at getting your prose in the Little Black Book of Furry Fiction, visit baddogbooks. com for submission policies and advice.

Oh, and André 'Badger' Blaireau, whose story "Bitch-Boy" takes such a prominent position in this volume, has had his novel "Everybody Loves Luther" published as part of the FANG Presents line of novels. Featuring cover art by Grimal, this spunky tale of college romance is scheduled to be followed by a sequel, "El Burrito de los Muertos".

Visit baddogbooks.com for more information!